WAS SHE CREATING
THE FIRST SUPERMAN . . .

She stood in her laboratory surrounded by glowing computer banks, test equipment, laser transmitters, holographic projectors, and TV screens. . . . Around her, like a charnel house, bits and pieces of adult males littered the floor . . . tendons, limbs, feet and hands, knuckles, fingernails. She was ready now.

She used the power controls to lift Lance's unconscious form and move it into a great human statue. The first complete ManFac, powered down, brooding, shockingly lifelike. It looked alive because in every sense, save motion, it was alive. All it needed was the spark. . . .

OR A COMPUTER-CONTROLLED
FRANKENSTEIN?

Samurai!
The Ragged, Rugged Warriors
Black Thursday
Thunderbirds!
The Long, Lonely Leap
The Long Arm of America
The Mighty Hercules
Let's Go Flying!
Cross-Country Flying
Test Pilot
Hydrospace
The Winged Armada
Air Force
Golden Wings
Thunderbolt!
This Is My Land
Everything but the Flak
A Torch to the Enemy
The Night Hamburg Died
Barnstorming
Boeing 707
Flying Forts
Flying
Messerschmitt Me-109
The Zero Fighter
The Mission
The Silken Angels
When War Comes
It's Fun to Fly
The Power of Decision
Ju-52/3m Flight Manual
Bf-108B Flight Manual
Rendezvous in Space
Man-in-Space Dictionary
Spaceport U.S.A.

The Astronauts
War for the Moon
I Am Eagle!
Rockets Beyond the Earth
Red Star in Space
Jets, Rockets and Guided Missiles
Rockets and Missiles
Planetfall
Destination Mars
Vanguard!
Countdown for Tomorrow
The Greatest Challenge
Aviation and Space Medicine
By Apollo to the Moon
Man into Space
New World for Men
Why Space?
First Flight into Space
Worlds in Space
Overture to Space

etc.

MANFAC

MARTIN CAIDIN

A DELL BOOK

Published by
Dell Publishing Co., Inc.
1 Dag Hammarskjold Plaza
New York, New York 10017

Dell ® TM 681510, Dell Publishing Co., Inc.

ISBN: 0-440-15587-8

Printed in the United States of America

First printing—October 1981

Hey, Paisano!
Roger
For you . . .

BOOK ONE

Chapter 1

He couldn't see. No, that was wrong. He couldn't focus. His eyes worked, and there was vision, but everything before Lance Parker *blurred*. He stared vacantly, then blinked rapidly and again tried staring, forcing his eyes not to blink. No damn good. He still faced that eerie shimmering, the kind of blur that comes from heat waves screwing up a horizon. Or if the air itself was shaking. Jesus, this was crazy. Lance squeezed his eyes shut tightly, and strange spirals and whorls danced along his inner retina. The redness increased from the blood pooling in his eyes.

Now he felt and sensed and tasted what was happening.

He had that deep-gut sensation that makes dogs howl and birds dart about swiftly on wings of panic. He understood why the air blurred before him, and it didn't have a thing to do with vision. He opened his eyes, and instantly he wanted to vomit. His equilibrium staggered, and vertigo knifed from his brain to his stomach. Bile appeared in his throat, hot and choking. He threw out an arm in an instinctive and hopeless motion. He saw the walls about him quiver, felt the floor tremble beneath his feet, and then quietly he said, "Oh, shit," because an earthquake makes a man so goddamned helpless.

There was no way he should have experienced more than a mild shock so far down in the bowels of this mountain in northern California unless there was enough punch in the quake to have kicked the Richter scale right in the nuts. And Richter was getting the hell stomped out of it. He listened, every muscle straining, his nerves taut. No doubt now. He couldn't hear the deep, thrumming thunder always present within this thick-walled and reinforced assembly of steel and concrete—the thunder from the underground river that sliced through the enormous pipes. He couldn't hear the familiar thunder because that other thunder was louder. The first knifepoint edges of claustrophobia cut into his mind. He was way down in the belly of the land, and an earthquake could swallow him, mash him, crush and pound and squeeze him until his bones and teeth would flow with scrunched concrete and steel rods and raw granite.

The only things louder than this thunder were the shocks that pounded his ears and inside his skull with great ringing peals. Did a man's brains really shake like jelly inside that cranial packaging? He stared in fascination at the dust dancing in the air, and he cursed himself for his fascinating but useless perceptions.

He lurched like a drunk to his left. At least he was moving. He stumbled to the readout control panel and a nearby control console. Every damned light was flashing red. For the first time he realized sirens were screeching through his hearing, and two small speakers in the same control room wailed their danger cries. He'd heard these sounds individually before, but never in this insane chorus. Smoke shimmered up from broken circuits, and sparks flashed from metal, and he discovered he was staring at one large brilliant red light that visually drowned out everything else.

The rad level was climbing like a baboon with its ass ablaze. That meant that somewhere deep within this hydroelectric power system—or what the world had been *told* was hydro—the mighty nuclear fast-breeder reactor was suffering the horrors of having its radioactive innards wrenched. The fear welled up in him, and he forced it back. Hell, he had confidence in this system. He'd designed the major safeguards himself, had watched them built, had tested them through every phase of assembly and operation. The great power system was built on a massive hydraulic platform that would easily have balanced both World Trade towers in lower Manhattan. *I hope,* he said to himself. The world rattled about him, and he had that mental picture he hated: his body being shaken like a helpless rat in the jaws of some mighty terrier. He focused his attention as best he could on the display panel with its myriad lines depicting tunnels and elevators and even stairwells that traversed five hundred feet before a man could open a sealed thick-armored lock and peer into open air. Then he lurched and stumbled, fell, climbed to his feet, and lunged for the doorway to an adjoining equipment room. Hanging from a rack was his personal salvation.

His flailing hands reached what looked like an armored version of an astronaut's space suit, but it was more complicated, designed for surviving killing agents tougher than vacuum and cold. The entire suit was woven with a double-walled interior layer of coiled lines filled with water, power packs hanging about a belt that ran heaters, coolers, dehumidifiers, radios, tools, and enough complicated gadgets for a small submarine. A man in that suit was intended to survive freezing cold and winds, even naked flames, to be able to absorb physical punishment, and above all, to have protection against the invisible juggernaut of lethal atomic radiation. Lance looked at the rising scale of surrounding radiation on a wall counter. Just one glance was enough to make him climb into the suit. Within two minutes he was sealed, solid canisters pouring fresh oxygen under pressure to the helmet. He studied himself in a dust-covered mirror, pressed a row of suit-test buttons on his right forearm, and picked up and hooked several more oxygen canisters to the suit belt.

He had half turned to leave the equipment room when the wall to his immediate right cracked wide open. Rock and crushed concrete spewed out in a frightening stream, and a blast of thunder penetrated even the suit. The shower of rocks and dust rattled in a grisly rain against the suit as he leaned forward, compensating for the weight and mass of his radiation armor, to get the hell away from that increasingly violent jet gushing from the smashed wall. He made it through the doorway back into the control room and turned to slam shut the heavy door between the two rooms. The alarms and sirens were dulled considerably by the pressurized suit, and he ignored the flashing red lights. He knew only too well what they meant. He was drawn instantly to a television monitor, ablaze with the strobe and repeated flashing of a sign that had to be the absolute understatement of the moment: URGENT. He lumbered to the set, reached to his side for a coiled power line, and plugged in directly to the TV system. A scanner picked up his picture; instantly the URGENT sign blinked out, and he saw the face of John Matterly, the power plant director. Matterly's expression, a mixture of horror and honest concern, made all preliminary conversation superfluous. To his credit he didn't even try. His voice stabbed through Lance's earphones within the helmet.

"Parker! Goddammit, man, the whole thing's coming unglued! You'd better—" Matterly's eyes blinked, and he paused but a second. "Thank Christ you're already in that suit. Lance, get the hell out of there. Some of the tunnels and shafts are already blocked. You'd better use the D system. It's the strongest and your best chance. Take the D tunnel from your present position to Shaft Sixteen. I don't know if the power is still on, but there's enough battery juice to keep some lights going. Be sure to plug in as you reach the successive contact points so we know where you are and can update you on any changes. Got it? Don't even answer. Just nod to me and *move*. Now, *go*, dammit!"

As Lance yanked the plug and started for the doorway, a wild shock smashed everything about him, and the floor jerked away beneath him. He tensed for the fall. The whole feeling was incredible and at the same time absurd because while he was falling, suspended, an invisible fist struck him along the side of his head and a black fog swept through his brain, a strange warm fog that kept him just short of unconsciousness, a long-held daze in which he wasn't sure of anything, and his mind was pinwheeling. . . .

Then it snapped back sharp and clear to him. Falling—*but it was beautiful.*

God, they were crazy. Jesus, crazy like no one else. There were eight of them, and it was a gorgeous day, and they were over the lake at ten thousand feet, eight maniacs laughing and grinning in the DC-3 jump plane, outfitted in goggles and wet suits beneath their parachute harnesses. It was a contest like that which no one had ever tried before, and it demanded skill and experience and, above all, the kind of timing that had to be perfect or you were going to bust your ass, baby, and that was for sure.

They were all pilots and sky divers and scuba divers, and they climbed mountains and went on hunting and fishing trips in desolate and angry country, and they were always trying to find some new gimmick, some new way to test themselves and challenge one another in a unique or, best of all, in a completely unprecedented way. They had their own private jump club.

Al Collins was jumpmaster for this gig. He wore a crazy wet suit of rainbow colors. He looked insane. But like Lance Parker, he had had more than four hundred jumps, and he was very, very good. "One last time," he said, "and I want you cats to listen carefully." He glanced outside the DC-3. "We're coming around for the jump run, and I want no mistakes about the rules. We go out in two-second intervals, right?" They nodded to one another and Al. "Good. From ten grand everybody has a chance to spread wide. You've got to crack your canopies no lower than six thou. That gives everybody a chance to get good separation, and you've got to go by the numbers. One through eight, just like we've set it up. Okay on all counts?"

They nodded. Yeah, okay on all counts. Lance felt a thrill of anticipation wash through his body like a cool wind. He glanced through the DC-3 window at the deep blue of the sky and the scattered cumulus clouds below. A perfect day, wind about twelve knots, but they'd be dumping toward water—except for their crazy target.

Everything seemed extra-sharp, extra-bright. He could almost feel the seconds ticking away. He was mad with a sudden desire to hurl himself from this clanking winged monster. He felt the short jabs on rudder, the aft fuselage swaying as the pilot held course; he could *feel* the moment of jump coming. He was number five in the string, and the guys were lined up, tensed, alert, ready to go, and Al's voice called out the seconds: "Five, four, three, two, one, GO!"

Benny went out first, Al's voice barked, "GO!" and Mike was next, and then Roger, and Milty, and then Lance hurled himself through the open doorway into the teeth of the 120 miles an hour roaring by the jump plane, and God, it was marvelous as the blast hit him, and he moved his arms and legs and twisted his body and went into perfect free-fall position, arms wide, legs spread, back arched slightly, the wind pushing up against his clothing and shoving against his goggles and distending his facial skin, and he was grinning as he saw the other bodies below him, and there, he heard the slight popping sound as the first chute opened, and Benny's square-rigger, a parasail chute that flew like a glider, was open, and then one after the other, the bright canopies deployed, and he was coming up fast on six thousand feet; he glanced at his altimeter and pulled and heard the whooshing sound of the shrouds and the canopy whipping away from his body, and he was no longer falling but floating in a dreamlike world.

Time to concentrate, baby. His own words, unbidden, as he rode the wind. For now came the maniacal part of all this—because of what they were going to try. The trick was to aim the chute, flying as if it were a hang glider, to a point nearly above a trampoline floating in the water. They could all handle that well enough. But next, well, it was crazy, all right. Just before he touched the trampoline, the jumper was to cut away from his chute and drop onto the trampoline, and then bounce into an inflated rubber tube anchored off the trampoline.

Lance watched Benny coming around into the

17

wind, dropping toward the trampoline. He was playing it smart; he'd cut away one shoulder hookup, leaving only one connection to the chute, so he could drop perfectly at the precise moment. But it didn't work. A gust of wind caught the chute. Benny couldn't control it with just one hookup, and he splashed into the water a good six feet short of his target. Right behind him, too close for comfort, came Mike, who released his chute too high and fell like a rock, flailing wildly to avoid hitting the edge of the trampoline. Roger dropped perfectly, but his bounce was too strong; he landed clear beyond the waiting target. Three down. Milty also got a good drop and bounce, but he hit the edge of the inner tube and skidded into the water off to the side. Lance judged it carefully. He made a final steep turn and headed for the trampoline, hands ready to cut away. The others had all tried to land feetfirst into the inner tube, and it hadn't worked.

The trampoline came rushing up at Lance, and he cut away. Immediately the tension of the harness was gone, and he fell, keeping his legs together. He hit dead center of the trampoline, got his bounce, and instantly arched his body as he went back into the air in a bastardized sort of a jackknife dive. But the trampoline had shifted with a wave, and he was going up and over in a crazy twisting turn. He swung wildly to regain his aim, but he was off, and instead of the inner tube below him, he saw the edge of the trampoline, and he hit it with a crash against his shoulder and . . .

He knew there would be pain. But he didn't expect the savage electrical shock that tore into his legs. He screamed with the sudden agony. He couldn't understand the pain because he'd hit with his shoulder, and why were his legs hurting him like this? My God, what in the hell was happening? He snapped open his eyes, and it all came back to him instantly. He'd jerked away with his mind to escape the terrible reality of being deep under a mountain in a nuclear control complex with all hell breaking loose. Now he remembered the floor snapping away from beneath him, and that timeless moment he had waited to feel the impact against the floor, and he yelled again with the sudden agony, but in that last instant before blackness swallowed him he felt the ultimate anguish of knowing there was no one to hear him save himself.

Chapter 2

Somebody with enormous hands and unimaginable strength jerked his legs violently. He kicked wildly, an idiot besieged with muscle spasms, and he tried to sit up and punch an armored fist into that giant's stupid face and . . .

His head cleared. He lifted it from the trembling concrete floor and stared in disbelief at the heavy electrical panel that held him captive to the floor. Now he understood those insane spasms. Wires still led from the panel to their wall source, and they were hot, their shocks keeping his legs jerking crazily. If he continued to lie there stupidly, he was inviting electrocution. He groaned and tried to sit up, his eyes catching sight of Matterly's disbelieving face on the television monitor, and then the man's frantic gestures for Lance Parker to *move*. He tried, but he couldn't get balance or leverage from the still-shaking and rolling floor. Dust settling about him and clinging by static electricity to the faceplate didn't help. Neither did the shrill clamor that knifed even through the thickly armored and padded helmet. *That was the master alarm for the nuclear reactor—the core proper.* Something had come very loose in the heart of this entire system, and hell was about to spatter violently in all directions, and not even this massive armor could save his tender ass if radioactive sludge were to flow like artificial lava over his pitifully defenseless form. He struggled to a sitting position, grabbed a wrecking bar attached to his equipment belt, pried it beneath an open space of the heavy panel still pinning his legs, and shoved with all his strength. The scream came involuntarily from his throat as the electricity tore through the bar into his hand, and the wrecking bar flew from his grasp. No way; no way. He gathered all his strength and rolled to one side. He didn't make it all the way, but by God, *he had moved*. Again; another violent side motion, and one leg was clear. He kicked and squirmed and dragged himself out from under, and he made it. He rested, gasping for air. He looked up so that Matterly would see his face through the television scanner, but the light was dead, and so was the screen. He climbed with rubbery legs to his feet. The damned world was going dark on him. He looked around, baffled, then realized that lights were fading about him. *Klutz,* he told himself, and turned on the suit lights, one in the helmet and another at the front of the equipment belt.

The shaking movement of the floor had lessened, and he found he could move without that drunken gait. He got through the cracked entranceway, turned along a squared room, and headed straight for an oval opening with a large D SHAFT above the oval. It was a tunnel constructed of massive steel piping with an overlaid flooring of thick rubber to insulate any occupants from the thick cables running beneath the floor panels. A long row of lights overhead illuminated the tunnel, but they flickered on and off. He wondered what the hell had gone wrong with the backup systems. Then the electrical mains to the lights failed completely, and the battery-powered systems winked on. Lance moved in his steady stride along the tunnel, forcing down the urge to run madly toward safety. He'd just heat up the suit until he saturated the life-support system, and that would seal his doom. One step after another, each one measured and careful—the only way to go and keep on going. Signs on each side of the tunnel marked the distance he'd covered since stepping through the oval entrance. They helped.

But all the signs in the world wouldn't do him any good if this mountain kept disintegrating about him. The thunder boomed hollowly along the shaft, and every new detonation set the dust floating again in midair, casting strange rays and beams from the battery lights, all intermixing and clashing silently with the lights from his suit. One moment he moved onward in his measured stride, and the next he was rolled off-balance as the tunnel shuddered beneath him. He kept his arms wide for better balance, sometimes rocking off the side walls of the shaft. A series of sharp reports banged through the air and the tunnel beneath him, almost staccato in their repetition. He paused by a monitoring panel as he kept moving toward Shaft 16. A single glance told him the grim story.

The earthquake shocks were gone. The thunder and cracking reports came now from a man-made system that was tearing itself apart: the core of the reactor. The radiation levels in the air were climbing steadily, and he knew the very dust in the air about him was already dangerous. Without the suit . . . He pushed away the thought. He didn't need to dwell on maybes and mights. *Just get the hell out of here.*

Concrete dust and chips of metal showered through the air. The long tunnel shaft rocked and then twisted before his eyes like an enormous writhing python in some infernal death throe. Metal rods appeared suddenly, tearing through the sidewalls of the tunnel shaft; he lunged forward to escape a jagged steel rod that nearly impaled him. The world about him had gone insane as more rods bent under tremendous strain and snapped free of their restraints, piercing the tunnel walls and quivering madly. Over the booming reports and through the thick suit he heard their cries, these huge tuning forks that sent strange groans through his body.

Then everything went ominously quiet. He started forward, running now. To hell with the heat inside the suit. Death was near and all about him and threatening to appear in a dozen different forms.

He hadn't run fifty feet when he knew his instincts were terribly true. He stopped and turned as a new and different roar began to fill the tunnel about him. The blood drained from his face, and with a muttered oath he turned again and ran with all his strength. Far behind him the tunnel shaft had ripped completely open. Water thundered like molten steel down the tunnel in lethal pursuit, and he hurled himself forward, the hatch to Shaft 16, leading upward from the tunnel, beckoning to him. His chest heaved and his sweat showered against the inside of the bubble visor as he reached the hatch. He grasped a vertical handle and threw all his weight against it as water thudded against his boots. It took three complete turns. The water was at his knees when the hatch yielded. He shoved it upward wildly, feeling the holding mechanism lock into place.

He climbed the ladder, using everything his arms had to give him, his legs swept away by the water. Each step was a huge victory, and then he saw his boots clear of the water. He was in the shaft, his heart pounding, his body screaming for relief. Not yet. He had to close the hatch. Six more steps up the ladder, and he turned, kicking madly at the hatch. The holding clamp let go beneath his weight, and the hatch slammed down with a deep muffled clang. He lowered himself to the hatch, standing on the curving metal, cursing the lack of room and his clumsiness. Then he had the locking wheel in his gloved hands, and he twisted until metal refused to move. He leaned back, eyes closed, refusing to budge. Cooling oxygen flooded his face, and he felt it moving through the suit. *My God. I made it.*

Above him extended a long, dangerous, and muscle-straining climb. Then he remembered the footholds and the hand clamps from the power lift. He set his feet into the slots, grasped the clamps, and squeezed, bracing himself for the upward movement. *Nothing.* The power was dead.

He forced himself to breathe deeply, steadily, measuring every move he made. The old mountain-climbing trick. You go up one step at a time. Nothing exists save your present position and the next step. One, then two. One again and then two again and back to one, every step a careful, selective process. One hundred feet straight up. That's climbing a ladder in a hundred-pound suit the equal of a ten-story building. Jesus Christ. What the hell did they expect from a man! Ten stories below him. Take a step. Stop. Breathe deeply, keep the system flushed with oxygen. You're burning energy like water spewing from a garden hose. Don't run out of adrenaline, goddammit. Another step. Twenty stories straight up from the tunnel. Two hundred feet. He'd done it. He stopped, stars flashing before his eyes. He was dizzy. He *must* rest. He did. It would be easier from here on. The shaft bent now at a forty-five-degree angle. He started climbing; the vertical ascent eased greatly.

Continuous thunder, the mountain shaking like jelly, then quieting down, resting for its own renewal of angry tremors. One step after another. Climb, crawl, keep moving. Sweat poured down his neck. He'd long overloaded the cooling capacity of the suit. Screw it. He was making it. He reached Level F. Five more levels to go, and he'd be at the surface control room. He paused at another station. The power lines still fed energy to the console report panel.

It was a full-blown holocaust within the earth. Power breaks everywhere, tunnels flooding, radiation hot spots already lethal to any unprotected personnel. Different parts of the reactor system were coming under more and more enormous pressure and collapsing. The pressure squeezed metal, and the steel shapes groaned and bent and finally exploded.

The very system that had made this entire project safe—*so they had predicted*—had now become its own worst enemy. The vast water flows in the coiled and serpentine paths of the great pipelines recirculated heat with an efficiency constant several times greater than ever used before in any energy-producing complex.

That was the way they had managed to create the largest nuclear energy plant in the world in complete secrecy. They'd told the outside world that the enormous electrical dynamos within the mountain harnessed huge underground rivers. Had they announced their decision to build a fast-breeder reactor, even under a mountain, the project would never have seen the first stirring of construction, thanks to the antinuclear forces.

So they had gone underground in more ways than one. And felt secure. Because what the hell could be safer than a nuclear plant *under* a mountain? My God, they had billions of tons of shielding! Well, it had been one hell of a theory. Now it was collapsing under the awesome forces of a crunching earthquake and a mountain with severe stomach cramps. And when billions of tons of granite growl, man's machinery suffers the same acute indigestion—and comes apart at the seams.

Lance reached Level E and stopped. He pushed everything from his mind. Breathe. Again; deeply and slowly. Let the adrenaline pump. That's it. The ringing in his ears subsided, and the tortured heaving of his chest eased to a normal pace of respiration. He looked blankly at another report console. MAKE IMMEDIATE CONTACT. The glowing letters blazed at him. He forced the fog from his mind and plugged the suit connector into the unit that connected him to control center.

Static. Electrical hissing; no contact. Screw it. He unplugged and began another long slanting ascent. The report console at Level D repeated the same flashing request. MAKE IMMEDIATE CONTACT. He was moving more slowly now. God, he was tired. He looked at the rising radiation levels with stark dismay. They were going through a slow, murderous outward expulsion. He plugged in. To his surprise he had immediate voice and television contact. On the screen before him he saw Matterly's drawn face. A group of white-coated technicians, their faces wan and frightened, was visible behind him.

"Lance! Thank God you called in!" Matterly sucked in air. His eyes were unnaturally wide. "Listen carefully, Lance. The reactor core is going through a meltdown, and it's a bad one. Worse than anything I've ever known. There's very little time. The rods have broken in the central core, and what we're getting is a severe crushing of material from the collapse of the heavy rock masses. Lance, we're getting a severe *compression in the core*."

Lance Parker felt an icy wind through even the steaming heat of his suit. He wiped a gloved hand across the helmet visor to clear away some of the dust.

What kind of nightmare was this? He was poised in a slanting ladder that ran straight down into hell and—

"I know it sounds impossible," Matterly's voice droned into Lance's brain. "But we're getting an extraordinary reaction, and—"

"Goddammit, wrap it up," Lance spat.

"We have, uh, a high fission reaction. It's breaking into loose."

Lance stared at the television monitor. "Short and sweet, John, is there an approach to the K factor?"

The silence was just long enough to confirm the worst. "Yes. We have an open end of reaching critical mass."

"Jesus Christ . . ."

"The automatic controls have failed, and so have the remotes." John Matterly's words tumbled from him in a rush. "Lance, you've *got* to get into the reactor control center to the manual overrides. The only way we can save this whole situation is for you to set off the imbedded charges and flood the core from the storage tanks. It'll blow apart the rods."

"We'll get one hell of a radiation output," Lance said, and he realized his voice was literally a snarl. What the hell, they were talking about *him* being the hero, and that was so much crap.

"But it's the only thing that will work!" Matterly's voice reached almost a waspish whine. He was frantic. "It will stop the rise toward K, and from that point on we can contain what's already happened."

Silence. The magic letter. *K. K* stands for critical factor. When there's enough uranium compressed to a sufficient density and mass to transform a reactor into a fucking *bomb*.

"You're not giving me much of a chance, John," he said finally.

"I know, Lance, *I know.* Your chances are slim—"

"They stink."

"But you're *the only one* who can do it! I've already started the rescue crews on their way to the core room. They'll work through from the A Shaft."

"Not a chance, John. It's a one-way trip for them."

"We don't have much choice."

He didn't have to say that Lance Parker had the choice. He could tell them to go screw and keep right on climbing to the surface.

"Lance, no one can or will blame you if you decide not to go back into that thing. Most people would call you every kind of fool for even trying."

Lance heard a short, harsh laugh from his own mouth. "Well, John, they say one fool begets another. You started this whole mess, and I was your golden-haired boy, so I guess we're fools of a feather. Look, I'll punch in as I go along, but I won't stop to chitchat."

He jerked the connection free. If he talked anymore, he knew his own common sense would take over and he would tell John Matterly to screw off. He twisted in the shaft and started his descent back into hell.

Chapter 3

He fought against every tumbling second of time. The suit cooling system was on overload, and not even the cool oxygen could disguise from him the stink of his own sweat. *And fear,* he murmured to himself as he scrambled down the ladder to reach an escape shaft still sealed off from the choking water that had almost snared him. He didn't need the position consoles. The emergency system routing had been established firmly in his mind long before this moment; indeed, he was responsible for the rule that every man who worked in central core had to memorize the emergency routes between the core control rooms and the exits to the outside world. Twice Lance had to stop in the smaller tunnels, where he had barely enough room to proceed in his cumbersome armor; he had taken alternate routes because the selected tunnel had suffered a breach or had been crushed in the deep shuddering of the earthquake. Nevertheless, he moved steadily toward the core, noting, as he went, the continuing rise in radiation levels measured on wall monitors and through the instruments of his protective suit. The heaviest explosions were now a thing of the past, but there was no escaping the steady rumble transmitted to his feet and the manner in which dust danced along the floor of the emergency tunnels, cavorting senselessly in the twin beams of his suit lights. At each station he passed he paused long enough to bang his gloved fist against a wall signal stud to let Matterly and the others know both his progress and his position at any one time. No messages flashed at him to call in. They didn't have the time to waste in conversation.

Forty minutes after he had abandoned his near reach to safety and started his return into the belly of the mountain, exhausted, eyes smarting from the salt of his own sweat, he stood before the crumpled metal door of the central control room. He could hardly believe what lay before him. In every direction bodies sprawled awkwardly, frozen in their grotesque last moments of violent death, limbs twisted beneath torsos, eyes bulging as they were struck down in the midst of their fear. Strange, the door had been crumpled as if it were paper, but there was little physical damage within the master control proper. He scanned the boards. Whatever had happened here had swept through a peak and then subsided after performing its grisly mission. He stood before the videophone panel, punched in the emergency line to exterior control, and watched the anxious faces of John Matterly and his aides come to life on a flickering, ghostly screen.

"Everybody here is dead," he said by way of salutation. "The main door's been torn apart, but not much damage inside. From the looks of things we took a tremendous electrical overload. It must have flashed out of the equipment like ball lightning. Most of the people look as if they were hurled about and killed by shock at the same time."

Matterly ignored the dead. "Have you got condition readout?" he asked without preamble.

Lance scanned the gauges. "Looks like almost everything's on the line. Air circulation and cooling are gone, though. Immediate temperature in here is a hundred and seventy degrees, and it's still climbing." Even as he spoke the words, he knew Matterly understood the meaning of that temperature rise.

"Lance, I know it's supposed to be impossible, but we're getting a fast reaction from that core. Do you agree with the compression effect?"

Lance nodded to himself and looked up again at the video screen. "Only one thing, John. We've had a physical collapse into the chamber with the fuel rods. They've been jammed together by God knows how many thousands of tons of rock, so what we have is the equivalent of plutonium being imploded, but on a greatly expanded time scale from a bomb. But what you're worried about is that if we get any further collapse, we get a real crunch, and the squeeze could give us a critical mass."

"I wish you were wrong," Matterly said.

"Shit, so do I. What about the computer evaluation?"

Matterly took a deep breath. "We've been staying real-time with the computer. According to our electronic oracle, the pressure is still increasing, and in something like twenty minutes from now, we'll have so much squeeze the plutonium will begin uncontrolled fission."

Lance felt the icy wind again through his suit. "No question on critical mass?" It wasn't so much a question as a useless prayer.

"None."

"Give me the predicted yield."

For a moment he saw John Matterly trying to speak, finally sucking in air to force out the words.

"The computer can give only variables, of course, Lance, and we don't know how many input circuits are still functioning, but—"

"Jesus Christ, the numbers!"

Matterly swallowed. His answer was a solid kick to the mental groin, and it came in a staccato read-off of the numbers. "Minimum yield three kilotons. Max yield curves off the graph at fifty-four kilotons."

Lance's response was unexpected. *"Holy shit—"* That meant an explosion on the lowest side of the scale of three thousand tons of high explosives, along with the accompanying shock waves and the jetlike release through the tunnel vents of some pretty nasty radioactivity. But that was the *low* side. If the computer slide-off was accurate in the opposite direction, then, as the core continued to compress under the grinding weight and pressure of the surrounding rock, they would have an explosion equal to that of fifty-four thousand tons of TNT erupting in the bowels of the mountain. It was more than an explosion. A hell of a lot more. *It was three times as powerful as that grim beauty they used to pulverize the cities of Hiroshima and Nagasaki.* My God, they had a city buster on their hands! The shock could trigger another earthquake in an already unstable situation, and the radioactive release would far exceed tunnel venting—it could be catastrophic on a scale all its own.

The clock gave him all of eighteen minutes to prevent the nuclear disaster. He knew what he must do and without any further delay. He ignored Matterly's useless words. He turned from the video console and went back into the reactor master control room, stepping over and around bodies. A glance at the digital temperature readout didn't help. Since he'd walked into this area barely five or ten minutes ago, the ambient temperature had climbed another 12 degrees; it

34

was now 182 degrees Fahrenheit. The goddamned chain reaction was beginning and pouring out enormous waves of heat. An energy reactor was being transformed into a bomb. It was that simple. And the instant it achieved the status of a bomb it would explode.

And he was the only poor, dedicated son of a bitch who might be able to slay the dragon in its nuclear nest.

He punched the computer code before the steel blast doors to the emergency control room. The heavy door released its catches, and he had to tug with all his strength to open the steel mass. It grumbled on roller bearings as it slid slowly and ponderously aside. He pulled it closed behind him, and it thunked into position with a finality he didn't like at all.

The spherical emergency control room was a tomb within the tomb of the mountain, a chamber sealed off from the outside world, near or distant, save for plug-in cables that would, once he activated the override controls, be snapped away by steel blades crashing into place. The great sphere was festooned in every direction—like a woman gone mad with hair curlers—with massive springs of the type used to shock-mount enormous intercontinental ballistic missiles in their underground silos. With its honeycomb anticrush material and other protective systems, the chamber was intended to withstand the force of any impact save that of a close hit with a nuclear warhead. Which was what was going to happen unless he quit this idiotic reflection of his and pulled all the right handles.

He went through an elaborate cross-checking of trigger locks and had several more minutes of safety preparations to complete when a great gong sounded and lights throughout the chamber began flashing. There could be no more waiting. The plutonium had now been squeezed together with such force that the fission process was getting out of hand. Critical mass could be only moments away. Lance threw himself into the master seat, a thickly padded seat built like an enormous throne, pulled restraints about his legs, arms, torso, and helmeted head, opened the cover to the ultimate button, and squeezed that button with one finger, while he pulled a spring-loaded toggle switch with another. He had to hold down both the button and the toggle for twelve seconds and not interrupt the electrical command from either during that period or the final safety process would never go through. He counted down backward from twelve to one, reached zero, was befuddled when nothing happened. He started to curse and never completed the thought.

The world blew up in his face.

Chapter 4

Shock waves, hard as steel, punched outward to blow apart critical control rods in vertical assemblies, severing rods, hurling them into a tangled mess like an enormous pipe organ tearing itself to jangling junk. The tubes of lead so essential to damping the rise of heat and the rate of radioactive emission were shredded and melted by the intense heat of the explosions. The radioactive outpouring flared in a mushrooming glow, but only for an instant, for as the intricate and finely balanced assembly became a boiling caldron of lead, steel, plastic, and other debris, there remained no chance that the fission process taking place from imploding plutonium would continue. The dangerous runaway fission ended as swiftly as the blast tore apart the concentrated mass. The explosion was everything it had been designed to be.

Nevertheless, a great dragon simmered and writhed in the midst of the shattered nuclear cornucopia, and its name was radioactivity. Within the massive spherical shell of his survival chamber, Lance Parker was unaffected by alpha and beta particles; they could not penetrate the layered sludge born of the contrived

37

devastation. But there were gamma rays and neutrons that could slice through the miasma of boiling rock and magma as if it were little more than wisps of fog. The gamma rays flashed outward, ghosted through rock and steel and glass and the body of Lance Parker, doing their cruel damage to his organs and body systems and bones and eyes. Then they were gone, and their presence remained only as a legacy of physiological disaster.

The neutrons had the ability to render other objects radioactive. When the blast itself was spent and the earth was grumbling under the job of settling its unequal pressures, the effect of the neutrons remained. Much of what existed about Lance had been rendered radioactive, thereby continuing the radioactivity affecting him and beginning a deadly cumulative effect. The breakdown was as insidious as it was dangerous, for Lance Parker felt nothing of its effects.

Yet.

Lance was occupied with other matters: loud, physical. The explosive shock ripping through the dense material surrounding the reactor core had rattled him in his seat like a helpless spastic undergoing a jolt of electricity. He could feel the liquid sloshing in his body. He shook, palsied, jerked wildly to and fro within the securing harness of his seat, and finally realized the punishing "ride" was over when his vision began to clear.

He sat quietly for several minutes and tried to take stock. The chamber had retained its structural integrity. That meant he had proper air and pressure and temperature control, and the complicated life-support systems were functioning. He had a decent chance to remain alive there for weeks to come, if that bleak prospect were to be realized. And despite the head-rattling and body-sloshing punishment of the explosion, he had no more injuries worth any worry.

What he must do, he realized, was to understand just where he was and what his relationship was to the outside world and the future. His power systems were self-contained. Fuel cells and batteries: no sweat on these. He existed in what was the perfect equivalent of a spaceship. Self-regulating temperature, humidity, and pressure systems. He had scrubbers that would clean his lung exhalations, that would literally eat carbon dioxide and water vapor exactly like the systems in an Apollo spacecraft. Fans would circulate and recirculate the air. His body wastes and other debris would be dropped into a deep receptacle beneath the chamber floor, sealed, and then instantly ionized by a short-lived but intense electromagnetic flash. Even feces converted instantly to free molecules aren't a bother. He had food and water and medications and—

But no communication with the outside world. If he had been claustrophobic, he would have long since been foaming at the mouth. All cables leading to and from the chamber had been severed just before the deliberate explosion. *Face it. You're locked inside a mountain. Buried, impounded, sealed, imprisoned, trapped, wedged; whatever the hell you want to call it. And there's no way out. They will have to come to me.*

But he had no way of knowing how extensive the damage was from the explosion he'd triggered, if he had collapsed the tunnels and shafts leading to the chamber, just what access the rescue teams had—or *didn't* have. Yet time was against him. The longer he remained in this chamber, the fewer were his chances for survival. The radiation would continue to work its deadly effect on his body systems, and the greatest of all dangers lay in radiative accretion—the cumulative effect.

He laughed aloud at the absurdity of it all—now

that the radiation levels were no longer immediately lethal, he would be trickled to death by accumulation. He sighed, released the seat restraints, and stood upright. There was no need to wear his suit of dusty armor anymore. He studied the control panel and set all contact alarms to their maximum sensitivity. There was always the chance that Matterly and the rescue teams would deliberately set off a series of minor explosive shocks in a coded number to let him know they were on their way. He rechecked all the life-support systems, made a mental checklist of what to scan and service every four hours, and was astonished to discover that despite the reality of his imprisonment and the great likelihood of his death, he was hungry.

He turned on a cassette player to fill the dull acoustic atmosphere of the chamber with music, swung down a sleeping cot from the curving sidewall behind him, inflated the mattress, and pored through the food stores. Ten minutes later, thanks to his autoelectric food heater system, he was having a bowl of mulligan stew, fresh crackers, hot tea, and fruitcake. The only thing missing was a good cigar, but tobacco had never entered the list of survival rations. He leaned back, belched, scratched himself comfortably, and pondered the reading library. But he couldn't concentrate on a book while all about him there prowled a radioactive monster.

He had a better way. He was an expert self-hypnotist, thanks to the technique he had developed years before to aid his engineering studies, improve his relaxation, even be able to listen to recorded lessons while in a hypnotism-induced sleep state. Never had he been more grateful for that ability. He knew he could slip away into a world of self-mesmerization and yet be sufficiently alert to snap back to unpleasant reality if that were necessary.

Close your eyes.

Relax.

That's it, just let it all go. Let's start down now.

One hundred.

Ninety-nine.

Ninety-eight.

You're starting to float down, a deep and long descent, wafting downward like a feather, down, down.

Ninety-seven.

As you float down, you will drift off into a state of complete relaxation. Easy, easy. Floating, drifting.

Ninety-six.

Floating . . .

Chapter 5

He was still accelerating as the jump plane flashed up and away from him. He held out his arms and extended his legs in jump position, and then, from all the sensory inputs of wind and sound and the way his body reacted even to so much as a palm flashed upward or downward, knew he was at flat-bodied terminal velocity. He maneuvered his limbs to turn slightly. "Hey! Over here!" he heard. Even with the wind tearing past him and the jump helmet, he recognized Lee Grazzi's voice. There weren't that many beautiful women with crystal laughter in their tone. His body turned slowly, and they maneuvered closer, grinning at one another. Wisps of dark hair fluttered from the sides of her helmet. He had never seen anything so beautiful in his life; even within that wind-tugged jump suit and helmet and goggles there was no way to mistake this woman he loved.

They touched hands, a light caress as they fell earthward, two human forms floating under perfect control. Their world above a world was a feather bed of infinite softness. She pushed away, laughing, and quickly she pulled her knees up to her chest and he did the same, and they rolled through a lyrical somersault, then spread-eagled again. Lance moved his palms outward and slid backward and away from Lee. She nodded. Time fled swiftly in these carefree leaps through thin but friendly air. The trick was to engage that massive planet below them with gentle greeting. They grasped the D rings of their main chutes and pulled. A spring snapped away a small pilot chute that blossomed instantly and whipped away. They could hear the fluting whistle of rubber bands, an easy, gentle shuddering sound as the shroud lines followed the pilot chute away, filled quickly but also gently, and that quickly their fall was ended, and they floated like great nylon dandelions, wafting toward earth.

Eighty-four.

Eighty-three.

Eighty-two.

Floating, falling gently, drifting down ...

Lee came off the high board with flawless grace, her body shamefully sinuous as she arched at the high curve of her dive, twisting through and head coming down. She sliced into the clear waters of the pool with no more splash than a cavorting silent dolphin. She came out of the water, and he greeted her with a wild hug, and they laughed together. "You're getting your clothes all wet!" she protested, pushing him back gently. He hugged her all the tighter. Who cared about getting wet or the clothes or all the smiling people watching them and laughing with them? He kissed her deeply.

Seventy-seven.

Seventy-six.

Floating, floating ...

Their clothes seemed to slide from their bodies. Not all at once, but piece by piece, in between sweet kisses and deep embraces, until only their skin and souls came together. They joined and they moved in love and it was *complete,* and he soared to a gut-wrenching climax and floated along a lofty cloud and the wild surging of his loins became gentle warmth, and he eased down slowly, floating back to physical touch, floating down gently, ever so gently. . . .

Sixty-three.

Sixty-two.

Sixty-one.

Hiking along high mountain trails, joining the sharp-hooved and surefooted creatures that pranced and leaped along jagged rocks, tugging and struggling to crags and ultimate peaks, and coming down slowly, carefully, linked together by strong safety lines, bound even stronger by what passed between their minds.

Fifty-seven.

Fifty-six.

Lance looked down from the weathered balcony of their apartment on a high hill overlooking San Francisco Bay; off in the shimmering distance, a floating Camelot in the foggy haze of San Francisco, rose lofty spires and needles of buildings. He glanced at the winding road to see a bright yellow MGB curling its path upward, saw that flowing dark hair of Lee, felt again that sense of miracle, luxuriated in the feeling of love and oneness that always rose so quietly in him. She had worked late in her laboratory. Lance was home early from his gleaming chrome and plastic and electronic environs of Coastal Dynamics, where he labored to produce new designs and machinery for the great power systems that might slake a nation's insatiable demands for energy. He was a chemist and a nuclear engineer and an aerodynamicist, and he had his Ph.D. in fluid mechanics, all of which seemed to contradict his athletic prowess and competitive spirit. But at least he and a friend owned a twin-engine plane, and he and Lee owned a boat and a sumptuous van. Thirty-two years old, nearly six feet tall, with curly brown hair and 190 pounds of muscle and sinew on his frame, he appeared more the star slugger of a major-league team than the young scientist.

He had been called brilliant and innovative by his colleagues, but those were the words he reserved for the slim dark-haired beauty who was driving to him now. In her chosen fields she was considered just one short step over the boundaries of genius. He thought now, as he often did, of how much she had achieved already.

Lee had begun her college studies in medicine and physiology, added bionics and cybernetics to her learning burdens and then judged accurately that she was sorely deficient in human engineering systems and electronics. So she had learned and taught herself as much as, if not more than, had been provided her through her skull-squeezing years at MIT and UCLA.

Lee Grazzi had put into her career future the same incisive judgment that had marked her academic years. There existed a wide-open market for a new commodity, and Lee swiftly stepped into the vacuum: produced, and patented, what she called her AHS— Automated Human System. Her robot figures were indistinguishable from living persons. They were built with such detailed systems that they could bend, twist, rotate, rise, sit, stand, and, for the limited distances of entertainment dioramas, even walk and execute a series of commands imprinted within their computers. She developed artificial larynx systems that gave individual voices to her near androids, as she was so fond of calling them, and the Grazzi Dioramas became the rage of the entertainment and industrial demonstration worlds. They were so startlingly real that technical industry bought them for special tests with cars and aircraft and a hundred other uses, and Lee became a woman who could have rapidly grown wealthy —had she not found so much pleasure in pouring the incoming finances right back into new and ever more advanced research.

For if Lee found real pleasure in any endeavor, it was in the challenge of improving what lay behind her: prosthetics and exoskeletal systems and modifications of computers with their silicon chips jammed with the memories of motions of living human beings. She was the creator of modern-age benevolent and faithful Frankensteins, and she searched constantly for plastiskin with human hair embedded in the material; she perfected artificial eyes that narrowed and enlarged their pupils, and she gave those eyes tear ducts with saline solutions. Her Automated Human Systems were near androids that might slide across the invisible barrier to real life if only she could brew up a new stirring of electrical juices.

He thought of the elaborate hoax she had played on him one night he had returned from a trip to find her standing behind the bar of their Sausalito hillside apartment. He had started toward her for an embrace and a kiss when she extended her hand. "No, don't. Not yet, Lance. Let me bring a drink to you first. Take the couch, please." He had studied her in the half-light of the apartment, then nodded. Lee was unpredictable in her moods at such moments, and he enjoyed yielding to her desires. He had watched her lithe movements as she brought the drink to him. Ordinarily she wore no clothes when they were alone late at night. She slept in the buff, and so he was surprised, but in some different way quite pleased, when he saw the outline of that lovely form beneath a brief sheer nightie. She slid close to him on the seat and extended his drink. "Welcome home, darling."

He had held the drink. God, she'd never been more beautiful, more sensuous than at this moment, and he waited to drink, leaning closer to her, their lips touching. She fell into his lap. He was so astonished as she collapsed across him that the drink tumbled from his hand, and he blinked as the room lights snapped on full and Lee stood before him. "Dammit, I thought I had that balance problem licked. But when the torso bends like that on a soft surface, the center of gravity shifts, and—" She had stood before him and sighed. "Hi. I love you. Do you like your welcome-home present?"

The human facsimile had lain warm and gurgling in his lap, and he stared up at her. "I don't know whether to kill you or love you," he had said finally. He looked morosely at the spilled drink. "Was that real? A shame to waste it."

"Kiss me and I'll make you another. And close your jaw, love. Did I really surprise you that much?"

He had refused to kiss her until the ersatz Lee, still warm and still gurgling his name, was dragged off to a closet and its power systems were disconnected. He shuddered. "I still don't believe it."

Forty-four.

Forty-three.

Forty-two.

Down.

Down . . .

He handed her a drink as she came through the door, easing packages onto the couch. She held the drink and kissed him warmly, then saluted him with her glass. "I detect all manner of bubbling sounds and strange pleasant smells from the kitchen. Do I hasten or lie here like a smiling wastrel?"

He grinned at her. "Waste away, lovely one. This evening is my once-a-month plunge into gastronomical adventures. You sit and sip, and then we both sup."

She chewed the end of an olive with glistening white teeth. "During the time of your last such adventure," she purred, "I recall fervent prayers of thanks from both of us that this place has two bathrooms."

Lance winced. "A slight miscalculation, my dear."

"A vast dumping of the wrong spices, as I remember it."

"The wrong time of the moon. Weak stomachs and all that."

"Mine wasn't weak *before* you cooked." She joined him in the kitchen and nibbled at his earlobe. "All right. Living dangerously is fun, I suppose."

He sniffed with mock disdain. "You'd rather jump from an airplane?"

"At least *that* doesn't upset my stomach. What do you boil in your toil for us, lover?"

"Ah, an ancient recipe from the witches who ghost through forests, from their friends and trolls, from the elves and the creatures that go bump in the night. It is what I call a challenge recipe."

She studied him, holding back her smile. "You pique my interest. I didn't know you were a warlock."

"Only in the intestinal sense, my dear."

"You sound like Dracula with a belly fetish. What's the challenge?"

"You can't—"

"No, wait," she interrupted hurriedly. "First tell me what it's called."

"Chicken nuggets."

The silence held for a long moment. "Chickens don't have nuggets. Roosters may, but I really haven't looked lately."

"Chicken nuggets, dammit," he repeated.

"All right." She sighed. "My interest is yours. What's the challenge with your fowl testicles?"

"I'll ignore that if you'll pay attention," he rebuked her.

"Horrors. I promise good manners from here on. The challenge, Mr. Parker, tell me."

He showed the trace of a smile. "The recipe is from my grandmother. If you're with me while I prepare the meal, there's no way you'll eat a full dinner at the table."

"Why?"

"Once you start tasting, you can't quit. You munch your way through. No way to stop."

"You mean, I can't take just one bite."

"That's it."

"I don't believe it."

"You get the wine. We drink while we cook."

"*We* drink and *you* cook."

He rolled his eyes. "You test your chef."

"The better to observe." She looked about the kitchen. "This is all preparation or has the ship been launched?"

"I have waited patiently for your return. Now, first I beat two eggs with a whisk in a bowl of precisely two and a half quarts' capacity, and then—"

"Do you know how to make a Hungarian omelet? You're on your way. First, you steal two eggs, and—"

"Shaddup. You whisk the eggs for one minute until they are a precise golden yellow. Presto, we add one cup of water, one and a half teaspoons of salt, two tablespoons of sesame seeds—"

"*Yuk.*"

He ignored the barbs and swept on. "And one cup of flour, measured precisely. We mix thoroughly until the flour is mixed into the proper batter. Ah, just right." He moved the bowl aside, moved another large bowl before them. "These shall become nuggets."

"My God, you've chopped the chicken." She drank a bit more hastily.

"Of course, m'love. Eight chicken breasts into cubes of approximately one inch size."

She waved an empty glass before working on a refill. "You, my engineer of micromillimeters, are saying approximately? Why not precisely?"

"Dead chickens yet uncooked squiggle like sponges."

"I yield the point. Continue."

"We use these handy tongs, here, to dip the chicken cubes in the batter. Over here you will note I have been preparing one and a half pints of oil, within a three-quart Corning Ware cooking pot."

"*Uh-huh.*" She sipped noisily.

"Now we cook the nuggets until they become a fascinating golden brown in color. The stove is on medium heat, the level of oil is precise, so we shall cook for four minutes." He moved quickly to another bowl. "Here we have the sauce, into which I have combined one cup catsup, one half teaspoon dry mustard, one tablespoon of brown sugar, six tablespoons of margarine—"

"You've got to be kidding."

"And one, no, make that two tablespoons of vinegar. We cook over medium heat in a saucepan for five minutes, stirring constantly with the left hand until it is a dark russet to red in color."

She blinked her eyes. "Russet? And why the left hand? Oh, I see. You're playing catch-up. Stir with the left hand, and use the tongs with the right hand to remove the nuggets. What happens if you want to scratch your nose?"

He ignored her as he removed the first cooked chicken nuggets and placed them on a paper towel. His left hand kept stirring, and with his right hand

51

he placed more chicken cubes in the pot. He grinned at her. "The sauce isn't set. Watch that chicken. It's hot, so don't burn yourself."

She picked up one with extra caution, bit gingerly, showed surprise, moved it from one hand to the other. "Like I said, hot," he warned again.

"My God, it's delicious. All that witch's brew." She reached for a second piece. "I can't believe it."

"Try the sauce." He smirked.

"Too hot yet. I'll wait. *Umm,* I'll just try one more."

He laughed. *"Uh-huh.* I told you."

She tried to talk through a mouthful of hot chicken nugget. *"Mmrf?"*

"I told you. You can't eat just one. You keep eating these damn things fast as I make 'em. Pour me a nice triple martini, will you? I'm a prisoner in my own kitchen."

"Smrgff. Umm. Sure thing. Here."

Thirty minutes later they were both stuffed and more than well on their way to being smashed. They giggled and sat on the kitchen floor, mixing nuggets with martinis. Lance sprawled on the floor.

"I'm horny," Lee said.

"I'm stuffed. Call for help."

She undid his belt. "Help," she said quietly.

"My God, I'd die."

She pulled away his clothes. "What a way to go. You lie still. Slaving over a hot stove and all that." Her clothes tumbled by his. She wriggled her toes. "Nice and cool. Lie still, dammit." She slid onto him, leaned forward to grasp his hair with both hands, and kissed him deeply. He didn't, he couldn't move. He was a giant bowl of contentment as she took him at her own leisure, and he nearly went mad as she brought them both to climax. She lay beside him, her head nestled in the crook of his arm, instantly asleep. He felt himself drifting away, drifting down, down . . .

Thirty.

Twenty-nine.

Twenty-eight . . .

The small boat drifted through stygian darkness, floating with the black current beneath them. They were awed, enchanted, as their lights moved across the miniature cathedral spires of the deep cave.

"The colors." She spoke in a half whisper. "I don't really believe the colors. Where could they come from? There's no sun down here." She flicked him a glance. "And don't start reeling off your list of elements and chemicals. I'd rather be a kid again in fairyland."

He smiled. "That you are. We both are."

She turned her head suddenly. "What's that sound? It sounds like thunder. But it can't be that."

He flashed a light on the water, watched it swirling by the boat. "We're moving faster. It could be a waterfall."

"Then we'd better put on the brakes."

He turned his light again to the narrowing tunnel before them. Sparkling motes drifted downward. The thunder became louder, and now they felt vibrations in the air and through the water. Lee had time only to cry out, "Lance!" when the thunder became a terrible roar and the world began to pulverize its own innards and rocks fell into the river and the cave was collapsing all about them and a wave capsized the boat and the icy water struck him with the shock of a billion frozen needles and he felt himself going under, *going down, down, down . . .*

Nineteen.

Eighteen.

Seventeen—

WAKE UP! YOU DUMB SON OF A BITCH, COME OUT OF IT!

His own voice, his subconscious, screaming at him. The built-in warning at the back of the mind. He blinked his eyes, startled, moving only his eyes, and oh, Jesus, the world *was* coming apart all about him. Just outside the surface of his spherical chamber, enormous rock masses were shifting. Alarms clamored shrilly in his ears because not even the incredible strength of the sphere could endure that kind of pressure without breaching its integrity, and when that happened, his air would become heated radioactive fog. *Christ, man, move it!* He was moving immediately to where he'd hung his armored survival suit, and he was closed in, completing the pressurization and power systems, when he heard a devastating *TWANG!*, the cry of a bowstring a mile long releasing its energy, and he heard it again, and even in the face of certain death he marveled at the sound that he knew no man had ever heard before, those massive springs coming apart under unbelievable pressure, and he clambered into the seat and tugged all the straps and the restraints as tightly as they would go.

He stared at the spherical wall as it rocked violently, and when the blurring eased, he saw the first spidery cracks appearing, and as the suit cooling system kicked in, he could almost feel the awesome heat. A crack widened into a true fissure, and the edges of some enormous boulder punched through what had become an eggshell, and the rough-edged rock ground inexorably toward him and slowly, deliberately, as if the pushing finger of some angry deity, broke his leg once, twice, and still a third time, and the sweat stabbed in agony from his face, and he felt the heat coming through the crushed suit. Shit, why die like this? He could at least go without thrashing about mindlessly like a creature burning alive while all those granite teeth were closing on him.

He found the control for the morphine syringe and stabbed it wildly, felt the drug sluice into his system, and he stabbed a second one, and a third, and it was a race between powerful opiates and maddening pain, and then the pain came from a distance, and he wasn't all that sure it was his pain, and he really didn't care anymore. He heard the roar again, the roar he'd heard in the river with Lee, but when had they died in that river? The sound was the same, an angry mountain collapsing upon itself, a paroxysm of final convulsion, and there, over there, another crack in the eggshell and he saw a steel-hard jet of water under all that pressure rip into the chamber, as straight and true as if it were a steel rod, and it came at him. He tried to move his head out of the way, but he didn't care and it missed his head anyway and he knew someone was grinding a knife into his shoulder and he fell faster and faster into a black whirlpool, and he knew he was thinking his last, his final thought.

Thank God, I'm dead.

Chapter 6

"He has an even chance. No more, no less." Dr. Martha Foster held Lance Parker's chart. She turned to look directly at the distraught face of Lee Grazzi.

"Fifty-fifty," Lee intoned. "Not much of a chance, is it." No question there. Statement. Announcement of almost certain death. The physical injuries were only part of it. Lee looked up through the thick glass window separating her from the hyperbaric chamber that had for nearly three months contained the broken, abused, even savaged form of Lance Parker. Three months during which broken bones refused stubbornly to knit together. Three months of almost constant struggle between a body that had quit long before and the miraculous tools and weapons and knowledge of modern medical science.

Dr. Foster shook her head. "How can I discuss this with you on a medical basis? That's not a patient in there. It's a man you love. You're too deeply involved on an emotional basis to—"

Lee's head snapped around to lock eyes with the doctor. "After all this time you're *not* emotionally involved?"

Martha Foster sighed again, held her hands clasped before her. "Of course I am. Very deeply. Let's just say I have more experience in that twilight zone between life and death. And the most important thing for you to remember, for all of us to remember, is that we're not using machinery to keep him alive. Lance isn't a vegetable. He's been hurt in the cruelest way. But the very fact that he's alive is a great victory. If this were thirty years ago, perhaps even ten, he would have died. Not from the physical injuries. The radiation. We know so much more now." She looked through the window, into the chamber where they had kept Lance under an atmospheric pressure of thirty pounds per square inch, double that of normal, and with the oxygen content at fifty-five percent instead of the normal twenty-one percent. Oxygen under pressure to saturate tissues that couldn't receive enough oxygen because the blood didn't work well, because too many cells of too many kinds were missing, because the circulation system was a physiological plumbing nightmare, and—

How could he have lived through it all? Any other man would be dead. Any sane man would have quit, would have pulled the switch inside his own mind. But he hasn't. He doesn't know what's happened to him. If he did, he would have willed himself to die. If only we can keep him alive long enough to gain his strength, he may not be able to close off his mind to life. He may live despite himself. Lee Grazzi forced down the lump in her throat. It had been there too many times. She had even learned to close off the tears. Even in the darkness of her lonely bedroom at night. Even when she lived in her own imagination what had happened to Lance deep under that mountain.

Right ankle crushed.

Right leg fractured.

Left leg fractured.

Pelvis partially crushed.

Seven ribs broken.

Organs damaged; healing slow, dangerous.

Large intestine pierced. It had bled for two months.

Right collarbone broken.

Two vertebrae crushed.

Left side of the skull fractured.

Concussion.

Left arm broken in three places.

Right wrist fractured.

Lance was a complete medical catastrophe of broken bones, crushed bones, burned skin, punctures, abrasions, massive bruises, mashed capillaries, severed arteries and veins, thermal exhaustion, chemical burns, lung damage from inhalation of poisonous gases, damage to the retinal structure of one eye, still possible loss of hearing, and—

Disfigurement, bodily distortion, scarred skin.

A host of wonders awaited life for what had been a superb physical specimen. Would Lance hate her when he emerged from the fog in which electrically induced sleep had shrouded his ability to think? He was a maze before her eyes, a slowly pulsating biological mass with tubes and lines and wires running from and into and through his body and connected to row after row of life-suppporting machines. Electronic and mechanical angels ministering life. An artificial heart kept blood and oxygen moving until electrical shock and chemical stimulants could bring the weary, abused human heart to resume its nearly impossible task. Wires fed electrical impulses through his system. A kidney machine dribbled away wastes. He did not lie in a bed. His body could never have taken that. He lay suspended in a sutured net that constantly

59

shifted the weight and the pressure of his ravaged body. Bedsores alone could kill him.

For the worst damage had been invisible. Not in its effects, but in its cause. Those unseen sprays of radiation. Gamma radiation and X rays and neutrons and all the hellish fury they had wreaked in his unconscious form.

He had been unconscious, trapped, still mind-isolated through the morphine and the shock to his own system when they had reached him. A paramedic had drowned him in opiates, so that they could ease his form, like the skin of a cat with every bone inside broken—they could *feel* and *hear* his insides grinding and moving, his body liquids sloshing—out of the smashed spherical chamber and on that long, terrible ascent through the broken tunnels and shafts to the outside world. Plasma and IV and oxygen and adrenaline and anything else they had in the medivac helicopter, even a machine to pulsate the heart with electrical shocks timed to his heartbeat, and a steady flight directly to the great hospital on the outskirts of Oakland, where they placed him in the hyperbaric chamber and suspended him like a breathing, slowly heaving mass of bloody meat and stuck in the lines and hoses and wires and—

The radiation should have killed him. Lee felt a harsh and grating laughter in her own mind. Should have? It did; twice, maybe three times. Invisible, insidious, horrifying, defying the struggle to live.

He vomited again and again, and they had to be with him constantly so he wouldn't suffocate on the vomitus and bile that clogged his throat and threatened to add even more liquid to his already treacherous lungs. He lay unconscious, and the only thing they could bring within his body had to come via tube and needle. Glucose through a constant slow feed. Massive injections of vitamins and minerals and iron and God knew what else, and a small river of antibiotics. It was a time for knuckle-biting hellish frustration when diarrhea racked that already crushed and mauled body, when the insidious effects of the ionizing radiation began to manifest themselves. There was no way to hold back the bilious upheavals or the diarrhea and the raw and bleeding surfaces of his mouth and throat. The bed would have been worse, but the sutured net itself was a special torment; *any* surface against that outraged skin would have been terrible, creating bleeding beneath the skin. He had been flayed and cut and lacerated and scraped and bruised. But he had been strong, powerful, in perfect physical condition, and they knew gratitude those first few days when healing signs showed quickly and scabs formed, and they knew his body was fighting its own battle, and very well indeed.

Then the radiation emerged through tissue and liquids and bones and organs, and the scabs sloughed off and away, and wounds that were almost healed and already forming scars turned to mush before their eyes and bled freely. His eyes stared sightlessly from huge red pools because his retinas had begun to hemorrhage.

His fever went wild, and they could not bathe him in ice water or alcohol or whatever, and they dared not fill him with aspirin or its equivalents because his blood refused to clot and even aspirin could have killed him. Fans. Old-fashioned fans saved his life against the raging fever. Hanging, suspended through his benevolent meat-hook-like sutures, the fans could blow air about and around and across the tortured living carcass and carry away much of the heat and cool the skin.

Several weeks after he had been sealed within the hyperbaric chamber they almost lost him when, un-

61

Martin Caidin

seen and unnoticed by them, the lining of his mouth
and throat began to disintegrate and slough off into
spongy, mushy clumps of material that almost choked
him to death. A spasmodic coughing alerted them,
and the very act of coughing almost killed him. It was
a bizarre and brain-rattling Catch-22; to save him
from one immediate stab of death, the cure itself
could be lethal. They continued to balance along that
razor-thin tightrope of survival and final utter collapse.

"It's as if he's suffering from a terrible *internal* sunburn," Dr. Martha Foster explained to Lee Grazzi.
"It burns not only the undersurface of the skin but
also the tissues of his entire body. The worst of it, of
course, is that the ionizing radiation has such a devastating effect against the blood-making cells at the center of the long bones of the leg."

Of course. Lee already knew that. She had spent
sleepless nights studying the effects of ionizing radiation on the human body. She had crawled back in
time to those hours and days after the suns stabbed
into existence over Hiroshima and Nagasaki. Lance
suffered much the same as those Japanese who were
in the open in the Japanese cities anviled by the early
atomic bombs, with the exception that he was spared
the thermal outpouring that would have burned him
to a crisp.

What drove her mad was that Lance was showing
all the symptoms of final decay of those victims in
Hiroshima and Nagasaki *who had died.* Why, then,
did *he* live? The answer lay, of course, in his own superb physical condition. That, plus the fact that the
medical staff did not grope blindly amidst the horrendous thickets of radiation damage. Thousands had
been there before Lance Parker, and their deaths had
at least built up a working knowledge of what ravaged his body. There was no guesswork anymore, and

since the doctors could anticipate, they could also plan their steps well ahead of time. They knew he would lose between sixty and ninety percent of all his white blood cells; they protected him with antibiotics and massive transfusions. They knew skin would deteriorate and mucous membranes would manifest acute inflammation, and they were ready with the necessary steps to ward off final disaster from that route. They prepared for the onslaught of inflammation of his gums, mouth, and pharynx. They were ready with cooling air when his fever rose. They could only hope that both their attention and his strength would fight off the temporary ulceration of his lower gastrointestinal tract.

Lance had broken several teeth years earlier in a bad fall from a mountain climbing accident. Dr. Martha Foster pondered that matter, and then memory rang a bell. She had the gold fillings removed at once from his mouth. "He took neutron exposure," she explained to Lee. "The damned gold is radioactive. It could have killed him."

Any small straw could break the back of his remaining tenuous thread of life.

The slightest cold, an onslaught of sneezing, could now kill Lance Parker. His survival was a race against time—just how swiftly and effectively his doctors could keep fresh blood pumping into his veins with the white cells he needed to combat infection. The score so far was a tenuous standoff.

The ionizing radiation—that superinternal sunburn—not only had wrecked his ability to produce white cells but had also wreaked havoc on the ability of Lance's blood to coagulate. Thus, the internal bleeding. Even if the condition was temporary, it was impossible to escape the grim reality that the gamma radiation Lance had absorbed reduced drastically the number of platelets in his blood. Again it was the source of reproduction that took the beating, the bone marrow, now suffering the equal of terrible tiny furnaces raging through their roots. Platelets, so small, so insignificant, so essential to life. Tiny cellular protein bodies that played so indispensable a role in clotting tiny wounds in the capillaries and the smaller blood vessels.

Scratch a man and watch him bleed to death.

Goddammit. The man was Lance.

The pumping system was breaking down inside the biological machinery of one Lance Parker. But by some miracle the crushing of his rib cage, the damage to his lungs, all the grueling knives of injury, had somehow escaped directly punishing his heart.

Lee sat up brooding one sleepless night, trying to reduce her own emotion-racked heart to vital statistics by which she might anticipate the survival of the man she loved. Strange, but statistical parody helped. She could in those times think of Lance much as she did of her Automated Human Systems, except that she dabbled with a biological computer in terms few people ever realized epitomized their own bodies.

Blood. Heavier than water, half plasma and half corpuscles, three times the viscosity of water. A body with the mass of Lance Parker should contain some thirteen pints. Easy numbers. She nibbled at the computer and brooded at numbers. She already knew the hellish drought of white cells and Lance's ghastly helplessness before infection and disease. *Forget it,* she told herself. They've got the machinery and the drugs and the systems to make up for that. She studied the other side of the coin, red and rich. *Supposed* to be red and rich, she mused. The lack of red was as potentially lethal to Lance as was the drought of white.

Blood is red. *Only if it's flowing through that miraculous circulation system; only then. Don't forget that.* She remembered. If you take a quart jar of blood, remove its ability to clot so it loses ability to retain its color, you also change red to a triple agent in the jar. That wonderful red color plops to the bottom of the jar. Atop the wonderful red color, like icing on some liquid cake, is a thinly sliced layer of white. Those white corpuscles. In Lance's case they were so few that if the jar had been filled from his body, the thin layer might not even have been visible except for the slightest discoloration. *Anyway. Yes, anyway. What about the top of the jar?* Slightly more than half will be colored like straw. That's the plasma. Forget the plasma. *That's right. There's no shortage. The hospital has pints, quarts, gallons, whole vats of the stuff, and most of it has already been in and through Lance.*

Life would remain, or it would ebb away into cold and gray meat if that rich, heavy liquid weren't replenished sooner or later by Lance's own systems. For now, the scientific biomedical machinery would suffice, but only for now. After that, the astonishing miracle of his own body must repair itself and resume its miracle of output, or he would wind down like a spongy clock choking on itself.

She stared at her own hand, picked up a needle, and pricked her thumb. Lightly. Just enough to produce a dot of blood. She adjudged it as being a cubic millimeter, the same size to which she and Dr. Foster had referred when they discussed the white blood cells that Lance needed so desperately and that had thinned to fog. One pinprick, one cubic millimeter, and a respectable average of 7,000 to 8,000 white blood cells.

A few snowflakes in an otherwise clear sky, compared to the blizzard of red to be produced continually, all his life, by his own body systems. She tapped the computer keys to study the digital readout displayed before her. Wonderful, life reduced to digits. But they were astonishing.

One pinprick equals 8,000 white blood cells.

One pinprick, the same one, equals 250,000 platelets. Platelets kept a man from bleeding to death from a scratch. They did other wonderful things, but she ignored that for the moment.

One pinprick, the *same* one, also contained for a body the size of Lance Parker on the order of 5 million red corpuscles.

More numbers. Lance had 13 pints of blood coursing through his body. That meant about 65 billion white blood cells, more than 1.5 trillion platelets, and some 35 trillion red cells.

The red lived longer than the white. Perhaps four months. Lance had been in that triple-damned hyperbaric chamber for four months, during which his blood had circulated throughout his body more than 170,000 complete round trips.

To stay alive and reasonably healthy, 9 ounces of bone marrow from his entire system had to replace 20 billion red cells *every single day*.

Every minute of every day his heart shoved and pushed and pumped 27 trillion cells and platelets through his mauled body. The distribution system was all screwed up as well, and the heart and the body, understandably, had more than once simply wanted to quit.

But the circulation had to be maintained, for the red cells were chock-full of dandy little things that made up hemoglobin, and hemoglobin is the magic voyager that distributes oxygen throughout the body tissues. Lance desperately lacked hemoglobin, and so he desperately lacked oxygen, and without the hyperbaric chamber and oxygen saturation and the machines and pumps and vats of blood and the doctors and nurses and technicians he would have—

Don't say it.

Right. Let's stay with the numbers. Let's pick out one lonely little red corpuscle. Just one out of 35 trillion. That one corpuscle—she jabbed into the computer for the digital readout on the screen—carries nearly 300 million molecules of hemoglobin. And each single molecule is bulging with some 10,000 atoms of oxygen, and therefore, Lance Parker needed 60 sextillion atoms of oxygen every minute of every hour of every day of—

Just to stay alive. And she hadn't even considered the nutrients, the hormones, the antibodies, and God knew what else.

Her fist raised as if it were possessed of its own command and banged down on the CLEAR READOUT button. The millions and billions and trillions and sextillions winked out. Lee sucked in long, shuddering gasps of air, the very act of recognizing the impossibility of life coming close to strangling her. She sat in the dim glow of the waiting computer control console, and she looked up at the gleaming cybernetic system and how neatly it had doodled electronically about a living, thinking, loving human being, and very quietly she stood and looked again at the computer and said, "Fuck you," and it helped.

Chapter 7

Stanley Newsum was a big man, broad in shoulders and ample in girth, and his three-piece suits were tailored to his great bulk so that he moved through rooms and amidst people with all the grace of a well-oiled whale. Stanley Newsum was a Ph.D. in nuclear engineering, but he was also an administrator for the Atomic Energy Commission, and he was smart enough to have forsaken his slide rule and salary pittance as a scientist for the fat wages of the man who directed the Alamitos Nuclear Generating System. Of course, that wide and smiling face with its thick, wavy gray hair was regarded as something of a monster by the ordinary citizens who feared the atom just a bit more than they did Stanley Newsum, but he really didn't give a damn. Not at $300,000 a year, because Newsum could deal in the harsh inner sanctum of nuclear power with the best of the press, and he never lost a word duel with what he considered the jackals of the media. He was very big, very fast, very smart—and as cold as ice when it came to wielding the ax.

"He's made it, Lee," Stanley Newsum told Lee

Grazzi. "No one ever believed he could survive his injuries, but he did. No one ever believed he could survive the radiation he took, but he did. Even his hair has grown back! He was bald as a babe, and we both know that the best overt sign of recovery is the regrowth of hair." Newsum grinned. "Why, he's going to need a haircut pretty soon if he keeps improving like this. I'm delighted, really delighted. I want you to know that."

"Kill the big smile, Stanley," Lee told him with a bluntness that caught the big man off guard. "It's not in your character."

Newsum's eyes narrowed. "You mean something more than you're saying, Lee."

"Stop the shit. How's that for starters?"

"Not very nice." Newsum smiled coldly at her. "I don't know what misconceptions you've already built up in your mind, Lee, but you're being unfair."

"My God, pretty soon I'll need a crying towel. Poor dear," Lee said, matching the humorless smile, "we've hurt his feelings." Her tone changed. "Now you listen to me, Stanley. We both know what you are. A smart engineer and a good scientist and a man who preferred to use his body beef and shrewd mind to pick up a lot of money instead of laboratory blisters. Okay, that's your bag. But in the business your fame isn't being an administrator." She watched his brows raise. He pursed his lips and made a steeple of his fingers, waiting. "We know what you are, Stanley. The word is hatchet man. In the old days you'd be a collector for the mob."

This time his smile was broad and meaningful. "My dear, you save me a great deal of unnecessary conversation. I'll preface my remarks by reminding you that for one year the Alamitos board of directors has been paying all medical bills for Lance Parker. They—"

"You mean," she said angrily, "the insurance company has paid the bills."

The smile faded like a light dwindling away. "No insurance. The policy specified hydroelectric. It didn't mention nuclear. The policy was voided."

"Then Alamitos—*you*—lied. Not Lance."

"No," he said with a realism she couldn't reject, "we *all* lied. Lance went into this with his eyes open. He knew we were hanging a big blanket of wool before the public, waving the banner for underground rivers while he was working on the reactor system. That's not the issue. That's history."

"I have a sinking feeling I know why you're here," she said.

"I always said you were a smart girl."

"Don't patronize me, you son of a bitch."

Newsum blinked several times and delayed answering. It was an old and tried trick that worked. The opposition studied the eyes and wondered what the hell the blinking was all about, and that gave Newsum time to select his next line plunge. This time he went dead through center.

"The till is empty, Lee. All of us at Alamitos are the modern-day gangsters. There's no complaint. It's a fact. We're going to be indicted. That, too, is a fact. We'll beat it. But there are also other facts of life. We consider Lance Parker to have survived the accident. He was severely injured; he made it. He took one hell of a blast of radiation, and he made it out of that. Presto, anything from here on out is a handout. We can't afford to do that. Part of our defense is to establish clearly that Lance is the victim of an accident that left him with the same problems that could have come from a car wreck, or an accident with a tractor on a farm, or an airplane crash, or whatever."

She took it silently, absorbing it all, considering the counterthrusts, knowing it wouldn't do a damned bit

71

of good. She knew Stanley Newsum's *modus operandi*. Leave nothing unresolved *before* you stick it in.

"You're throwing Lance to the wolves. Isn't that it?" Newsum nodded. "That's it."

"You're a filthy bastard."

"That's how I earn my keep." Again there came the steepled fingers and the hard-eyed study of Lee. "Of course, there is one thing."

"You're too big for a spider to be playing come-into-my-den."

"True." The great bulk leaned forward. "The long and short of it, dear lady, is that Lance Parker is the only man who may be able to shed some light on what happened *inside* the core of the reactor. Don't forget we're not dealing with a situation like the one we had with St. Helens when it exploded. There we had a bona fide volcano and lots of warning, and it was very spectacular, and it didn't kill as many people as die driving on a quiet Sunday. *This* is very different. That earthquake and all its aftereffects spread out over a wide territory. The direct shock and the floods and avalanches—well, more than eight hundred people died from that quake. Lance Parker *lived* through it. He's the only survivor, for God's sake! It's like, well, it's like his surviving the explosion of St. Helens while he was inside the crater. So he's all we've got. He's *everything*. His testimony, in response to the indictments, proving that the fault lay in the hands of God, that the reactor was sound and that nothing could have withstood the effects of that earthquake . . . well, it could make all the difference. So far Lance Parker won't talk about it. You can make him talk for us."

"The rest of it," she said, gesturing impatiently.

"He testifies, and we arrange for a bank deposit of one hundred thousand dollars. That should give him a nice fresh start. We're off the hook, and he starts again."

"You're forgetting something. Physically he's a wreck. Emotionally he's a disaster."

Newsum shrugged. "That's the breaks." He locked eyes with Lee. "Goddammit, woman, it could have happened skydiving or in a car or *anything*."

"But it *didn't*," she said quietly.

"Will you talk to him about this?" Newsum demanded suddenly.

"Yes. I'll talk with him."

Newsum pondered her words. "Do you think he'll play ball?"

"Play ball?" Her laugh was shrill. "What a goddamned stupid choice of words about a man who can no longer *walk*. Play ball. You amaze me."

"Never mind the sparring, Lee. I—"

"If he doesn't testify, or *does* testify about basic faults with the reactor, you people may go to prison."

"Yes. That's why we're willing to lay down that hundred thousand."

"I don't think he'll play ball. He doesn't like you people very much."

"We don't care what he likes. We're talking a hundred grand."

"You're talking blackmail. You're talking coercion. You're talking putting the screws to a man who's gone through incredible pain and torture and who faces life as a cripple. He can't play ball very well. But there's one thing Lance Parker does with style."

"And what's that?" demanded Newsum.

"It's called getting even. Now get out."

He swung around slowly on the swivel chair, a twisted parody of a human being condemned all the more for his gnarled hand, the head subtly askew from a permanently misaligned spinal cord. There

was no way ever to accept that this disfigured wretch
had been the athletically superb, the ruggedly handsome Lance Parker. What emerged with greater impact than ever before was the intensity of his
emotions. Before his collision with a mountain, his
drowning under radioactive steam, Lance had been
strong but easygoing, powerful yet gentle, and, above
all, unencumbered with any problems of self. Now
the inner fire burned more fiercely, bitterly, sluiced
and fed by torrents of naked anger. "What I want
you to do, Lee," he said slowly, for he could not
speak quickly, nor could he manage clarity in his
speech—his damaged vocal cords had altered a beautiful baritone to a rasping growl—"is to leave me one
last gift. Do you understand? I'm asking you for a favor. Stop helping to keep me alive as Mr. Supervege-
table, dammit."

She sat across thick carpeting in her living room,
matching his eyes. God in heaven, that blazing hatred
was a flame pure and bright; his eyes had gained an
intensity she would never have believed possible in a
human being. She'd gone through this argument before with Lance. She fought down the pity that had
been shoved harshly into a corner of her mind; she
rejected it as worthless to both of them; it would only
have directed his hatred of life against her. That face
. . . disfigured, lips twisted, some teeth still missing
and awaiting further dental surgery. Flesh torn and
scarred, his left hand gnarled through its fingers, one
leg slightly shorter than the other. Strangely enough,
the musculature was still there: bent and clumped,
not the smooth flowing lines of the running athlete,
but in some ways even greater than the strength he
had known before, for the new demands imposed on
his body created new areas of powerful muscle and
greater sinew and tendon.

"Do you really expect me to help you in dying?"

She had planned to speak softly, gently, much as her fingers had caressed his body before and wanted to caress them now. But the velvet was wrong. He had to have his response in kind. "If you do, you're as stupid as the desire."

He shook his head slowly, fingers gripping his cane until the scarred knuckles showed skeletal white. "Look, I know we've gone over this before," he rasped. "Maybe you don't understand all of it. Maybe you think my wanting *not* to remain alive in this stinking husk of a body is self-pity."

"Isn't it?" She almost purred the words, but the sarcasm came through.

"You know goddamned well it isn't!"

"What is it then, Lance? What is this desire for complete destruction? It's nearly two years since *it* happened, and you have miracle upon miracle behind you, which is why you're here. You have miracles waiting for you. You'll regain all your teeth. I've told you about the vitreous implants. They—"

"Spare me. I know."

"You have most of your life still ahead of you! They washed the radiation from you. It won't get worse. It won't keep chewing and tearing at you—like you do with your *mind*. You . . ." Her voice trailed away, and the rasping sound from his throat gained a plea, a gentle call, for deeper understanding.

"I am not a goddamned hero." The words were carefully spaced, each distinct, each a verbal entity demanding its own attention. "I didn't go to the moon. I never stormed a beachhead. I didn't win any medals. But I do have a right to put a value on my own life. It seems to me that the choice of living or dying is mine, and I am *not* scrabbling around emotional ice to find a footing. It's a ledger. Assets and debits. Before, I had the assets and the debits were minimal. Now it's the other way around. When I add

75

it all up, this wreck in which I'm trapped just doesn't appeal to me. Do I want to live this way? Do I want to limp and scrape and twist and bend and walk like a broken doll? Do I want to scare the shit out of kids with my voice? Is giving people nightmares when they look at my face an acceptable solution to *not* living?"

She didn't hide her scorn. "You forgot leprosy and bad breath."

He blinked at her words. "I'll put it another way then. There's nothing wrong with dying if living isn't worth the candle. Dammit, Lee, we've both lived on the edge of wiping out—in balloons, skydiving, water skiing, mountain climbing—"

"Driving in traffic, eating in fast-food restaurants," she thrust between his words.

He sat quietly for a moment. "I'll ignore that. You and I, we did what we wanted. We took our chances. Now I can't do what I want, and life has lost its sweetness because I can't even walk up to the risks. I'm a wreck and not a man. I'm alive by a fluke, a long procession of miracles, if you like. The truth is that if you had found an animal in the condition they found me in that sphere, you would all have nicely agreed to be merciful and blown it away." He grimaced-smiled naked hatred at her. "Why don't you be kind to the nice doggie, Lee?" Laughter grated in his throat. "Be nice to the doggie and blow out his fucking brains."

"You forget something. I care for you and I love you and—"

"I don't owe you shit, lady."

Her pause was brief. "No, you don't. And *I* don't owe *you*. Nor do I pity you, no matter what you may believe. You needn't glare at me, Lance. Like it or not, what I just said is the truth. What I do find so repulsive is this farce of dying you keep on prattling about."

She might as well have struck him across the face. "Farce?" He blinked in disbelief. *"Farce?"* he repeated.

She nodded. "That's right. You want the easy way out. Like someone overpowering you and throwing you off a boat so you can be eaten by a shark. Or jumping out of a plane without a chute. Or best of all, taking a bottle of sleeping pills. Slip off into the eternal twilight on clouds of opium poppies."

"Not bad," he said quietly.

It was going too far. They were like two animals with fangs bared, constantly circling each other. It led nowhere but down. She bit the bullet.

"I'll make you a deal, Lance Parker."

His fingers squeezed the cane, relaxed, squeezed again. "I'm listening."

"I'm going to help you kill yourself."

"I don't believe you."

"You'd better believe, friend. Right here in this room, tonight, *now.*"

He looked at her with suspicion. "What's the hook?"

She smiled coldly. "I pick the weapon."

"You're playing games with me."

"The hell I am. But there's a condition."

"I said there was a hook."

"If there is, Lance, then it's all yours. I'll give you the means to kill yourself right here and now. *But I don't believe you really want to do that.* I don't believe that down deep in that mind of yours, you really and truly want to die. So I'm going to test you. No, don't interrupt me. I'll tell you the terms."

He waited.

"If you don't go through with it, if you don't kill yourself—and I swear to you I won't intervene, no matter what happens—then you give me your word you'll go back into electric sleep and let me continue the plastic surgery and other medical work I had planned."

He took several deep, shuddering breaths. "No gimmicks?" he said finally.

She shook her head. "None. Thousands of people die this way every year."

"You really mean it then?"

Her face was set in stone. "I damned well do."

"All right. Let's do it."

Fear stabbed her heart. But there was no backing down now. She *must* gamble on two things. The first was, as she said, that deep inside him he did *not* want to die, no matter what he said. The second was the reflex of the body itself to resist death, an instinct that howled deeply in the furthermost recesses of a man's mind. Fight, struggle, kick, bite, kill—but never give in.

The selection of the weapon was everything. That was why she had made the sudden decision. If she brought him a gun, it would be too easy. There's no defense against the angry, sudden, blind squeezing of a finger that sends a bullet into the brain. No knife. He could fall on that like the samurai of old.

She stood up. "Wait here."

She returned from the kitchen and placed a low table before his chair. On her next trip she brought a large tub in which she normally mixed plastic chemicals. He sat in silence, and she kept her lips tight, as she made a dozen trips to and from the kitchen, each time returning with two large pots of water.

"All right, Lance. It's full. Two feet of water. You need only hold your nose and mouth an inch below the surface. Just breathe it in and keep breathing it in, and you'll drown right here in front of me, and as God is my witness, I will sit here and watch you."

"You bitch."

"Why?"

"I know the reflexes as well as you do! I—"

"Do it."

His eyes blazed at her. Abruptly he flung aside the cane, leaned forward, grabbed the sides of the tub and, in a final gesture of hatred and rejection, slammed his head deep into the water. She forced herself to keep her eyes open, to watch. She saw it all, the fingers going through spasms as he fought desperately to keep his head immersed, the convulsions as his lungs took in water and autonomic functioning rejected the killing fluid. She heard him snarling, screaming under the water. His body twisted from side to side, and he was a broken, mangled doll moved by some satanic force, and *oh, my God, he's doing it.*

Blackness began to envelop Lance, and he felt his muscles shuddering and his body jerking to and fro, but he fought back racking coughs and the primal scream in his mind to let go, to come up, *up*, out of that last breath, and then he smiled to himself because he knew his lungs had too much water, and he let the blackness take him and he—

She bit through her lip as he retched violently, already unconscious, the violent subconscious lunge throwing him backward and away from the water, and he collapsed on the carpet, soaked, his body twitching and convulsing, choking. She couldn't take the chance. She rolled him over and bent to him for mouth-to-mouth resuscitation. For a moment she thought he had won. His body went limp, without so much as a tremor. Then she felt his heart give a sudden jerk, and another, and he was fighting madly to come up from that deep water in which he was drowning.

When, finally, he could breathe again, when he

could see, he focused his eyes on her. She sat quietly in the same chair. He shook his head. He could think only that he'd lost.

"Goddamn you," he said.

Chapter 8

Dr. Milton Sapperstein stood by the silent form of Lance Parker. Across the bed, her brow furrowed, her eyes dark from sleepless nights, Lee Grazzi looked up at this strange doctor who had flown in from Israel. "He rests," Dr. Sapperstein said in broken English. "He rests well. His sleep is deep. There is no trouble or pain."

"I—I don't understand," she said. "I know the induced sleep, the brain wave machine, and I don't see how it could do what you say."

The doctor smiled and gestured to dismiss her protests. "We do not use the machine. It is good. But it is not what we need now. We need more."

"But how could you—"

"You watch." He leaned forward, and his voice took on a gentle sound. At once he was loving mother, caring father, sworn brother, friend of all friends, angel to be trusted without question. "You are hearing me, Lance. Nod your head, please."

His eyes remained closed, but the head nodded. Slowly but without question. "Very good. Do you remember where you are? Of course you do. You are at the gym. Your high school gym in Pennsylvania. That's right. The gym. You're wearing your gym clothes, no? Blue and white. That is good. You are lying on your back, and it is time for your leg exercises. Ah, you see that you remember. When I tell you, you will open your eyes, but you will remain asleep. I will count to three, and then your eyes will open. One, two, three."

Lance's eyes opened. *They were clear, but he was still asleep.* "Very good. Look to me now, please. Ah, you remember me. Jim Reed. Your gym instructor. And it is time to exercise your legs. They hurt a little because you were running track, no? And you gave yourself leg cramps. But we will work them out now with some exercise. Lift up your left leg, ah, good. Hold it there. Now bring it down slowly. Very good. That doesn't hurt, does it?"

Lance shook his head. "No. No pain."

"Now the right leg. That is even better. And the leg, it feels better, right? Good. You will exercise like this for fifteen minutes. I will be here to watch you. First the left leg, and then the right leg. When you are through, you will sleep again. Now exercise. The left leg. Good. The right leg. Good, good. Keep exercising. Fifteen minutes."

He motioned to the astonished woman and led her into a small anteroom. Through the glass they saw Lance exercising his legs, raising and lowering one and then the other.

"He acts like he's hypnotized!" she exclaimed.

"Of course," Dr. Sapperstein said. He looked from Lance, his legs moving in slow but definite rhythm, to Lee. "We wait," he urged. "Let him finish the exercises with the legs. Then we let him rest and we talk."

"I was able to place Mr. Parker in deep hypnosis only because he was more than willing to fight his way out of his situation. I did not argue with his actions." Lee looked in wonder at this gray-bearded, slim, gentle man. "That is why it is working. You told me yourself how much he said he wanted suicide. But you never believed him."

Lee shook her head. "No. I didn't then, and I don't now. But for a few moments I admit I was terrified."

The gentle man patted her hand. "What you did was a risk. But everything is a risk. What you did was very good. You brought him a mirror of himself and"—Dr. Sapperstein shrugged—"he emerged. That told me much, of course. He could be reached far below the level where he hates. This man, he lusts for life. His burden is very heavy. But it is that lust we need. You see, my child, he goes deep into hypnosis because it is a way out. Now we let his subconscious take over. It is a new technique. We developed it for our soldiers who were burned and shot badly. You know, like Mr. Parker. In some ways much worse. Blind, paraplegics, terrible burns. *Ach,* who wants to remember? But we discovered that deep down, if we could make the trip through the outer layers of the mind, there was a way. A man could give in; he could surrender to himself. His subconscious would produce great amounts of what we call body morphine. Resistance to pain goes up enormously. It is the brain taking control of the body's defenses."

"Is that why he can move his legs, I mean, what I saw?"

Sapperstein nodded. He fished a cigarette from a crumpled pack. "An old habit. Excuse me. It will probably be the death of me. But since I am seventy-four years old, I will take the risk."

She couldn't help the gentle laughter at his words. "His legs," the Israeli doctor went on. "If his conscious mind was involved, he would scream with the pain. But the subconscious, like the brain itself, does not know pain. So it blocks out the signals. Mr. Parker exercises his legs, he stretches muscles, he strengthens his body, with no pain. He is stronger now, and he will get stronger. Unfortunately hypnosis will not do many things. It will not strengthen his spine. Even the subconscious has limits."

She gazed at him intently. "How long can he remain this way?"

"Why, for months. For a year. Perhaps two. Only his subconscious can answer. I believe a year is practical for him."

Her eyes had come alive. "And he won't feel pain?"

The old man shook his head. He coughed on his cigarette; she waited patiently. "No. Believe me. I know you love him and you worry about his pain."

"That isn't my reason, Doctor." His raised brows showed the question, and she hurried on. "Yes, I love him, and very dearly. But I am also a realist. This year you can give him can mean everything to him."

"Tell me how." He avoided her gaze and toyed with his cigarette.

"Why, all the medical work we could do," she said, honestly surprised with the question. "Most of his teeth were broken. He would never accept dental bridges. But carbon vitreous implants, with the blade edges for dental caps, would give him teeth as good as his own. They would be his own, in fact, as the gums grew about the implants. That would be an enormous step forward."

"Go on."

"He needs plastic surgery. We may even be able to implant one or even two vertebrae, pass the nerves around them so we can straighten his spine. Not as well as before the accident, but it will take away from him that terrible twisted walk he now has. We can transplant hair even better than what he's grown back since he overcame the effects of radiation. We may have to break his fingers, so that they can be repositioned and brought to knit together—" Lee stopped abruptly. "But you know all this. I apologize for lecturing you."

Fingers of surprising strength gripped her wrist. "No. *Never* think that. No man knows so much he cannot learn. Why is the hypnotic state so vital in all this?"

"Because then he's *cooperating*."

"Ah. Excellent. Tell me more."

"We can't keep him drugged all the time. It won't work. We need him to exercise to prevent muscular atrophy. We need him to accept more pain than he's willing to endure or may even be able to endure. We—"

"We need the other Mr. Parker, no?"

She thought swiftly, then understood. "I see what you mean. That part of him that fights self-destruction."

"Yes, yes. So we are in a race. We must get as much done for him while his conscious mind is willing to bow to his subconscious. The moment there is conflict, I must warn you, he will emerge from the hypnosis state. When he does, you must never forget that no matter how much time has passed for us, for you, for me, for *him* he will have gone to sleep, and he will come awake as if only a night had passed. His mental attitude, you see, my young lady, will be the same. *That* is what you must never forget. Inside his head"—Dr. Sapperstein tapped the side of his head—"very little, if anything, will have changed. That is when the real struggle will be decided."

She was astonished, and her surprise let words slip unguarded from her. "What the hell is going on *now*? A game?"

She was even more surprised with the response. "Of course. A game. That is what life always has been. A game of life and death. That is the history of all men. We are born to die, and we most certainly will die. We cannot change that. Deep in our minds we know that. So what happens between being born and dying is a game. *We can never win.* That is what you must understand, especially since you are playing God. Me, I am maybe a small Moses, if even that. I am here because my government says to me, Milty, you go to America, where there is this man who is hurt very much, who has survived enough radiation to kill ten men. Find out how he lives. Find out *why* he lives. Find out all these things, for Israel has been in many wars and there will likely be many more wars to come. They are right. And if I can learn these things, maybe I can save the lives of many young Israelis who must fight our wars and suffer very badly."

"I'm playing God?" It was as if she hadn't heard another thing he'd said.

He held out both hands in supplication for her understanding. "You are surprised? A man wants to die and you bait him, you trap him in a suicide pact, you gamble with his life, and you are *not* playing God? What is it then? A game of gin rummy?"

"I . . . I never thought of it, like that, I mean. I never *wanted* to . . ." Her voice trailed away.

He patted her hand as if he were offering tender care to a child. "Ah, my dear young woman. You have been hurt. This man, whom you love, tells you to go to hell with your love, and this is like a knife in your heart. It is true; we both know this to be so. Since he will not listen to your love, since he turns his back on your help, you have no choice. You will help him no matter what he says. No matter what he does. No matter how much he wants to die. You say to yourself, God will not help him. What else is there to do? You become God. *You.*"

"I—"

"*Shush*. Listen to an old man who has learned a few things from life. You think you are the first to meddle in other lives? That is our heritage, all of us. Meddle and interfere, criticize and give advice. That is our way. You are no different. Even your reasons are no different. And if they were, what would it matter? Do you know what you do?"

She stared at him, numb, shaking her head.

"You deny him the right to decide for himself. You decided he should not decide. And why? Because you are afraid he will decide to die. So you interfere. You do not play gin rummy. You play with his life."

"It's hardly *playing*," she said coldly.

He was unfazed with her sudden ice. "I study this man you love. Ah, but he is a *man*. He has *chutzpah*. He loves life; he lives it; he challenges it. It is the sweetest of all wines. Never did a vineyard give us wine so sweet. Now it turns to vinegar for him. Sour. Sour inside his mind. You are trying to convince him you can turn the vinegar back into wine. Am I wrong?"

She sat quietly, her hands now folded in her lap. "No." The word could barely be heard. She cleared her throat. "What else can I do? I mean, what you're doing with him, it's incredible. I can pay for the surgery, all those things. *But how do I get through to him?* How do I convince him that destroying himself is the worst thing he could do!"

He looked at her with a sadness that seemed thousands of years old. For the first time she saw just how thin, how much like parchment, was this man's skin, how the lines were embedded so deeply along his eyes, how long and how much he had lived. Then he answered, as men like him must have given the same answer all through history.

"You are asking me? Who do you think I am? You think that maybe I am God?"

Chapter 9

For the first time in more than a year she was able to remove herself, emotionally as well as physically, from the presence of the man who so completely had dominated her life. For the first time her absence provoked no onslaught of guilt. She didn't wolf down her food because the possibility of savoring her meals would make her feel she had no *right* to such pleasure while Lance suffered. She no longer avoided the pleasures of a swimming pool where her lithe limbs and strong young body moved her through water like a creature of the sea. With Lance in the clinic and the subject of total study by the weathered old man from Israel, she shed guilt at being alive, at being well, at being healthy. For a week after her meeting with Dr. Sapperstein, she indulged herself in a quiet, private orgy of tasting, feeling, hearing, touching, enjoying. She basked in a tub brimming with silky bubbles and perfume. She treated herself to massages, to the fingers of manicurists, the delights of fine restaurants. She turned off her telephone; she slept late; she listened to her favorite music as if it were a wine she had long and desperately needed.

Then she went to work at what she did best.

She rearranged her laboratory, a scientific housewife putting everything in new order. On a wide curving wall before her desk, which functioned also as a control console for her many electronic and other devices, she set up both direct screen and holocubicle receptors, so that she could project photographs or motion films within the cubicles in the full three-dimensional reality of the laser-beamed hologram. Tied into her computer memory banks, the holographic projections snapped into being a three-dimensional figure so realistic that the eye could not distinguish the projection in any way from a solid object. But it was a past event being re-created. And, there was something else that could be done. If a computer were fed sufficient data to establish a pattern over many occasions, it could anticipate what its holographic figure must do. Lance walked in his own particular manner. The computer had been fed that information so the memory banks could instantly retrieve and present in any one of several dozen ways the manner in which Lance Parker walked. His tread, stance, balance, stride, lean, adjustments to varying speeds and for varying terrain and loads he might carry, adjustments because of temperature or to speed up or slow down because of a companion—all these were in the ghostly electronic patterns of the computer brain because, Lee sighed with relief, she had this crazy penchant for recording just about everything she could on super 8 mm film. Now it was offering up a reward she had never anticipated.

Because she had a living record of the physical motions, characteristics, and mannerisms of Lance. She had his voice from a hundred or more occasions, serious, laughing, intent, free and easy—the wide gamut of aural identification. She had more than his voiceprint; she had his complete soundprint to be mixed in with the other data. She had captured and recorded and impressed into the biomedical computer his skin color and tone, the reflectivity of his skin under different lighting conditions, the amount, fineness, and depth of body hair. And she had film that ordinarily would never have existed. She and her lover had taken films of themselves in the nude, bathing, caressing, massaging, making love. She set her video cameras on full automatic so they would take up to an hour of film without interruption, one camera switching automatically to another so that the film records were long and meaningful. A private eroticism of theirs—they found tremendous pleasure in watching these films of themselves that no other person had ever seen—was now an invaluable deposit in a bank of knowledge about Lance Parker. From all this information and data she produced a realistic ghost companion of the man before his grisly accident.

She had a bad moment when watching the films of herself and Lance embraced in their lovemaking, then cursed herself soundly for regressing to this insufferable pity. The stronger her own positive approach to Lance's future, the greater their mutual chances for success.

Slowly, almost mystically, the computer began its transfer of memory banks to shimmering reality. A curving row of computer TV screens stretching to either side of Lee Grazzi presented different aspects of that information. On one screen appeared color photos of Lance, showing different angles. On another a gridwork pattern developed, a three-dimensional computer impression created from the photographs with data down to a thousandth of an inch as to facial feature sizes. Another screen interpreted in numbered gradients the hues and reflectivity and nature of facial surfaces. Still others, the movement of the mouth, the flexibility and limits and patterns of skin stretch and distortion, eyebrows, muscle and nerve movement. The computer was creating a literal mathematical model of the human being in terms of Lance Parker's physical structure, movement, balance, flow, expressions, and other elements that made up the man. *Not* the person. There remained that fine line not even the computer could cross.

It was a magical thing, though, this "capturing" of a human structure into a flexible, flowing three-dimensional printout. The computer fed its data into the laser-beamed holographic projectors. Fifty-seven light beams from laser transmitters in a large control room all flashed their light toward a central point six feet high. When they came together, blurring and shimmering, they began to match their pressure of light and color and shading with a touch as exquisitely light as the caress of an electron.

Lance's head and shoulders materialized in the shadowy gloom of the hologram cubicle, suspended in midair. Soft lights appeared and brightened slowly to bring into sharp relief the eerie, startling "living statue." Lee sucked in her breath. It was more incredible than even she had imagined, for she was looking at Lance before her. Something tore cold and deep within her heart, and frantically she suppressed the rush of emotion. She swallowed the lump that had appeared in her throat with the "sight" of Lance. For a moment she froze as if ice were trickling down her back. Then she identified the new onrush of emotion.

The bust of Lance wasn't moving, but it had a sense of life that defied every failing conviction of disbelief. *For the head was breathing.* It was a motion barely perceptible, but then she understood. To the computer memory section, any holographic projec-

tion of this numbered sequence, unless directed otherwise, would be in animated presentation.

She worked the controls before her. Again that incredible impact of reality. Lance began to turn
slowly, as if he were wearing a cloak of absolute
black, and all that was visible before her was the
head and shoulders of the man. His head made a
complete rotation and she was again struck dumb by
the reality that even the small mole behind one ear
was there. Her fingers moved steadily through the intricate system of controls. The figurehead stopped in
profile view to her with the gentle touch of a button.
She ran through the programming sequence. An electronic tapestry creating an Adam before her eyes. A
celestial sculptor working with forces as tenuous as
light and as realistic as a block of granite. She wondered if this were how the first two figures had
materialized in the Garden of Eden.

The computer followed her orders, and it was
watching the darkness below the broad shoulders
flowing away, like sand draining through unseen orifices at the lower darkness. Again the touch of sor-
cery. As electronic data flowed and was converted to
light beams, more and more of Lance materialized
until a breathless, awed Lee Grazzi studied a *real*,
nude Lance Parker before her. The impulse to rush
into the holographic cubicle and throw her arms
about this man had to be suppressed.

She set her teeth grimly and worked the controls.
Lance's body began the same pirouette, the silent
gliding turn as if he were standing on obsidian that
turned slowly. She recognized every mark, every scar,
every line and texture of the body that she had loved
and that had so many times embraced her own.

Enough! she cried to herself. Now came the part
she had dreaded. There was the need to produce the

Lance Parker of this moment, the remains of that beautiful male animal before her. She worked the controls again. Alongside the beautiful male animal there began to coalesce in eerie flickerings of holographic light the man who had survived the mountain and the glowing fog of radioactivity. During Lance's stay at the hospital she had continued, without his knowledge, to take her thousands of feet of film. They were taken in visible light and in infrared and in ultraviolet, so that even in the dark she was recording his physical structure, his changed movements, his twisted deformities. She now must establish a working and viable comparison between the two. From the before and the after she might yet create her dream.

Of which Lance knew nothing.

The second Lance, the ravaged man, materialized, with its terrible cataloguing of scars and burns, the torn flesh and ripped ears, the twisted shape, the hair still growing back, the tilted head and gnarled fingers. From the computer-fed numbered data, the glowing digits of injuries. For these, too, were necessary. As Lance was changing under his long hypnotic control, as plastic surgery and other repairs were being made to his body, that information was also fed into the computer. When she had compiled the latest changes, up to this very day, she worked the computer to produce the third Lance Parker.

He was grotesquely less than the first, but measurably improved upon the second. To the left was the peak, the beautiful male animal before the mountain fell. In the center was the worst, when he was little more than a cruelly deformed and helpless creature of agony. To the right was the new changeling, the emerging man from what had been nearly a total wreck.

Her hand moved with a sudden angry motion and

stabbed controls. The beautiful male animal vanished as if he had never existed. A moment later the crushed and torn animal also was gone.

There remained the present. Lee sat back for a moment, making coffee from the small bar behind her, sipping slowly. What had Jacob Bronowski said when he examined man's role in life, his accomplishments, and his mastery of his environment and his future? She searched her memory, and then the words came back to her.

"Man masters nature not by force but by understanding. This is why science has succeeded where magic failed: because it has looked for no spell to cast on nature."

But magic would have been a damned sight easier, she decided. She looked again at the long and terrible list of injuries. This was her key and the lodestone for Lance. From what she had gathered together, she would produce a means to give to Lance Parker mobility denied him, strength torn from him, an acceptable physical appearance ripped from him as effectively as if his face had been bathed in acid. Steel cables would supplant withered and burned sinew and tendons; there would be new plastics and alloys and implants and power systems and plastiskin and massive continued injections to build up the body systems over long periods of time.

She would call it *ManFac*.

Man Facsimile.

The name felt better, more comfortable, the more she toyed with it. She tapped it into the computer, presented it in glowing letters suspended in air.

M A N F A C.

She had much work to do. Weeks to prepare, assemble, test, integrate, link with small computer systems that would disappear into and within the exoskeletal framework of a *new* man. The preparation would be but the first phase in her growing hopes. It would be as nothing without the cooperation, the deep willingness of Lance to endure yet more pain, to attempt new experiments, to suffer possible indignities. The hope and the promise were there, but only with the total involvement of Lance.

Lance must become a willing disciple of the gods of science—and the unknown.

They brought him through her door only five weeks later, hunched in a wheelchair, his eyes dark and malevolent, brooding, his open bitterness now a colder, deeper stone within him. Five weeks! And she had hoped for at least six months, perhaps even a year. Oh, God. The old doctor had driven to her home, had met with her in her laboratory. Dr. Sapperstein's hands trembled as he scratched a match into flame and lit a cigarette. "I do not know where to begin," he said, his sorrow intoning his words like peals of death.

She sat across from him and took a leathery hand in hers and held his gaze steady.

"What happened?" she pressed gently.

Anger appeared in his face. "He quit."

She waited, and there was no more. "That's all?" she pushed.

"All? How much more can there be? *He quit.* Inside him. The hypnosis no longer worked. He went under, but he twisted and he turned, and the sweat broke out all over him, and it was no good, no good at all, because now he was fighting us. He has a towering will, this man of yours. He may be broken and bent, but inside that head"—Sapperstein tapped the side of his skull—"there is a giant, and the giant fought us, and there was no use continuing. When we went to help him, he refused. His hands are still twisted, but he struck a doctor so hard that the doctor was unconscious from the blow. Such a lump he gave him. If he could only use that same spirit to build . . . *Ach,* I have nothing else to say. I must go. I can do you no more good here. Soon the ambulance will be here with your man, and you will need the help of God this time. God and a good woman. That can accomplish miracles. It has in the past, and it can do so again. I do not want Lance Parker to find me here. He will associate us with a plot. He thinks that way. It is all a plot. We are scheming against him."

"Why would he—"

"No, no, you don't understand," Sapperstein said, his hands fluttering. "We are plotting to keep him alive, to make him better, and all he has left is to fight against it, against us. Getting better is a long and terrible trip. That is not a fight; it is a struggle. It is easier to burn down a forest than to chop every tree one by one. So he must not associate us together. But remember this, my good woman. Remember that we have passed one major point. He will not harm himself physically. That much we have done. The challenge is there. He will not commit suicide with a gun or a knife or a bomb. The violent self-destruction is no longer a problem. What *is* a problem that you must understand is that he is going to will himself to die. He will try to will himself into death, and he is strong enough to do that. I have seen it happen before. A man turns off his heart, he squeezes it with an invisible hand that reaches inside his chest and, *ach!* it is over. Be careful about this. His spirit is powerful, but it has become both his ally and his enemy."

Sapperstein was gone, and twenty minutes later the ambulance arrived. The twisted figure in the wheelchair looked at her with coals of dark fire from his eye sockets.

Martin Caidin

She set up Lance in a room alongside her laboratory. The bed moved in a hundred different directions through electric controls to keep pressure points from building painfully along his torn body. He could heat the bed or cool it from within by punching buttons or twisting dials. A console along the side of the bed operated room temperature controls, slid drapes back and forth, turned on and off and dimmed the lights, even opened windows to the fresh air and heavy tree growth just beyond. Lee even built a curving set of rails that enabled him to bring himself to and from the bathroom without her physical aid. If he preferred not leaving a bed to urinate, he had a version of a "motorman's friend" at bedside.

It was all there, and more. Magazines, papers, books—all could be held by hand or read through projected wall screens. He had television and a vast library of video films from which to choose.

But the screens remained silent, and the books unread and the music unheard. He ate sparingly, only to attend to hunger pangs that became too troublesome to ignore. Even the leanest hawk must eat more than the fattest sparrow, and he ate no more than would a sparrow. He was wasting away. The overwhelming determination to quit was winning.

Until, finally, Lee lost her temper. She told him of her talk with the old doctor from Israel. He showed a death-head's smile. "Ah, yes. The feeble Jew from the desert. The crier of holy words. The paragon of philosophical wonders. Healer and man of faith, and a pain in the ass."

She had trained herself not to wince with the gravelly sound of that torn throat. "He may have been all those things," she said in quiet response, "but he sure had you pegged."

"Did he now?"

"Yes. Right on the button. He nailed your description right to the cross."

"Fitting for an old Hebrew. The cross, that is."

"You didn't need to explain."

"I forget. You are a wise woman and learned in history as well as science. Tell me, lover of mine, woman who is enchanted by this grotesque and maggoty body, with what pearls of wisdom did he describe me?"

Lee leaned back in her chair, studying her nails. "It wasn't that important, Lance."

"Tell me, dammit!" That face, the starkness of lines, the rasping demand—she was shaken to her soul. She forced herself to hang in there.

"He said you were a little shit."

Lance gaped. "He *what?*"

"A little shit. A quitter."

He looked at her with that brooding glare he had adopted as a constant thing. "I'd expect a foreigner to say something like that."

She took a deep mental breath. "Oh, I don't know. I'm as American as apple pie, and I'm not a creaking old Hebe from the desert, and as far as I'm concerned, Milton Sapperstein is absolutely a dear, and I agree with everything he said."

He struggled up to one elbow and snarled at her. It was literally that: a guttural, uncontrolled snarl, a rasping, choking gurgle. So great was his anger that his damaged vocal cords could not control the intensity of his sudden rage. He fought to speak, and one hand reached out in a crooked talon, and he croaked like a dragon born newly of its cracked egg.

Instantly she was on her feet. "Shut up! *Shut up, goddamn you.* If you want to speak, then do so like a man, instead of like an overgrown chicken scratching in the fucking dirt!"

His mouth remained open, but he no longer tried

to speak. He had no words for this sudden, totally on-expected reaction from Lee. Her finger stabbed out to him. "I'll tell you what, you self-pitying little shit! You want to tell me what you think, I'll damned well give you the chance to do exactly that. Now lie back and just shut up until I'm through!"

As she spoke, she reached behind her to a drawer and extracted a wide copper-glowing metal band. It looked like an extravagant wide neckband, but inside the thin metal was a vast and complicated maze of wiring, silicon chips, receivers, and vibrating mechanisms that had been prepared by the computer that now carried so exhaustive a file on Lance Parker. She moved swiftly to the bedside, rudely shoved him back against the mattress and pillow as he grabbed for her. When she was ready, she grasped his hair and jerked him upward. Startled, so frozen with surprise he could not move, he sat upright, and the metal band snapped about his neck, molding to his skin shape. The instant the metal touched his skin, the chemicals in his skin and on his body generated a trickle of electrical current in the neckband. Only a trickle, but enough with the advanced systems, the electronic miracles she had created, to lend it all the power he needed.

But he didn't know he had until he croaked again at her. "What the hell do you think you're doing!" he roared at her, and went as white as a full moon *as his own voice boomed across the room.* He stared in astonishment at her, at the walls, at anything. His hand moved to the metal.

"I . . . I'm talking. *It's my own voice!*"

The computerized system had picked up the vibrations welling along his larynx, had converted the whispers, the rattles, the hints of sound into the memory chips of what had been his voice, had converted his feeble speech into the full and resonant tones of the voice he knew before his accident.

"That's right," she snapped at him. "Your own voice. It comes from that band around your neck, but it's your own voice, and it can't be told from the way you spoke before. But get something straight, you son of a bitch. Now you've got one less thing to complain about, to feel sorry about. You've been wanting to tell me how much you hate me, how much you want me to go to hell, how much you hate living, how much you want to die! Well, damn your hide, now you can tell me. Go ahead! Tell me, *and then do it!*"

She ran from the room and threw herself on the couch in her office. No longer could she hold back the tears, the frustration, her own rage, the helplessness. All of a sudden, hearing him talk again with his own voice, her willpower had disintegrated, her resolve had fled, and she was willing to accept his own decision not to live.

She had *quit.*

And she didn't give a damn because fighting to give a man the desire and resolve to live ended at its own time and place, and that was right now. She could keep him alive in the medical sense, in the biological sense, but this was a mind with which she was dealing, and when it wanted to quit, that was it.

Sapperstein's voice echoed in her mind. *Who do you think I am? God?* She answered herself. *No, old man, you're not, and I'm not. And I don't care anymore.*

She didn't hear the scraping sounds. She didn't hear a thing out of her own soul until she heard his voice again. Not shouted. Quietly.

"Lee?"

She turned slowly, an immense effort, moving a thousand tons of deadweight of her own body, half-lying, half-sitting on the couch, and framed in the bright light of the doorway, twisted, in pain, he stood there before her. On crutches—*but he had made it all the way from his bed to this doorway*. Her hand flew to her mouth, and she bit down hard, desperately, on a knuckle, and tasted the saltiness of her own blood.

"Look at you," he said. "Now . . . now I can talk, and you can't."

Chapter 10

"Slip your hand into the system as if you were putting on a glove. That's it. Try it for movement now," Lee urged Lance. He had eased his gnarled right hand into a facsimile of another, larger hand that defied description as artificial. Lance moved his fingers gingerly within the "glove" and grinned at Lee.

"It feels like a hand within a hand," he remarked.

"That's precisely what it is," she confirmed. "It *is* a hand. Not simply a prosthetic. That thing has almost as many nerves and connections as your own. How does it feel?"

"Inhuman." He chuckled. "No pun intended. It feels like I've put my hand inside another human hand. It's, well, comfortable. I thought it would feel warm, maybe even hot. But it doesn't. It feels cool."

"Good. It's a new synthetic material that undergoes a chemical change when exposed to perspiration and heat. It stays cool, oh, for about two hundred hours. Then we change the lining. Now let me see you move your fingers."

He hesitated. That once-strong and supple hand of his was gnarled and misshapen, knuckles bulging at crazy angles. "Don't be afraid to move it," Lee urged. "Remember, that hand is an electronic interpretation of your own hand as it existed before, except that it's slightly larger to accommodate your own hand and its equipment. Go on."

He moved several fingers. He stared in wonder. The hand at which he looked moved with his own thought. A human hand. Perfectly proportioned. Large, strong, supple. Lines and creases and hair. He moved his index finger. His own could move only through a fraction of its former freedom. But the hand he watched moved easily, and the index finger went through full and complete movement. "How did you manage that?" he asked quietly.

"The computerized record of full manipulation is locked into the system. Any input on your part functions through the memory circuit. The hand 'remembers' that it's supposed to move through certain arcs, twisting, torsion—the works." Lee leaned forward. "Extend your fingers and thumb fully. Make an arc of your hand." The powerful hand did precisely what he tried to do with his own. It was a strange paradox. He couldn't, but he could.

"Make a fist."

He did. He knew he had enormous power in that hand. "What's the material?" he asked.

"Flexmetal. Think of the old woven armor of knights. This is stronger, doesn't rust, and the sections where bones, knuckles, that sort of thing would be are duplicated right down to the nth degree." Lee placed both hands behind her head and regarded him carefully. "It's more than a hand, Lance. It's also a tool. There's enough power in the small micromotors for you to use that hand as a wrench, a pliers, as wire cutters, a hammer; whatever. So it's also a weapon. I built a curving steel plate into the side. It's cushioned on the inner side. But if you were to use the hand as a karate expert would, you'd have much more striking power." She leaned forward again. "But don't ever make the mistake of inertia and mass. This isn't a Disneyland diorama. You can't ignore physical laws. For example, let's say you wanted to strike out with your fist, and we had power systems built into the wrist, forearm, elbow, upper muscles, even the shoulder. Believe it or not, you wouldn't be much faster than a trained boxer. You fought in the Golden Gloves."

He was flexing the hand, squeezing a rubber ball.

"You said you never hit a man on the chin. Why?" Lee asked.

Even his grotesque features couldn't dim his sudden grin. "I didn't say it quite that way. I said you never aim for a man's chin. There's an instinctive reflex to pull your punch, and that's a fast way to lose a fight. So you aim for the back of a man's head, *through* his chin. One good shot, and you can put him out. Even kill him if you're not careful."

"Charming," she said dryly. "All right, Mr. Parker. You're the expert. How much damage could you do with *this* hand?"

He looked steadily at her. "You made this better and stronger than you think. It's deadly."

"Could you hit as hard?"

"Not the way I am." He kept bitterness from his voice. "I don't have the balance, the rapid turning motion on the balls of my feet. I don't have the automatic crouch, the leaning forward into—"

"But if you did have all that?"

"I could bludgeon another fighter. Oh, there's always the problem of keeping *him* from beating me half to death if he's faster and a better boxer, of course, but if I ever nailed him one good shot, I'd slow him down and—"

She held up a hand. "Enough. I get the idea."

He nodded, very sober. "How . . . how far have you gone with this system of yours? This facsimile of a human."

"I call it ManFac."

He waited until she went on. She let out a long breath. "Not as far as I could have gone, Lance. You fought us too hard." Quickly she touched his arm. "No criticism intended. Please. We don't need that anymore. I'm only trying to answer your question with candor."

He set his jaw. "Go on."

"We'd hoped for a year of medical work. That way we could have used bionic implants in your spine, where the two vertebrae were damaged."

"That could have taken two years. Maybe five," he countered.

"Agreed."

"So I walk funny," he said.

She was delighted, nearly overwhelmed, with these first bare touches of self-humor. "But not if you're a ManFac," she said.

"Not if I *am* one?"

"That's what I've been trying to get you to understand. The ManFac isn't simply a fancy suit of armor. When we bring together you, a human being, an individual, with the ManFac, it's not like donning that suit of armor. It's a symbiotic act in principle and in reality. You become what you are. Does that sound crazy?"

"Yes."

"All right, we want green. You're blue, and ManFac is yellow. Stir them together and—"

"Okay. I wanted the semantics clear. Once again, please, as to why it's just not putting on a system, though. If I were to wear an exoskeleton, like those they've been using in industry for years, it's simple enough. I 'wear' the exo system. It's a metal-ribbed framework in the basic shape of a man. If I want to lift five hundred pounds, I apply lifting force in the normal sense. A detector picks up the attempt to lift, senses that my own muscles can't do it, and adds energy."

"Which comes from a direct electrical plug-in with motors, reduction gears—stuff like that," she broke in.

"Right. I've got to be properly balanced and that sort of thing, which is why exoskeletal systems have such big feet. How is ManFac different?"

"Wearing an exoskeleton is a bit like snuggling into an MGB sports car," Lee said. "You're operating power systems: the motor, brakes, windshield wipers, horn, air conditioning, whatever, through your control of power devices. You've got to make the effort to push this button, press that pedal, twist this dial. When you go the next step upward, you're into the exoskeleton. It's the ultimate-fitting MGB, let's say. But it's terribly clumsy. It gives you enormous strength, but you move slowly, you're awkward, you climb stairs like a drunken polar bear, you can't run, your sense of balance is ridiculous, you have virtually no torsion in body twisting and—"

"And you can't really leave home," he said, thinking hard. "That means your ManFac has mobility."

"*Your* ManFac," she corrected hurriedly.

He chose to let the remark slip by. "What kind of power?"

"Batteries, different types. Inertial systems. Tied in with memory metal for spring-reflex action so that a little bit of muscle push goes a long way. A spring coiling and recoiling and coiling, but operating all the time, always ready."

"Neat. How long?"

"Early stages yet, my love. Fourteen hours, and you wind down like a toy soldier jerking to a halt."

"Recharging?"

"Dual systems. Battery replacement on the modular principle. Snap out and snap in. Two to five minutes at the outside. Located at different points."

"Electrical charge?"

"Yes. The batteries can recharge from exhaustion to full power in a few hours. If you slam in a charge, you overheat the system. I think we can improve on that."

"I know we can," he said. The powerful hand flexed fingers, squeezed the rubber ball. Her eyes widened as she saw it coming apart slowly, shredding under his grip-relax-grip-relax-grip.

"All right," he continued. "The facts of life. The spinal column is distorted. Vertebrae missing and we have a twist, what you could call a permanent torque. Does ManFac compensate for this?"

"It does. You wear it; you slip into it; you fit into the mold waiting for you. It's like wearing an outer skin. It is *not*, repeat *not*, a shell. It is not a suit of armor. It is an outer body of yourself. The interior adapts your frame, distortion and all, and receives body input. Leaning, twisting, torque, balance. The receptors have all been memory-banked with a computer built into the suit that has a record of every physical movement you have ever made or your body *could* make."

He looked up. "All those thousands of feet of film," he remembered aloud.

"Yes. That, and the ability of the computer to extrapolate. The life sciences systems can produce literally more than thirty million possible combinations of movement, without going into the even more subtle actions and reactions. We don't need to go that far. Randomness is an acceptable factor here."

"I can assume basic physiological requirements," he said, making the statement and the question together.

"Cooling, heat supply, thermal protection, variations to the extreme and compensation for immediate, even instant changes, as fast as physiological receptors." She leaned forward again, her own expression tense, her eyes bright. "If necessary, it's possible to accept and store body wastes. Urine and fecal. They can also be disposed of in normal fashion if time permits."

His eyes widened slowly. "You mean even with—"

"Let's not be childish. We've made love too long. I have the films of us. The ManFac system accommodates for thermal change. The penis fits within the penis with compensation for engorgement and erection."

He shook his head. "You didn't include tactile response, I hope."

"Don't be silly. The girl wants the inner man."

"Yeah," he said heavily. "I don't know about that, but I'll buy what Raquel Welch once said."

"Which was what, love?"

"Someone asked her, it was on a television talk show, what she considered her most erogenous zone. She pointed to her head."

"She's right," Lee said. "It ain't up there, it ain't nowhere."

They moved into an awkward pause. These two had made stirring, wild, tender love. They'd planned their lives together. Lance's genitals were unaffected by his accident. His suit had been heavily armored, and his groin protected with steel plating. The radiation had made him sterile, but that was the same as a vasectomy without the knife. Yet since the accident they had never even approached a sensual or a sexual attitude between them. She knew better. All the words in the world, all the responses she could offer, wouldn't get past that built-in barrier that the princess doesn't want to get laid by the horned toad. So she had let it alone, hadn't rocked that boat.

But how she wanted him . . .

He held up his arm with the hand still moving, marvelously alive. "There's more where this came from then?"

"An entire ManFac. *You*."

"What's the next step?"

"Slow and easy. I can't work miracles. I need your cooperation. The basic system is ready. Now it requires *your* input. You need to develop new muscle tone, new reception to movement, to shift in body mass, to kinesthetic response. You've got to grow *with* the ManFac. It's the only way it'll work. Slow, steady progress all the way through."

He squeezed the hand as hard as he could. Dust trickled from his fingers with the remains of the rubber ball. He had crushed it to a pulp. He looked up at her. "You're better than you thought you were," he said. "All right, woman. I'm ready. Let's go."

"Not yet. I need a new attitude from you."

His eyes narrowed. "Like what?"

"No failure syndrome in your head. It won't work if you hedge."

"I didn't plan to—"

"You walk. Crutches. You work out. You progress to two canes, then one. The ManFac is you only when you two are together. But you can't be together, the symbiosis, all the time. You've got to be what you are *now*. You've got to face that reality. You must learn to be two people at the same time you emerge as the new Lance Parker."

"I remain a cripple."

"You're no more a cripple than you accept."

"I can't run, I can't climb, I—"

"Oh, fuck off," she snapped. "You want pity, try

the paraplegic ward. To them you're superman. To me you're my man. That's the deal, straight out."

His face was a twisted statue. "You're pushing."

"That's right, Lance. It's the only way. You're out of ManFac, you limp. Your spine is twisted. Your lip is scarred. Your hand is gnarled. You flunk as a tryout for *Swan Lake*. No leaps, no pirouettes, no graceful motions. *So what?*"

He started to speak, bit his tongue. But she seized on the facial expression. "What were you going to say? It's easy for me to speak?"

"Yes," he grated.

"Why don't you add up the plus side of the ledger? The past is frozen. The ledger gets black ink from here on with ManFac. It's that simple. It's a new world, a new life, a new *way* of life. You're a cripple, and you're ManFac. You can't be one without the other. But if you choose to quit now, then *all* you have is cripple. And you can walk. You can learn to walk with no more than a cane. I know the human body better than you do. I know *your* body better than you do. You have the chance now to make head-way on both counts. But I need a man to work with. The question is whether or not you're man enough."

He sat quietly. Then he sighed. "It's better than a sharp stick in the eye."

It was an old line from their past, from that time *before* the mountain fell on him. It was an *inner* acceptance. She could have shrieked with joy.

"Okay," she said.

Long, slow, arduous, demanding, painful, necessary, frustrating, repetitive, maddening, torturous.

One step at a time to be mastered. Then the next step. Then another phase. And another, and another. He had to learn each one separately and master that one item before he could try two. He had to learn to walk and chew gum at the same time. It wasn't easy.

She fitted him in a special chair that braced his torso, that adapted to his unequal weight, and he sat in the chair with two ManFac arm systems. In this fashion he wasn't out of balance. The chair restraints were his equal of weight, of mass. When he wore both arms, she made him perform the same action with both hands. It was like driving a car with someone else's hands on the wheel. Or watching one television screen while listening to the sound from another channel. But he stayed with it, hammered at it, anviled it.

He wore the legs in a torso brace. He stood between parallel bars and braced himself with gnarled hands, one wrist twisted, and stood on the legs that could think better than his own goddamned legs could. "It's simple, really," Lee said with infuriating patience. "Your legs teach the ManFac legs what to do. The ManFac legs learn, and they know what to do. They start doing it from memory, pressure points, the extrapolation possibilities of the computer. Your own legs then have to learn to catch up with the ManFac system. When that happens, well. For now, wiggle your toes. Go on, dammit, wiggle your toes. Good. Very good. Now let's see you wiggle just your big toe. The right leg. Try it."

He tried. The powerful legs, toes and all, refused to cooperate. He tried to move just the big toe. He struggled until sweat poured from his face and neck. "Goddammit," he swore, "I *can't*."

She laughed at him.

"What's so goddamned funny?" he shouted.

"Did you ever try to wiggle just your big toe, *ever*, without the other toes also moving?" she asked him. He stared at her with a blank expression, and she laughed again. "You can't. Not you, not me. Maybe someone who's a freak, but not a normal person. Toes aren't fingers, and your big toe isn't a thumb. It's impossible to get individual movement from a single toe out of the group. Don't you see the point, Lance? If *your* body can't do it, then the ManFac can't do it. You just made another step up on that ladder."

Slowly, surely, he gained new perceptions and depth control. He matched the amplitude of his own physiological signals and muscle contractions with those of the ManFac systems. They were like identical twins separated at birth and just brought together again, and now they were trying to mesh both bodies into a single unit. Amplitude, impedance, floods of energy, subtle ticklings, massive blows, gentle caresses. Stand, walk, run, stop suddenly. Twist in place. Balance on one leg and then the other, and *that* was easier than he could have dreamed, for there were small, swiftly spinning gyroscopes built into the system, and they compensated for what damaged kinesthetic senses could no longer handle.

Sit, stand, lie, roll, fall, and roll, tumble, jump. Not all that simple. For a while he wore a knight's corset, a torso supporter molded to his body so he would accommodate his damaged system to improved balance. Little by little he added bits and pieces and parts. Sometimes he would work with just the fingers and a hand. Sometimes with two hands. Then he would attempt to manipulate a single side of his body, but that always made him uncomfortable, a half-sided slab of a man and—well, whatever. But he tried the assemblies as Lee continued her development. He wore different skeletal systems with wires bulging, but by God, he sat and stood and lay and rolled and fell and tumbled, and when he jumped, he found he had the equal of powerful coiled springs in those legs, and the problem was in not overdoing it, for he would leap into the air and come down with a terrible cumbersome crash. He worked with pens and pencils to write without mashing them into the paper and tearing it into scrap. He balanced while he walked. He put on clothes and took them off. Manipulate, test, experiment, compensate.

Learn.

He was getting edgy. The days became weeks, and the weeks became months, and she was exhausting her funds and their mutual patience. Their relationship was deep and meaningful and horribly frustrating. They were celibates, and she twisted and moaned in her sleep for the want of him. *Him,* not the damned ManFac. But the latter was the only way to bring him around. They were deeply attached and sensuously walled off from each other.

One morning she found an experimental model in the making in her mind. She assembled the systems, looked up to see Lance on his crutches, awkward, watching her. "What's the new gimmick?" he asked.

"It's an FR system," she said.

"What the hell is that?"

"Frustration release. I've put together the various limbs and a torso foundation. Each hand and arm has steel edges. The motors are at three times normal for response and movement of mass. Get into it." She suspended the ManFac test system from an overhead rack, like that of a superpuppet. He eased into the ManFac, and she watched him tightening straps. "It's only a temporary rig," she told him.

He was within the system. "Now what?"

"Come with me." He followed her through the laboratory and to an outside yard. She had a large shed she used for storing excess materials. Without all those wires and open panels he moved like any large, powerful man, but he really didn't know it yet. She stopped by the laboratory exit. "Hold it for a moment. Release your neckpiece, please."

His hand hovered protectingly about the device that let him talk like a human being. "It's all right. I have a new one I want you to wear." He removed the neckpiece, refusing even to try to talk. She placed the new band about his neck. "It's flesh-colored. I used scar tissue to let it blend in. How does it feel?"

He hesitated. "Like . . . like before," he said cautiously.

"It's not the same. I've modified it. Improved it. It can do something you never did, that no human being ever did."

"What?"

"You'll have to find out yourself. That's part of the program," she said offhandedly. She turned to a panel, opened it and adjusted several controls, then closed the panel. She pointed to the work shed. "I'm going inside. I said this was a frustration release process. You're all pent-up inside you, Lance. Boiling and angry. You've come a long way. But you've got to release your feelings."

"This a psychology program?"

"If you wish. Here's what I want you to do. Wait until I leave. Then I want you to tear that building apart. Use only yourself. Lance Parker. ManFac. Let it all out. Shout, yell, anything you want. I won't be here watching, so there's no need to be self-conscious. Tear the goddamned building apart. It's all yours. The main thing to do is to *let go inside your head.* Be a madman. Be anything you want. Just level that building. Please wait until I'm gone."

She went inside and closed the door behind her. He looked at the door, somewhat bewildered. He couldn't figure out what she had in mind, but whatever it was, he trusted her and her instincts. And the more he thought about it, the more he knew she was right. He *was* tied up in knots. He turned slowly. Okay, he'd go along with her. He knew what to do. He began to blank out his mind to everything except that building. That's all that existed in the world. That goddamned building. He hated it. *It hated him.* If it could, it would destroy him. He advanced slowly, menacingly. He had to destroy it first. The building. Nothing else existed in the world but the building. He stood before a corner, and he threw back his head, and he burst into a primal scream, a bellowing roar, the cry of a Viking berserker, and his fist lashed out and thudded into the heavy upright wooden beam and splintered the wood into kindling, and he shouted mindlessly and proceeded to demolish his enemy utterly.

That night, his soul cleansed, something bitter and black torn free from inside him, he came full circle with her. He watched the films. She had kept her promise. She hadn't watched. But she had had cameras and microphones set up. He watched in wonder as a furious madman possessed of maniacal strength ripped and smashed and pounded heavy wooden beams. He heard an incredible screaming thunder. He turned to her. "What the devil is that noise?"

"You."

"Me? That's crazy."

"No, it isn't. It's the new system I built for your neck. It amplifies, oh, about ten times more than it did before. You can make as much noise as a locomotive if that's what you want to do."

"Why would I want to do that?"

"That's for you to figure out." She turned on the lights. He sat in an armchair he had found most comfortable to his body when he was, as he had come to say it, "on his own." "I got a letter today," she said without preamble. "It's for you. I didn't give it to you

right away because I didn't know how you'd react.
Then I decided that I don't think for you. You make
up your own mind about what you do and don't want
to do."

He sat quietly, lighting a cigarette. "Who's it
from?"

"Carruthers. Congressman David R. Carruthers of
the House Committee on Safe Nuclear Energy, to
give you the whole title."

His face darkened. "He's a scumbag," he said nas-
tily.

"I'll throw it out." She held her breath and said a
silent prayer.

"No," he told her. "Let me see what the son of a
bitch wants."

The congressman didn't want much. Just everything. He read the letter twice and looked up at her.
"You know what this bastard wants from me?"

"I can guess."

"He wants to know what went wrong down there
in that mountain. But that's not all." He rushed on
as though she'd never said a word. "Oh, no, he wants
a *statement* from me that he can carry to the
President, that he can take to the people, to prove
that there was nothing wrong with the concept we
worked with."

"Well, there wasn't, the way you explained it to
me."

"Well, no," he admitted grudgingly. "*We* failed.
The design, I mean. We should have compensated for
the possibility of the earthquake. We diverted the
rivers and figured that would absorb any local shocks.
We were wrong. We *could* have built that system so
that if it had to fail, then it must fail a certain way. It
would have shut down its own operation and sealed
itself in."

"You mean there wouldn't have been any radiation leakage?"

He shook his head angrily. "No. Not a damned bit. But the fact of the matter is that seventy people died inside the reactor complex alone."

"How many of those would have been killed if the power system were straight hydro?" She studied her fingernails. "If there had been no nuclear reactor?"

He mulled that one over. "None, really. We would have had the same explosions. I mean, the steam system, the pipelines, the pressure. The explosions that tore everything apart weren't nuclear."

"But they screwed you, didn't they?"

He looked at her, astonished. "The AEC did, yes. And so did Alamitos." He tapped the paper. "But I can't blame Carruthers. He had no part in that."

"What's he after then?"

"A statement from me telling him what I just told you. But he also wants my recommendations as to how the system *should* be built. The long and short of it, Lee, is that he wants me to roust the atomic bogeyman from the public's attitude."

"That's a tall order. Maybe too much for one man," she offered.

"Christ, I have the answers, Lee. I had them all the time."

She stood up. "Hey, you don't have to convince *me*. Remember me? I'm on your side." She glanced at her watch. "It's late, and I'm tired, and I need a hot bath and a good sleep. Good night, love. See you in the morning."

Before he could say a word or protest her leaving, she was gone. He sat quietly, and then he read the letter again. He let it rest on his lap. Then he folded the letter and tucked it into his pocket. He struggled to gain his feet, balanced on the crutches, and walked slowly to the engineering office they shared. He dragged himself to an engineering chair, a high stool before a drafting table. Without thinking consciously of the movement, he snapped on the bright, close lights. He fingered a pencil, toyed with it, tried to make rough sketches. Fumbling, he cursed and hurled the pencil from him. He sat quietly, then walked on the crutches into the laboratory. He returned with a ManFac wrist and hand. He took his seat at the drafting table, picked up the pencil. This time he held it firmly.

But he hadn't done this before, and his pencil strokes were crude. He tried again, making a sweeping curve. It wobbled. Again. Better this time. Again, and again and again, until his lines were smooth and flowing. He used his scarred left hand to hold a ruler and began drawing straight lines, squares, rectangles, the beginning of basic schematics. He pulled a desk calculator within reach of his ManFac hand and switched on the power. The fingers moved slowly at first, then faster, more surely. He worked for three hours, and the papers began to fill with lines and curves and formulas.

In the morning Lee found him fast asleep at the table. He was unconscious. About him was a floor littered with torn and crumpled paper. But to his left was a stack of other papers, filled with graphs and charts and lines and symbols—the pathway through the maze where the atomic dragon lived. He had pinpointed the faults, highlighted the weaknesses, found the necessary safeguards. Right there before him was a vital key to a nation's search for clean energy.

Lee left quickly. In the kitchen she microwaved a steak sandwich and poured a large mug of cold beer. She knew his working habits better than he himself did. She brought the sandwich and the beer back to the office, placed them on a table to his right, within

119

his reach, and left again. Back in her room she pressed the message buzzer.

He awoke slowly, fighting off grogginess. He looked about him, coming out of his stupor with difficulty. Then he saw the sandwich and the beer. Yet he was alone. Lance smiled; it didn't take a genius to figure out what Lee had done. He ate slowly, thinking, doodling as he consumed the food and the beer. He worked for another two hours and turned off the calculator. He removed the ManFac hand, placed it on the table, patted it fondly. He removed the letter from his pocket. The congressman had included his home telephone number. Lance looked at a wall clock. A quarter past six in the morning.

He pulled the telephone closer to him and used his *own* fingers to tap the number with direct dial. A sleepy male voice mumbled at him. "Is this Congressman Carruthers?" Lance demanded.

"Yes, *yes*. Who the hell is this? Do you know what time it is?"

"This is Lance Parker, Congressman, and I don't give a damn what time it is, and—"

"Parker?"

"Yes, dammit. Will you wake up, for Christ's sake!"

The sleepiness was gone. "Parker, are you calling about my letter?"

"Congressman, I'm calling about your letter, and your questions, *and* all the answers you want. I can tell you not only what went wrong at Alamitos, but why, and why it didn't have to happen, and why it shouldn't ever happen again. You awake?"

"You're damned right I am, Parker. Go on. *Please*."

"All right. I have it all down on paper. Schematics, tables, computations, the works. It's all yours."

They talked for thirty minutes. The congressman would have the papers picked up that same morning by special messenger. He was deeply grateful. He—

"Congressman, I'm bushed. Let's talk about it later. The papers will be waiting for your man."

In her room Lee Grazzi had no way to keep the tears from coursing down her cheeks. She had listened to it all. Oh, dear God, *it had happened*. He had fought his own way up and out, he was thinking constructively, with purpose and—

This night he had changed from a mutilated caterpillar into the beginnings of a butterfly never before known. Crippled and mauled and in many ways still chained to his grievous wounds.

But more a man than he had ever been in his life.

BOOK TWO

Chapter 11

Lee Grazzi stood alone in her laboratory. It stank of rubber and creosote and vinyl and molten glass, of burned metal and welding equipment and propane and other gases.

That was bad enough. She turned slowly, the floodlights and spotlights and banks of dazzling lights on all about her. She was standing in the center of an insane charnel house. An unprepared visitor would think that the woman who ran this modern dungeon had a penchant for hacking, slicing, cutting, ripping, tearing, and savaging different limbs, parts, skin, and organs of the human body. Bits and pieces of adult males littered the floor, were scattered about shelves, strewn on tables, hung suspended from hooks and cables. There were pieces of skeleton, cranial sections, tendons, limbs, feet and hands, shoulders and stomach sections, knees and wrists, knuckles and fingernails; the lot. Artificial, surrealistic reality to fool the unknowing eye.

Lee looked about her and chuckled suddenly to herself. Evolution and development and the billion-and-one miracles of what is life swept over her. Cherished myths and superstitions and theology and nonsense, and, good grief, what a fumbled ball of wax is this small gray mass between two human ears.

"Last night I spoke to God, and She say, lissen heah, honky—and I been careful evah since."

Does God wear skirts? Is male the dominant theme in the act of creation? Does the womb of life exist in the male belly? Can there be even godly creation without sexual union?

She looked up. *I don't know, Lord, but thank you for this chance with Lance. I'll do my best. And if my humor seems a bit irreverent, it's only because I approach you with love and not fear. Besides, I'm tired, and you forgot to give me unlimited endurance.*

She worked for another two hours in the lab. When she was done, she took several minutes to study everything with great care. She nodded with self-satisfaction, turned on just a few dim lights, and switched off the brilliant overhead fluorescents.

Lance looked at her. He shifted in his seat, an automatic gesture to accommodate the almost constant discomfort that filled his life. "You've got something up your sleeve," he told Lee. She sipped wine slowly, her eyes wide, looking at him across the rim of her glass. They'd had a light dinner of steak and salad and had followed their old tradition of always spending a quiet half hour afterward. She noted the thirty minutes were about over.

"Yes, I do," she said quietly, placing the glass carefully on the table. "I need your cooperation."

Lance shrugged. "You've had that for a long time."

"I need it blindly this time."

He took on a wary look. "You've got more red herrings up your sleeve than the whole Russian fishing fleet."

"True," she said casually. "However, it *is* what I need."

"Full cooperation, huh?"

"Blind obedience would be more like it."

He sucked on a cigarette, let the smoke drift slowly from his nostrils. "You're asking a lot."

"I give a lot. This isn't a debate, Lance. Yes or no will do very well, thank you."

His eyes widened. "Testy, aren't you?"

She shrugged. "I'm waiting."

"No explanations?" He frowned when she shook her head; then took a deep breath. "All right."

She leaned forward, her elbows crossed on the table, her head resting on her forearms, locking his eyes with her own. "You may not like it."

"You've made that clear," he admitted. "I said okay, didn't I?"

"I want you to be sure."

"I'm sure, I'm sure! What the hell do you want? An affidavit, for Christ's sake?"

She rose to her feet. "Let's go to the lab." He followed her, his movement swaying and forced. But he was using one crutch this time, not two. He'd worked on that little problem for weeks. On his own he'd developed a different type of shoe with a high ankle and calf support that carried side weights effectively, and he had started moving with but the one crutch. It was tough, he pulled muscles and there was considerable pain, but he was hardening up even more and determined to stick with his new goal. *And that's all it takes,* she told herself.

They walked through the laboratory door. Lee stopped by a control panel, stabbed a number of buttons, studied the console readout. Lance watched with interest as she activated intruder alarms in the infrared, shock wave, ultrasonic, and rolled the heavy steel door to the laboratory closed behind her, sealing them within the lab. He turned to look about him.

"Why the special lighting effects?" he asked. He'd never seen the lab like this. A great hulking shape lay in shadows off to one side of the lab. He nodded in its direction. "Something new?"

"Yes," she told him, and her lack of words heightened his interest even more. She turned to him and motioned to a chair.

"Please undress and take that seat," she said, her tone already noticeably distant.

"What?"

"You'll catch flies with your mouth open like that. Take off your clothes, and sit in that chair."

Nudity meant nothing to him with her. Exposing his racked and, to him, grotesque body meant everything. "Bullshit," he said.

She sighed. "You agreed, remember? Full cooperation and all that?"

"For tests, yes. For a circus, even if it is private, *no*."

"You don't even want to know why I'm asking?"

"I don't *care* why."

"You're not leaving me much choice. All right, forget the clothes. For now," she added, and he didn't like the tone. But she didn't press the issue. He sat in the chair, one hand holding the crutch idly by his side. She snapped a switch, and a light shimmered across the room from him. "Please focus your attention on that light," she instructed.

He nodded, then concentrated. Anything along this line was all right with him. "Something special?" he asked. The light expanded and contracted and expanded and contracted in a strange, mesmerizing manner. Good. She wanted him to try to figure it out, to fight it if he wanted, but, above all, to concentrate upon it. She moved closer to him, stood by his side.

"Can you figure out what it is yet?" she queried.

He squinted. "No. I—"

His attention was total. As he stared at the light, concentrating, she brought the hypodermic needle neatly into the fleshy part of his upper arm. He jerked back from the sharp penetration, turned to look at her. Confusion crossed his face. "What the hell did you do that—" Then he saw the needle, and alarm leaped into his eyes. At the same moment the drug raced through his system, and he realized what she had done. "Goddamn you!" he shouted, hauling himself to his feet, eyes wide and his face contorted. "I'll—"

A talonlike hand reached for her. She stepped back, her face without expression. He grasped at her, and the crutch slid clumsily out from beneath him. "Relax, Lance," she said finally. "It works quickly. Just relax and go with it."

He snarled something without words, and she stepped forward quickly to catch him as he slipped into unconsciousness even before his collapsing body could reach the floor. She dragged him to a couch and laid him prone. She checked his pulse and heartbeat; things were fine. Quickly she removed his clothes until he lay naked before her. Damn, but this would have been so much easier *with* his cooperation. *Bloody stubborn bastard.* She wheeled a wide body-carrying device so that it rested over and straddled the couch. She slipped supports and webbing beneath his arms, crisscrossing his chest so his body would not slump, and he could be raised with most of the lifting pressure beneath his arms and through his torso. She placed soft webbing beneath his buttocks and legs. Electric motors whined as he was lifted slowly to a cradled horizontal position. She wheeled him across the laboratory to the shrouded shape, now illuminated by dazzling lights. She removed the shroud, paused to study the creation that had taken months of careful, exhausting, and secret preparation. She breathed deeply several times. She had to complete this before the drug wore off.

She used the power controls to lift Lance's unconscious form and move it into a great human statue. The first complete ManFac, powered down, quiescent, brooding, shockingly lifelike. It looked alive because in every sense, save motion, it *was* alive. Just the spark, just the spark . . .

The cradle brought Lance up into a vertical position. With the gimbaled ring at the top she was able to slide his legs into the ManFac legs, ease his torso into position, place the crisscrossing crotch webs firmly and tenderly against his body. She held his head in the hands of an angel of love and mercy. She made every move with sure but tender care.

She mated the two.

Symbiosis.

Fingers, wrists, arms, elbows, legs, calves, ankles, jaw, ears, nose, temple, shoulders, pelvis—all had to be joined smoothly and meaningfully. She went through an elaborate checklist, a technological-human manual of joined creation. Power flow, motor operation, oxygen, and pressure; of *both* these men. The crippled living human. The lifeless facsimile of a man, about to be joined as never before.

He was starting to emerge from the drug-induced stupor. She moved carefully but swiftly through the remainder of her checklist. When she was through, she closed the panels; she completed the form until it was human. She stood before the ManFac. It *breathed*.

She stared at what she had done, checked the biological monitors, the power systems. She held a small mirror beneath the nose of the superbly muscled specimen before her. Fog showed on the glass. How strange. She laughed shrilly, a vocal alarm in the laboratory. She was surrounded by the most advanced automated, synthetic, bionic humanoid systems in the world, and yet she had to reassure herself through an ancient but tried proof of exhalation.

She saw his eyes flicker. My God, the vocal system! If he regained consciousness without being able to speak, he would be *trapped*. It would be the mountain crushing him all over again. He could lose his sanity in a single moment of entrapment. Swiftly she threw the switches that activated the entire head system; now he could speak and hear and—

"What the fuck have you done to me!"

The outcry without profanity would have alarmed her. His instinctive choice of words confirmed to her he was expressing more anger than fear. She moved directly before him, saw his eyes move from side to side and then look at her. She gestured to be certain the movement captured his attention, no matter how momentary. "Lance. Listen to me. You won't be able to move your arms and legs for a few moments. Just a few moments. I swear it."

Critical point. Her words brought his attempt to move, and he was encased in a steel coffin. He couldn't understand what was happening, and the explosive urge, the subliminal claustrophobia from his long terror under the collapsed mountain could yet emerge full force. She had to thread the needle because if she activated him fully, he might not yet have sufficient control to think his actions. He would move instinctively, angrily, with fear, and that could ruin everything.

"Let me out of this goddamned thing!" he shouted. His eyes moved rapidly from side to side as he struggled within the ManFac. She watched the biological monitors. Jesus. Everything was sliding upward dangerously on the scale. She moved to the side, away from his vision, ready at that moment for a desperate gamble. He would start to shout now; he'd rant and scream at her. She moved the throat control to full output, rushed back to where he saw her. His eyes were wild, frantic.

"Lance! Please *listen* to me. Don't struggle. Trust—"

"I'LL KILL YOU, YOU BITCH! JUST LET ME GET MY HANDS ON YOU AND—"

She fell back as if struck with a terrible physical blow. Fell back, her legs like rubber beneath her, her ears ringing, her head feeling as if a vise had closed about it, and she tumbled sideways to the floor. The crashing thunder rattled through the laboratory, and they could hear glass still falling from where it had broken, could hear metal vibrating. It died away slowly. She lay on the floor, sucking in air, aching in every bone. A truck had run over her. Her arm raised weakly, and her voice issued forth like a half-drowned cat.

"Lance, please. I . . ." She struggled up to one elbow. "In the name of God, don't do that again."

Frozen, as immobile as a stone statue with a living face, he stared at her, the shock of her pain overcoming his own anger. "What—what happened?"

She made it to her feet and stood, swaying, before him, looking directly into his eyes. "That new throat band. I told you. Remember? It has more power."

"But . . . that *noise*. It was incredible."

"It was you."

He looked at her blankly. Instantly she seized the moment. "Lance, you trust me. You always have. Will you bear with me a few more moments?"

The eyes became hard. "Get me out of this . . . whatever the hell it is first," he said with swiftly renewed anger.

"All right," she said, nodding. "But let me get something first. You may change your mind."

"Lee, you promised—"

"And I'll keep my promise! Just wait a moment, will you?" She hoped there was enough exasperation in her voice to keep him at bay a precious few more seconds. She moved from her peripheral vision, and he heard her wheeling a large shrouded board that she stopped before him. It looked like a sheet of plywood. "What's that for?" he demanded.

She held the corner of the shroud in one hand. "I want you to meet someone."

"Screw your damned games," he snarled. "Just get me out of this thing and—"

"Lance." Ice in her voice stopped him again. She jerked away the shroud to reveal a large flat mirror. "I want you to meet Lance Parker."

Chapter 12

He was—beautiful.

Disbelief flickered in his eyes as the mirrored reflection looked back at him. His face resembled what he had been before, yet she had introduced subtle differences. He looked as if he might be a brother to a different Lance Parker. She had avoided the error of attempting a true mirror image, facially, of what he had been before. *That* umbilical wouldn't need cutting.

His neck was thick and powerful. If he was a remodeled Lance Parker, the most obvious difference was that she had added mass to the body configuration. His neck was thicker, his shoulders were broader, as was his chest, but the latter was also deeper. He had immense arms and powerful forearms. She had wisely avoided the weight lifter form in the ManFac body; he was more the solid, massive trunk with ribbed stomach musculature. A lumberjack with the superb muscle conditioning of a Roman gladiator. His thighs were thick and powerful; his legs, columns of sinew and corded muscle.

He struggled to move, and Lee moved quickly before him. "You're not trapped, Lance," she said evenly, looking directly at him. "You've got to understand that."

"Why can't I move?"

"I've locked the systems until you've had the chance to *see* what you are," she said quickly. "That's the *only* reason. I had to talk with you first, let you have some time to adapt. I apologize, I really do, for having to bring you through this with so little understanding, but—"

"Then why did you?" The anger was gone; he was questioning, seeking now.

"You heard your voice. *Your* voice. You used it without realizing how much power is added to the ManFac system, the bionic larynx, really, by tying it with your own. If you can be so dangerous with just your voice, try to understand what would or could have happened if you woke up and panicked with the ManFac systems fully powered up."

Until this moment he had worn only bits and pieces and parts, gaping skeletal frames, had had bundles of wires and controls taped and snugged to his body. It had been highly advanced flotsam and jetsam, a far cry from a completed package. An automobile becomes starkly naked and skeletal if you remove only the outer shell. The comparison fitted here. She noticed that his rapid, almost frantic eye movement had stopped. Relief swept through her.

"Give me just a few moments, Lance."

"Go ahead."

"All this time I've been working toward this moment." Her voice came across crisp, sharp, fully controlled now. She had his attention between his ears instead of fighting only his gut reactions. "The first correction in the artificial physiology, the bionic aspect, was to use manufactured systems, microminiaturization and amplification, plus the memory

136

circuits, to enable you to speak as you spoke before. Now you're complete, in terms of the ManFac system. There's more power available. And just as the neck-band corrected and amplified your own injured vocal system, so the ManFac is another step up the line. Thus, the volume while retaining your, well, let's call it a vocal signature."

"Wrap it up, Lee." His attention span was lousy while he felt trapped. She hurried on.

"You'd be no more than a fancy exoskeleton except for the most critical factor of all. The ManFac has a total memory bank on you as you were and can interpret every aspect of what you were before and then extrapolate what would be a normal movement in response to a nerve signal." She took a deep breath. "I—"

"Let it wait. Right now this is a very attractive prison." His voice was low, controlled. A shade too ominous. "Let me out."

She nodded. "All right. One last thing. *Do nothing rashly.* Do you understand? Do it slow motion. Think of what you want to do, and then stop right there, and pick it up again slowly. I'm releasing the holds. You'll be fully powered. There won't be anything mechanical or robotic about your movements. Slow, please. Very slow."

She left his direct vision again and disappeared to the side. Several moments passed. Goddammit, when would she—

His right hand balled into a powerful fist. The action caught him by surprise; he realized that he'd been attempting to make a fist from the moment he'd regained his senses. He started to move his arm, remembered what Lee said. Slow, easy, then even more slowly. He stared into the mirror, blinked. He took a deep breath and saw his great chest rise and fall. He turned his head to the right, saw his face

137

partly in profile. Then to the left. He stopped. He didn't really want to move, not yet. He flexed his arm muscles.

Biceps bulged at him from the mirror.

Holy Jesus . . .

He raised one arm, full above him, brought it down slowly. Then the other. He brought his open hands together and rubbed his palms briskly. He looked up, surprised. "I don't believe this. I can feel the movement. Even the slight heat from the friction."

"You have kinesthetic receptors, thermal receptors, pressure points, and feedback, all linked to your own hands, and *they,* in turn, are sending the signals to your brain."

He leaned forward slightly, testing his balance. Then backward. Hands on hips, he repeated the motions, then rotated the torso in calisthenics movements, but all very slowly and deliberately. He did a slow knee bend, nearly fell off-balance. He looked up at Lee, questioning.

"It doesn't happen all at once," she said quietly. "You're still in the category of the experimental model. You'll need practice again and again, and likely we'll have some modifications of the system. All in due time. Now keep the mirror before you. Walk toward it; judge what you see. That way you can compensate from what you experience and what you can see."

He walked, stopped, bent down, twisted in different positions, squatted, sat on the floor, lay prone, exercised his powerful limbs. "Tight in the pelvic area," he noted.

"We'll modify the plexisteel frame."

"When I do a full shoulder twist, like this"—he grunted—"something pushes into my shoulder."

"We can cushion that. Try some push-ups."

They were ridiculously easy. "There's no effort," he told her, looking up as his body, held absolutely rigid, pumped up and down through his arms.

"Jog in place."

He ran steadily. "Slight imbalance," he told her.

"Experience takes care of that. Faster," she directed.

His legs thudded like pistons into the floor of the lab. She studied the physiological monitors. "How much strain?" she asked over the sound of the pounding legs.

"Almost none. Oh, I can feel it, but it's easy. Almost too easy. I feel like I'm disengaged, like I'm a passenger."

"We don't want that." She scribbled notes on a clipboard. "We'll need some more resistance. Otherwise, you'll be unable to judge accurately your own speed or even speed of body motion."

He stood still, breathing normally, then walked slowly to the mirror. "I can hardly believe it. I'm sweating."

"Thermal sensors. At certain temperature levels the ManFac begins to release a synthetic perspiration. It's the same chemical composition as your own, with the ingredients of saline material, the odor-producing chemicals, that sort of thing. You'd never pass for long in society without such levels of normality." She gestured to her right. "Stand over here, please."

He followed her bidding, and a powerful fan hurled cooling air at him. He found himself leaning forward, blinking in the sudden blast. "Your own eyes are feeling the air, of course," she explained. "I'm pleased. The temperature system is working perfectly. Your perspiration has just about stopped." She switched off the fan.

She pointed again to another area marked with a circle on the floor. "Over here, Lance. Now stand perfectly still. Face that wall, please. Remain completely still, and listen as best you can." He nodded. A barely perceptible hum came to his ears.

"Can you hear that?"

"Yes."

"It's far below the ability of the human ear to detect," she said. "Feel the area on your face just ahead of and below your ears, where you would find the normal bony structure."

His hand probed, touched, pressed. "I feel it. What is it?"

"Implanted acoustic sensors. They work far down in the infrasound level, the superlow frequencies, and they go right on up to beyond what a dog can hear in the higher bands. However, you have a built-in sensitivity control. If you press against the left ear, you double the sensitivity input. Now be careful. It can get to be too much. The system is designed to let you detect pressure waves, what we call sound, but to bring the sound to you without harmful levels. Any time you want to return to normal hearing, press the unit on the opposite, the right ear. For the moment give me two levels in the left ear, and tell me what you hear."

He followed her instructions. He shook his head in wonder. "Your breathing, Lee. It sounds like an air-conditioning system. I can hear a deep pounding, and—"

"That's your own heart. I was afraid of that. We'll have to find some way of filtering that out."

"The same with my ears. I was once in an anechoic chamber. You know, without any echoes? Right now I can hear the blood rushing through my ears, just as I did then. Can you block that out as well?"

"We'll have to. What else? Concentrate outside your body."

He stood absolutely still. "How thick are the walls of this building?" he queried.

"Two feet. Concrete, steel, foam insulation. Soundproof."

"But they transmit vibrations." Any good engineer knew such characteristics. "Lee, you won't believe this, but through those walls I can pick up the sound of a jet. It's high, very high. It's like a distant echo, but I know a jet sound from anything else, and I can *hear* the damned thing."

"Excellent. All right, Lance, over here." She led him to a rack of clothing. "Use that chair. Your balance will take a few days to become automatic. You're moving more mass, and you've got to compensate for inertia—well, you know the data. What I want you to do now is to start coordination exercises." She handed him clothes. "Jockey shorts first, please."

He looked up with a sheepish grin. "I forgot I was naked," he said. "Know when I remembered?"

She smiled. "When I gave you the clothes, I imagine."

"No. When my ass hit this cold chair. It's incredible. I could feel *myself*, the cold against my body, I mean, even though I'm wearing, or inside, or whatever . . ." His voice fell off, and he slipped on the shorts. He followed with baggy gym trousers, a sweat shirt, socks, and sneakers, then went back to the mirror and stared at himself.

He turned to Lee. "I'd get a lot of help from videotape."

"You can look at yourself later. All this is recorded. But from now on nothing goes under the camera unless you say so."

"I appreciate that. What's next?"

"What may be the most difficult, strangely enough."

It was. He slopped water like a clumsy child when he tried to drink. She stopped him and placed a straw in the glass. "Try that." He sipped through the straw, felt the cool water within his own body.

"Piece of cake." He grinned.

"You'll need work with using glasses and cups. We'll schedule that. I think you'll need some time with food. The distance your arm travels, the heft of your muscles. The computer can do only so much. The rest is practice, experience, then compensation by reflex until you do such things automatically." She smiled. "I think we deserve a toast to tonight. Ever try champagne through a straw?"

His laugh was that of a child who has just discovered magic can be real.

The next several days flew by. Lance moved through a bubble of enchantment at the incredible new life given him by Lee. He went through dozens of exhausting tests, and where before he had quickly reached limits he refused to exceed, now there was no stopping him. He came to hate those moments when he had to withdraw from the ManFac, for each such withdrawal was its own traumatic nightmare of returning to the crippled body that would be his the rest of his life.

"It's like being Cinderella," he said wistfully. "The clock strikes midnight, and suddenly I'm a pumpkin again."

"Do I register that as a complaint?" she asked.

He shook his head. "No, thank God. I'm beyond that now."

"That was the most critical part of all," she told him. "If you fell victim to the reality of yourself, we had big troubles before us. Because this is *not* magic. It's materialistic in the cruelest sense, if you want to think of it that way. Look at what we've done, though. In a few days you've become as natural in the ManFac as you were before the accident. In some ways your own body mass and balance were better. For example, you'll never be as agile or as splendid

142

on the high bar or in tumbling as you were before. A fourteen-year-old girl has more grace and flow and rhythm than you can ever have, but—".

He broke in with a wide grin. "I yield to the young lady. I look lousy in leotards anyway."

"Excellent. Your attitude, I mean."

"Why, thank you, ma'am."

"Gallant, too. But I meant what I said. The worst enemy you'll have in creating a whole new life-style is understanding your limitations. The envelope of your experience and possibilities, to steal a phrase from some dashing test pilot."

He nodded. "I've got to be the kind of a pilot who flies, but whose airplane is not a machine. At first that sounds like a paradox, but it isn't. Not really. It's like being a living extension of one. There are pilots, and there are pilots. The best of them recognize the ultimate, and they all say the same thing about them: they don't get into their airplane—they *wear* it."

She nodded. "Like that air show we saw with Bob Hoover. I still don't believe that one."

"Great example. Hoover in an airplane is a living extension through his machine of his desires. *He* can't fly," Lance emphasized. "He needs the machine. So he blends in, and he uses all that power and fury and skill, and he flies in a way that gives a bird envious ulcers. He's the perfect match—"

"He's the man-machine gestalt," Lee interrupted. "In the case of a man like Hoover, it's almost as if the airplane anticipates his responses to the controls. Gestalt—a final product that is so much greater than adding one on one and so forth. You, one. The ManFac, one. Putting you together doesn't just make two. It squares and compounds and magnifies enormously. One on one, Parker and ManFac, creates something entirely new. You're a body-surrounding alter ego, an extension of self. Maybe"—she grimaced—"I'm taking someone else's words out of context, but you get my meaning. Come with me. Let me show you another thing you haven't seen yet about your new self."

In the laboratory she wheeled a cradling device to room center and picked up a steel bar. "ManFac," she said crisply. "Experimental systems only." She looked ruefully at the experimental body before them. "I vent my frustrations on him. Take out exasperation."

The giant by her side stood quietly. "I could have used him myself," he reflected.

She shook her head. "Not the same thing, love. Different intents. I mean, he's not just for bashing about. There's purpose in all this."

She hefted the steel bar. "Take a good look at his skin. The hair isn't synthetic. It's human. It burns, and it stinks the way human hair does. Most people don't realize how endurable human hair can be. The best wigs aren't synthetic. They're homegrown, clipped like a sheep, and sold elsewhere."

He glanced at his burly forearms and then brushed his head with his hand. She laughed. "Don't ever bother to ask. You, too. Head, eyebrows, body, pubic —all of it. But pay attention. This skin is the same as yours. It's not as finely developed, but the structure is the same. Flexmetal, plastimetal surfacing, thin woven honeycomb, accommodations for connecting and supporting areas where there would normally be muscle, tendon, bone, sinew—that sort of biological glop."

"I hadn't quite thought of myself, at least the *new* self, as glop," he protested.

"A rose by any other name," she said, shrugging. "Watch, will you?"

Before he could answer, she stepped forward like a

slugger at home plate and brought the steel bar up and then down in a wicked, devastating blow against the left shoulder of the ManFac before her. The heavy structure rocked backward slightly, seemed to shudder, and finally was still.

"Christ, *I* could almost feel that," Lance said. He went forward to examine the deep crease she had pounded in the shoulder area. "You've pretty well crushed it," he noted. "Was that necessary?" He turned back to Lee.

"Look not at me, sir." She had a satisfied smirk on her face. "Observe carefully yon damage to your bosom buddy."

He looked, and then he stared, and then his fingers brushed lightly across the shoulder of the ManFac—because the deep indentation was slowly but surely vanishing, the form was filling in again, and as he kept watching the shoulder returned to normal shape. "Holy Christ," he muttered. "It's even got a *bruise*."

"Well, it looks like a bruise, but that's simply an unexpected effect. A bit of cosmetic serendipity, you could say. In real life that blow would leave a bruise. This one does the same. I told you the material was a mixture, a compounding of plastimetal, plastiskin, and that new honeycomb sandwiching, and it's all constituted of memory molecules. Unless the material itself is destroyed molecularly, it will always regain its shape within twenty to forty minutes. The difference is determined by temperature and pressure."

She turned to a control desk and began flipping switches. "We have some important work to do. I need to mix the physiological reports of you in that thing with the computer inputs and the feedback. Think you can stand about two hours of testing? You can start by punching holes in those wooden panels over there. And then there's some wood and metal I want you to bite through."

"Bite?" he echoed.

"A German shepherd has seven hundred pounds per square inch biting force, lover. You have nine hundred or so. You can literally bite your way through thick ropes and lesser cables, to say nothing of the steaks you accuse me of murdering."

He felt incredibly good. "You name the test, and I'll play the tune," he told her.

"Like I said, two hours."

"What then?"

No fun on that face at which he looked. "Then it's Cinderella time, and you become a pumpkin again."

"Yeah. I know," he said quietly.

Chapter 13

Cinderella time was a bitch. He didn't believe just how tough it was. Not merely the first time, but the second and the third, and it became worse with every occasion when he had to quit being a human specimen in many ways beyond even his wildest fancies as a kid. Lee felt his deep searing introspection, the soul-searching to which he subjected himself. There was the kind of withdrawal he went through *every time*—each separate occasion—that could have broken a will less strong than that of Lance. It was like losing an arm or a leg forever. It was a deliberate acceptance of torn face and scarred lips and gnarled ear where moments before there had been a rugged face that didn't scare the hell out of children.

His past was gone forever. If he accepted that deep within himself, he could apply that marvelous mind to the future; he could face life with an altered but wholly viable zest and appeal that had marked his days "before the mountain." The rules were the same: Live fully or die slowly. There were really no in-betweens.

"You'll have to learn to bring together the two personalities of yourself," Lee warned him. "But you can never go through a constant shifting through this diaphragm of Jekyll-Hyde. You've got to stay in full control of both men, the before and the after, no matter which role you're playing at the moment."

"Tough," he murmured.

"History is filled with people who were told they could never again do this or do that. Men who couldn't walk and ran the world's fastest mile," she reminded him. "Pilots who failed air cadet school and tried the back door and became great heroes. And so on. You know this. Can you imagine the world losing that beautiful brain of Charles Steinmetz, the ultimate genius of electricity, because he had the poorlittle-me syndrome? He was partially a hunchback, he was ugly and scrunched up, and the greatest men of science in all the world sat adoringly at his crooked feet."

He growled at her. "There's no self-pity here, Lee."

"But there *is* a struggle," she persisted.

"Jesus Christ, do you expect me *not* to have one?"

"No. I'm just trying to let you know you don't stand alone at your personal crossroads."

He looked at her, and he didn't smile, but there was something deep and warm in his eyes. "I know that. I have for quite some time now. I suppose"—he sighed—"even when I fought you, I knew it."

"You never fought me," she said quietly. "It was always yourself."

"Yeah," he agreed.

He wondered about himself. He toyed with the theology of it, if there was anything of that nature. Was it straight out of cards dealt blindly in life? He could accept that. Fate dealt the hand, and you played or bluffed or drew new cards, but ultimately you had to play those in your hand.

He laughed aloud, and Lee studied him. "There was some deep humor in that sound," she observed.

"I was thinking of the fanciful and wonderful celluloid world of television," he said.

She smiled. "I can guess. The bionic man."

"*Uh-huh.* The old Six Million Dollar Man smoothie. Old stone face mumbling at the camera. The made-to-order idiot."

"Leaping over tall buildings."

"Not without ear-stabbing sound effects," he added.

"And his bionic girl. Falling out of the sky and waking up supergirl."

They laughed together. "And who could forget the bionic boy, and the bionic dog, and the bionic asshole?" he said.

"Well"—she tweaked him lightly—"you *could* have a bionic dork."

"What?"

"To use the terms I overheard when my dear father was playing poker with his friends, and I was a young girl who was *supposed* to be asleep," she explained, "a dork, pecker, cock, schwanz, meat loaf—"

"Good grief," he said, honestly taken aback.

"Every word except penis," she added.

He looked quizzically at her. "And you think I want some electronic dildo hanging between my legs, springing pinkly erect when I press a hidden button?"

She showed sharp teeth. "Don't you?"

"Hell, *no,*" he said with unexpected vehemence. "There are some things a man wants to do on his own."

The toughest exchanges weren't with Lee. They were in his own head. Because the fact of it was that sometimes he felt like the bionic village idiot. He had so much more than great strength. He had brains and intelligence and training and knowledge and capabilities built into the ManFac over which other men would have drooled. But, and it was a deeply meaningful "but," were this ManFac system and all its promise really more than a glossed-over supercaricature of a man? Beset by doubts and honestly questioning the future, he wondered if he could truly, deeply within himself, be something more than polished ceramics. What had he called himself one night? A computer-prodded ghost of a lost Lance Parker. In a way the ghost of Christmas past.

Not so long ago he had wanted desperately to kill himself. That weakness, no matter how real and terribly urgent, was behind him. Strange. Now that he had the strength to storm the future, the greatest doubt he faced was—himself.

Lee didn't give him that much time to wallow in his own thoughts. You don't create a quantum leap in the Man Facsimile system and just leave it wandering around. If there were a dozen improvements, there were a thousand changes and modifications to be made, and all of them could emerge only from testing, experimenting, trials, and failures. No one ever succeeded until he had, in one way or the other, failed. Success is handling all the little failures with ease and confidence. It's what gets you through the dark nights.

There was little, indeed, on which either of them could draw for advice or counsel of true guidance. It was as if he had sidestepped the rest of the human race onto another plane of existence. But there was no other way than to return to square one and take that giant first step. It was called understanding the system and the environment. Like climbing a mountain. All the best equipment in the world didn't mean a damn if you didn't know how to use it. And you had to understand mountains as a mass as well as the tiny details of rock, and what weather would do, and you always had to watch the clock because climbing a sheer, slippery face in daylight was really not the same as clawing your way up the same wall with a flashlight gripped in your teeth. That was just a faster way to get killed.

Or flying an airplane. Once you knew what to do, it was easy. Flying a 747 was a hell of a lot easier than handling a tricky training plane with a tail wheel that cavorted and danced and whipped about madly in a crosswind. But it was a long road to being easy and comfortable in the 747. The long road was the experience and the know-how and the confidence you acquired en route.

He needed to know, understand, comprehend everything about the ManFac system that had emerged from the genius and the love and the patience of Lee Grazzi. Yet where she was brilliant, she also had moments and quicksands of inadequate knowledge. He was an engineer and looked upon their problems with a perspective different from hers. He was the man who became the ManFac, and that gave him a hell of a different view. Now it was time, because they had come so far together, to apply their talents as a team. He knew engineering and power systems, he knew trusses and bridge-building and cantilevered designs, he knew pressure and flow and materials, and with all this he was, as he had always been, swift to learn, quick to seize on the most basic as well as the most advanced systems. He was as much a mechanic and an electrician and a tinkerer as he was a professional engineer. He'd worked with remote control systems, and he understood intrinsically the highly complicated and advanced intermeshing systems created by Lee, and quickly, much more quickly than either of them had expected, he became as much the teacher as Lee had been to him.

He could judge the ManFac both as a collection of parts and as a single unit unto itself. He could think in parallel lines, and every time he discovered a fault or a weakness he was able to bring his own input into the problem. Rubbing, chafing, hard points were small problems in comparison to channeled power and sensor systems. That was *wrong*. A man can handle a broken leg a lot better than he can a sharp cinder in his eye. The first will inconvenience him and diminish his daily envelope of performance; the second, unless it is removed, will drive him insane.

The prosaic is more often the seemingly insuperable than the exotic problem. Those pressure points drove him to distraction, much as they had the astronauts who went through one generation after the other of high-altitude flight suits and then the suits tailored specifically to the hard vacuum of space. "We're not facing the same conditions," Lance complained to Lee, "so why are we trying to solve things the same way? No matter what you do, like eliminating a chafing point in one place, it seems just to shift it to another. I think I know a way to eliminate that."

And he did, and it was surprisingly simple. If a chafing point built up, he was able to seal the suit, to pressurize the system slightly, and bring a layer of air between his body and the suit. It was as if he rode within an invisible layered cushion separating parts of his body from the ManFac system.

After slopping and splashing for several weeks, he mastered the techniques of eating and drinking in normal fashion. The technique that had so long defied Lee's design was in the interface between Lance's scarred lip tissue and the inner layers of mouth and chin and, above all, the upper lip and those of the ManFac. The lips and mouth are astonishingly flexible, even wildly rubbery, and they depend as often on liquid lubrication as they do on this facility of extraordinary and misshapen movement. The ability to pucker up, to whistle, to open wide, to operate tongue and palate and the edges of the cheeks, to move air as well as liquid and physical objects in and out is one of nature's most ingenious engineering feats, and nature just didn't accept Lee's ManFac meddling. At least, nature refused to yield without a fight. It was slow, tiresome, and often painful, for the scarred skin tissue rubbed raw, chafed quickly, and healed slowly. The solution again appeared from an unexpected source. Lee used pigskin tissue and designed the ManFac for easy replacement of this tissue when necessary. Lance came up with the idea, not from ingenuity, but from memory. Pigskin, the closest product of nature to human skin. They'd used the hapless porkers for atomic bomb tests, tethering them in the open so they would be seared by the violent infrared radiation of the exploding fireballs, and the more they learned, the more amazed they were that pigskin was less than one percent variable from human skin. Pigskin found its way into burn wards, surgical wards, and the like. Treated with chemicals to sustain its beneficial characteristics, it could stand in for human skin for weeks at a time. Presto, that problem went into the solved ledger.

"I think," Lance grumbled uncomfortably during a suit test, "that the toughest problem with this suit is what we're doing now." He shifted his weight and grimaced at Lee.

"Little boy doesn't want to make cocky?" Her voice was sugary, and her expression one of torment. His, not hers. He gaped at her choice of words, to say nothing of her leer.

"Little boy doesn't—" His echoed response stopped dead, and he glared at her. "Goddammit, Lee, I—"

"Oh, shut up and just try a dump, will you?" she demanded. "Or would you rather I revert to clinical terminology?" She stepped back and curtsied. "Please pass the feces, good sir. Is that better? Or would you have me ask you to spill the stools into this liquid-filled ceramic receptacle?"

"What the hell's gotten into you!" he shouted.

"There's nothing polite about taking a crap!" she shouted back. "Do you need privacy? At this point of the game, for God's sake? I've just about crawled through your intestines and your bowels for a year, and *now* you get cute. Jesus, Lance, if you're ever going to adapt to the ManFac system, we've got to *know* if you can pass physical wastes through the anal interface or if we have to store the bulk in containers, and that means germicides and sealants and all that nonsense, and it would be a lot easier if we could—"

"I hope to God we're recording this," he said, exploding into laughter. "Great moments in history. What a terrific show for HBO."

"HBO? Hot bowel offerings?"

"I can see it now," he said, making a grand gesture with one arm. "Ta-da! Lights, action, and camera! Proctoscope!"

"A rear-end view of the news!" she cried.

"No shit!" he shouted.

"*That's* the problem," she reminded him. They sobered quickly, and she snapped her fingers. "Idea time. We can't quite go to sphincter to sphincter. Tough tango to handle. But what if we created a partial vacuum—which you could set up through a separate control—about the buttocks when you did have to go? That would keep the ManFac interior buttock area firmly against your own skin, and there'd be no interference with the anus—"

"I hate this," he murmured.

"And there'd be no interference with passing physical wastes," she pressed on. "In fact, elimination and cleaning would be about as normal as one might expect." She patted him on the arm. "I'll make the preliminary drawings, love. In the meantime, you just grab yourself a handful of privacy and have your own quiet little dump. See you."

And she was gone. Not so flippantly, he realized later. She had managed to make him emerge through the emotional thicket with a half grin on his face. That woman was incredible, he thought with renewed admiration. He had, with her help, overcome a savage determination to end his life, in a hundred different ways, and she had anticipated that all their success to date could have been tossed through the nearest window if he had become hung up on a subject that had all sorts of psychological hooks to it, going all the way back through dark emotional passageways to childhood. He brooded on the subject, and the more he thought about it, the more he came to appreciate just how carefully Lee had guided him. Human nature was a most curious beast.

The man who napalms an entire village of men, women, and children won't say "fuck" before his mother. That's really *bad*. And it *is* if the taboo has been cemented in his mind structure so heavily that the very act of verbal utterance triggers a guilt complex.

She had teased him on the matter of bowel movement. Just something to pass by, right? Good God, how badly were people hung up on these social thorns?

There were people who would rather die, literally, than shit before an audience. There were people who *had* died because of their mind-frozen inability to climb over a wall of social-emotional no-no. And what was even wilder was that through their exchange Lee *had* produced the engineering-biological

155

answer to the problem. The air seal, that pocket of partial vacuum, would work.

Except that he had spent so much damned time thinking about it that he, well, he just couldn't go. It was the next day before he could even bring himself to talk about it with Lee.

"I'm, ah, well, I got a problem," he muttered. By way of answer she raised her brows and waited.

"I'm constipated," he blurted out.

She laughed so hysterically tears ran down her cheeks.

She didn't miss many tricks. To Lee the ManFac wasn't just a system, but a way of life into which Lance would have to fit and then function without detection. Those were the magic words: "to function without detection." She also thought far ahead of his own hopes. The ManFac would provide Lance with many physical capabilities that were far beyond what his own body could provide even before his accident. But he had been capable of certain graceful movements and rhythms she could not infuse within a ManFac system. So he had to adapt to what would be the new system, the new Lance Parker, while being always those *two* men—the inner and the outer.

She had spent countless hours on this matter of great strength. She understood Lance in the emotional and psychological sense far better than he would ever know himself. Deep within the mind of the man she loved there still lurked a primal hatred of what had happened to him. Someday, and that would be soon, he would emerge from all this self-control she had brought him to develop. And when Lance slipped into his new self, that mighty new being, he would be possessed of great destructive power. There was every chance he would, subconsciously at least, seek the opportunity to enact a form of revenge.

She envisioned scenes that would ensue from the use of the ManFac strength, and she sighed because oftentimes the only real difference between enraged boys and men is their size or the stubble on their chins. The anger and the rage are often the same—and so is the vulnerability.

She had given to Lance, as a ManFac, an attribute few men enjoy: the ability to take a tremendous kick in the groin and be unaffected by the blow. She designed into the ManFac a groin cup of flexisteel and ceramics that would absorb any such blow. In fact, the man who ever kicked Lance in the groin would probably break his foot.

Lee poured coffee for them both and turned back to the holographic projection and computer controls. "Fantasy time," she explained. "I've been working on systems we can incorporate within the ManFac. Not immediately, but projects that will need your input even more than my own. The kind of stuff with which you're a lot more familiar."

He glanced at her as she brought a full-size holographic ManFac into the three-dimensional reality before them. It stood suspended in thin air, glowing slightly, transparent so that all inner systems as well as the exterior showed. "Sounds like some more therapy," he said suspiciously.

She shook her head. "Nope. Straight engineering, Mr. Bones. For example, the plastiskin." She touched controls as she spoke. Before them the external skin surfaces of the holographic ManFac glowed brighter than the rest of the assembly. "As a nuclear systems engineer you had to develop linings, pumps, pipes, holding tanks, valves, controls—the whole works—that would be reliable for years, without any servicing of any kind, because they carry radioactive solutions and chemicals, right? Right. So, how are they different from chemical plants?"

He nodded. "I see what you mean. Ceramic liners, special alloys. They can withstand pressure, thermal extremes, shock, just about everything we can anticipate as a disruptive or destructive force."

"Can you improve the plastiskin the same way?"

"Sure," he said lightly.

"Not so fast. Let's say you make it able to endure ten minutes of open flame. Will it retain the flex characteristics after that time?"

"Not completely. You've got to compromise somewhere along the line," he said.

"Right now," she went on, pointing, "that plastiskin can take ninety seconds of open flame. Then it undergoes a drastic chemical reaction. It stiffens and assumes undesirable brittle characteristics. How long can it absorb flame, beyond ninety seconds, and still retain the flexibility it has now?"

He sipped coffee slowly. "Three to four minutes max."

"That's at least twice as good as we have right now. How long would it take you to mix up a batch of your new plastiskin?"

He looked at her. "I never said *I* would do it. Stan Loren at Global Synthetics. He's the absolute genius of this business. I worked with him. *He* could do it."

She studied him. "Without asking personal questions?"

"Yes."

She made some notes. "You call him then. Now let's look at a system that can endure open flame for, *um,* let's say three minutes. What about the eyes all this time?"

He leaned forward. "I see what you mean. Sure, what's the use of walking through fire if you gouge out your eyes?" He gestured at the glowing eyes of the ghostly ManFac. "Same source. Stan. He can give us, oh, maybe sixty seconds of a Plexiglas material. They use it for supersonic aircraft. Takes more heat than steel without breaking down."

"That means," she said, operating her controls, "that if you were walking through a fire and you *had* to do it, you could snap down a Plexiglas shield over the eyeball? And at the same time maintain the Man-Fac integrity to prevent heat and gases from invading the suit?"

"That's not nearly as tough as it sounds. We dealt with those kinds of seals all the time inside the reactors."

"All right. Breathing then. We don't want this system limited to the oxygen duration of a man holding his breath. Especially if he's exerting energy. What's the answer?" As she spoke, the nostrils, mouth, and respiratory system came into sharper glowing relief.

"Snap-shut ports for the nasal passages. Same for the lips, mouth, ears—all body orifices. They'd have to be stronger than the basic plastiskin because after exposure you'd want them to snap back into their storage receptacles. And, *um*, see there? Where the back muscles are? The area to the upper side of the back? You could build solid-oxygen containers in there, one to each side. Closing the nasal passages would open the oxy flow automatically."

"Can you do it?"

"Of course, Lee. Look, it's not a *new* system. I mean, I don't have to play boy genius about that because the armored suits I wore, even when"—he faltered for a moment as he recalled the mountain crushing him—"even when I had the accident, well, any high radioactive or heat level triggered the same sort of thing we're talking about now. Automatically. In fact, we built three *days* of breathing oxygen

159

and air scrubbers into the system. The trick, strangely enough, is not what to get to breathe. It's what to do with the exhaled gases. You want the suit sealed so you can't just pass them into the air. You have to store them, scrub the air, remove the unwanted gases and water vapors and—"

"Can you fit it into the ManFac system?"

"Easy."

Perhaps not easy, but easily within their technical grasp.

If they could build in resistance to enormous heat, even open flame, it was much easier to build in resistance to terrible cold. Power, heat radiation wired through the inner system, defogging—it was, in fact, a simple modification of astronaut and deep-sea-diving systems.

"The skull," Lee murmured. "Ah, what a treasure."

"Mine?" Lance asked, nodding to the hologram. "Or his?"

"Yours is more lovely than fascinating. Besides, I like to crawl around inside your mind to tickle your fancy." She gestured at the hologram. "Him? A little trickle of electricity here, a pseudosynapse there. Lots of things that go snap and pop, but no real fun."

"What did you have in mind?"

Instantly, in that way he knew so well, she was serious again. Her fingers flew across the control panel, and a glowing image appeared within the holographic ManFac. "That's you. The yellow area. Your skull inside the ManFac housing. See how much space we have there?"

"So I'm empty-headed."

"Not you, dummy. Between the two."

"Oh," he said with a touch of innocence.

"There's enough room there for an awful lot of printed circuitry. Remote sensing systems and—"

"No," he broke in. "Bring that stuff down into the torso." He used a flashlight-illuminated arrow that moved about the hologram. "You put the sensors both in the cranial area and in the torso, but the main system, where everything is processed, well, if you put it into the torso, you can protect it a lot better and make access much easier. Using modular plug-ins, that means maintenance, *um*, well, you know."

"Do I ever!" she said, enthused. "Do you realize the ideas you've just given me? I'd forgotten about available space within the body system. I could build in ultraviolet, infrared, even ultrasonic systems. With the power boosters and the new lenses, we could—"

He curled a lip. "How about X-ray vision? Then I could see through your clothes."

"Your *Playboy* subscription run out?"

"I could see through a *lot* of clothes."

"You're not funny, stud. You're right, but you don't even know it."

"Meaning what?"

"Meaning, on a limited basis right now I could adapt an X-ray system to ManFac."

He shook his head. "You're talking too much power. You're also forgetting processing, plates, a few little items like that."

"Forgetting, hell. I could *do* it." She rubbed her cheek, thinking hard. "Oh, not right away, but down the line, I could damn well do it, all right." She turned to face him. "A combination of fluoroscopy. With an X-ray capability. Do you realize what that could mean?"

"Sure. You'd go crazy trying to figure out how to present the information to the inner soul of the ManFac. You know, like me."

"Present it?"

"Sure. How do you transmit the optical readout of

an X-ray, or even a fluoroscopic system, to the bearer? You can't have a screen, a cathode panel, or anything like that incorporated into the ManFac. It would be clumsy, it couldn't take any heavy shock, its thermal envelope would be restrictive, and, well, presentation of data is the real snag here. It wouldn't be worth the effort." He drained his coffee. "I don't think the X-ray thing *should* be a part of the system. Everything is a matter of degree, and we could keep right on going, and we could overload a beautiful system. Even ManFac has limits."

"Go on," she urged.

"I think we should draw a line with ManFac," he said, finding his own convictions as surprising to him as they were pleasing to her. "The X-ray system couldn't be a part of the biological system. So it's got to be an addition, a carry-on, or even a plug-in. Just like placing a pacemaker in the chest of a heart patient, except that the pacemaker is essentially a bionic device to aid a failing physiological system."

"And the X-ray ability—"

"Is packaging, pure and simple," he finished for her.

"Very good. *Very* good," she said, genuinely pleased. "I'll add to that. I'll drink a toast to it. The X-ray system is possible, *but not now.* I want to emphasize that. One day it will be possible. Of that I'm sure, but we'll have to wait for electronic microsurgery of the human body, and we're still a very long way from that stage. So it's a future far down the line, not a factor now. I think," she said slowly, "that the line you want to draw is that the ManFac systems are limited to the gross extremities, the limbs, and the major skeletal and structural elements of the body."

"I'm not ready to buy that," he said in an easy counterpoint. "You're working with electronic systems; you're using wires thinner than human hair, memory chips for the computerized systems smaller than a pencil dot—that sort of thing. It seems to me that in some ways you're exceeding some of the really small, intricate, even the exquisite systems of the human body." He was surprised with her continued insistence that still, she was right.

"Look at it this way then. God made the human eyeball of jelly and water and, well, let's call it superfine catgut and biological fiber optics, and out of all that glop we get the truly incredible optical system of the human being, all neatly connected to a computer center just loaded down with batteries of sensors, memory banks, and all those goodies we take for granted. Maybe God can string both celestial tennis rackets and human eyeballs with all their connecting systems from those few materials, but *I* can't. One day it will happen. It wasn't so long ago that flying and walking on the moon and television and computers were completely insane ideas but"—she shrugged—"who knows? Maybe you're right. Maybe we ought to draw limits."

He nodded. "Not because we *shouldn't* try these things," he emphasized, "but only because we're not capable of joining them all together with meaningful reliability."

"A large mouthful very adroitly spoken. That packages our thoughts well," she added. She sat up straight, leaned forward, and the hologram vanished. Lights glowed brighter about them as she adjusted the lab system. She turned to face Lance, slapping both hands against her knees. He recognized that gesture. Lee was about to lay something on him. He couldn't help it; he tensed.

"Are you ready for another mouthful?" she asked.

"With you I expect only the unexpected," he parried.

"Rough one, lover."

163

"I've grown accustomed to your smile," he side-stepped.

"This one is different, Lance." Her tone changed so quickly, gained warmth instead of that fencing they did so often, that he *was* caught by surprise.

"Okay," he said. "Go ahead." It was the first time in many weeks that he'd seen doubt in her eyes.

"I have an experiment I want you to try. You're ready for it. You'll never be more ready, in fact"—she tapped the side of her head—"than in there."

"Big mental barrier to break down, *huh*." It wasn't a question, and she recognized it from him.

"That's it."

"Well, don't play cat and mouse, woman. You don't need to anymore."

She sighed. "I hope you're right, Lance Parker. Because this is a low blow. I want you out of the Man-Fac system."

"I don't get you. I go in, go out. So what's—"

"Two weeks out."

He took that one slowly. He didn't like it. "Why?" he asked after the long pause.

"Lance Parker, survivor, has to test himself in the world out there."

"Well, sure, I could—"

"Survivor," she broke in. "*Not* ManFac."

"You mean—" He couldn't even finish it.

"That's right. The man with the cane. The guy with the scars. The guy who has a rough time walking. But he's learned how to drive again. And he can walk. He can do a lot of things. But he hasn't learned how to get out and mix with that world. It can be cruel. People stare at scars. They ask indecent questions. They can be absolutely rotten. It's tough, getting up and down stairs. Going into a rest room. Eating with kids whispering about that man who looks so strange. Talking to—"

"Enough. I have the picture."

"Will you do it?"

"I don't have much of a choice."

"What?" Her reaction was total surprise. "Of course you do! I can't make you—"

"Not you, Lee. *Me*. You see, I'm not sure if I can handle it." He faced her with a crooked smile. "And the only way to find out is to try."

Her hand touched his. "Oh, Lance, it could be so difficult. Maybe we're rushing it just a bit. We could wait until—"

"Fish or cut bait. That's what time it is." He stood up and looked down at her. "No. You're right. About meeting the world head-on. But I got to admit, lady, it scares the hell out of me."

Chapter 14

He had a long heart-to-heart with himself. The Lance Parker he'd known was dead. *Make that fact a meaningful reality. You died.*

Yeah. Life's a bitch. *What? How can that be? You died, so how can you be discussing this?*

That was something to mull over. Okay, okay, so his inner soul's position as a devil's advocate was forcing the issue. *You're here because you got what the other poor bastards don't get. A second shot at life. But right now you've got to do it as what you really are. Not with that walking suit of armor Lee Grazzi whipped up for you. You've got to do this one on your own, baby.*

Fact of life. He walked, but only barely. With a foot-dragging and shuffling gait that rested for its pivot point on one leg and that cane. He swore he wouldn't use a crutch. He didn't care how much it hurt or what the hell it looked like to anyone; he was going to do it with just that one goddamned cane. He twisted and dragged and shuffled, but by damn, he was walking on his own.

When you should be dead, right?

167

Lay off, will you?

I can think for myself. That's the key. Think for myself.

It was. The reality was that he had been given a prison sentence for life, trapped in this grotesque parody of what had once been a beautiful male form. But if he *did* think about it, he was alive, he had accepted life, and screw the poor-little-me syndrome.

Right on. What's next?

A mind becomes sharper when the demands increase. And he knew he must use his mind as never before because it was the only way to go. A blind man hears better and a deaf man sees better because of a factor called compensation. Nature's compensations are real.

So are the minds of men, he argued with himself. *And since the mind is every bit as important as the rest, since it's the absolute fulcrum for the rest of this body, what the hell is so wrong about depending upon that ManFac system?*

Because, dummy, with all its wonders, without you as the motivating element it's so much chrome-plated junk. It's a plumber's nightmare that doesn't go anywhere or do anything. The key is the catalyst. That's you.

Then why the hell am I going through all this?

Because you have to answer a question. Can you handle life without ManFac? If you can't, then you're more of a cripple than we ever dared suspect. That's what cripple means, baby. Not being able to handle life when you're at rock bottom.

He yearned for the ManFac. In that thing he was—

Knock off the crap. I know what you're going to think next. You mix the physical cripple and the beautiful mind with the machine, and we get some sort of low-budget superman, right? Well, you're wrong.

ManFac

He was surprised by his self-vehemence. He knew better than his own yearnings. Superbeings have always been a fiction, and in respect to contemporary society that's the way it would always be. He was an engineer, and he couldn't shake his own reality. Superman is a violation of nature's own laws. Entropy works for biological-intellectual systems just the way it does for the clockwork of the universe. You never get something for nothing. You don't build castles on thin air or upon mental quicksand. If you run from reality, you're a sop to fairy-tale dreaming. Before you give orders, you've got to know how to take them. Before you learn balance, you've got to experience the loss of balance and get up off your ass.

A man and the ManFac become a superior system only with full preparation, training, and knowledge of what's involved. Superiority exists only with a complete grasp of the environment.

You're learning.

He nodded to his mental self. Under certain conditions the best of the ManFac could be a liability. If he weighed 190 pounds and had to cross a rope bridge that could hold 200 pounds, he had it made. But in the ManFac system he weighed 320 pounds, and that meant—

Right to the bottom of the gorge.

The first day was pure hell. He hadn't used his own body for more than an hour or two at the most. Then he could lie back, relax in a whirlpool, wait for Lee. Before the first hour of driving, even with power steering and power brakes and air conditioning, even with all those things, the mountain roads reached inside his body and his brain, and they rattled him good. Coordination drained his energy. Wheel and accelerator and brake and centrifugal force and depth perception and thinking ahead and driving ahead

169

and matching his speed to the mountain roads and turns and upgrades and steep slopes. He wasn't that certain how long he'd been driving when he pulled to the ride of the road. A clearing overlooked a stunning stretch of a deep valley ringed by peaks. Once he'd been able to *run* up those peaks. They were duck soup to the mountains he'd climbed. Now he was grateful to sit in a car and suck in air and rest after just *driving* through the place.

He had a coffee Thermos. It helped. He ached through his arms and his legs, and his back had a red poker jammed through it somewhere but—

Remember, that first step is the bitch. The first hour is the killer. You're on your way.

But he wasn't about to try out for an Olympic record. Screw that stuff. There was also common sense. He drove slowly for another hour, and the road turned and came out in the midst of a tourist camp. He had never been so glad to see a motel, and when he saw a drive-in registration window, he could have whooped for the joy of it. The thought sobered him. Drive-in registration? He'd forgotten . . .

You sure have. There's a whole world of people out here who can't walk. Not even on crutches. They use wheelchairs, and that's why they can register this way. Then there are those without legs or arms and others who are paralyzed, and would you believe there are still people in iron lungs? Tell you what, Lance, baby. The chaplain's on leave. Tell it to Jesus.

He grinned at himself and drove to the window. It went easily enough, but he *felt* crippled, and he hated that.

Oh, shut up. You could always have parked and walked on that cane into the office. This is how you wanted it.

He clammed up to himself. He registered and paid with a MasterCard. He was amazed at how exhausted he was. He knew he wouldn't want to drag himself to a restaurant because—

Because you're not ready yet to try eating before other people. Face it. No crime there. Take it slow.

He quit arguing with himself, stopped by a small all-night food store in the tourist parking area to buy sandwiches and milk. Getting back into the car was a herculean effort. So was making it into his room. He dropped the food on a table, pushed the door closed, and sank gratefully into a wide armchair. Before he knew it, he was asleep.

He came awake with a clutch of cold fear about his neck. *Voices. What the hell . . .* Dark outside; he saw the lights from the parking lot through the window where the drapes weren't fully closed. He started to get up. Every muscle in his body howled at him. He gasped with the unexpected pain. He gritted his teeth, made it to his feet, hobbled to the drape cords, and pulled them closed. He turned on the room lights and stared at the door. The lock. All this time he'd been in this goddamned room without throwing the bolt. All this time he'd been so helpless—

His face whitened, and he felt his fingers squeezing the cane. He squeezed his eyes as tightly as he could until he knew tears ran down his cheeks. He forced down the thoughts that came swimming up from somewhere far down in his skull. But there was no denying them. They swam upward, a billion tadpoles carrying their dark and ominous message. *The truth. Dammit, you've got to face it sooner or later! The truth. Admit it. Admit it! It's the first step to beating what you've refused to admit.*

He was soaked in his own sweat, and he hadn't moved an inch. *Oh, God . . . make it go away.* It refused to leave. It was here now, full-blown and sitting astride his mind, grasping it with suckers and

171

cups and talons and claws and teeth, and it wouldn't go away.

You're afraid because you're so helpless. That's what scares the shit out of you.

He heard himself gasping hoarsely for breath. It was true. The terrible awful nightmare. He had visions of a body twisting, turning, running, jumping, wrestling, snapping gloved jabs into another man's face, feeling leather against skin, feeling leather against his own skin, laughing off the blows.

That's what you were. No more.

No more. What? The truth.

He had a mental picture of a premature infant, wet and blood-slimed and not fully formed, thrust naked and wet and totally helpless into a world filled with gnashing teeth and hungry stomachs, and he wanted to scream because the tiny twitching form was premature, but the face was full grown and developed, and he looked at himself, and then he felt the floor coming up at him, and he lay on the carpet, dry-heaving with this stinking, terrible truth.

Helpless. Everything in the world out there was an enemy. He had a vision of looking at himself in the full-length mirror, and it showed him the rippling muscles and thick neck and powerful body of himself, ManFac, and he felt dizzy with the longing for that great form covering this shriveled hulk of what he really was.

It took him an hour to get off that floor. He dragged himself into the bathroom and sat on the floor by the tub, washing himself with a cold, wet towel. It took an enormous effort to return to the room, to force himself to eat the sandwich and drink the milk because he knew he needed the energy. He sat quietly, his back against the bed, dozing, waking fitfully at any sound outside. Finally, he summoned all his strength and pushed and dragged the armchair before the door. His muscles were knotted like twisted ropes, and he went back to the bathroom and ran a hot tub and somehow got his clothes off and carefully, every so carefully, eased himself over the edge of the tub and slid gratefully into the hot soaking relief. He would have remained there for an hour or more, but the fear knotted his stomach. What if someone tried to come through that door? What if he broke it down? He forced down the sudden panic, opened the tub drain, waited until the water was gone before lifting himself slowly and carefully. He went on hands and knees into the room, dragging his towel, drying off slowly, kneading muscles, one eye always on the door. Dry, he slipped into his clothes, brought his cane with him, propped up the pillows, and half-reclining, the cane in his hand, dozed and slept and awoke with sudden alarms before again falling nervously into sleep.

The morning sun brought his eyes fully open.

Well, well, sport, you survived your first night. One down.

On the fourth day he shaved.

On the sixth day he ate a sandwich and drank iced tea through a straw in a small diner by the highway. He didn't know that he was already moving with far better confidence and strength than when he'd started this local trek. The waitress let her glance linger barely a moment longer when he'd pulled himself into the diner seat, but it was enough for his paranoia to turn the glance into a long, sneering stare. He pushed it aside. He froze with sudden fear when several boisterous Mexicans came into the diner, laughing and shouting among one another. He had visions of fists and boots and knives, and he gripped the chair with white knuckles until he could breathe without gasping.

Leaving the diner, he nearly slipped on a wet spot, and banged his hand painfully on the door trying to prevent a fall. A strong hand gripped his arm, and he turned, eyes wide, trying to defend himself against the swarthy face. "Hey, man, you okay? You could have hurt yourself there. You need some help to your car? I be glad to help. Which one is it?"

He tried to pull his arm free. The Mexican sensed the pull and immediately released his hand. "Hey, no sweat, man. *I know*. I know, *amigo*."

He stared at the dark face. "What . . . what do you mean?" he forced out.

The Mexican laughed. He made a fist and banged his knuckles against his right leg. Lance heard a metallic sound. "I know, *amigo*. I left mine in Vietnam. You going to be okay, man. I see it in your eyes." He was gone. Lance went painfully to his car, sat without moving for several minutes.

Fists, knives, and boots—and a metallic sound where there had been a leg. He knew, and he understood. Lance rested his forehead on the steering wheel and wept.

He knew where he was now. He'd looked down from Lee's office atop the mountain ridge and seen this town before. Stanley, that was the name. It lay in the valley far below the ridge. The one road through this mountain pass bore the town on each side of its constant curves. He drove slowly into town, debating whether to stop here for a bite and stay in the small motel or to eat and then make the drive back up the mountain roads to the laboratory. Thirteen days. He was stronger, the haunted look in his eyes had been replaced with animal caution, and the fear lay deep in his system instead of struggling at the surface to break loose. The gun had helped, to be sure. On his second day he'd stopped in a sporting goods store and bought a .22 automatic. "Comes in three sizes," the clerk said. "Got it in .22, .32 and .380, but you need a license for anything over the .22. That size is considered a plinker. Ain't much use for anything else."

The hell it wasn't. He knew enough about guns to know that a .22 in the forehead is just as good as a .44 in the belly for stopping a man. He bought a box of ammunition, and while he still pushed a chair against the motel door every night and kept the gun on the bed by his side, at least now he slept.

Red neon lights glowed at him. Stanley Tavern. It had sandwiches and beer. He felt suddenly hungry, and parked. He went inside slowly. He had the uneasy feeling this was a mistake. These weren't the usual tourists. There must be construction somewhere nearby. The clothes were too rough-hewn; the voices, too loud and raucous. Not even the jukebox turned up full could disguise the voices, the shouted laughter, the squeal of waitresses being grabbed. He slipped into a booth, waiting. He ought to get the hell out of here. He didn't like this. He wasn't being paranoid now. The place smelled of trouble. It always had some before the night was out. You could *feel* it.

He ordered a hamburger and a beer. He hadn't taken three bites from the hamburger when he felt something tugging at the cane he had in the crook of his arm. A snarling sound came to him. It was a dog under the table. A goddamned dog with its teeth clamped on the other end of the cane. He pulled it abruptly. The animal yelped. "Get the hell out of here," Lance snapped.

Then he knew trouble had found him. Two longhairs off some construction crew, just as he'd figured. "What the hell you hit my goddamned dog for, you fucking queer?" Tight tank shirt, tattoos, beery breath, and a grinning sidekick.

"I didn't hit him," Lance said quietly. "I just pulled my cane away."

Two heavy fists rested on the table. "You calling me a fucking liar? I ought to shove that cane right up your queer ass. For two cents I'll—"

"Leave him alone." They turned to the waitress, disgust on her face. "You got a whole bar full of people your own size. Go pick on them. This guy can't help it he's crippled."

The word tore through him. A waitress having to defend him against *this*. It wasn't much defense. "Fucking broad." The man said it without concern as his powerful backhand split the girl's lip open and sent her sprawling against the wall. "You're next." The man grinned, reaching out for Lance.

He didn't really think about it, but he got some leverage and brought the cane around to smack against the man's head. There was a cry of pain as the wood split and went flying off into some dark corner. "So the fag wants some action." A powerful fist moved again, and Lance felt a terrible blow against his face. He was slammed into the back of the seat and then jerked forward brutally and struck again. He heard voices shouting and curses and men coming to his help, but he didn't know much else because his body was tumbling crazily over the edge of the booth, and he hit the floor with bruising impact.

It went quiet. A state trooper stood over him. He saw the shiny boots and wondered what the hell was going on. He looked up and saw the big revolver held level to the other man's stomach. He heard voices, but they came to him from a distance. Then someone laughed, and the gun was being returned to its holster, and the trooper was picking him up. "How you doing, fellow?"

Lanced looked about him, bewildered, aching. "My . . . my cane. I need my cane."

"That drunk said you hit him with it."

"Yes. After he hit the waitress."

"She's gone. Splitsville for her, mister. You want to press charges?"

Lance knew the routine. Barroom brawl. Fifty dollars would bail out the construction tough. It happened all the time here. Lance shook his head. "No. No charges." The tough stood in the background, grinning, then walked off. Lance looked back to the state trooper. "I can use some help in getting to my car."

"Of course. Let's go." The trooper carried Lance more than helped him. Lance knew every eye in the place was glued to him. He stared straight ahead as they reached the parking lot, and the trooper helped him into his car. "You better get some ice on your face," Lance heard. "You got a bad bruise. Going to be a goose egg unless you get to it."

"Sure. Thanks," Lance mumbled. He couldn't wait to slam the goddamned door and get the hell away.

The drive to the hilltop laboratory was another hour. By the time he eased into the driveway Lance was no longer shaking with fury and pain.

You made it. Don't you know you made it? Your worst fears came true, and you made it. It's all downhill from here on!

He looked inside his own head. *Shut up,* he told the voice that had been with him since he'd left the lab thirteen days ago. *I don't need you anymore.*

He kept blowing the horn until the driveway lights came on. He pulled into the garage as Lee opened the doors and he waited until they closed behind him. Lee entered through the side door and stopped in her tracks, staring at his bruised face and torn clothes. She bit down hard on a knuckle to keep from crying out.

"Just don't stand there, dammit. Get me a cane." He pushed the car door open and glared at her.

"Are . . . are you all right? Lance—you're hurt. I—"

"Just get me a goddamned cane, will you!"

She rushed inside, returned quickly with another cane. "What happened?" she asked as they walked together into the laboratory.

"I flunked my test for the job of Sir Galahad," he said.

She was so astonished she stood dead still. "You *what?*"

He turned, leaning on the cane. He looked ridiculous with that swelling bruise and a lopsided grin. "I defended a lady," he said. "Or at least I tried to. I got to get me a stronger cane. I busted the one I had over that bastard's head."

"Wait a moment," she pleaded. "Start from the beginning, please."

"Can it wait, Lee? First things first, okay? A quick kiss hello—"

"Of—of course. I—"

"And a lot of ice. Some in a bag for this bump and some in a glass. My God, I need a drink." He walked past her, twisted, hobbling, dragging a foot slightly behind him.

And whistling.

Chapter 15

"But you've only been back an hour!" Lee spun on her heel, furious, frustrated. Helpless. She turned back to him. "Goddammit, you're not ready to go out again! You're crazy. I don't care what happened down there, but—"

He held up a hand. It only worsened the sight of the ugly bruise on his head. "*Unh-unh,* lady. We made a deal. I was out there floundering like a fish out of water, and I learned to breathe air and talk and walk, and I got my diploma. I did it your way. *All* the way. Now, do you help me, or do I get into my tin suit by myself?" He watched her wavering, torn by indecision. "Lee, if you don't help, you're going to have to stop me. Physically."

Her shoulders slumped. "You really mean that?"

"Damned right."

"Nine feet tall and a yard wide, *huh?*"

"You bet your sweet ass. Isn't this what you wanted? No more bellyaching. No more lamenting, right?" His face hardened. "Maybe it's time for *you* to graduate, Lee."

Her eyes blazed. "All right," she said grimly. "Let's go. I'll get things started."

She walked off stiffly, and he followed, not rushing, moving with that swing he'd developed. The cane was a part of him now. He could make it. It would take more time, but he knew he could devise a brace that would give him better balance, and—

He forced the future from his mind. What he wanted was *now*.

He looked at himself in the mirror. He grinned. A thick and broad face set on a neck almost as thick. Stubble on the chin. Just what he wanted. "The clothes, Lee. Any workingman stuff?"

"Corduroy jeans, boots, a plaid shirt. You'll look like a lumberjack, for Christ's sake."

"Just what the doctor ordered. Get it, please." He felt an incredible freedom. He knew Lee had several complete ManFac systems in the lab. She could change heads, change faces easily enough. He could choose any one of them. He chose this one. She returned with the clothes, and he dressed quickly before the mirror. Five minutes later a stranger looked back at him. He grinned. So did the stranger. He liked the son of a bitch. About thirty years old. "Hi," he said, and so did the man in the mirror.

"You're going back there," Lee said.

He held her gaze. "Yes."

"Is it really that important? I swear I'll never understand men!"

Strong hands held her arms gently. "You don't need to understand men. Just keep working on me."

She stood without moving.

Lance shrugged and walked from the laboratory. He went through the garage, along the ridge, then turned east until he stood at the last trees at the edge of the steep slope. Far below him he saw the lights of

Stanley. He could make out the red neon sign of the bar. He was going to walk unannounced into that town. He started down, sliding, slamming his heavy boots into grass and dirt for balance. He felt he could do anything. He reached a dirt road and started across. He stopped dead as a huge shape rose before him in the dim moonlight. "Holy Jesus," he swore quietly as he looked into the eyes of a great bear. The animal rumbled a snarl deep within its chest, sniffing him out. He saw teeth, coming closer. He didn't know if he could outrun this beast. Something was wrong with it. Bears in these parts didn't mess with humans. This one wasn't following the rules.

The snarl deepened. The son of a bitch was going to charge him. Lance reached up to his neck, felt the hard point beneath plastiskin, pressed it several times. He almost stepped back as the bear advanced menacingly. No more time to waste. Lance threw his arms wide and stepped forward, toward the animal. Face to face with the beast, Lance roared. The power system picked up the vibrations, magnified it ten times over the volume his own throat could ever produce.

A thunderbolt of sound, the scream of some impossibly huge primal beast, shattered the night. The bear reared back, terrified, rolling in confusion from this unexpected adversary. It rushed off into the brush.

Far below the roar carried through the streets of Stanley and rattled windows. People stared up in wonder and unexplained fear.

He walked slowly into the bar. Idle glances met him. The roughnecks sized him up. Elbows nudged friends for attention. A stranger; big bastard. No one knew who he was. Lance leaned against the hardwood bar. A man in a dirty apron looked at him. "What'll it be, mac?"

"Beer."

181

A bottle banged down before him. "Two bucks, mister."

Lance brought the bottle to his lips, drinking lightly. "Run it up," he said after a pause.

"Pay now."

Lance leaned forward and quietly gripped the bartender's wrist. He applied the pressure slowly and steadily. The first attempt to pull back the arm didn't work. The bartender's eyes widened. "Stay quiet," Lance said to him. "Just stay quiet."

"Jesus, you're killing me," the bartender said in a hoarse whisper, trying not to draw attention.

"Run it up," Lance told him.

"Yeah, anything you say. Just let loose. *Please.*"

Lance turned around, elbows against the bar. Then he saw him. The long dirty hair, tank shirt, the tattoos. Lance walked slowly through the drunken crowd, and finally, he stood before the table, looking down, smiling. The tough looked up. Conversation at the table fell away.

"Whaddya want, buddy?"

"You."

He said it so quietly the other man was taken aback. Then he roared with laughter. "Me?" He turned to his friends. The grins spread. It promised to be good. This crazy son of a bitch was alone. Oh, man. They got ready. "You want *me*? You one of them fags or something? Take your fag dick and get the hell outta here before I take you apart."

"Get up."

The smile was gone. "Mister, you're messing wrong, you know that? You're alone, you're crazy. You want me up, you get me up."

Lance's hand shot out faster than the man could follow. Two steel fingers closed on the tough's nose. He yelped in pain, trying to move, his hands grabbing at the terrible pressure. Blood was already running down his face, trickling through Lance's fingers. Lance looked around the table. "Nobody move. He's mine."

He squeezed tighter. There was a shrill scream as flesh and bones pulped together. Blood bubbled out in a froth.

"What the hell's he doing to him?"

"Look at the blood! He's killing him!"

Lance pulled his hand away. He looked at white bone showing through torn flesh, and then it was all covered with the bubbling blood. The man staggered to his feet, still screaming, stumbling blindly.

"Kill 'im!"

But Lance wasn't there. He did what nobody expected—he went forward swiftly, his foot coming up into the table, and a loud crack snapped through the room like a shot as wood splintered and flew wildly in all directions. The man on the opposite end of the table seemed to levitate as the heavy boot crashed into his groin. He crashed to the floor a dozen feet away, writhing in agony.

Lance whipped about, ready for whatever would come at him. They were faster than he believed, every man jack among them an experienced, tough brawler.

He grinned. So much the better. But he had hesitated too long, and a fist crashed into his mouth. The impact jerked his head back slightly, but the man who had swung howled in dismay as several finger bones and knuckles cracked against the impact of hitting the equivalent of a lightly padded steel pole. Caught by surprise, Lance hesitated but a second, and it was a second too long as several bodies hurled through the air to slam into him. Their combined weight staggered him backward, and he crashed against a wall, splintering boards and shattering glass. He came alive with a startling fury. A short chop to the side of a nearby head, and the man fell like a poled oxen. Lance moved expertly, starting finally to bob and weave, his powerful left hand stabbing outward into chins and noses and cheekbones and foreheads in rapid-fire fashion. Every blow struck sent the hapless recipient sprawling or tumbling wildly backward.

He had his back solidly to a wall. As men rushed forward, they were smashed with steel battering rams. Lips split, cheekbones were laid bare, knees and legs broke under the pistonlike feet of ManFac strength. And still they came, several from each side. Lance ducked and bobbed and weaved, his fists great steel poles. Then an ax handle came from nowhere to smash across his own nose. The splintering sound was both wood and plastiskin and flexmetal, and the blow was so severe Lance felt his own blood within the ManFac. He bellowed with his own pain and threw himself forward, scattering his attackers with a terrible fury until he reached the one he wanted.

He hauled him upward until the other man's feet dangled above the floor. Other men rushed Lance. A madness was upon them, all of them, including himself, and he knew that soon people would be killed. He didn't want that. He held the kicking, dangling figure higher, and Lance stood erect, and he used that strange other weapon again. One word.

"STOP!"

That terrible noise hit them with brutal impact, its effect heightened by the total surprise of an explosion in their midst. They looked about them, bewildered, ears ringing, befuddled, still feeling the vibrations common to sudden severe overpressure. It began to dawn on them that the roar had indeed come from this incredible stranger in their midst.

Lance snapped his arm from one side to another so they might have the full effect of a large man hanging from a hand, hanging and being shaken as if he were a featherweight rag doll. For the first time a touch of fear began to spread through the midst of brawlers who would normally fight to the point of unconsciousness before they gave in to any such weakness. They watched silently as Lance drew back a hamlike fist, held it poised to destroy the twitching figure in his other hand. He waited several seconds and released his grip on the man's hair. He never hit him. He didn't need to. That long hanging in air had done it. The man on the floor scrabbled away on his hands and knees.

They stared at each other—the stranger and the brawling mob—and it was an impasse that lasted but a few seconds more. Then sound intruded to break the eerie standoff. Sirens and the squeal of tires. "Holy shit! Police!" The shout was unnecessary; this mob knew only too well its one common enemy—the law breaking up one of their spirited "parties." Lance stepped backward slowly until he felt the wall behind him. Scuffling and running and overturned tables and chairs, men yelling and women screaming, and people who'd done this a hundred times before diving through windows and climbing out bathroom exits and hitting the fire doors to stream away in all directions before sheriff's deputies and state troopers poured in through the front entrance and a fire exit of the building opposite him.

He couldn't afford to be one of those standing up before a judge. No identification. No name. And a lot of trouble. But he didn't want to attempt a break-away through a rear exit. Not smart. They'd be in position now.

He had to do something completely unexpected. The deputy and trooper cars would be out front, strung along just off the highway, headlights pointed inward. That group at the opposite end of the building to him was the only smart way out. Beyond them was the fire exit. He remembered the area. Not big enough for cars. They wouldn't bother posting anyone out there. Lance moved with the milling crowd toward the lawmen. He crouched down to mix in with the noisy, shuffling group. Then he was about as far as he could go without being detected. He tensed up, remembered his training, the effects of mass and acceleration, reminded himself he was 320 pounds packaged into a compact form. He leaned well forward, dug in his heels, and hurled himself forward like a small locomotive boosted by a powerful rocket charge. He went through unsuspecting bodies just like that locomotive going through wheat. People flew in all directions to his right and his left, and more than a few sailed over his lowered bull-like shoulders. He burst from the crowd without warning and charged madly into the thick of the unsuspecting lawmen. Before they could bring their clubs or guns into play, Lance had hurled them wildly aside and was through their middle—and through the door standing between himself and freedom. The instant he was in the cold night air he spun on his heel and cut a sharp left, taking the steep upward slope without even slowing down. Seconds later he was high in the thick brush, flat on the ground, silent, watching and listening with an impish grin as they tried to sort out what in the hell had happened down there. He waited several minutes. No one was coming up that hill. Another hard scan of the area. Lance grunted with satisfaction, turned, and went up the hill at a steady pace.

Lee stared at him with wide eyes when he walked into the lab. She shook her head slowly. "Satisfied?" she asked finally.

He sprawled in an armchair, dwarfing it, nodding

slowly. "It took a lot of barbed wire out of my belly, Lee."

He said it so quietly, with such meaning, she knew he had been right. She was prepared for boasting, bravado, war stories, the lot, but he'd brought back none of it. Just that quiet remark. There could be no argument with that. She went to him, looked at the blood and the ripped clothing. "You must have done a number down there. I could hear the sirens. Sounds like they called out the National Guard." She studied his face. "My God, what hit you?" she asked. Her fingers probed the smashed nose. "Is some of that blood yours?" she went on, feeling sudden fear.

"First question: an ax handle, I think. Second question: I think so. Third question before you ask: Yes, it hurts."

Without thinking her hand moved through his hair.

His hair. He's become that gestalt I hoped would happen. Even I accepted it without thinking. How incredible . . .

"You smell, Lance. Bad."

"Beer, booze, sweat, blood. Lousy combination."

"Time for a bath."

He looked up at her. "Time, long overdue, for a bath together."

She nodded. She had her man again.

Chapter 16

He ached more than he would ever admit to Lee. Ached through every muscle and joint. His teeth ached where he had unknowingly clenched them during the fracas in the bar. Even his bones seemed to wash pain through him. But he found as much pleasure, perverse though it might be, as he did his aches and pains. He felt that he had struggled back to life, instead of lying prostrate like a wounded animal. His were the signatures of living, of movement, of greeting a shining and warming sun he had almost obliterated from his mind.

He refused Lee's help, no matter how stiffly he moved, no matter what new pain rippled through him as he hooked the ManFac supports to the system. He pressed the necessary releases to swing open his access panels to the ManFac. Once supported from the overhead cables, he powered down the system. *For the first time since he had activated a ManFac, he felt no pain inside his heart or his mind by withdrawing. He had found himself, and he would be himself, walking half-crippled on his cane or striding*

189

with magnificent power as the combination of Man and Facsimile.

He withdrew from the ManFac, shedding an outer epidermis, marvelous and intricate, of beauty and strength. He hobbled back a short distance, and he had a new appreciation of that marvelous system. *Lifeless. No angel to blow beautiful movement into those limbs. It lacks the fire, the divine spark.*

He nodded, at peace with himself.

She lay sprawled in the long and wide tub, as lithe and yet as relaxed as a large jungle cat, her limbs moving gently to and fro by the force of the whirlpool jets. She in the tub, Lance still outside, very much in need of assistance. But she knew that the worst thing he could have happen to him right now would be *her* assistance. He was still nearing the summit of his personal mountain. He had laughed off his bruised pride and torn skin; he had gone forth again to seek his own personal catharsis. And he was back. Now, in the height of that new strength, there had come Lance's greatest struggle. To remove by himself that awesome ManFac power. For once that happened, she mused behind narrowed eyes, he would have gained a strength he had still not yet guaranteed.

Strength of self. If he could complete this psychological maze, the highest obstacle yet of them all, the original Lance Parker, only stronger in spirit and resolve and inner confidence, would be here with her.

Great events at times occur without the searing flashes of light, minus the blare of trumpets, free of the adoring roar of the crowd, unattended by announcements of proclamations. To Lee Grazzi this was such a moment. Silent except for his labored breathing, the creak of equipment, the occasional sound of metal against metal, he disengaged himself from that awesome physical might to return to the harshness of his own physical disfigurement, and then he was nude again before her—and without a shred of the self-consciousness that had always attended this occasion before.

She looked up at him as he sat on the edge of the tub, feet in the water, content for this moment simply to sit, to regain his breath. She watched him without comment, and he chose not to intrude with words on this moment. Somehow it felt special. On a sudden whim he dragged himself to his feet, walking laboriously, more stiffly than was normal, to a worktable. He returned to his former position, feet in the water, but this time he had a slim cigar in his teeth. He lit up slowly, savoring the smoke and the taste. Then he held her eyes.

She lifted one eyebrow. "You look like hell," she told him.

Lance's reaction was laughter. *Yesterday it would have been pride-begotten withdrawal,* she reminded herself. He dragged deeply on the cigar, removed it from his mouth, and looked at it vacantly. "I guess," he said after several moments, "I do look sort of silly. Clint Eastwood I'm not." He threw away his cigar.

"That's not what I meant," she said, stirring the water with her legs. "You should see yourself. You've got a bad bruise across your nose, and you're black and blue in a dozen places."

He grinned. "It was worth it."

"Get the hell in here, lover."

He slid carefully into the water, supporting himself by his arms until his body rested on the tub bottom. She nodded approvingly. "Did you know your arms are stronger? Come to think of it, you've improved in almost all your physical conditioning."

"Still a little short of leaping tall buildings in a single bound." He grunted. "Maybe a hop, skip, and a jump first."

She ignored the remark. "Turn around. I've got oil. Time for you to get woman-to-man treatment."

"What happened to the doctor?"

"She doesn't take baths with her patients, dummy." She pulled gently on his arm. "Here. Sit between my legs with your back to me." She waited until he was able to sit as she had instructed and still be able to lean his weight on the side of the tub with one arm. Without that bracing he would have lost his balance. He had come far; there was a hell of a journey still ahead of him.

She kneaded his sore muscles, beginning with the back of his neck, working heat and love into his arms, then down his back and along his thighs. He leaned back, turning and moving as she prodded gently with her hands. He rested against the tub, his eyes shut with deep pleasure. Her hands moved slowly and lovingly along his ribs and about his stomach, and she placed her straightened legs beneath his body to bring him out of the water so she could work his groin and his legs with the oil. Through it all, not a word, not a sound, only that message clear and unmistakable on his face. Then she was done, her fingers caressing lightly along his toes and the bottom of his feet. His eyes opened wide and clear. He pulled himself to a higher position. "My turn," he said finally, and if he had struck her a wicked blow, she could not have been more stunned with those two words.

"My turn."

To rejoin the human race . . .

Her neck; slowly, lovingly, with more strength than she dreamed he had regained in his hands. Still, he needed the back bracing, and she sat with her own back to him, between his legs, as his hands moved slowly with the oil, kneading tenderly, working her skin. He moved his finger beneath her arms and along her ribs, and then he froze, his hands cupped beneath her full breasts. Her nipples hardened instantly. She dared not move, afraid to break the magic spell. He remained as he was, and she could almost hear his own heart pounding.

The miracle. He felt her move closer.

She felt him hard, unbelievably marvelous, against her back. *It had been more than two years*. Her hand reached behind her, down his belly muscles; then with infinite slowness she moved her fingertips over the entire surface of his penis. She felt him throb, heard his gasp of intense pleasure. *Oh, God, not right here, not yet, please, not yet . . .* She moved from the tub, not turning to look at him, and she walked, her body glistening from oil and water, into her living room, where she kept a great spread of pillows on a thick rug. She was afraid to turn, afraid to see if he had followed her, if that marvelous, throbbing hardness was there. She heard Lance moving and then his body next to hers. She turned slowly, and their lips came together in a deep and searing kiss that had been torn from her life all this terrible time. His body moved to hers, and she shifted to ease his entry.

"*No*." The word spit from him as if he'd thrust a knife at her. "Don't move. Don't do a thing. Lie there. *Be* loved."

She avoided even an answer as he explored her body, caressed and kissed and touched as if each movement of his own body were an exploration never before made. In a way it was and—

She closed off her mind and sank back, a feeling of woman rolling over her body and through her mind and within her like a fog that penetrated and absorbed and brought mystical wonder with its touch. There was no clumsiness from that racked body slowly joining to hers; even his pain was a joy for them both, his struggles not to be imprisoned by his infirmities; all was love. She reacted, she responded, she gave utterly of herself, and individual movements flowed into a single creation of love across the pillows and that rug, and then she felt the muscles through his body hardening, his breath dragged into laboring and tortured lungs, and now, without his knowing, she could move to ease this wonder for them both, and he moaned and the sweat poured from him and all the weeks and the months and the years erupted from him in a violent, stabbing, explosive orgasm, and he screamed in the wrenching, sweet pain of total release.

He eased down from his savage heat without knowing, without awareness, reduced to utter limbo in his mind, and slipped into a coma, and from that state of unawareness, of the loss of consciousness, was deeply, uncaringly asleep. For an hour, perhaps two—she didn't know and cared not at all—the only sign of life from her man was deep, undisturbed breathing.

He awoke, unmoving, his only physical action the confused opening of his eyes. He looked at her, and he remembered, and he understood it all. He raised himself to one elbow and looked across the pillows at her. Then, slowly, beautifully, he winked.

"If you smoke a cigar now," she said, "I'll kill you."

He bit her on the neck, and their laughter was crystal.

Chapter 17

"I haven't been this hungry in . . . well, in years," he said, toast in one hand, sausage speared on his fork. He lifted his third cup of coffee, sipped the hot liquid, stuffed his mouth again.

"You're mumbling," Lee told him.

"*Mrrf*," he said.

She rolled her eyes in mock despair, brought her coffee up slowly, cradling the cup in both hands. He ate like the Lance of old, grinning between bites, anxious to clean his plate as if it might get away from him if he delayed. Finally, he was done, leaning back in his chair, his grin wrapped about a fresh cigar. "My God. I don't believe I ate the whole thing." He belched.

"Watch it. That'll put out your cigar."

He patted his stomach. "Worth it." He still had that foolish-happy grin of his. The lines of his mouth narrowed slowly. He studied her with sudden alertness. "Something's wrong," he observed.

She shook her head, her hair gleaming in the morning sunlight through the kitchen window.

"Nothing so bad it can't wait. This is all too wonderful for—" She smiled. "Later."

He didn't reply for several moments. Cigar smoke wreathed his features. "That isn't your style," he said after the pause. "Let's have it." His brow furrowed. "Was it anything last—"

"Last night?" she finished hurriedly for him. "God forbid. Of course not. It's not a tragedy, Lance."

"Then spill it."

She leaned full back in her chair and sighed. "All right. It's mundane, prosaic, but the kind of bullshit that won't go away."

"Jesus, you're dragging it out."

She nodded. "I thought that if I ignored it long enough, well, you know."

"The hell I do," he said with a touch of exasperation.

She held a level gaze with his own. "All right. The long and short of it is that we're broke."

He blinked several times. It didn't register at first. He hadn't even *thought* of this subject for— It sank home then. He hadn't thought of money for years, literally. Broke. The till was tapped. Where had his mind been all this time? He knew, but it didn't do any good to realize the fact—after the fact.

"How bad," he asked finally.

"Busted. Flat. Cleaned out. Bare cupboard. Empty purse and pockets."

He was still riding high enough to coast on his good feelings. "Short, *huh*?"

She shook her head. "Not short. Stubbed out. Flat, like I said." She became serious. "The fact of the matter is that a healthy bank balance is a velvet lining. I've worn mine out. The cabinet shelves have only splinters left."

"Just how much *do* we have left?" He was coming down fast now.

"Loose change."

"What happened?" His eyes flicked from the kitchen to his right. To the home. To the laboratories. To the staggering power bills. Taxes. Equipment by the truckload. Food, expenses, medical treatments, tests, travel, professional help. He could add to the litany if he exercised a modicum of plain old common sense. *Someone* had bought the groceries and the clothes and the gasoline and paid for the cars and—

"I see you just added it up," she remarked, judging his thoughts from the changing expressions of his face.

"Yeah. Rude awakening," he agreed. "Christ, I'm sorry, Lee. How could I have been so blind? I mean, I'm a big boy. I knew money's not from trees." He shifted position in his chair. "Come to think of it," he said, thinking as quickly as he could unravel memories too long put aside, "how did you manage all this time?" Another memory stepped forward in his head. "You haven't been working," he announced aloud, knowing the statement was more for his own benefit than hers.

"I've been working," she contradicted him. She stared into her coffee.

"That's not what I meant."

"I know, I know. I didn't mean to sound the martyr. We've made it all this way because I had a very fat bank account, lover. Very fat, indeed. Then royalty checks have been coming in steadily. And then I was able to borrow. And finally, I managed to get some heavy advances on future contracts. But—" She shrugged.

"More goes out than comes in."

"My accountant *and* my lawyer," she added, "refer to it in kind terms as a negative checkbook. My lawyer has been very active. I don't even know of all the collection agencies after me. He's kept them at bay. But that gets tough with the Infernal Revenue Service."

He smiled at her shift in description. "How infernal is the Internal?"

"They've been trying to seize my property. Monte's held them off. He doesn't know how much longer. They want to grab all this," she said, gesturing to include the house and the lab.

"Can he hold them off? I mean, long enough for you to get back into the swing of things?"

She eyed him carefully. "What does that mean?" she asked, a bit more harshly than she had intended. But she knew in what direction this conversation was moving, and she didn't like the words, the meaning, or their inevitable end.

"It means precisely what it sounds like it means," he said matter-of-factly. "Money doesn't grow on trees. There's no secret admirer filling your bank account. I'm not only broke but a drain. The government screwed me. Us, really. The insurance company was backed up by the government, and they got off laughing. They must have laughed pretty hard when they tore up my policies."

"Is that bitterness I detect?"

He studied his dead cigar. "Once," he said with a shrug. "But not for some time now." He brought up a lighter in a strong, gnarled hand. "I graduated, remember? Ain't no use getting mad. It's a whole hell of a lot better getting even."

"I *do* have a way out," she said quietly.

"I'm listening. I'd also like to know what I can do to help."

"I have a new contract from the Disney people. At least they're offering me a new contract. They opened a Disneyland in Tokyo, oh, about a year ago, and the Japanese, to put it in un-Disney-like terms, have gone apeshit over the Automated Human Systems. They want me to design a complete diorama for the Japanese project and also start on plans for another one in South America."

He looked puzzled. "That's great. Why the sour face?"

"I have to get cracking immediately."

"Jesus, do it."

"You don't understand. There's a trade exhibition opening in San Francisco, and they also want a diorama. But I have to start on it within the next two or three days, or I lose the contract." Her eyes were pleading. "It means I've got to leave. For weeks, maybe even months."

"Does it get you out of the hole? Come on, Lee. Straight out."

Her voice was so low he barely heard her reply. "Yes."

"Then there's no question, is there?"

"I don't want to stop what *we're* doing, Lance. We've come so far and—"

"Hold it, please, baby. You just said the magic words. Look, we've come a long way, and there's more to go. But the worst is behind us. You've been wiping my nose and playing nursemaid to my busted ego for a long time. We can't avoid the realities, Lee, and in the system under which we live, the long green is what makes things go 'round and 'round. We've made a dream come true because of what *you* did. No, don't interrupt me. This has got to be said out loud because life itself can bring you down from the biggest high there is. You're broke, the creditors are banging on the doors, and your lawyer is dazzling the opposition with fancy but temporary footwork. You have the way out. There's no choice. I've got to get off your back."

He regretted his last words as quickly as he said

them, but the more he thought of that sentiment—
I've got to get off your back—the more he realized
how true were those words. *There's an old saw,* he reflected in the long silence between them, *that the real
heroes in life aren't found on battlefields. They're the
people who awaken to bleakness and problems and
plodding that simply won't go away because life is
more than a series of valiant bugle calls and charges.
It's getting up every damned day and facing the grim
reality of cleaning a man's body, trying to rebuild a
shattered wreck, fighting his own mind as well as her
own problems, dedicating herself, giving everything
of herself—her,* this woman, this magnificent human
being, with her back bent badly beneath the weight
of problems of which he hadn't even been aware.

He chewed on the one thought that rolled around
in his head like a broken medicine ball, heavy and
rumbling and erratic. The same thought he had
voiced aloud. *Get off her back. Give her breathing
room.* It felt unreal, impossible, that the miracles Lee
Grazzi had wrought in her automated exoskeletal human designs could be brought to a halt in such a
fashion, but cash flow for technological development
is just as critical as is water flow for irrigation. Somebody had to pay the piper, and Lee had been doing
all the paying for them both. *Well, sport, listen to
your own words. Get off. The gravy train has just
come to its last stop. It's time to earn your own keep.*

Lee saw his thoughts in his facial expression. "I
know you, Lance. I know you perhaps better than
you think, and what you're thinking is *not* the way to
go." She slammed her hand on the table, sending
dishes and silverware rattling. Her voice rose as her
anger ascended swiftly. "Goddammit, I haven't gone
through the last two years to let some stinking petty
cash get between us *now!* Stop being Sir Galahad,

and start thinking reality. We're a team, and we're a beautiful team, and we love each other and—"

"And you need room to breathe," he said slowly. "I know what *you're* thinking. We both know each other too well to play the game. You have a shot at getting your fiscal nose clean. Jesus, love, you gave my life back to me. What's wrong with our both taking a break for a while? I've got a long ways to go. I want to experiment—"

She shook her head, close to tears of frustration. "Dammit, if you could work with me on the Disney project, but . . . but it's design. I'm not going to do the construction and assembly. It's all headwork, but I've just got to be *there*. Why can't you stay here, Lance? There's still so much work to do." She rushed on in fear he would produce some argument that would draw him further from her. "Dammit, there's got to be *something* you can do that will let you work on the ManFac designs and also let you help with the bread and butter. You know, I just thought, I mean, well, we could work with the government and—"

"*No.*" Short, quiet, and implacable from his tone. His hand gripped hers. "The government?" The word was a loathsome profanity to him. "Haven't you learned your lesson *yet*? You can't trust those bastards. They have no sense of decency; the word 'loyalty' to them is something spoken in a foreign language. Where would you begin? How would you work with them? The moment those sons of bitches find out what you've got here in the ManFac system, they'll—"

"What *we* have in this system, you mean," she broke in, her eyes snapping.

"So much the worse then! Remember *me*? They sacrificed me to the wolves once. They'd like nothing better than to rake me over the coals again. I told you, I'm telling you again, once those animals find out what you have here in ManFac, they'll drop a mountain on you just like the one that buried my ass. They'll invoke some national security regulation they keep handy for moments just like this one, and they'll take over. We wouldn't have a chance. Right out on our ear, and we couldn't do a thing about it. We couldn't even go to court, for Christ's sake, if they used the gambit of national security. They'd hogtie and gag us, and that would be the end of that. *Unh-unh*. No way. They'd—"

She held up a hand to stem the flood of anger, and she nodded slowly. "I can't argue with you about the government."

Silence eased between them once more, leaving them to their own thoughts. They needed more time for that, and they both recognized the need. "Lance?" She waited until he looked at her. "Can we, *uh*, sort of put this aside until tonight? I mean, I know we've got to come to a decision of some kind, but I was planning something. A surprise for you. I still have a few hours' work to do and—" Her eyes widened and she froze as the floor beneath them vibrated. He felt it also. They heard a rattling of dishes and glasses, and then it went quiet.

"That was a warning," he said quietly.

"I know." Everything else had been forgotten with that ominous rolling, vibrating sensation. She looked around. "It's stopped."

He nodded slowly, warily. "Yeah." He was breathing deep and slow, every movement measured with animal caution.

"Lance, you all right? I mean—"

"No, no, I'm fine," he reassured her quickly. "It's not the same as being *under* the mountain." He was also looking about him. "But you're right. It was just a tremor."

She plunged right in. "You're the expert on quakes in this family. Is there more coming?"

He was climbing to his feet. "No way to tell. I'll call the seismology lab in Sacramento and see if there's any pattern to it."

She nodded. "Good. I'll be getting dressed, and then I'll be in the lab. Oh, by the way, I don't want you in there until I give you the word."

He wouldn't mess up her plans with demanding questions. Besides, he'd been less than completely open with Lee. He had his own plans, his own inner determination to take off for a final test of himself and on his own. So he let it ride; he let the severe emotions of the moment, the earth tremors and their possible consequences, dominate their conversation. "Okay," he said easily, "I'll be in your office."

The confrontation of fiscal crunch started out as a damper for the day, but they had been through too many of life's obstacles to stay down for long. Lee disappeared into her laboratory with the doors closed behind her. Lance had a brief conversation with the seismology crew in Sacramento. He was less than pleased with what he heard.

"There's no way to tell, Mr. Parker," he was told by a technician. "We're in an unstable area and—"

"I don't want to sound short," he broke into the telephone exchange, "but I *know* that. We all know that. What I want to know is if today's shock shows any indications of continuing. I mean, was it dislocation well belowground, or simply a shear shift, or what?"

"I'm sorry, sir, you're asking me to predict a roll of the dice. Unfortunately we don't have any prophets in this office, and anything I would say, in the absence of any real indications, would be, well, I guess

203

you could call it theoretical hearsay. I don't think that's what you want."

"No," Lance said. "Thanks anyway."

"Just a moment. Where are you calling from?"

"We're high. In fact, we're on a ridge pretty well inland."

"Then I wouldn't worry. At least you won't have any mountains falling on you. Bye."

Lance went cold with those words. "If you only knew," he murmured at the dead telephone. He shook off the sudden chill and went to the bar. A good stiff drink would help. He took it straight, then poured another shot of Scotch into a mug of steaming coffee and balanced his drink precariously to his drafting table. Ideas had been swirling about in the back of his head ever since his excursion into Stanley and that glorious melee of busting bones and heads in that bar. The rest of the day went by with surprising swiftness as his mind transferred concepts and proposals to paper. Lee's voice brought him out of his deep preoccupation. He looked up to see her smiling.

"*Uh*, that apron," he said in reference to her attire. "You starting dinner?"

"Not starting. Finished. It's ready. Do you realize it's dark outside?" Her smile broadened. "Apparently work's good for the soul."

He stretched and shook his head. "No wonder I ache. I've been at this six hours." He was immensely pleased with the day. He'd made significant progress; he was getting a better grasp on improvements for the ManFac system. He climbed slowly to his feet and leaned on his cane. "You got a hungry man on your hands, ma'am," he drawled.

He devoured his steak and home fries and topped off the meal with black coffee. He rounded out the repast with a slim cigar. He eyed Lee carefully. "You ought to play poker," he said. "You can keep a secret better than anyone I know."

His remarks delighted her. "I *do* have something special. It's a new ManFac. I'd like you to become this one without looking first."

He nodded. "Lead on," he said, and followed her into the lab. A ManFac stood supported beneath its overhead supports, but every visible part of the system was covered with hanging drapes. He removed his clothing and went easily into the ManFac. By now changing from Lance Parker to—well, to whatever she'd created was a move he made easily and quickly. There was that extraordinary sensation again of shifting personality *and* body once he was within the system. He settled in comfortably. "Okay. I'm ready," he told her. He pressed the power switch beneath a finger. The magic wand passed over him; he could feel, even without any further movement, the tremendous strength that had become a part of him.

"Seal up, please," she instructed.

He pressed the power system again, and the entry area of head, torso, and legs sealed behind him. He was no longer occupying a ManFac—the miracle had happened; the gestalt was real; there was only one personality, one body, one entity.

"I'm turning out the lights," Lee told him. She sounded as happy and pleased as a child. "Then I'm removing the cover. Just hang in there for a moment."

The lab went dark, and he felt the heavy drapes being removed from his body. "All right, Lance, I'm bringing in the lights slowly. The mirrors are right in front of you."

He saw only a shadowy form as she turned the lights up to their lowest level. A powerful shadow, if there could be such a thing. He strained to see better, but there was no rushing her. And then he stared, caught completely by surprise, as the lights came up to full brightness, and he was still staring when he gasped.

A powerful young black man stared back at him. "My God . . . I don't believe it. Lee, this is incredible."

He moved, and the strong young man moved, and they were the same. He went closer to the mirror. A deeply toned brown skin, short, curly hair, a rugged face. He wore snug jeans and boots about a slim waist, and a weight lifter's body moved rippling muscles before him. "Somehow Logan fits you," he heard Lee saying. "Logan Scott. That's your name on your security pass for this lab, and your driver's license, and the rest of those things in your wallet." She hesitated. "How do you like yourself, Logan Scott?"

He bent, twisted, moved swiftly, turned slowly. "Marvelous. Absolutely freaking marvelous. You sure do good work for a honky, woman."

She laughed. "This is just part of it, Mr. Scott." She stepped to the side and pulled away a concealing drape. In their cubicles stood a hulking, bearded Swedish seaman, a huge Japanese with a startlingly large stomach and shaved skull, and, finally, a thick-necked young German.

He studied them carefully, life forms awaiting the touch of life. He turned back to Lee. "I don't know what to say. Really."

"You don't need to. I can see it in your eyes." She clasped her hands together, sharing the moment with him. "This was my surprise. Not just the systems. But the fact that you now have something, you and Man-Fac as a single being, that no one else in the world can have. Something that makes you so special, so different . . . Lance, don't you see it?" She clapped her hands in delight. "You can be anybody you want to be. *You're the man who could be anybody.* Or anyone," she amended. "You can live just about any life you choose and you can shift from one to the other. You can be anybody, and you can be as anonymous as you select to be."

He turned to her again and held out those marvelous, powerful young black arms. "Come here, love." She ran to him, cradled in his strength, her head resting against the broad chest.

"You're incredible," he said quietly. "Just incredible. I don't know how you do it, but you—"

The tremendous earth shock jerked the floor out from beneath them. His voice froze as the savage jolt hurled him from his feet, and he twisted desperately to keep from falling onto Lee. One arm stiffened to absorb the fall, and as he half rolled, now to protect her, he felt the new sound, the grinding rumble building to a roar. Glass and metal and wood were breaking all about them, and directly before his eyes a wall split open in a long, jagged tear. Thunder from far below hammered at them.

"Outside!" he shouted. "Let's get the hell out of—"

He didn't make it. Another terrible blow rolled through the hills, and the earth danced in its agony of spasms, and he threw himself over her body as the roof collapsed. He felt a chunk of concrete slam into his back, and even that splendid system could not keep the pain from reaching the inner body. But Lee was safe. He turned his head. The wall that had split was now tumbling outward, and the rest of the roof was coming down. He was on his feet swiftly, still protecting Lee, dragging and carrying her through a doorway that fell with a crash just as he made it outside the building.

All about them the earth screamed.

Chapter 18

He stood like a hulking monster, covered with dust
and bits of plaster, holding her tightly to him. Lee
had gone numb at the sight of her beloved laboratory
and home collapsing in wreckage, a tumbled monu-
ment to years of total dedication. Lance turned her
slowly, pointing. "We're lucky," he said simply, and
her eyes followed his gesture. In the distance below
them they saw the intense flashing of power lines torn
down and arcing. Green fire speared the night sky as
transformers exploded. Yellow and orange flames began to appear along roads where there were individual houses; the flames leaped to trees and grass and
would become raging fires running loose along the
steep slopes.

But up here they were safe. The ridge ran long and
wide and provided protection from even the worst of
the fires that might come their way. Lance looked
around the horizon, seeing the same signs of erupting
fires everywhere. He turned back to Lee.

"It's over."

A moan escaped her lips as she stared at what had

been her home and laboratory. "I know, I *know*," she said quietly.

"That's not what I meant. The earthquake. It's over. That tremor this morning. That was the warning; this is the result. I know this kind of shock. Somewhere the fault had too much pressure, and it adjusted itself. The shock was the result. There won't be any more. I mean, nothing strong."

She had turned back as flame speared upward in the distance. "What about that?" she asked.

"It's not the flames that worry me. But if it rolls up this slope, on either side, and if there's any kind of a strong wind, the heat and smoke could be damned dangerous. Our best bet is to get down from here, make it to some relatively open areas. They'll be evacuating people any way they can because of the fire danger, so there won't be that much time to waste. We'd better move." He glanced down at his own body and then at Lee. "And we need some clothes. I'll go back in for them. You wait here."

"I'd better go with you. My purse, cards, money. I—"

"You stay *here*," he said firmly, blocking her way with a powerful arm. "That whole place could come down around our ears, and I can handle that a lot better than you can. Now wait for me."

He was back in several minutes, carrying a shirt and leather jacket for himself and a jacket for Lee, as well as her purse and some personal belongings he'd seen in the rubble. Lee pointed down the mountains. "It's spreading faster than I thought," she said. "See that road? We'd have to go through there with the car."

He shook his head. "No way. The flames will be there before we will. We walk down."

She stared doubtfully down along the darkened and

precipitous wooded slopes. He grinned. "Don't forget who you're with, lady. Logan Scott. Remember?"

She smiled wanly as she slipped into her jacket. "I guess I forgot something," she said, her voice self-accusing. He waited out her thoughts. "All I could think of was getting out of here because of the danger. But there must be so many people hurt, and, Lance, they'll need me down there."

He squeezed her hand gently. "Then we'd better move out."

It was a tough descent, and she would never have made it safely without the brute strength of the Man-Fac with her. As it was, she lost a shoe, and tree branches and brambles made a wreck of her clothes, as they did of his. Several times she fell, and only that powerful arm kept her from tumbling dangerously into God knew what rocks or trees. All about them they heard animals scurrying through the darkened woods, fleeing the growing flames. Sirens sounded thinly across the mountains, seemingly to float on the night air from every direction, and they saw headlights mixed in with the garish hue of the spreading flames.

They emerged from thick underbrush onto a road winding along the mountain and smelled the smoke already rushing before the wind. Lee stood rooted to the ground, then pointed. "Lance! That fire? Do you see it?" She looked up at him with an anguished cry. "It's the school. A girl's school and church, and *it's on fire*! Lance, go on ahead of me. I'll be safe along the road. Please . . . do what you can."

He hesitated only a moment, kissed her on the cheek, and took off downslope at a dead run, his weight of more than three hundred pounds crashing through the thick growth. Branches kept tearing at his clothes and skin, but he felt no pain or even a scratch in the ManFac. Despite the power systems, his

211

own body provided the basic impetus to his movements, and he was breathing hard, sucking in air, when he burst out of the heavy growth onto the leveled area, where the school and church presented a catastrophic sight. The adjoining structures had been ripped up by the quake, walls broken and tilted crazily with chunks of concrete strewn through the area. Thick smoke poured from the crazy quilt buildings, and he saw tongues of flame mixing with the headlights and searchlights of cars and trucks. An assortment of men, teachers, nuns, and children struggled with hoses from which water trickled ineffectually. The pressure was gone, and the lines from the water tower, which by some miracle was still standing, had been broken. Lance saw men trying to break through the rubble of the school entrance. A slim hand was suddenly upon his arm, and he turned to look at the grief-stricken face of a nun.

"Please . . . you're strong, please help me," she begged, her other hand fluttering at the knot of men struggling to fight their way into the tottering building. "In God's name, sir, there are more than fifty young girls trapped inside there. With the flames. *Please.*"

He jerked free of her arm, and his feet pounded against the asphalt of the drive. Without conscious thought of anything but this moment, this need, his powerful hands tore at chunks of concrete and flung them away, ripped free jammed timbers. The bloodied rescuers stared in awe at the human battering ram thrust suddenly into their midst. Lance saw their stares and rage filled him. "Get to it, dammit. *Move!* Clear away this stuff!" He turned back, pulling, tugging, ripping a pathway clear, ignoring the smoke now pouring from the building. Thin screams and cries of pain and fright reached him. He tried to see the children. There was some light from fires, but the thick smoke thwarted his attempts to get within. He turned back to the entrance. "Get me some lights, quick! And get a hose in here!" Again he turned and went inside the building, stepping over wreckage. A huddled form lay at his feet. He scooped up an unconscious child, ran to the narrow entrance, and thrust the body at another man. Back inside the smoke, he shouted, "Come toward my voice! That's it, come toward me. Hurry!" Another man was by his side with a powerful flashlight. It acted as a beacon. Several children stumbled toward him, toward the light. He passed them on to the other rescuers.

He was kicking his way through the wreckage, the smoke blinding, embers flying about him. There was no time to be gentle. Wherever he saw or felt a body he scooped up a child, one in each arm, and forced his way back to the entrance, where there were now more lights and a spray of cooling water. Ten, twenty, more than thirty children were dragged and pulled and carried from certain death to the line of men who continued the rescues. There were more! He grabbed a flashlight, plunged back into the smoke. Weak voices guided him, a hand raised above the rubble, a torn white dress. Each caused a frenzied hurling aside of splintered wood and glass and stones and another stumbling rush back to the entranceway. Again he returned, this time farther into the building, where he found several terrified children, huddled in a group within a storeroom that had so far staved off the flames. He couldn't carry them all. They looked as if they could walk.

"Hurry!" he called to them. "Follow me. We can get out if you hurry!" He scooped up a bleeding, fear-frozen youngster and started back. Screams tore at him as a wall collapsed in a great shower of blazing sparks. He turned, horrified, as he saw a thick pipe erupting from the broken ground, lifting up into the air. Even as he shouted, *"Down! Get down!"* and dropped his body over the child in his arms, the ruptured gas main exploded with a deep booming roar. In that last instant he remembered to snap shut the clear covers over his eyes and seal off the ManFac, activating the solid oxygen system. Flames ravaged the remaining children, setting them ablaze where they stood, human torches dancing and shrieking madly as fire seared their lungs and stabbed their eyes and enveloped their skin.

The explosion killed them where they stood or hurled the small bodies with terrible impact against the wreckage. Lance lay flat on the ground as fire tore past him and wreckage pounded his body. Time ground to a stop and then resumed its passage in soul-shattering slow motion as the explosion slowed to a hissing roar, and he saw the skin and clothes and hair of the children become all-encompassing fire, and he reached instinctively to save them and froze as several bodies whirled and bounced across his own body in their ghastly incineration. And then there was the final blast, the ultimate thunder that blew out another wall and tore up the ground beneath, and Lance felt his own form flying madly through the air, exploded upward and outward, encased in flaming debris and flung beyond the collapsing structure, beyond the chain-link fence at the edge of the school grounds where the earth dropped away sharply.

He felt the fence breaking and a thousand hammers slamming at him and then an incredible blow as he struck a tree, spun wildly off the bending wood, and crashed downslope through heavy undergrowth. He came to a stop in near darkness, fighting for air, pain stabbing through every muscle and bone, and sank into darkness.

* * *

Lee had arrived just moments before the final tearing explosion. Teeth biting into her knuckles, she had watched in horror as flame speared outward from the erupting building, and then, with a blast of fire and smoke and a ground-shaking crash, the remaining walls had collapsed onto the children still within the school.

Burying Lance with them in that sea of fire and wreckage . . .

She had heard someone screaming, and her voice had choked off as she recognized the sound from her own throat. She saw blood on her hands where her teeth had ripped her own skin. She started forward when hands gripped her shoulders, and she turned to look into the soot-streaked face of a nun. "God help you if there was someone you loved in there," she heard.

Her hand motioned weakly, and the hands gripped her more tightly. "And God knows the children that man saved need all the help they can get if they're going to live. Can you help? Do you know something about first aid?"

"Yes," Lee said weakly.

"Then *hurry.*"

Chapter 19

I think I'm dead. He lay absolutely still, afraid to move, not sure he could even if he so desired. *But if I'm dead, why the hell do I hurt so much?* The thought brought a giggle up from his throat and a stab of new pain everywhere. *This is ridiculous.* He forced his mind to go blank, to let everything loose so he could start over again. *My name is Lance Parker and I—*

The hell it is. *Logan Scott's the handle, and don't you forget it.* He laughed aloud with the thought, and it all flooded back to him. Well, he'd learned for sure that being sealed within the ManFac wasn't any guarantee for escaping the bruises and groans of physical abuse. It was like going over Niagara Falls in a plush barrel, double-chambered, fitted out with harness restraints and thick padding and a pressurized compartment—the works. You were still going to take your lumps because there was a physiological reality Lance hadn't considered. Acceleration—that was one of the nasty keys. If you're going so many miles an hour in a direction and you come slamming to a stop, there's no way you don't pay the piper. Even if

217

you stop in a ManFac that can take the bruises without so much as a twinge, you have body liquids that have gained mass from your momentum, and when you stop, they want to keep going in the same direction, and that means broken blood vessels and a severe impact on the heart and the air pounded out of your lungs and all those whirling stars before your eyes. You can't escape an inescapable force. The ManFac took the brunt of the punishment in the form of physical blows. A fist to the jaw of the ManFac wouldn't really hurt the jaw of Lance Parker residing within, but if there were a sudden snapping motion, his own head would undergo acceleration and all its resultant problems.

But without this ManFac I'd be squashed flat and torn wide open. Thank you, old buddy.

He sat up slowly to take stock of himself. He held out his arms. Caked blood. *Blood?* Sure, he realized. That artificial blood Lee had designed into the system so that to an observer a cut would appear to bleed. But there was human blood on him as well. That child in his arms when the explosion ripped through—

He climbed to his feet. Hey, everything worked. He slid back a panel on his forearm just above the inside of his wrist, pressed a button, saw miniature instruments flashing digital reports on the ManFac system to him. Damn, he'd forgotten. He punched off the oxygen system, released the eye covers, and opened the suit ports. The cold night air reached him, and he drank deeply and went into a coughing spasm from the smoke filtering through the slopes. Sounds filtered to him. Sirens across the hills, voices far above him where pain and death and misery stalked the remains of the church and school. Something tugged at his mind. He again studied the suit status report. The ManFac had barely an hour of full energy remaining.

If he didn't recharge the system or replace the power packs, he'd have no choice but to return to what he was—semicrippled, clad only in underclothes, and nearly helpless on a cold mountain slope. His thoughts centered suddenly on Lee. Where was she? Was she safe? Had something happened to her? Did— He cut himself off in midsentence. *Stick to what's immediate, what's critical.* With just that one hour of power remaining in the ManFac system, he didn't have the time to go traipsing about the countryside looking for Lee. He couldn't help her with rampant emotionalism. *Always consider the alternatives.* He had no choice but to trust to the fates, until he could *do* something about Lee, and hope fervently she had made it. His survival syndrome took over his thinking, cleared his mind, made him objectively judge his situation.

He looked about him. He didn't want to return to the mob at the remains of the school. There would be too many questions and too much attention. Down below then. Roads wound their way through these hills and mountains. He saw headlights, and he had his direction, moving steadily down through the heavy growth of the steep slope.

He emerged on the road a garish figure, a powerful black man with clothes torn and singed. He wished desperately for a car to show up. Several cars rushed by, their headlights illuminating his great bulk, but the drivers continued on. Every minute ticked away in his head like a time bomb reaching its penultimate moment of disaster. *Goddammit it . . .* He was determined to stop the next car if he had to stand in the middle of the road like a bull. He saw headlights coming around the turn below him, and he stood in the road center, his arms wide, signaling. A pickup truck screeched to a halt, and a voice shouted at him.

"You crazy or something? I almost hit you!"

Lance—Logan Scott—walked up to the driver's side and saw an older black man returning his gaze. The driver shook his head. "Man, I don't know who you are or even—what the hell happened to you?"

"I was up at that school," Lance said. "Tried to help them. Then some explosion. I'm not sure."

The man studied him briefly. "Les Seaver is my name. Get in." He waited until the giant black was seated next to him and started off along the road. "You hurt? You sure as hell look like you've been through the grinder."

Lance shook his head. "Some. Not too bad. But I need help."

A sudden, sharp glance. "You in trouble? You running? Don't sweat it, brother. Just keep it on top of the table with me."

"It's straight, man," Lance said. "It may even sound crazy. I need juice."

Seaver's eyes widened, then narrowed. "You crazy like this because you're on the sauce? Don't sound right to me."

"No, no. Nothing like that. I told you it's crazy." He looked straight ahead. "Hell, I don't know."

"What you need is a doctor. I know just where—"

"No doctor."

Seaver nodded slowly. "Okay, brother. However you want it. But you're gonna have to wait some before we can do anything. I work for the county, and everything that can move is on emergency call." He pointed along the road. "County garage is just down there. I got to pick up some emergency gear and get it to an evacuation center. But it's safe here. You can wait or come along. Nobody's gonna be here except them folks picking up supplies. Anybody questions you, just give them my name."

Lance nodded. "All I need is some rest." He

paused. "The garage have power? The lines were down everywhere I looked."

"We got it. Generating station of our own." Seaver pulled into the county garage, backed the truck to a loading platform. "You okay enough to give me a hand?"

"Sure."

"Got to load blankets. Two hundred of 'em."

Seaver's eyes widened as heavy boxes of blankets seemed to fly into the truck bed. He studied the stranger. "Never did get your name, brother."

"Logan Scott."

"Well, Logan Scott, you just rest easy here and wait for me. Most of the roads are down, so I'll arrange to get some food into your belly." Seaver waved good-bye and drove off.

Twenty minutes. Jesus, only twenty minutes. He heard a gasoline-driven generator banging away somewhere in the building, and the lights were on. Juice. Electricity. He had twenty minutes to go before he wound down like a toy soldier. He slipped into a back storeroom, thanked the deities for a sign, and found it—a wall receptacle in a corner of the room. He wedged the door shut, slid to the floor, and opened a panel in his rib cage. He extracted the slim plug and power cord and plugged himself into the wall socket. It was an incredible experience. A transfusion of energy. IV into the ribs. Life flowing through a cord. He sat quietly, knowing he must remain this way for at least four hours to regain a full charge. Maybe Seaver would be a whole lot busier than he'd planned. Lance shifted position to be more comfortable. Minutes later he was fast asleep.

"Maybe he's in here. Goddamn door's stuck. You guys give me a hand, willya?"

Lance came awake with a start. He glanced at his

wristwatch. Nearly five hours had gone by. He looked up at the door, heard the voices closer, felt the door tremble as several men on the other side pushed against it. Swiftly Lance unplugged, let the inertial reel snap the wire back into place, and slid the rib cage panel closed. He let his head droop as the weight of the men shoved the door open. "In here! He's in here!"

A hand touched him gently. Lance feigned deep sleep, came out of it groggily. "Gimme that damn bottle. He needs a drink bad." Seaver hunched down near him, close, eye to eye. "Here. Do it slow. Just a short one. Snap a bit inside you."

Lance nodded slowly, held the bottle. Whatever it was in there went down like honey fire. It *did* snap something inside him. He opened his eyes wide, saw the circle of men behind Seaver. "Les, that him?" the one asked.

Seaver turned his head and nodded. "It be him, all right. You people give him a hand getting up. He might be weavin' yet."

Lance heard two men gasping with the effort of trying to raise him to a standing position. He tensed his leg muscles to help. A big man released his grip. "You must be made of solid stone, mister."

Lance grinned at him. "Heavy grits, I guess." The other man shook his head doubtfully but shared the grin. He helped Les Seaver guide the powerful young man into the office, where they led him to a chair. Lance sat back and looked up at Seaver. "What the hell's the matter with you people? I ain't no damn cripple. I—"

"You hush." Seaver fussed over him. "Somebody get a clean shirt back in supply. Get the biggest damn one you can find. Even that ain't gonna be big enough, I suspect." He turned back to Lance.

"Logan Scott, huh?" The dark face creased in a

wide smile. "I guess I'm the only one knows your name, Logan, but sure as God made green apples the whole damn state of California is trying to find out."

Lance tensed and Seaver clapped his hand to his shoulder. "Son, we been looking *everywhere* for you. Came back here once. Forgot you might have crawled back somewhere to rest. Anyway. The TV's full of you. You some kind of very special hero, Logan. You know you saved more'n forty kids in that church school?"

The other men nodded. "One of those kids," said a tall, thin man, "was mine. I thank you, mister. More than I can say."

Lance nodded and turned back to Les Seaver. "I ain't hurt none," he said slowly, "but if there's one thing I am, it's *hungry*."

Seaver grinned hugely. "Figured that might be the case. My woman's got a table heaped high at home. You sure that's all? I mean, you don't need a doctor or nothing?"

"Food," Lance repeated, sharing the smile. "Food, and one more thing. It may be strange, but I'd appreciate it." He looked around the group, and they nodded. "Just don't tell anyone who I am or where I'm going."

They didn't understand. "But you're a *hero*," one man protested, "and people want to thank you, and—"

"Knock it off," Les Seaver broke in. "That's his business, not ours. You men doing as he asks?" He waited as they nodded and murmured their assent. "Good. Let's get him out to the truck. Got an empty belly to fill."

Three wide-eyed youngsters stared at him throughout the meal despite admonitions from their mother and several glares from their proud father. Whispered asides among the children went between bites, most of the conversation juvenile comparisons between an obvious favorite in this home, Ali, and the stranger. "He got bigger muscles." "But Ali, he got bigger *hands,* and he *faster.*" "But Logan, man, look, you ever see muscles like that on Ali? No way." Seaver's patience ran a touch ragged, but Lance favored him with a subtle shake of the head. Seaver smiled and let his kids be. Their mother had little to say. Her husband had told her of the events preceding this visit, and she was content to listen to the two men talk. There was little enough of that no matter how hard she listened.

"Never saw you around these parts before," Seaver prodded gently.

"Never been here before," Lance-Logan Scott told him. "I was making a delivery to the laboratory atop the mountain. Earthquake ran my truck off the road, I looked down and saw that school coming apart. Ran down the hill, done what I could."

Seaver shook his head admiringly. "That's all, man? Just done what you could? You were, as the TV is saying, incredible."

"They say many things," Lance replied, smiling.

"You drive a truck, I mean, that's your job?"

"Some. Mostly warehouse stuff. But it's the way to learn the business." Lance was trying desperately to deliver a picture of blandness, but it wasn't working too well, and the last thing he wanted to do was seem offhanded to this wonderful family. "I mean, I want to learn about warehousing. Stocking, shipping. It's all going to go computer, so I study a lot at night."

"Studying give you that body, I think I'm gonna crack me a big mess of books," Seaver retorted, and they shared laughter.

"Well, I do work out some at the gym, and there's surfing, and mostly I run a lot."

"You'd be dynamite in the ring."

Lance leaned back. "I don't like fighting." He said

it in such a way as to end that line of conversation. Lance stood up and turned to the woman. "Mrs. Seaver, that was a marvelous meal, and I thank you. Would you mind if your husband and I took coffee outside?"

"Go ahead. I'll bring it."

They sat on the steps, drinking slowly. Seaver toyed with his cup, finally turned, and held his eyes on Lance. "I don't mean to pry, Logan, but I know men, and you did some storytelling at the table in there. Now, hold on," he said, holding up a hand to prevent interruption. "Don't take me wrong. What I'm getting at is that if you got some kind of problem and don't want folks to know where you are, that's good enough for me. That's what I'm trying to tell you."

Lance sighed. "Thanks. You're right on the first count and I'm glad to say you're wrong on the second. But that's all I can tell you."

"Good enough."

"One more favor. Would you drive me a couple of miles from here, let me off your truck, and, as far as the world is concerned, just forget we spent this time together?"

They held a long look between them before Seaver nodded slowly. "Okay." He sighed. "I don't know what's coming down with you, Logan, or whatever your name might be, but I got the feeling there shouldn't be any more questions."

"I appreciate that."

"Whatever you want, you got. Those kids in there"—he jerked a thumb toward his house—"could have been in that school. We'll play it by your rules. I'll tell the wife we're—"

"Could we just go?"

Seaver motioned him to follow to the truck. Ten minutes later they clasped hands. "You got a funny way of talking for black skin, Logan. All I want you to know is that if ever you need someone or somewhere, my door is open to you. Peace, brother."

He watched the powerful figure disappear into the shadows of the trees, and then he was gone. Perplexed, Les Seaver drove home, carrying with him the strangest feeling no one would ever again see Logan Scott.

His decision was made before he climbed and pulled his way up the mountain slope to reach the now-silent wreckage of what had been Lee's expansive home and laboratory. As he'd predicted, the leveled area was safe from fire, but smoke hung thick and heavy along the ridges, and he moved through a smoke fog that became heavier as the night continued. There remained damned little here for Lee to find on her return. She wasn't here now, and Lance didn't expect her to be anywhere but in an emergency hospital attending to the hundreds of injured from the devastating earthquake. So much the better. At this moment the wreckage was isolated from outside contact. The telephone lines were down, and all roads would be strictly controlled. As he picked his way through the wreckage, he felt it might be a blessing in disguise. Lee was heavily insured, and while nothing could truly replace what she had assembled painstakingly through the years, at least her financial collapse would now be averted. He realized this was also the perfect moment to unshackle himself from her, to give Lee the breathing space she needed, have that shot of rebuilding from the ground up.

Do it.

No need to obey his inner voice. It was just a matter of translating decision into action. He pulled aside smashed wreckage and broken timbers and great concrete chunks to fight his way into the garage. Dust covered the truck, which had taken its share of

ManFac

knocks and dents, but only surface damage. He cleared away the entrance and pulled the truck around the tumbled mess to where the wall had collapsed. Now it was a matter of steady and meaningful labor. Into the truck went the overhead trestle from which the ManFac systems were suspended in the laboratory. He would not take the ManFac Lance. He wanted only his own true identity or totally different ones. He secured the beams and rods securely to the sides and roof of the truck and carried first the Japanese ManFac into the vehicle and braced it firmly. The thick-necked German followed next, and when he was in place, Lance tossed a casual salute to two personalities of himself. Back into the wreckage and repeated trips into the truck with power supplies, tools, test equipment, clothing, cables, ManFac system parts, medical kits— Damn, he'd almost forgotten clothing for Lance Parker as himself when he was *not* a ManFac. Several canes, identification and credit cards, all the cash he could find—a paltry $340—driver's licenses, and other papers. Lee had prepared separate identification packages for each ManFac. He buried them in a padlocked box deep within the truck for later use.

It was done. One more step to follow. He returned to the wrecked laboratory and removed himself from Logan Scott. The powerful dark figure stood as he was, a lifeless statue. Lance dragged himself to the figure of the bearded Swedish giant. He struggled into the ManFac, powered the system, and went through that always startling regeneration into a powerful human form. He closed off the entry ports, checked out the ManFac, and slid smoothly into the transition of Sven Andersen. He went through the papers, slid licenses and credit cards made out to the laboratory into his wallet. Keys, handkerchief, comb, cash: the usual, the ordinary, the prosaic. He carried the inert

227

form of Logan Scott into a corner of the lab, moved it carefully within a steel locker, and closed the combination lock. Only Lee, aside from himself, knew the right numbers.

And that was his message to her. He had considered a letter to be left for her, or even a tape recording, but dismissed both for a better choice. As soon as she could, Lee would return to the top of the mountain. With only a glance she would see that three ManFacs were missing. When she opened the steel locker and found the form of Logan Scott, she would know. Lance had returned safely to the lab. The ManFacs would be gone along with documents and papers *and* the truck. She would read the signs better than any words he might leave for her.

It was done. He looked about him slowly. Strange. This had been his womb, and in a very real sense Lee had been his creator. But the cord was cut, frozen in memory, committed totally to the past.

Now he must cut the mustard, as both Lance Parker and whatever ManFac he might choose to be. He had what he needed. An open mind with which to start out along an open road. He didn't delude himself that it would be easy.

What the hell, Parker. If it ain't got thorns, it can't be a rose.

"Damned right," he said aloud, climbing into the truck and starting the engine. He eased away from the wreckage about him and drove slowly down the mountainside. He didn't look back.

BOOK THREE

Chapter 20

He drove at a leisurely pace along the southern route of the country, keeping as much as possible to the interstate highways, where he would always be within easy driving distance of fuel, food, and motels. He was heading for the Ponce de Leon Inlet on the Florida east coast; it was an isolated beach where people minded their own business and the fishing was great. It was the perfect place for catching up on himself.

He eliminated one worry before his first day was over. The ManFac power system was limited. He kept power packs in the truck cab for emergency use, but he detested the idea of being restricted to limited hours of movement and driving, having to come to a halt when he was dangerously low on guaranteed movement. He shopped in a small-town hardware and auto parts store, ran a power cable from the engine generator into a regulator bolted to the underside of the cab dashboard. Presto, when the engine was running, he had a constant source of regulated electrical current directly into the ManFac. Hooking in or out was a matter of only seconds. It removed the nagging worry of keeping going.

He had plenty of other thoughts with which to occupy himself. Like what he was going to do with himself. His money supply had its own limits. He was an engineer, but he had sworn never to use his own credentials. If ever there were a background survey or a security check, his past would leap up like a screaming goblin, and no one was going to keep on a payroll the man who had been pilloried in the media as the son of a bitch mainly responsible for that nuclear blowup beneath a California mountain.

So he had a new ID. Sven Andersen, big and strong and very impressive. And what do you do, Mr. Andersen? Why, I eat electricity. That's for starters. And I'm very strong, and I worked at a laboratory in California, and no, I don't have any credentials or an engineering résumé, and sorry, I don't have any professional or personal character references, and the construction crew hiring office is where?

That was about as good as pissing up a rope. He wasn't going to be any muscle boy on a road gang or any damned kind of construction. He'd have to start way down on the bottom of the pile, and he'd earn just about enough to feed himself food, gasoline, and electricity, and he could do that for a month or three or six, and when the time was behind him, he'd be nowhere. The merry-go-round wasn't on his trip ticket.

When the thinking furrowed his brow and he felt the headaches starting to crawl behind his ears, he quit. Just quit cold. No use building up huge walls. He had ideas. Hordes of them. But there was no way he could settle down and tinker and test and experiment without a big fat bankroll. That problem would have to be met squarely in the future.

File it. He did. He'd open the file when he had to.

232

He danced on wings of imagination, though. He already knew how to improve the ManFac, improve the systems, gain more flexibility. He had crazy ideas. Direct use of force fields. An idea for magnetic or microwave lift came into his thoughts. It would be interesting. He could tie it in with several gyrostabilizing systems, and he could—

File it.

Yes, sir!

There were new problems much more immediate to be solved. He'd lived for two weeks as Lance Parker, hobbled and needing his cane, and he'd gone through a whole series of wide-screen nightmares that were just as real as he'd imagined. That was well behind him. He'd made excursions as a ManFac. Twice, the last occasion as the dark-skinned rescuer of children. Too much notoriety there. He didn't regret his decision to lay Logan Scott to rest.

But this was his first voyage into the daily world as a ManFac. Endurance was a new test. He had to maneuver not only on a day-to-day basis but one day after the other. There were compensations. As the crippled Lance Parker he was horribly vulnerable. But a man would have to be crazy to mess with his formidable bulk and obvious strength as the hulking Sven Andersen. He didn't spend his days looking over his shoulder. It was beautiful.

Not so the long hours and the days that sometimes seemed never to end. He drove until he chafed and twisted uncomfortably, and then he stopped the truck and sat amidst trees or on the edge of roadside camps where he could look across mountains and desert and sometimes just look up at the sky, remembering when he had fallen through that same sky with Lee, fallen and balanced and whirled before pulling the D ring and waiting for nylon to blossom, and then the quiet cushioned gentle float to earth.

There was no rush on that rolling eastward trek, and he had just the company he wanted. Himself. The small things in life were a constant challenge, and the acceptance and meeting of each such challenge were a growing list of successes and victories. He ate rarely in restaurants, preferring to pick up his food and drinks and eat in solitude. It went well.

The times he *had* to stop were the killers. And there was no way to escape that harsh reality. After long hours of driving and eating and walking and functioning as a ManFac he drifted into the ManFac being. Lance Parker and Sven Andersen coalesced into an entity that defied identification. When he looked into a mirror, the mighty face and form of Sven looked back at him, and he *was* the Swede. Not merely in appearance or in actions but in subconscious thought and intent as well.

But there was no living as Andersen. Every so often the giant Swede had to be put aside. His own biology demanded its due. Rubbed and chafed skin, aching muscles, bleary eyes, the need for oils and ointments to work their effect. It was a rotten, stinking time for him to emerge from the ManFac, always behind doubly locked doors and alarm systems rigged for each room that for a time became a terrible prison and also an eggshell that could be cracked when he was his most vulnerable.

Every occasion caused a paranoid shriek of helplessness in his mind. He backed up the extra bolts and bars and security alarms with a repeating shotgun and a .38 revolver. He never went anywhere without the handgun. He slept with it; he kept it by his side when he bathed; it was within instant reach when he sat on the john. Standing to urinate was rough on him. Balancing with one hand on his cane or leaning against the wall and using a twisted arm to handle himself and his clothing left him glaringly naked to any intrusion. He never relieved himself standing unless he was Andersen. He felt safer on a toilet seat. No crazy balancing act. His eyes always on the door. The gun always within a split second of his hand.

No showers. Too helpless. Baths, because this way he could heat-soak; he could soak in oils, and the gun was always on the edge of the tub or on a stool by the tub. He was thinking constantly of his security. The bolts weren't enough. Neither were the alarms. He might be in a deep sleep and someone could come crashing through his defenses, and he had nightmares of a great fist smashing into his scarred face or a knife slashing at him, and he would jerk awake, soaked in sweat, his eyes darting about like a wild, cornered animal, and he would clasp the shotgun and take the whole goddamned night to come down to coherent thinking. He forced himself to use what he had in abundance—engineering know-how.

He rigged an electrified matting that he hung across any motel window and along the floor just inside the doorway. The netting received its charge from both a wall socket and, in case the local power went out, a high-amp twelve-volt battery. There was enough juice in that battery to slam a water buffalo against a wall. Any interruption of the electric current snapped on a bright floodlight he always directed toward the windows and door and set off a clanging alarm. It brought him extraordinary relief. No one could ever reach him without running that gauntlet.

Paranoia eased well back from his immediate thoughts when he sealed himself into motel rooms. It cleared his head for thinking instead of reacting.

Yet a man couldn't escape the harsh realities of life in the form of people who *liked* trouble and actively sought its company. He was driving slowly through a small town in Louisiana, forced to take back roads because of construction blocks on the interstate, when he learned that all the electronic miracles and technical advances could not dismiss certain cardinal sins. Like, don't mess around in the wrong town, meaning simply, don't attract attention. That was pretty tough with the truck and his own brute size.

River Keys was an out-of-the-way shitpot of a town that had managed to avoid the attention of modern expansion. No big shopping centers, no new industry for years, no wide-laned highways crowding the town. It was holdout country for rednecks and spoilers, and it was a century in the past, enjoying its privileged position of being able to hate "niggers" and strangers—and get away with it. It was a world of "good ol' boys" to whom whomping strangers was good sport.

Lance drove slowly into the town, unbelieving of the ramshackle buildings, the closed gas stations, the proliferation of small bars on each side of the one street through River Keys. He was beat, his skin chafed in several places, and he needed desperately to return to Lance, no matter how appalling the thought of emerging from the form of the powerful Swede. He pulled into the driveway of the Rivertown Motel, parked and locked the truck, and went into the lobby to register for a room.

A pockmarked face with stubble and buckteeth met him across the greasy motel counter. *If the rooms are like him,* Lance thought, *I won't be here more than time enough to bathe and get some oil on my skin.* "What kin Ah do fer ya?" He could hardly understand the drawl. He tried his best to ignore it.

"A room," Lance said, towering over the Adam's apple bobbing beneath the protruding teeth. "A room with a bath."

Tobacco juice spattered on the floor. "Cain't help you none," he was told.

Lance's eyes narrowed. He could feel the *wrong* about all this. If he had the first ounce of sense, he'd be back in that truck and on his way, but—

"You got a vacancy sign outside."

"Don't matter. Ain't got no baths here. You want a shower?" The pockmarked face twisted into a high giggle. "You smells like you needs one. That's fer sure."

Lance looked coldly at the clerk. The sense of *wrong* was stronger than ever. What the hell would make this beanpole so cocksure of himself that he'd deliberately taunt someone of the size of Sven Andersen? He had his answer when two dark-faced men came into the lobby through a side entrance. "You got some problem with this stranger, Luke?" one asked.

Luke nodded vigorously. "He like to tell me we ain't good enough for him. Ain't got no bath. He needs one. Told him he oughta shower, the way he smell. Maybe it's his beard, being blond and pretty and girlylike."

Jesus Christ . . . Lance took a deep breath. "Shove your shower up your ass," he said quietly, turning to leave.

Two more big bastards, one with a chain hanging from a dirty fist. "You got to apologize to Luke, sonny," said the chain handler. "You a big motherfucker, all right, but you done hurt his feelings. Now apologize to him."

Lance glanced to his side. Sure enough, the other two were moving closer. And Luke was grinning hugely, a baseball bat appearing in one hand. "You shoulda stayed on the interstate, boy, and not come messin' around and insultin' good people."

Lance backed up to a wall, already knowing what he was going to do. He faced the five men. About fifteen feet to the doorway leading to the truck. He nodded. "I suppose I was wrong," he said.

Jaws dropped. Good. "I mean, what the hell, no harm intended. Luke, you got my apology, just like your friends want."

"Why, the yellow-livered polecat is sucking—"

Lance came forward with unbelieveable speed and fury, leaning forward into his run, catching the man with the chain along the bridge of his nose with his knuckles held tightly together and protruding. Even over the sudden thunder of his feet slamming onto the floor they could hear the terrible cracking sound as the bones splintered and blood sprayed out. Lance didn't hesitate as he continued. The second man caught a tremendous backhand that hurled him off his feet and through the wall to his side. Lance threw himself into the run and did just what the remaining two men would never expect. Six feet from them he hurled that massive body through the air, hands outstretched with his fingers in great claws. His left hand caught one man by the shoulder and spun him about, but the other was a dead-on catch, with Lance's right hand squeezing about his face along his temples. And he squeezed with force enough to break wood. The skin split, and the bone beneath shattered, and the scream told Lance he could ignore this son of a bitch. He felt as much as heard the feet behind him. He spun off to his right, turning as he did so, and caught a glimpse of Luke's enraged face as he swung wildly with the heavy bat.

Lance went forward, beneath that stupid swing, and did no more than to plant a great fist solidly into the ribs beneath that still-upraised arm. Luke never made a sound, and Lance knew he'd done more damage than he planned, for his fist not only punched into ribs but went on through the rib cage.

A chair crashed over his head. Damn, these were

tough bastards! The man he'd spun around moved like a big cat and had already grabbed a chair and slammed it across Lance's head and shoulders. Wood cracked, but Lance stood his ground and came upright slowly, then pointed a finger at his attacker.

"You ever do that again and I find out about it, I'll bust your head, understand?"

The remains of the chair dropped to the floor, and his assailant took off at a dead run, tearing away a door hinge as he hit dirt outside and kept running. Lance had no time to enjoy amusement. These towns stuck together, and he was a sudden challenge, and if they ever got their act together, he'd be in trouble up to his ears. He went swiftly to the motel desk and ripped out the telephone wires. Then he ran outside to the main power line. He went up the pole, hauling himself along the metal rungs as if he were weightless. He braced himself, and then the ManFac arm came down in a great sweeping arc with all his strength. No danger from the lines; the plastiskin was nonconducting. But sparks showered out wildly, and a great greenish light flared, and the town fell into blackness. The only lights to penetrate the sudden dark came from the headlights of cars cruising through town. Out of sight of anyone who might be seeking the loss of power, Lance dropped back to the ground. Four cars, that was all. One hand ripped open the hoods, and the other hand tore away the electrical wires, and Lance was running for his truck. He unlocked the door, started the engine, leaving his lights off. There was still that one polecat who'd run from the motel, and it was time for Sven Andersen to haul ass away from this snake pit. He slammed the truck into gear, spinning rubber as he fishtailed wildly until the tires grabbed asphalt.

And just in time. He heard the shotgun blasts fired through the darkness as he accelerated along the highway. Someone shouted obscenities as the dark mass of the truck bore down on him, and he jumped aside with only inches to spare. Lance grinned and then turned on his lights. He hit eighty, screeched to a crawl at the first intersection, drove several miles on the back roads, and picked up an interstate going north. He drove the legal limit for the next two hours and then eased off the interstate to follow signs leading to an all-night truckers' stop. There was safety in numbers in the long rows of heavy rigs. Twenty minutes later he was within his motel room, doors and windows locked, his electrical defenses alive and humming.

He filled the tub, poured in body oil, rested the shotgun on a table alongside the tub, and slid gratefully into the soothing water. He afforded himself the luxury of a cigar. He looked vacantly at the smoke, his thoughts far away, and then a wry grin came slowly to his face.

It had been one hell of an education.

Chapter 21

Shigura Sato drove steadily at fifty miles an hour along the wide highway leading to Atlanta, and he made certain never to exceed the speed limit. The big Japanese sat easily behind the wheel of his truck, eating a hero sandwich with obvious pleasure and sipping from a Thermos of steaming coffee. Wherever he stopped for fuel and oil he drew curious stares. A six-foot Japanese with a shaved skull and massive arms isn't your everyday neighbor on the highway. He remained at each stop just long enough to service his truck and use the men's room, and he was gone.

Lance chuckled. He'd been a bit absentminded the first time he walked into the men's room. The hulking Japanese looking back at him from the mirror startled him. For a split second he looked frantically for the face of Sven Andersen, and then the cobwebs vanished. Sven was secured within the truck along with his lifeless German companion. The need for the fast change before Lance left the truck stop hadn't been so funny.

He hadn't planned to shift to another man. Until he watched the early-morning television news. According to still somewhat confused reports, the small town of River Keys had been the scene of an invasion of biker hoodlums led by a bearded giant. No one knew just how many bikers were involved, but a motel clerk had been critically hurt from a kick in the ribs that punctured his lungs. Another man had been stomped in the face and was in a nearby hospital. There was more, but Lance leaned back in his chair, ignoring the details. He, of course, had been the "gang." Those swamp yokels weren't about to admit to anyone that just one man had wreaked such carnage. But it posed a serious problem spelled "All Points Bulletin," with descriptions of the "large man with the blond beard" sent to all law enforcement agencies on a dangerous fugitive charge. Lance waited until no one paid attention to the parking lot, walked casually to the truck, and disappeared inside. As Sven Andersen.

When the truck drove off, Shigura Sato was behind the wheel. Lee Grazzi had been right. He was the man who could be anybody.

His ease of slipping into the physical shell of another man didn't blind him to harsh realities. Until the time came that he could live uninterrupted within the ManFac for a week at the very least, he was still a Cinderella prisoner—would return to being the pumpkin with dragging foot and twisted body and eye-catching scars. What would he do if he were arrested? A night in the slammer would expose who and what he was and draw incredible attention to him, and if there was any defense more vital than anonymity, he couldn't think of it. If a situation arose where a cop wanted to play rough, Lance feared he'd have no choice but to play even rougher. He would have to, he absolutely must, prevent coming under the control of any agency or individual that restricted his movement.

He would play it clean, and he would play it straight unless his own survival dictated otherwise, and survival was spelled out, among other things, as having his multiple identities remain unidentified.

Well, he sighed, all this was fine as to sorting out future modes of personal conduct, but it did damned little to settle that other nagging problem: the tough four-letter word spelled "cash." Cash on the line. He couldn't live indefinitely off Lee's credit cards, and he didn't want to, because that signified to him that if nothing else, his financial umbilical was still intact, and he was still sucking on a fiscal tit. More than that, the continued use of such cards meant a warm trail, and if he was going to be fair to Lee, he *had* to cut that cord, leave himself isolated from any contact.

The question that loomed phantomlike before his mind's eye remained. How was he going to perform that little miracle of making his way through life without that dependency upon the credit rating of Lee? He didn't like some of the alternatives. ManFac was a most effective instrument for strong-arm tactics. One blow of his hand could smash through a wall or crush a man's head. Was he going to embark on mugging to earn his keep? Rob stores? Use that strength to break into jewelry stores or whatever? Dillinger was hardly his hero, and the whole idea of living that way, spurred on by a bitterness he knew he had whipped, repelled him.

He turned off the convoluted thinking, for he could handle it for only a short period at a time. Driving was his solace right now. The freedom of rolling along, of becoming comfortable within the ManFac rather than simply extending the time he could bear the problems of disappearing within this outer husk of his new being, was tonic to him. He could hardly believe eight days of driving were behind him, but the highway signs announcing Atlanta were not to be denied. He rolled off a ramp leading to a small airport and industrial park on the outskirts of the city. The motels in such areas catered to workers, salesmen, and essentially a professional crowd rather than tourists, and that kind of crowd was more prone to mind its own business. To them motels were like fast-food restaurants that kept a man's profile acceptably low. He drove slowly past the lights of the airport pilots called Charlie Brown Airport, and then his foot came slowly to the brake as a garishly illuminated building caught his eye. He eased off the road and shifted into neutral.

A great neon sign blazed at him. DEKALB SPORTS ARENA—WRESTLING TONIGHT. He studied the building, the parking lot, the entrance. Jammed; thousands of people making the scene. Thousands of people means several times that amount in dollars. And the television receipts—

The grunt-and-groan circuit with its hysterical, loyal, crazy fans. He knew wrestling well enough. On his collegiate team he'd won the gold cup and been a serious contender in his weight class for the Olympics. But that kind of mat competition had little to do with the deliberate mayhem of professional wrestling.

Making it big in the squared circle meant a *lot* of money. Some of the biggest names raked in a few hundred thousand dollars a year and left behind them a trail of broken bones, torn skin, and battered opponents. There was that fine line. When you were good enough to cross it—which meant when you drew enormous crowds and swelled the gate receipts—you were allowed to beat the other guy senseless.

A key to the game was physiological. Lance had known some very big, very powerful men from the football ranks who'd climbed into the professional wrestling game and had the absolute bejesus smashed out of them. What you needed in this business was a natural ability to absorb punishment. If you had that, you might be *in*.

But you still had to come up the long and slow route, you had to meet the private rules in the back offices, and everything was ritualized. You played by the rules, or you were liable, one night, to find a spoiler in the ring with you. The spoilers were nasty, tough men with one purpose—to teach errant wrestlers the wisdom of playing the game the way the management called the shots.

And there were grudge matches, which the management also held dear to its fiscal heart. If two men were determined to tear each other apart, the ring, not the dressing room, was the place to hammer at each other. That kind of match, especially between the real pros, even brought the other wrestlers out of the dressing rooms to watch. It was one of the few occasions when the hype was absent from the ring, and one of the two men squaring off was likely to end up in a hospital bed.

Lance drove slowly past the entrance, watching the long lines of people. The card tonight in this arena, which seated some eight thousand people, featured eight matches. The openers didn't matter. Lance studied the poster. A winner-take-all contest. Likely it was hype to increase the frenzied fever of the fans, but that was unimportant. Igor Belenkov, billed as the Mad Russian, up against Big Jim Swigert, who did *his* wrestling in logging boots. There was some other nonsense about the southeast television championship on the line. He ignored that. The matches started at eight that night, and the main event would get under way at ten.

Wonder what ManFac could do in that ring? He was startled with the clarity of that inner voice of his. But what if he *could* pit his strength, abetted by his collegiate wrestling background, against the best the promoters had to offer? He needed time to think this through, to get past the problem of coming out of nowhere. You didn't just walk into the promoter's office and get a top match. The rungs had to be climbed one by one. He didn't have that kind of time. Not in a business as tightly controlled as IBM. He needed an approach absolutely different, unexpected, something that would blow the minds of the fanatical devotees of this orchestrated mayhem. Because if they demanded you in the ring, they showed their zeal in lining up at the ticket windows, and *that* opened the door to the promoter's office. Lance rubbed his hand against his chin in an old reflex. If he hurried, he could register at a motel and still get to one of the big department stores that sold athletic equipment.

Shigura Sato stood in the lobby of the arena, the subject of close attention by security guards and onlookers. He watched through the open doors as the two wrestlers climbed through the ropes into the ring. Perfect. Igor Belenkov, the Mad Russian, was probably born and raised in Brooklyn, but he displayed beautiful showmanship in his fleece-lined boots and brilliant red cape. He strutted about the ring as Big Jim Swigert leaned against the ropes in his corner, preferring a style of brooding nastiness. The referee was going through his own ritual of instructing the two men as to the rules of the ring, an accepted con act for the crowd. Shigura Sato, wearing black boots and black tights and a black karate robe with a bright band tied about his forehead, started down the aisle. A security guard blocked his way.

"Hey, you can't go down there. You ain't got no ticket."

Sato smiled coldly and kicked the guard in the knee. The guard yelped in pain and spun about to crash into a row of spectators. Heads turned at the sudden yell, and thousands of people watched the huge Japanese stalk menacingly toward the ring. Two more guards stepped before him and were smacked aside by open slaps that sent them flying off-balance. Before the astonished wrestlers could move, Sato was in the ring. The referee grabbed his arm, leaned up to speak into his ear. "I don't know who the hell you are, but get outta here."

Sato smiled at him. "Play the game, asshole. Who do you think sent me here?"

The referee, puzzled, looked at the other men.

Who was this Jap? He was too *clean*. Not a mark on him. No scars, no twisted nose or puffy ears. Not a welt or a bump.

Sato pointed a thick finger at Swigert and in broken English said, "I want you. Other man, you go away before you hurt."

The referee danced about like a bantam rooster, grasping Sato's arm and shouting for him to leave the ring at once. He was flung aside contemptuously, and the finger still pointed at Swigert, and this time the voice could be heard throughout the hushed, still-confused spectators. "I want *you!* Now!"

Swigert smiled. He'd been through every ploy in the book. "Okay, you got me." He leaned back against the ropes. "But first you gotta get rid of *him*," he said, pointing to Belenkov.

Sato bowed. "*Arigato*. I appreciate." He turned to Belenkov. "You please to leave ring maybe?"

"You crazy bastard," Belenkov snarled, "get the hell outta here."

"Too bad," Sato said. "You come into ring with laces untied. Not smart. See?" He pointed to Belenkov's right foot. Belenkov glanced down, and he never saw the great hand that came up in a blur to chop him with devastating force in the throat. He

247

staggered back, blood trickling from his throat, and he had no time to protect himself as a hand gripped his hair, jerked him forward off-balance. A kick to the ribs, and before Belenkov could react, he was flung through the ring ropes to crash in face-contorted agony on the concrete floor.

He looked up in mingled pain and astonishment, judged a hasty retreat to be long overdue, and limped back to the dressing room. The other wrestlers, who had watched the unexpected turn of events on the closed-circuit television screen, surrounded him with a babble of voices. "Hey, Igor, what the hell kinda gimmick you guys pulling?" one man shouted.

Another pushed his way closer to where Belenkov sagged against a dressing table. "What's that asshole promoter Rawlins pulling off now?" He stared at Belenkov. "Hey, you really got hurt up there, didn't you?"

Belenkov nodded, trying to speak, but another wrestler pushed forward. "Who is that gook son of a bitch in the ring? I never seen him before." He looked around at the others. "Anybody ever get a look at that Jap?" The others shook their heads.

"You dumb bastards." They turned to Belenkov as he spit blood on the floor. "I told you he busted a couple of ribs. I think he crushed something in my throat. Will you assholes get me a doctor or an ambulance or *something*?"

A youngster patted his shoulder. "I'll get the doc, Igor. Just hang on." He ran for the phone.

Then they heard the renewed roar of the crowd as another wrestler turned up the volume of the TV monitor. They saw the referee shoving both men apart, gesturing wildly and shouting for them to stand off until the bell. One wrestler pointed to the screen and shook his head. "Whoever that Jap is, he don't know Swigert very well."

"Yeah. Didn't he kill a whole bunch of people with his bare hands in Vietnam?"

"You got it. He loved it that way. He used to wring necks until he broke 'em."

"He'll kill that crazy Jap. Swigert won't play the rules." A finger pointed at the referee. "Look at Julius. Son of a bitch is like a bantam rooster. He'll milk this for everything it's worth."

Igor Belenkov sat gingerly on the dressing table, wiping blood from his mouth. "I don't know. I never been hit like that before. But what I can't figure out is where Mike Rawlins got this ape and how he kept him under wraps for so long."

"Rawlins knows how to make it a circus, all right," another man agreed. "He's the best promoter in the game."

Mike Rawlins burst into the dressing room, pointed his cigar at the television screen. "Who the hell is that son of a bitch?" he shouted.

The crowd was screaming wild. The arena reverberated from the pressure of thousands of voices, of feet stomping the floor and banging chairs, of shrill whistles. *Never* had a wrestler come into the ring without *some* warning, if not to his opponent, at least to the referee. And the way he'd put Belenkov into the pits! My God, he had power.

But Swigert weighed 280 pounds, and he was known as the fastest big man in the ring, and he went low and his arm swept forward, catching Sato just behind the knees, sweeping his feet out from beneath him, and by the time the Jap was flat on his ass Swigert was back to his feet and moving in. He grabbed hair and jerked the other man up, keeping him unbalanced, and Swigert with every ounce of his strength slammed his knee into the back of the neck before him.

Steel-mesh skull or not, Lance saw bright red when the knee crashed into him. He'd never expected this. Not this speed or this strength *or* the smart ringwise thinking behind Swigert's move.

Sato twisted away. His stiff fingers shot up into Swigert's armpit, forcing Swigert to release his grip on Sato's hair. Sato—Lance—came in fast with a mighty punch to the rib cage. It would have worked except that Swigert was the old pro and twisted with the punch. It gave him that precious moment to shift tactics and to do some good wrestling. An elbow smash under the chin stopped the Jap. Swigert twisted, and a snap mare brought the Jap high over his head for a solid crash to the canvas. Dust flew from the impact. Swigert dropped like a boulder with one knee into Sato's forehead and the other across his throat. He kept going down, lying like a stone blanket across the Jap, holding one wrist flat, his hand on the throat and his legs hooking him down. "Count 'em!" he roared to the referee.

Sato heard two sharp slaps on the canvas. Astonished at his own ineptitude, he took the only way out and rammed his one free arm upward with all his strength into Swigert's chest. Swigert flew wildly up and off to one side, and Sato had his shoulder off the mat even as the referee's hand was coming down for the third and final time.

Swigert, on his feet, realized something was very wrong in here. No human being could do that. Not with one arm. He'd faced champion weight lifters. This was crazy. He wouldn't try to pin this bastard until he was unable to stand. He watched Sato come to his feet and then charged, head down, into the Jap's gut to shove him backward into the ropes. As he rebounded, Swigert went forward, and his powerful arms encircled the Jap in the killer bear hug for which he was famous. He locked his enormous hands tight with knuckles jammed hard into the spine of his opponent, holding him off the mat, feet dangling in the air. But he could hardly lift this man. No matter. He gave it everything he had, twisting the Jap wildly from side to side to empty his lungs and bring excruciating pain to his spine.

Lance didn't fight it. He let go. He let all his body weight slump. He became a 320-pound sack of loose sand. Swigert's legs wobbled. Lance laughed and pushed forward with his stomach muscles. Swigert felt his hands losing their grip. Enraged, he spit into the other man's face.

The Jap smiled at him. "You *baka*. Very stupid man," he said, and a right hand came up, when it should have been dangling helplessly, and grasped Swigert's left ear. Slowly, deliberately, and with relentlessly increasing pressure the Jap began to twist the ear.

Swigert strained with all his might to crack the other man's spine. Sweat burst from his face as he exerted all his strength—and the son of a bitch smiled at him! He tightened the pressure to break the grip on his ear, but suddenly the pain was intense, and a knife seemed to be stuck into the ear. Blood trickled where the skin began to tear.

"You let go, I stop," the Jap told him.

"I'll kill you," Swigert grunted.

"Too bad." The Jap smiled, and a steel vise lacerated the ear. Swigert yelled in pain, and his hands flew to his ear as the Jap walked away, still holding the ear, Swigert following helplessly, the pain white and maddening. The terrible pressure had brought him bending forward when a mighty foot thudded into his chest just over his heart. The next moment he felt himself going high into the air, and then there was a sudden drop into a steel knee.

The grinning Japanese stood over Swigert, one foot

on his throat, and he pointed to his helpless opponent. A voice thundered above the roar of even this crazed, screaming mob. "YOU COUNT FULL! ALL TEN!"

Julius Goldsboro intoned the count through ten, the Japanese stepped back, bowed ceremoniously to him, picked up his karate robe, jumped to the floor, and ran ponderously toward the nearest exit. He brushed aside spectators and astonished police, hurled the exit doors open, and disappeared into the night.

Chapter 22

Lance waited until three o'clock the next afternoon before calling Mike Rawlins. As he expected, he had a tough time getting through. Rawlins's office was a madhouse, and until Lance told the secretary that he managed the havoc-wreaking Japanese, he was getting nowhere fast. Then Rawlins was on the line. "Who the hell is this?" he barked.

"The name is Parker. Lance Parker. But the name you're interested in is Shigura Sato. He's my boy who cleaned your house last night." Lance waited for the pause he knew would come. Because Rawlins *had* to talk to him. The newspapers normally paid as much attention to pro wrestling as to a dead cat in a storm drain, but they'd been piqued by what had happened. There was no doubt two men had been hurt seriously. Belenkov had suffered a crushed windpipe and three broken ribs; he had a lung filling with fluid and was on twenty-four-hour watch. Swigert showed signs of heart fibrillation; it had taken forty-three stitches to sew back that part of his ear torn free; and his small fractures filled a page. Hundreds of hysterical fans had called the newspapers and television stations, and something was bound to emerge from that kind of fever. It did. It made only a small paragraph in the sports news, but other news was light, and the TV cameras had rolled into the hospital room. The story kept getting better all the time.

"You son of a bitch!" Rawlins shouted on the phone to Parker. "You know what I had to do? I had to take a goddamned polygraph test for the wrestling commission to prove that wasn't any setup last night! The bastards thought I was lying to them!"

"You have the press there?"

"Huh? Well, *uh,* yeah, but—"

"No buts, Rawlins. That's a hundred grand worth of publicity, and we both know it."

"What was your name again?"

"Same as it was before. Lance Parker. And don't play cute with me. I have something we both can use."

"You're pretty sure of yourself."

"Cut the shit, Rawlins. I want to talk a deal and talk it face to face, and we do it today, and my boy is back in the ring tonight. That gives you time to hype up the television and radio with special ad announcements. Hell, you know the routine better than anyone else. I can hear the dollar signs clicking in your eyeballs right now. Tell me we have an appointment in thirty minutes in your office, or shove your phone up your ass."

The pause was brief. "You got it. Thirty minutes." The phone went dead.

Lance Parker drove the rental car to Rawlins's office. Not Sven Andersen or Shigura Sato or Otto Heller, the name he'd decided on for the brutish German yet to be brought to life. Lance Parker, limping his way down the corridor into the outer office, smiling with scarred face and lips at the secretary. She didn't blink an eyelash; her world was filled with faces punched and kicked to hamburger. "I'm expected," Lance said pleasantly.

"Mr. Parker? Yes, sir, you certainly are," she told him, leading him through the next door.

Rawlins's eyes widened as the twisted body moved into his office and sought out a comfortable chair. "You're Parker," he said.

"You win the cigar."

"No unkindness meant, Parker, but your shoulders and other things about you talk. What the hell happened?"

"A mountain fell on me."

"I can believe it. Maybe we'll talk about it over a beer some night. What about now?"

Lance shrugged. "We're businessmen. The longer we talk before agreeing, the more time you lose with your publicity, and the more of that you lose, the more bread you lose at the gate and for the television circuit."

"I'm listening."

"Good." Lance hesitated deliberately to light a slim cigar. "Last night was free," he said.

"Wonderful. Marvelous. You put two of my best boys in the hospital, and you tell me it's free. What's your next offer? Cancer?"

"You're a funny man, Rawlins. Tonight you can jack up the ante and whatever else you want. What *I* want is five thousand dollars, cash on the line, as soon as the match is over. Not even a cashier's check. Five thou in century notes, and you hand it to my boy."

"What's his name?"

"Shigura Sato."

"Never heard of the bum."

"He has excellent references. Go to room 229 in your local hospital. Let's not crap around. Do we dance?"

"We might. I got conditions. Your boy has got to win. He don't win, you don't get a wooden nickel."

"Fine. Just have the cash ready for him."

"Only if I get my money's worth, Parker. That's a lot of green for one man."

"All *I* lose is one night of my boy having fun," Lance said casually. "This conversation is being taped and broadcast to a recorder outside this building, so hear me good. You rent that arena for the rest of the week. Sato will fight *anybody* you got. He wins, he gets paid at the end of the match. He don't win, you got yourself a freebie. You can hype this thing to complete hysteria. We get five thou a night. If it's a deal, Sato will be there at ten sharp."

Rawlins shook his head. "He gotta come to the dressing room ahead of time. The commission insists on—"

"Buy them television sets, for Christ's sake. No dressing rooms. We keep everybody off-balance that way."

Rawlins chewed his lip, then nodded. "Deal. Where can I reach you if I need you? You just may have to take your boy home in a hearse."

"My problem, not yours," Lance said. "I call you each day at noon sharp." He climbed painfully to his feet. "Play it clean, Rawlins. Don't fuck up a good payday." He left the office.

He handled everything with the precision of a well-drilled team. He'd rented space in a large garage with attendants for the truck rather than leave it parked in the motel lot. He used a rental car, changed motels each day. No way for someone to get a really good tag on him; he preferred to remain identified but not known. Rawlins wouldn't sit quietly for *too* long when Shigura Sato ate his wrestlers alive—and neither would the other men facing him in the ring. Lance thought about that some more, registered and paid in advance at three different motels, and kept one extra rental car stashed in the lot of one motel. Now he had flexibility; now he could dodge and twist if that became necessary. When he was ready for his appearance at the sports arena, he'd leave directly from the garage. No one would pay any attention to that. *No*, he corrected himself. There's a better way. Take no chances on anything's pointing to that truck. What it held was his whole life.

Later that day he drove a rental car into the six-story parking garage. He left the car and slipped into the truck. Twenty minutes later he was again Shigura Sato, clad in a sweat suit. He drove from the garage and took the main drive to four blocks from the armory, where he parked in the back lot of a motel. He sat and watched the car clock. At 9:45 P.M. he slipped the keys under the mat of the back of the car, climbed out, and started jogging toward the armory. He arrived at three minutes before ten o'clock. This time the lobby guards stepped *back* from him. He pulled off the sweat suit shirt and baggy trousers, placed them carefully on a seat. "Don't let no one touch," he ordered the nearest guard.

"Yes, *sir*."

He stomped his way down the aisle. Not walked or ran, but stomped, more than three hundred pounds crashing like muted thunder against the floor. Halfway down the aisle, every eye upon him, he stopped, extended both arms wide, threw back his head, and bellowed, *"Banzai! Banzai!"* His voice carried like a massive foghorn through the arena, and then he grinned and waved at the crowd, and they answered his call, this almond-eyed stranger who was chewing up their most detested ring villains. The crowd built into a thunder, a monster surf rolling over everyone and everything, a chant increased by a rhythmic pounding of feet. Sato urged them on, his arms rising and falling as he walked ponderously, until it seemed the very walls of the building were trembling with the outpouring of mob sound. Just before the ring he stopped and turned to the spectators, holding up both hands for silence. He was a maestro leading a human orchestra. Silence fell. In an unabashed exhibition of pure hype, the big Japanese beat his fists against his chest and roared in Tarzan fashion. Normally his voice would have carried just loud enough to be heard through the arena. The ManFac system magnified it to a bloodcurdling cry that echoed and bounced off the walls and ceiling, that turned people white with shock and no small fear at this animal in their midst.

It was a beautiful move, and it earned for Shigura Sato a tremendous kick to the side of his head, delivered by none other than the Montana Kid, 340 pounds of meanness packed into a hefty frame of six feet ten inches.

Shigura Sato spun about wildly, his arms askew, spinning in a crazy circle. Behind the Japanese face Lance was dazed by the force of the blow. His ears rang with the sudden pressure that had slammed through the steel-mesh and plastiskin layers before the impact thudded into his own head. Before he could catch his balance, he fell backward, and the alarm bells clanging away madly between his ears kept him rolling, kept him moving as his body bruised and pummeled screaming spectators. He caught a blur of the huge wrestler leaping the ropes, and he was just to his feet as a folding chair came walloping toward his head. A raised forearm deflected the blow. The Montana Kid hurled away the splintered wood in his hands, grasped hair, and jerked Sato into a grueling side headlock. Both men crashed to the floor. Sato prepared to break the hold when he heard a voice in his ear.

"You bust outta this hold, okay? Then get inna goddamn ring where the TV can see us. Okay, make your move *now*."

You're damned right I will, Lance swore to himself. But for a split second he had to admire the other man. Montana had smarts between those pulped ears. Rolling around on the concrete floor kept the view limited and the television useless. Sato twisted for leverage, yanked a great hairy leg up from the floor, and sank his teeth hard into muscle. Montana howled like a mad dog, and there wasn't any act to that sudden uproar as blood flowed from the torn skin. The headlock was gone, and Sato crashed a forearm smash to Montana's chest to throw him backward. Sato hit the ring, rolled under the ropes, and was on his feet like a great cat, standing ring center and gesturing wildly for the other man to come in and fight.

The scream of the crowd was maniacal. The struggle went for an endless twelve minutes and Sato didn't spend one moment "carrying" his opponent. The Montana Kid had been told to wipe off this unknown gook. He tried. He tried with every trick he'd learned in eight years of bloody fighting, and Sato soon learned why the fight kept on despite the battering he was delivering to Montana. The son of a bitch hardly felt pain. He was bleeding from the bite on his leg and from where terrible punches had split open the skin on his forehead and his nose, he had a smashed lip, and still he grinned and fought. Jesus, this had to *end*.

Sato got a wristlock, spun the arm and twisted around and went high into the air, coming down in a devastating arm bar. There was no bend left in the arm, and they both heard it break. Montana roared with the pain. Sato measured himself and broke Montana's nose. The blood choked him, stopped his breathing. He gagged for air, and their eyes met, and they shared the unspoken agreement for Sato not to punish that broken arm anymore. Sato did the job as mercifully as he could. A handful of hair to jerk the other man off-balance and a crashing fist to the side of the head. Montana fell unconscious.

Sato climbed to his feet, again spattered with blood, and he walked about the ring slowly, holding up both arms in a visible signal of victory. He gestured for silence. He was magnetic, majestic, a great fighting pit bull standing on two legs. "I fight anybody!" he bellowed. *"Anybody!"*

He went through the ropes and walked up to a shocked Mike Rawlins. He towered over him, his body streaming sweat and blood and literally steaming. The package was extended slowly, and he took it, bowed slightly, and began running slowly, faster and faster, his head lowered, away from where he'd left his sweat suit. He smashed through closed exit doors as if they were paper and kept running, disappearing in the darkness, twisting and turning and taking a circuitous route to the waiting car. He yanked open the back door, grabbed the keys, went in behind the driver's seat, and was gone in a blur of smoking tires.

Two hours later, car changes and shifts behind him, he pulled up to another motel. Lance Parker climbed out stiffly, limping more than usual, and disappeared into his room. The electrified security and alarm system was already set up. Lance brought the shotgun into the bathroom and started his tub. Waiting for the water to fill the tub, he sank into an armchair and opened the package from Rawlins.

His face went rigid. Two thousand dollars. Lance felt his jaw tighten as he opened a scrawled note:

"If you take Montana tonight, then tomorrow

*night you get eight grand. Fair's fair. Call me at noon
sharp."*

Lance had no intention of waiting until the next
day. He picked up the phone.

"I figured I could count on your call," Rawlins
told him.

"I figured you wrong," Lance countered. "Especially for a welsher."

"That's bullshit, Parker. We both gotta protect our
asses. You got the eight thou locked up for tomorrow
night. If you don't believe me, all you gotta do is
check the papers tomorrow. Full-page ads. The works,
and we doubled the price for the seats, and already
we're sold out every night the next four nights. So it's
a two-way street. I got your eight grand, and you got
me by the shorts if you don't show." A pregnant
pause followed, and Rawlins rushed to fill the gap.
"Your boy *is* gonna show, ain't he?"

"I'm not so sure I can count on your word,
Rawlins."

"Jesus Christ, Parker, look at the fucking facts!"
Rawlins was shouting into the phone. "We're adding
another thousand seats in the damn arena, and nine
thousand screaming assholes will be out there paying
double for their tickets. We even got prime time for
that boob tube. You were right. The mystery Jap
pulls 'em in, but just so long as he keeps winning, understand? So why should I crap you? You ain't no
dummy. Two and two is four. So it's a deal, right?"

Lance dealt a new hand. "You can raise your prices
again. Tomorrow night we play doubles. That's why
I'm calling you tonight. You have time to change the
newspaper and television promotion."

"Doubles?"

"*Uh-huh*. You pay me three thousand you still owe
me and ten thousand for tomorrow night's work."

"You creep, I wondered when you'd jack up the ante," Rawlins said scathingly. "We made a deal, remember? Five thou and—"

"Jesus, just listen. I don't break deals," Lance said coldly. "You advertise that Sato will be taking on two men and all by his lonesome. He'll—"

"That's old-hat, Parker. You got one good man in a tag team match. What's the big deal? All he has to do is wax one of my people, and he's standing there with his big paw out for ten grand. No way. We stick to the rules we made."

"There's an old saw, Rawlins. Engage brain before putting mouth in motion. Will you just shut up and listen?"

"Okay, I'm listening."

"Sato takes on both men at the same time. He's got to beat them both. He has to be the only man standing when it's over."

A pregnant pause followed his words. "Even you, Parker, know better than that," Rawlins said slowly. "I bring in some rough people, your boy may get killed."

"One way to find out," Lance said quietly.

"You're serious?"

"I am. So let's fish or cut bait. Do we have a match tomorrow night? Two men in the ring against Sato and thirteen thousand on the line."

"Okay, it's on."

"Two more things. There will be guards with Sato. Bonded. You be sure to make the payment like before, and no fun and games, or they'll arrest you on the spot."

"Are you threatening me, you son of a bitch!"

"No. I want you to keep one thing in your head. There's a fortune out there if we play this together, and I got other people under contract. I also have an idea for tomorrow night that ought to flip that crowd on its ear. But I need you to set it up for me."

"I'm listening."

When Lance hung up, he was smiling. If he could get through the double cross he knew was on Rawlins's mind, it would be a good night's work. He picked up the telephone book and thumbed the Yellow Pages for private security services.

Everything was reduced to timing. He had to move along a set schedule of events and let nothing interfere with his movements. He parked his rental car in downtown Atlanta and waited by a bus stop. Not the nicest place in the world in the dark hours, and the form of Shigura Sato smiled as he saw the shadows moving in nearby doorways. No doubt they were considering whether that hulking shape was worth an attempted mugging. But he remained alone until the armored car pulled up to the stop. They drove steadily to the sports arena.

Sato left the vehicle at a back entrance to the building. "Take it around front, and wait for me there," he instructed the driver. Then to the four guards: "You know what to do. Three minutes before ten o'clock you four start down the aisle to the ring. Got it?"

"Yes, sir. We'll be there."

Sato went into the service entrance. No one around. He ran up four flights of stairs and went through a door that led to a catwalk running the length of the arena. The catwalk serviced lights and loudspeakers and crossed directly over the ring itself. Sato looked down on the sea of faces. Every seat was packed, and people were standing along the walls. Directly below him the only man in the ring was the referee, but at that same moment the crowd broke into a roaring thunder of shouted voices. Two men, very large in size and bulk, even from this distance and angle, were walking slowly from the dressing room to the ring.

Sato looked for the rope. It was there. By damn, Rawlins had kept his word. He'd prepared the heavy rope just as he'd been asked, coiled neatly on the catwalk. Sato squatted and studied the rope very carefully. Good, it would hold at least a thousand pounds without being strained. But he *still* didn't trust Rawlins, who had to be under heavy fire from his wrestlers to lower the boom on this unknown and obviously lethal Shigura Sato.

Sato stretched out his hand to grasp the line just short of where it hooked to a steel beam. He tugged slowly and steadily, and his eyes widened as the hook-and-eye began to bend.

That son of a bitch . . . I would have fallen forty feet straight down to that ring . . . and those two thugs just waiting for me to hit so they could swarm all over me and finish the job. Rawlins, you just better kiss your ass good-bye. . . .

A fine, cold rage stayed with him as he released the hook-and-eye and secured the rope to another beam. He tugged tightly, nodded with satisfaction, then looked below. Both wrestlers were watching the aisle, waiting for his usual appearance as if they knew nothing of the rope. They wouldn't bother to turn until they felt and heard his body crash helplessly into the mat.

Shigura Sato dropped the rope to ring center and without a moment's hesitation was off the catwalk and dropping down. No careful descent here. No worry about the skin burns as the ManFac hands scraped down the rope. He landed with a thundering crash. Two men turned to face the helpless man they were expecting—and had no time to react as an enraged Japanese charged them with murder in his eyes.

Sato struck the first man, a large bearded wrestler with red hair, square in his forehead with his right fist. Instantly his left hand gripped a fistful of red hair to jerk the man forward and down, and then Sato had him in both hands, one gripping his hair and the other squeezing his neck, and Sato placed his mouth over the wrestler's ear and roared. The ManFac-amplified sound tore through the man's body, tore ear tissues, and ruptured the eardrum. The wrestler staggered in a semicircle as he cupped his hands to his ear, trying to stem the flow of blood and yellow fluid. Sato moved to his side with unexpected speed, grasped hair again, and threw the man from the ring. He fell heavily to concrete, still holding his ear.

Sato turned and saw five hundred pounds of trouble coming straight at him. Rawlins's trump card. A sumo wrestler from Japan, one of those giants with flab covering his body and steel muscles beneath. A man who had wrestled and trained from the first days he could walk. He had matched his decades of experience with grappling styles for his new audience, and he was a mixture of rhino mass and ballet dexterity.

I've got to take him fast, or I'm in trouble. Don't wrestle this man, and don't let him wrestle you. Cripple him. NOW.

The great Buddha-like figure moved with measured speed toward him, arms outstretched but lower than the usual wrestler's reach. Sato waited until the last possible moment and stepped *into* those arms, aimed carefully, and drove a steel-booted toe as hard as he could kick into the left kneecap of his opponent. It was quick, dirty, and, most of all, effective; the kneecap cracked like a walnut shell struck with a hammer. Sato had an overwhelming sense of danger, an almost frantic need to get this over with at once, and the danger wasn't from within these four ropes but outside.

The great sumo wrestler's leg collapsed beneath him, and Sato spun around behind the other man and brought both ManFac hands together in a devastating double blow against his ears. The air pressure alone was enough to render the man dizzy. For a long and precious moment the wrestler remained where he was, one knee to the mat, striving to regain his footing to face his enemy. Sato gave him no chance. He came in again, both hands wide from his body, thumbs stiffened like small clubs, and brought them together into each side of the man's neck. He collapsed and fell backward slowly.

Make it look good, and when it's over you'd better move it, friend. Lance acknowledged his inner voice; the ManFac body went high into the air and came down with thundering force, elbow across the exposed throat. Five hundred pounds twitched helplessly beneath him. Sato looked up at the stunned referee. "Count 'em, you bastard!" he roared.

Goldsboro hesitated only a moment, then dropped down, and his hand slammed the mat three times. The crowd roar was insane. Sato was on his feet immediately. He went to the ringside, where he saw a white-faced Rawlins staring up at him. Too many big bodies all about Rawlins for this not to be a setup. Sato grasped the top rope and tore it in half. Rawlins's eyes widened with sudden fear. Sato stepped over the lower ropes and dropped heavily to the floor directly before Rawlins, one ManFac foot crashing onto Rawlins's shoe. He couldn't cry out as the breath burst from him. Sato's hand shot out and yanked the package from Rawlins's frozen hands. Then Sato spun about and ran heavily along the first aisle, brushing aside spectators and guards like wobbly tenpins.

Whatever you do, don't stop, baby. Keep it moving. He nodded to himself as he ran. They'd expect him to go straight for the armored car, and he knew they'd bushwhack him before he reached it. Instead, he ran along the aisle to an emergency fire exit, crashed like a maddened buffalo through the doors into the night air. He ran with feet thundering into the ground into the parking lot, where his rental car was waiting. He roared off, turned away from the exit, and bounced onto a grassy area, the car skidding and fishtailing as he kept the accelerator down. He made it to the service road, forced himself to reduce his speed to the legal limit, took the first road that ran off into an industrial park, and rolled toward the interstate ramp. The rental car vanished within the streams of headlights as he drove into Atlanta.

He eased into the parking lot of a motel, switched to another rental car he'd left there for this purpose, and was gone again, taking turns through a housing development. No one could have followed him now without becoming obvious about the move. He returned to the interstate, cut off two exits later, and drove into the garage where the truck was parked safely. He parked a floor lower, walked up the ramp to the truck, and disappeared inside. He had paid the parking fee for a month ahead of time, and the attendants paid little attention to the truck coming and going.

Thirty minutes after he entered the truck, Otto Heller was in the driver's seat and rolling carefully down the winding ramp to street level. Seven blocks later the truck was on the interstate again. Shigura Sato and Sven Andersen were locked securely within their servicing compartments.

Twenty minutes later Otto Heller, dressed comfortably in slacks and a Windbreaker, was on the open road and heading for Florida.

Grinning like a kid who'd stolen the cookies, jar and all.

BOOK FOUR

Chapter 23

Cash was the lubricant required by Lance to slide through the social and business structure and still leave the least possible turbulence in the wake of his passing. He could pay for fuel, food, motels, clothing, and all his basic essentials, and he would be free of finger-pointing records. No credit cards and no checks—and no one to report on a powerful German driving a truck.

Until he rolled out of Atlanta, Otto Heller had never existed, and Rawlins's legions would have no place to search for a man of whose existence they were unaware. There was no question but that they were beating the bushes in search of Shigura Sato. There had been too much mystery surrounding the enigmatic and impossibly strong Japanese who had devastated every opponent brought up against him— and vanished as inexplicably as he had appeared. Let them look, and let Rawlins shout his innocence, even as he cursed the heavy cast on his foot.

Otto Heller took his own sweet time. No long driving sessions. His inner self had borne too many aches and bruises to accept the punishment of long drives.

He selected his motels carefully, assured both isolation and comfort, barricaded himself behind his electrified defenses and shotgun, and gave Lance Parker the freedom of mind, and the time, to soak in hot tubs and keep kneading oil into raw skin.

He had time to rest and regain his strength, and he had time again to think. He had ripped $20,000 from the grasp of Rawlins, and after expenses he still had just over $17,000 in cash. Not too bad for a few days' work by a scarred cripple, he decided with an acceptable touch of humor. And $17,000 could last him a very long time indeed if he remained with the essentials and didn't go off half-cocked. The problem was that he still didn't know where to go or what to do. The immediate future ended every day when the sun went down. He couldn't just keep on running, even if he did so at a leisurely pace and without financial pressure. He had to find his vision beyond each sunset, and he was plagued constantly by his own impatience in seeking solutions. Jesus, he hadn't even defined the problems and he was scrabbling about in his mind for answers.

He needed definition, purpose, meaning, a challenge, a goal. He had to be going *somewhere.* In mind as well as in body. Before him, well down that wide span of ribboned concrete, lay the sprawling peninsula of Florida, small towns and large cities and every manner of country from rolling hills to seacoasts and citrus country and farmland and—well, a lot of space in between. He could lose himself in the cities and—

Don't be such an ass. You could lose yourself in any city.

He raised an eyebrow to that inner voice and felt chagrined at this relentless demand on his own self-discipline. But, he sighed, it was true enough. Any conversation on "losing himself" in any area was just another cop-out, his refusal to wrest a solution to life itself from whatever problems he accepted were uniquely his.

So are the advantages. . . .

Right.

And you really ought to consider the alternatives, you know.

Shut up. I know.

Well, there was always the squared circle, the grunt-and-groan routine. He'd left no doubts about his abilities there and— He turned off that song with a touch of self-contempt. You didn't work the wrestling circuit unless you worked *with* the system, period. And the first time they even suspected he was more than he appeared to be on sight, they would react the way all human beings react to a creature superior to them, especially one with that Frankenstein touch. A fine madness that permeates all thinking of everyone involved: Destroy the creature. History bulged with such incidents, and the burning alive of witches was still an element of fairly *recent* history.

So to any well-structured organization, if he intruded so violently that he assumed immediately the position of top dog, he must be eliminated. That phrase—"carefully structured society"—stuck in his mental craw. Perhaps that was the key he sought. He didn't need to be a member of the nameless and faceless herd. He'd never been that before. He was always something special. He'd made himself better than most. Talent, skill, discipline, learning, sweat—he knew and exercised the necessary ingredients. But one salmon racing downstream while the horde follows blind instinct in its struggle upstream is glaringly visible. That was the last thing he needed to be.

Time, peace, a quiet resolution of torments still in his mind. Ah, that was a neat and simple delay to the final answer. He needed the Ponce de Leon refuge where he could think instead of scheming and remaining animal-alert just to get through every day. And he needed to exercise his mind and translate what went on between his ears into something useful, practical, or whatever—so long as it produced meaningful results. The ManFac system, he reminded himself again, as he had a hundred times, no matter how great the miracles wrought by Lee—God, how he missed her—had vast possibilities for improvement. And he must never lose sight of the fact that he was now more than a thinker and a tinkerer and an engineer. He *was* ManFac, and he was able to comprehend what could never have been fathomed without his total commitment to this system.

He glanced at the road signs along Interstate 75. His face took on a puzzled look. Something was tugging at his mind. He tried to turn off his thinking, release whatever was that subconscious urge to step forward in his head. And then the spark ignited. *Alachua County.* The rest of it tumbled into place swiftly. He needn't be a stranger here. Because in Alachua County there was the city of Gainesville, and that in turn meant the University of Florida, and that led to— Of course! He snapped mental fingers as memory rushed through him.

Dirk Martin, and his wife, Deidre. *They* lived in Gainesville. If there was one man whom Lance called closest friend—even if, he admitted wryly, he had hardly kept in touch over the past few years—it was Dirk. Little matter their long absence of contact. They'd gone to college together, had worked and crammed together, had majored in engineering and played football and wrestled and won gold cups of all kinds, and, as a postgraduate prize to themselves, had spent their first year out of college journeying about the world on tramp steamers and trains and motorcycles and in the process had cemented their deep feeling that few men ever really come to know. Lance searched his memory. Dirk for the past several years had been a professor of engineering at the university, and, and—that was it. They'd designed and built their own home and laboratory for special projects, all on a large section of land in the forested hills of north-west Gainesville. He recalled the pictures they'd sent so proudly of the magnificent cubed home engineering shop and office. And Dirk didn't strain for payments, for he had created several engineering patents that paid him very well indeed, and on a continuing royalty basis. He earned a steady $400,000 a year in a quiet manner unknown to his contemporaries, who "assumed," as the overly curious are apt to do, that Deidre was an heiress and Dirk a lucky son of a bitch.

If Lance could go safely, and openly, to any two people in this world, then it would be Dirk and Deidre. He eased off the highway at the first rest stop, waited impatiently for a telephone, and called information to get their number. Before he dialed, he had a long self-searching moment with himself. Suddenly he was overwhelmed with that dark desire to remain away from the mainstream of life, to—

To hide in a closet. Grow up, Parker.

He soundly cursed his inner self—and dialed the number.

He had to do it. There simply wasn't any other way he'd walk into their lives. It was time to put ManFac to rest. They expected Lance Parker, and that, by God, was the only way he'd meet them face to face. They were wildly excited with the sound of his voice, and he fought down sudden overwhelming emotion.

"By damn," Dirk shouted into the phone, "all this time we thought you were dead!"

Lance grinned to himself. "You know the old story about my death reports being slightly exaggerated,"

275

he said lightly. "I'm sort of bent out of shape but still ticking."

"Where are you? *How* are you? Are we going to see you?" The questions poured from Dirk. "Jesus, Lance, let's not let this chance get by. It's been too long and—"

"Whoa, boy," Lance broke in. "I was hoping for the invitation and—"

"When the hell did you ever need an invitation?" Lance heard Dirk shouting to his wife. "Deidre! It's Lance!" A shriek could be heard in the background, and there was a babble of voices until Dirk hushed his wife. "Lance, where are you?"

"About twenty miles north of Gainesville on the interstate."

"You're *here*? Goddammit, we won't take no for an answer, Lance. Let me give you directions. You continue south on I-75 until you—"

"Hold it, Dirk. Let me say something first." His tone stopped the start of directions. "How much do you know about what happened to me?"

Dirk paused. Lance heard him letting out his breath before his friend answered. "We know, Lance. The way your body was crushed, the radiation. All of it. Like I said, we thought you were *dead*. How could you have let us believe that?"

"We can go into that later."

"Then you're coming, right?"

"Hold on, Dirk. I've got to say something first. You can handle it pretty well, but it may be rough on Deidre. I don't look anything like the man you know. I was chewed up pretty bad. There are a lot of scars. I can't walk without a cane. My face looks like a bulldozer ran over it and then backed up again. I—"

"So what?"

The intrusion stopped Lance cold. *So what?* Was

that all there was to it? Couldn't he convince him that—

"Lance, I'm on the extension. Not one word of what you said means a thing to us," Deidre said quietly. "Will you just end this nonsense and let Dirk tell you how to get to us?"

"Well—"

"Lance, listen to me," Dirk said with sudden urgency. "You said you can't walk without a cane and you're chewed up. But I *know* you better than anyone else except for, well, except for Lee. And you sound just like the asshole I knew in college. Will you, for Christ's sake, knock off the crap? Just take down the instructions, please?"

Lance dropped his shield. "All right. Thanks. Go ahead."

He wrote it down. Thirty minutes away at the most to plunge back into a life of people who knew him before, well—

Shut up and move it.

Yeah, yeah, he muttered to himself. He returned to the truck, started the engine, but sat without shifting into gear. That decision filled him. He shut off the engine and climbed through the hatchway into the back of the truck. He removed the ManFac of Otto Heller, cleaned off his body, and slipped into jeans and a sweat shirt. Back in the cab he started up and began rolling onto the highway. It was a hell of a lot tougher driving as Lance Parker, and he had a few fitful moments with that twisted leg beneath him. *Screw it,* he snarled to himself. *If I want to do it, I can.*

And he could, and he did. He hadn't realized just how much stronger he had become. Only then did he realize the strengthening of his own body from operating within the Manfac system. The Manfac did nothing without the physical input of the intent and the *body* of Lance Parker. It was a hell of a lot more complicated than simply thinking a facsimile limb into movement. The motivating factor was and had always been himself. To move a ManFac arm, he first had to move his own arm. To move a ManFac arm up and down three hundred times, he had to move his own arm up and down three hundred times. His own nervous system initiated the activity, his muscle system had to bring it to life.

Every time he functioned within the facsimile system he was going through a complete calisthenics and physical training program.

He marveled at the way his own body adapted so swiftly to driving the truck, and then he laughed aloud. *He was still within a Man Facsimile system!* When he turned the wheel, he operated the main wheels through a power-boosted servomechanism, the fancy name for power steering. When he applied pressure against the brake pedal, the same chain of events took place—he was simply sending a signal to a sensor that translated the signal into a power-boosted force to operate the brakes. In its crudest sense the truck *was* a system adapted to his body outputs, and it didn't matter whether he was a frail little old lady of eighty pounds or a hulking bruiser of three hundred pounds.

But he still had to make the input himself. He remembered his earlier days in the hospital when the biggest thing in his life was other people trying just to keep him alive. People moving his arms and his legs for him, up and down and forward and backward, and bend this way and that way. People moving his limbs because he was unable to do so on his own. And what was that process for regaining strength? They moved his limbs, and the very act of moving those limbs strengthened muscles and sinew and tendons and ligaments and nerves and blood vessels and bone and—

He'd been functioning within the concept of the ManFac system long before he'd ever seen or even heard of it from Lee Grazzi. The conclusions flowing through his mind were thundering revelations, for they freed him from the conviction that without the ManFac he was just a cripple.

You're never "just" anything, mister. You're what you want to be.

Man, was that ever the truth!

Another memory crawled up into his mind's center stage.

He'd been overwhelmed with the television films of the *Six Million Dollar Man*. Seeing the bionic man running at sixty miles an hour had inspired him to modify a ManFac with his own innovations. He'd increased the operating speed, the gearing system, of the ManFac legs, so they would operate many times faster than his own legs could. Observed only by Lee, recording everything with a video camera, he'd started out for his superhuman dash.

He had run at the same speed he had always been able to run. He couldn't get up an extra ounce of speed. Perplexed, he had jogged along hard ground, then run as fast as he could move in a sprint, straining his muscles, sweat pouring from him. It hadn't worked.

He had studied the video films. He was doing everything properly, leaning into the run as he had done when he ran track in college, but the effort produced no additional speed. And then he understood. The powered system would run just as fast and not one whit faster than his own legs moved because the ManFac was *responding* to his own output.

He had looked up at Lee, who was trying to hide a

smile. "Okay, it beat me this time," he told her, "but there's another way."

"How?"

"I'll run a gearing system through the leg motors. A power boost system. My output will be sensed by the ManFac system and increased by a factor of, let's say, three times normal. If I run at a certain speed, the ManFac will run three times faster. Ergo, *I'll* run three times faster."

"Won't work," she said matter-of-factly.

"Why the hell not?" he had snapped.

"You'll see. You're thinking in terms of mechanical engineering, but you're forgetting the restrictions of human engineering."

"You sound like a monk sitting on a mountain. Black is white and the sun is square if your eyes are crooked."

She laughed. "Go ahead and try. It's the best lesson."

He had slipped back into the ManFac and started running. Same old thing as he pounded along. Then he pressed the power button that would triple the speed of his legs. He felt the enormous power feeding back through increased movement, and for that moment he felt like a god with superpowers. But only for that moment. Suddenly he couldn't keep leaning into the run, his chest began to follow instead of leading the legs, and the legs churned madly against the ground, and his balance vanished in wide-eyed frustration, and he sped along the ground like a drunk weaving on a rickety bicycle at superspeed, ending up with a horrendous crash on his back while his legs pumped madly. Soon it wasn't funny as cramps seized his limbs and pain shot through him. In desperation he hit the power button and came back to reality.

Lee had been hysterical. Really hysterical with tears of laughter running down her face. She could hardly talk. His face was dark and mood even darker as he sat in the projection room to study the video films, but very soon he was laughing with her. It was completely ludicrous, a scene out of vaudeville and the Keystone Kops. His legs had run away *from* him. He had had no control. As well be a helpless passenger without control on a runaway motorcycle. "Do you understand now?" Lee had finally asked. "Did you ever see a grown man shaking the hand of a child and pumping the hand vigorously, through a full movement of up and down? The child is helpless. He can't keep up with the movement. He can't coordinate with that movement, and very quickly his muscles are cramping, and he gets a charley horse, and the pain becomes severe. That's what happened to you. Since your own legs can't function at three times normal speed, you can't run at three times normal speed. There can be a slight increase, but that's all. Let me put it another way. Any good track man will run away from you, but there isn't a man anywhere of your size and bulk and weight who could hold a candle to the way you, as ManFac, can run. And as an afterthought, remember the way you leaned into your running? That was *wrong*. It's okay for starting out, just the way track stars do, but what happens when they're on their way around the track? The head goes high and is held back and—"

"Spare me the sordid details," he broke in. "One comedy routine a night is enough for me."

"It's been worth it," she concluded. "You have an understanding of how to use the advantages of ManFac without trying to find something that isn't there and never will be there. Never forget that even if you worked out the balance and the rest of it, running at three times your fastest human speed would tear your own muscles and body systems into knotted cramps in seconds. I'll tell you something else."

He had looked at her and waited. "Don't you understand that if there had never been that accident, the same rules would apply? You couldn't really run that much faster if you were a perfect physical specimen in the ManFac?"

The words had sobered him but at the same time permitted him to distinguish the true advantages. Such as climbing straight up a thick rope. His own muscles would let him climb for only so long a time and distance before his body began to yield to strain and energy drain. The ManFac would let him climb with very little effort for hours. As he moved his arm, the ManFac would respond with a dozen times his own strength. When he grasped the rope, he needed only to grasp it without straining. A tenfold increase in squeezing power would keep him locked safely wherever he was. A 320-pound human fly.

So there were the advantages and the disadvantages. And now, driving south on I-75 to the waiting Dirk and Deidre, he had found another advantage to *not* being ManFac.

When he wasn't—he was himself.

He took the turns slowly, amazed at the thick forest growth and hills in the midst of a Florida city. Northwest Gainesville had retained its wilderness with fiercely aggressive laws prohibiting the destruction of trees and other growth. He might have been in far forest country of the hilly Carolinas. He eased up and down short, steep grades, crossed thick-beamed bridges, followed directions through a maze of lanes and courts and terraces and avenues, and turned onto the road that led three blocks farther to the Martin home. He drove two blocks, eased the truck to a stop beneath a large overhanging tree, and immediately turned off the truck lights and engine. In the darkness he sat quietly, studying the unmistakable cubed shape of the house and the workshop—and a half dozen sheriff's and police cars. He remained frozen, watching, and finally spotted what he had expected: two more cars, unmarked, but with unmistakable police radio aerials.

What in hell was going on here? Suspicions flitted darkly through his mind, but as quickly as they did, he dismissed them. Screw that kind of thinking. If ever he was going to trust anyone in this world in addition to Lee, it had to be Dirk and Deidre. He started up the truck and drove slowly the last block, past the police cars, and turned into the second driveway leading to a wide garage. As he made the turn, he saw several officers returning to their vehicles. One deputy looked at the truck as Lance parked. The deputy waved and continued walking. *So whatever they're doing here has nothing to do with me.* Relief flooded him. He'd had some bad moments, ideas ghosting through his head that perhaps one of those wrestlers in Atlanta had died and they had a search out for him and—

He turned it all off, climbed down from the truck. The night air was a heady tonic, filled with the smells of the woodland all about him. He waited several minutes as the cars left, and then he walked slowly, savoring every step, along a brick walk leading to the front of the house. Dirk and Deidre had seen the truck, had heard his footsteps, and were waiting for him. He stood before them, leaning on the cane, wary of their reaction. A long, long moment passed as they took in one another, and before he could prepare himself for the movement, Deidre threw her arms about him. Her loving greeting turned into mild pandemonium as Dirk wrapped strong arms about them both in a fierce bear hug. They all talked at once, hearing everything and remembering nothing, and finally, they separated, their eyes bright, Deidre's wet and sparkling.

"Well, do I get invited in?" Lance asked, smiling.

"The house, our home, is yours," Dirk said. But he was, well, hesitating, Lance noticed. He refused his own speculations and waited. "I've got to be level with you first. Nothing hidden, all right?"

Lance nodded.

"We knew what to expect," Dirk said. "I mean, the cane, all the things that happened to you, the accident and the surgery and all the rest of it. After we spoke with you, well, dammit, Lance, we just couldn't help it. We called Lee. I have to tell you that. We didn't know you hadn't been in touch with her, and it looks like we stuck our noses in where—"

Lance gestured quickly to stop his friend's words. "No, no," he said, his voice strangely hoarse. "You were right." He had to force himself to speak. "How . . . how is she?"

"In love with you. Lonely. But not, as we had thought, worried."

Lance looked up sharply. "Not . . . worried?"

"No. She said you had the best company in the world with you. I don't know what that means, but you"—he looked long into Lance's face—"don't seem surprised. Oh, yes, she also said she loves you more than life itself, and you're not to call until you're ready." He grinned. "I've got a hunch that won't be too long. Dammit, we all talk too much. Come on in, Lance."

He walked in slowly, and his eyes were wet, and for a while he really never did see that incredible home and its stunning design or, for that matter, anything else. He sat on the couch and did something he hadn't done since he was a kid.

Holding nothing back, face buried in his hands, he wept like a child.

And discovered he was now truly free. His last fears were gone.

Chapter 24

The Martins set up Lance in a wing of their extraordinary home, a bedroom suite on the second floor along with a masterful bath creation—a huge stepped wooden tub of thick planking and a concealed whirlpool Jacuzzi. He soaked in the tub, groaned with the pleasure of the water jets against his improved but still sore muscles, then carefully kneaded oil into his skin afterward. A great king-size bed with a softly glowing overhead canopy lured him with silken sheets, and Lance, spread-eagled on the silk, soothed by the sounds of surf from speakers within the bed, fell into a deep sleep. He awoke nearly two hours later, incredibly refreshed. He shaved and dressed and went slowly downstairs to join his hosts.

"It's like dying and waking up where you've always wanted to be" was his description of the guest facilities. "I'd forgotten what a luxury-loving son of a bitch you always were," he told Dirk, and his friend laughed.

"I'll take the credit for the electronics and other goodies," Dirk said, "but when it comes to the pure essence of luxury and comfort, you talk to my girl here. I built the tub; she added the Jacuzzi. I thought of music in the bed; she added a whole selection of nature sounds."

"Those sheets?" asked Lance. "Real silk?"

"Made to order in India," Deidre said. Lance looked at her as if never seeing her before. If there could be an opposite to Lee Grazzi, then it was Deidre Martin. Long blond hair, an athletic body, a dazzling artist. Golden Girl. And a real, meaningful, productive working brain between those lovely ears.

"Well, how about some dinner made to order?" Dirk prompted his wife.

Deidre nodded assent. "We have a cook, by the way. A magnificent Japanese cook. You know how Dirk is about Japanese food."

"We used to call him the Sukiyaki Slasher," Lance recalled. "He would stuff himself to where buttons would pop."

"Chieko's not here tonight. *This* evening," Deidre said firmly, "is our pleasure. *We* do the cooking for you."

Charbroiled steak over an open grill and crisp salad and unbelievable silver corn and garlic bread and deep red wine. Coffee and pimento brandy afterward with Lance sprawled in a body-enveloping armchair, touching off the wonder of it all with a long, thin cigar. Dinner's conversation had been of the old days, of college and their global adventuring, of Lee and Deidre, and then, abruptly, with smoothly shifting mental gears they were back to the present.

"You've always been high on my list for self-control," Dirk said without preamble, "but this time you've outdone yourself."

"How come?" Lance asked. He was still floating on his cloud of comfort.

"What Lee said on the phone. About your being in good company. You drove up in a truck. I looked at it," Dirk told him, "when you were asleep. Steel locking systems for the back doors and the entry from the cab. Very neat and very workable. So"—he shrugged—"I put together a whole bunch of twos and twos. There's no one else in there, you need volume for it, you're an engineer, and we all know how brilliant Lee is with automated human engineering systems and—"

"ManFac," Lance said abruptly. "Stands for Man Facsimile."

"ManFac," Dirk repeated. "That's all we get?"

Lance studied his friend. "How much do you want?"

Dirk laughed and turned to his wife. "I told you. Never play chess with him." He came back to Lance. "Until *you* open up what's in that truck, we don't go near it. In fact, while you were upstairs, we cleared out the garage. It's for the truck."

"I appreciate that," Lance said. "Is the garage by your workshop?"

"Door goes from the garage right into it. Any special reason?"

Lance nodded. "I don't want to impose—" He let it hang.

"However, you're going to." Dirk laughed. "I'll make it easier. We have nothing special going on at the moment. Just some tinkering. If you need privacy for the workshop, you've got it."

"*That* means everything to me. For right now," Lance added hastily. "I'm not trying to keep something secret from you. Please understand that. It's well, timing. The long and short of it is, Dirk, I'll probably be asking for your help on a couple of things."

Dirk gestured easily in agreement. "Just holler."

"I will. Now maybe you can tell me something."

"Shoot."

"What was all that fuzz about? When I got here, I mean. You had local police and sheriff's cars and even some unmarked jobs all around the place. It was like a policeman's ball out there."

Dirk lost his touch of light exchange. His mood sobered enough to bring on a deep frown. "It's far from being a ball. In fact, it's damned serious business. It's closer to a wake than a party." Dirk took a long drink of his brandy, held the glass in both hands, and studied the dark liquid as he spoke. "They came to see me because of my engineering background. The truth is that they're checking with every teacher, engineer, professor, technician—anyone who fits into that general category—who might shed some light on the matter. They—"

"Hold it, hold it," Lance broke in gently. "You've lost me, fella. I haven't any idea of what you're talking about."

"Oh. Of course. Sorry, Lance. It's being kept under wraps because . . ." His voice trailed away, and he looked at Lance as if seeing him for the first time. Dirk and Deidre exchanged glances, and Deidre nodded. "Yes, hon, I'm thinking the same thing. They didn't speak to the right man."

Lance leaned back and gestured helplessly. "Right man? Me? What about?"

Dirk leaned forward, his intensity heightened. "I can break the silence with you because our problem is right up your alley. In short, Lance, and please consider this confidential . . ." He waited until Lance nodded and gestured again for him to continue. "Well, we have a major nuclear reactor research program here at the university. Not in terms of producing energy on the scale of a commercial reactor. Nothing like those breeders or fast-fission systems with which you've worked. What we've been trying to do is to develop field generators, essentially portable units, that use the waste material from the bigger reactors."

Lance felt his interest piqued. "I know what you mean. Like the systems the astronauts left on the moon to work the remote stations. In fact, they've been working since the early seventies, and very well indeed, I might note."

"Precisely," Dirk confirmed. "We've been developing systems that use the highest-quality waste material. You know, there's enough radioactive decay in that material to be converted to electrical power for limited areas. Since we're using straight radioactivity, we're not producing something that's nuclear. The radioactivity is there. If we put a converter system between the radioactive materials and the shielding, well, one unit would be enough to provide all the stationary power requirements for, *um,* let's say, a very large farm. It would attend to lights, heating and cooling, pumping systems, that sort of thing."

"Are you going for straight conversion to electricity? Or photovoltaic systems? Or heat conversion? Or—"

Dirk held up his hand in surrender, laughing. "We're testing them *all.* That's the whole idea. We don't know what's best, what's most efficient, what's safest, what's the best combination. Someone is even working on a powerful electromagnetic field to curve the radioactive emissions in a force field, which could either generate heat for steam or convert directly to electrical current. You of all people can recognize what this would mean. It would be a tremendous breakthrough. First, it allows us to make good use of the radioactive by-products of the main energy plants, instead of just storing the stuff. Second, it could give us hundreds—no, make that thousands—of well-shielded portable plants that don't have plumbing or complicated systems of any kind beyond the immediate generator. All safely portable, I should emphasize. In other words, we'd be able to place these generators in remote areas where, right now, there's nothing at all except gasoline-fed generators with all their problems of maintenance, power output, and especially delivery and storage of large amounts of fuel. We—"

"I've got the picture," Lance broke in. "So what's the business with the law?"

Dirk's expression was clearly one of pain, and Deidre found the moment perfect for examining her nails. Dirk sighed. "You're not going to believe this, but"—he shrugged—"here goes. We had some six hundred pounds of radioactive materials here. Some of it was considerably purer than the bulk of the stuff, and there was at least two hundred pounds of some pretty high-grade—"

"What the hell do you mean, you *had*? That's past tense."

Dirk seemed to flinch. "You called it. *Had*."

"You mean it's *gone*?"

"Like the wind," Deidre broke in.

"Let me finish your scenario," Lance said. Of a sudden he was back in home field, set smack in the middle of what he had done for years. "You said high-grade. If I know the systems you're messing with you people requested the highest quality possible in two thirty-nine."

Dirk looked like a basset hound. "*Uh*, right."

"Plutonium," Lance said softly. "You had two hundred pounds of plutonium, *and it's gone*?"

"*Uh-huh*."

"I don't know what the hell to say." Lance's face showed his shock. "Do you realize what this could mean?"

Deidre was waving for attention. "Someone please tell *me* what it means!"

"Angel," Lance said in a soft and disturbing voice,

"it's not that hard to figure. Given the right engineering knowledge, which any really good engineering students certainly have, that's enough stuff, even if you're sloppy, to put together at least two or maybe even three old-fashioned, clumsy, dirty *atomic bombs.*"

Deidre turned white. "You can't be serious, Lance." Her hand had flown to her throat. "Please tell me you're not serious."

"Oh, I'm serious, all right, and—" Lance broke into his own conversation and stared at Dirk, who in turn was now bolt upright in his seat, staring wide-eyed at Lance. "What the hell's the matter with you?" Lance asked.

"You just said . . ." Dirk was gesturing frantically, trying to put together the words tumbling from his mouth. *"Lance, how do you know who stole that plutonium?"*

Chapter 25

"It doesn't take a genius to figure that out," Lance replied, disclaiming any crystal ball powers. "It's got to be the students. A process of knowing the system and then a process of elimination, I suppose."

"Just like that, huh?" Dirk threw at him.

"I'm sorry to blow away all the mystery, but yes," Lance said, "just like that."

"I wish the police were here," Dirk murmured. "Don't quit now, for God's sake."

Lance took the moment to finish his brandy and relight his cigar. He shifted to a more comfortable position in the chair. "Look, like most universities, you've got a pretty heavy contingent of students from the Middle East, right? And that includes many from the Arab countries. Syria, Libya, Saudi Arabia, Jordan; whatever. And I understand they've been making demands of the university: They want some of their own troublemakers reinstated. They want their leaders in the student council. Many of these students went through a lot of military training and engineering before they ever got to this country. Whoever took that plutonium has to be knowledgeable about the stuff. It doesn't work any other way. They must realize it has potential far beyond its use in an electrical producing system. Believe me, that leads to the next inevitable conclusion, which is that they know what it *can* be used for. Anyone going after bomb materials won't bother with anything less than the highest-grade uranium two thirty-five or the plutonium you described. In fact, if they were to try to steal that kind of material from a major power plant, they'd go after similar materials. That's the highest grade. It's too tough for students to get that, but all of a sudden Allah shows them the light, and they have a couple of hundred pounds of plutonium up for grabs. Now it's waste material, *but it can be used for a bomb if you know what to do with it.*"

Lance rubbed his chin, deep in thought as he spoke. "Consider the material. It can't be handled without an organization. Don't lose sight of that fact. This wasn't ripped off by a few excited kids. The radiation shielding is so heavy that you're dealing with packages that are dangerous, bulky, and very heavy. It means a lot of warm bodies to move the stuff, and it means one large vehicle or more, most likely vans, and it means a sub-rosa organization. You've got to move the stuff to a place where it's tough to find, where it can be worked on, where you can assemble your bomb mechanism. You need a machine shop; you need electronics, transmitters, and receivers; you need a broadcast frequency free of interference or else a direct detonator receiving system." He stopped suddenly. "Are you getting the drift of all this?"

Dirk's face resembled a white statue. "Only too well, my friend, only too well."

"I know it's happening," Deidre added, "but I still can't *believe* it."

"You'd better, love, because it's the *only* way," Lance said with unarguable finality. "Now every university has its student ghetto. That's for starters, and you could hide an elephant in those. You've got a lot of open country, and that means farms where you have barns and silos, and well, it would all fit, even if it's not the best location because there would be too much sudden movement of people and vehicles. Staying in the normal flow of things is more likely. Is there a black militant force here?"

Dirk nodded. "Small. It can be vociferous, but the blacks in Gainesville for the most part are local citizens first and blacks second. Those who argue that point are the militants. If you're talking and walking a discrimination line, forget it. There's the social pecking order, as you might expect, but you'll get a lot more resistance from that caste system if you're a redneck."

"So much the better," Lance told them. "That narrows it even closer to the group, or the type of group, I was describing. So," he said slowly, "let's back up. Let's *assume* we have hotheaded foreign militants on our hands. Nobody does things like this mindlessly. They need a reason to do what they did, and that means they have a goal in mind. Maybe goal is the wrong word. Call it purpose, dream, target; whatever."

"How," Deidre asked, "can you call making an atomic bomb a dream?"

Lance put up his hands in mock protest. "Hey, *I* didn't steal the plutonium."

Deidre flushed. "I'm sorry. That was emotional."

"It's difficult to be cold about it," Lance said soothingly, "but you might say I've been a lot more intimate with this stuff."

"Lance, I didn't mean to—"

"Hush. That's way behind us."

"This group," Dirk urged him.

"Well, the plutonium, as it's packaged, really isn't

that dangerous. Exotic, but not that much trouble. But they *can* make a bomb from it. Knowing about bombs is part of their groundwork before they ever reach this country. Let me repeat a few things. Remember what they need to make all this meaningful. They need a machine shop, electronics, metals, explosive or rocket devices, transport able to carry heavy loads, and above all, they need tight discipline and close coordination. And they need a voice. A single voice to speak for all of them. They don't want babble. They want to be able, when they're ready, to get their message through to wherever it's aimed."

He held out his glass for more brandy, sipped slowly for a moment. His throat was hurting. He wasn't accustomed to long speeches like this, and even with the corrective surgery he felt a rasp file rubbing his larynx. He took another sip of brandy and pushed on. "The odds are they've spent more time fighting among themselves and with each other, so they haven't been much trouble outside their own clique. But now they have a purpose. They're the skinny kid on the block ruled by the big bad people, and the kid suddenly finds a case of dynamite. Now understand one thing," Lance emphasized. "I'm only reacting to what you've told me. I can't, obviously, prove a word of what I've said in a court of law, but I can damned well extrapolate and, if I say so myself, with very good accuracy. I can go even further than that. I think there's every chance that I personally could get a handle on these people and maybe even find out where the plutonium's been stashed. The key to all this is that the very nature of the plutonium dictates what avenues they have to travel. They're restricted, so to speak, by what they're handling, what they hope to make with it, and how they can communicate their intentions to the right people. As far as

I'm concerned, every one of these elements is a red flare on a white snowfield."

"Lance, what about the local authorities?"

Lance looked at Deidre and shook his head. "They're way over their heads. This goes beyond cops and robbers."

Dirk motioned for attention. "I think it would do a lot of good if you would talk with Crippens. Charles Crippens, the university president. He can coordinate the law enforcement people with university security teams."

"You're talking parking tickets and crowd control," Lance said disdainfully.

"Well, there's more," Dirk said with a defensive look. "We've got the FBI and the CIA and the AEC and God knows what other organizations already involved in this. They'll swarm all over the area like an invasion of fleas on a small dog's ass, and—"

"Jesus, that's the *worst* thing they could do!" Lance said with sudden heat. "I've lived with radical students, and so have you. Don't you remember? Just panic them, and they go wild, like animals running before a forest fire."

A gloomy Dirk Martin finished off his brandy. "Okay, okay," he said fitfully, "what the devil would you do?"

"First, I'd ask Deidre for coffee. We've hit the end of the road for the brandy."

Deidre was on her feet immediately. "Coming right up. For the first time since this started, I feel useful. You two go on with it."

They waited for her to leave for the kitchen. Lance turned back to Dirk. "The *first* thing you do is get the best private team in the business in here. You let *them* handle it. A special crew trained and experienced to work in this business, and that includes all aspects. You turn them loose; you trust them; you let them have their own way. Go ahead; let the police and the other gumshoes fumble around in full view of whoever's copped the stuff, so they can sneer at the bumblers. That keeps them cool instead of on edge. Never forget they can panic and take this radioactive stuff and spread it all over the campus and throughout the city. You know what happens then? They call the papers and the radio and television and the police and tell them where to look with Geiger counters; they find heavy concentrations of radioactivity, and the whole goddamned town goes apeshit. You'd panic the whole university *and* the whole city. You'd have mass running. Never forget just how badly people are spooked by this stuff."

Dirk studied him carefully. "You said a special crew. Who are they? How do we reach them? Will they do it? What would it cost? What—"

"Hold it, hold it," Lance broke in, almost desperately. "This is my territory we're talking about. I've remained fully active in it despite what people think, despite what they're *supposed* to think." Lance was doing the fastest improvising he'd ever done in his life. Suddenly, right out of the blue, here lay the answer to the question haunting his life: *What the hell are you going to do with yourself?* He hated bending the bejesus out of the truth to Dirk, but that was of minor importance simply because he knew he could do the job better than anyone else. It was a remarkable revelation to him. He rushed on, mental fingers crossed.

"I get these people," Lance said carefully. "I've worked with them before. Out there in California where"—he gestured to his own body—"*this* happened to me. They were on special duty all the time. They have their own way of doing things. You won't ever meet any of them face to face because being anonymous is critical to them. You work through their intermediary, who, in this case, is me. The whole purpose is for them never to compromise their identity. They're masters at disguise and being faceless; mixing in with the crowd, any crowd, is their single most effective weapon."

He fixed his eyes on Dirk. "Now, as to one of those questions you fired at me. It will cost the university fifty thousand clams, on the line, *before* they even start to work. They can't go to any court to sue the customer if the customer reneges. Court appearances would destroy their effectiveness. Now, if, after getting their first payment, they don't deliver the entire package to the university, they'll admit it, and no matter what it costs *them*, it doesn't cost the university one thin dime more."

"And if they're successful?" Dirk pressed.

"In this particular case they've got to find the stuff, keep people from getting hurt, prevent panic, and return the plutonium. On delivery they get paid a quarter of a million dollars."

Dirk's mouth opened, and his jaw worked, but he didn't do well in a clear verbal response. He took a deep breath before he spoke again. "The university won't go for that kind of money."

"Then they'll have good reason to regret being cheap," Lance said quietly.

"You call three hundred thousand dollars *cheap*?"

"There's an old saw about people complaining about growing old. It's not so bad when you consider the alternative," Lance threw at his friend. "When did you lose your grip on reality, Dirk? Three hundred grand to solve this problem is *peanuts*. A panic alone would cost millions. It would bring the wrath of the state and federal government down on the school, create a mass wave of firings and new people taking over. And have you considered what happens *if they put together their bomb and detonate the damn thing?*"

"Well, sure, I've been thinking about it, and—"

"The hell you have. You've been thinking all around it. You're talking about a crater in the middle of what *used* to be a university. They'd wipe out more than half the population of this whole town and raze or wreck the university. It would cease to exist. Jesus, maybe living in ivy row has stunted your thinking." Lance shook his head slowly. "Maybe we'd better just forget it. I came here to be with people I love and trust, not to get into some contest with you." He looked up as Deidre returned with coffee. "I apologize," Lance said to Dirk, then looked again at Deidre. "Here I am fresh out of nowhere after all these years, and I'm afraid I've been chewing on Dirk. It doesn't say too much for my perspective or my manners."

Dirk waved off the apology. He drank his first cup of coffee in contemplative silence. Deidre refused to break into their momentary standoff. Finally, Dirk put aside his cup. "You said you worked with this special group, right?"

Lance nodded.

"That's worked *with*," Dirk persisted, chasing a new quarry. "Are you a member of the team?"

Time to play poker, decided Lance. "No comment, Dirk. Not now, perhaps not even later." A smile flickered across his face. "That's the official story. In this house, between the three of us, I, *uh*, recommend you answer the question yourself." Lance's expression appeared suddenly to show a parted curtain to his thoughts, and he became visibly bitter. "Who else in this world would hire *me*? Where do I go? Where the hell *can* I go? I'm blacklisted in engineering, thanks to my government. Maybe I'm built like a scapegoat. I can't get into research. I can't even do administrative work where government support of contracts is involved." He looked at them both, a confidence in himself showing where it seemed absent before.

"Now that's the name of the game. You can't slice it any other way, and neither can I. They left me with a smashed body, and if it weren't for Lee Grazzi, I'd have stayed a mental cripple as well. Let's put that behind us. Consider me a gumshoe or a decoy or even a ferret if it seems most appropriate. I nose around and I listen, I nudge and I nibble at corners, and I find out things few other people would ever discover, because there's a semantic key, a subliminal advantage to being what many people consider a grotesque cripple."

"Lance!" His name burst from Deidre; her shock was touched with anger.

"Hon, push it aside. That's what the real world is all about, and I've learned to take advantage of it. People look at me, and what they see they disregard as any kind of danger. It's perfect. They let down their guard. They let you peek inside their heads. If you know the subject, they tell you things without knowing they're doing so."

He held out his cup for a refill, waited until he sipped slowly, turned his eyes back to Dirk. "All right, I want to get this over with now. Whatever business is involved, I mean. I've let it go this far because you asked me all the questions. Now let's talk *for* the record, okay?"

Dirk nodded, and Lance continued. "The rest is up to you or to whoever calls the signals and says yea or nay. It's as simple as that."

"I'll call Crippens," Dirk said quietly, and left for his office. Lance sat back in his chair, his cigar unlit, dizzy with the prospects he had raised in a rush of talk and bravado. But, dammit, *he was right*. Even from what little he knew, he had to be right. This wasn't strange territory to him. He had threaded the thorny thickets of nuclear materials *and* radical groups for too many years not to know, by both instinct and by detailed examination, what these people were up against. Hell itself. And if—

"Tomorrow morning at ten," he heard Dirk say. He hadn't even heard him come back into the living room.

"Okay."

"Would you mind, Lance, if we made some notes before that meeting with Crippens? I think it would be more effective than going through a straight verbal exchange. University presidents are as guilty as anyone else in the academic life; paper carries its own special message."

Lance turned to Deidre. "You still the crackerjack typist?"

"The best." She smiled.

"I can dictate into a recorder. That way you can get started and I can keep going."

"Very good. I've heard enough to start an opening presentation, as it is. Very official, very formal, very impressive."

"Good." Lance turned back to Dirk. "I'd recommend that part of the presentation include a recommendation for a cover for me. Guest professor, or lecturer, on nuclear reactor systems, with just enough material on bombs thrown in to attract a special sort of student. You can spread it around, even offer a credit or two for attendance on the group of lectures. I'll make up the notes on my professional background, and I'll also include the Los Alamos labs. That looks best of all."

"Looks? I don't understand," Dirk said. "If I remember, you *did* work there."

"I sure did." Lance grinned. "In fact, a long time ago, I was one of the bright, young, and upcoming scientists who, with no formal weapons training what-soever, built a homemade atomic bomb. We—the other students and myself—machined the bomb parts. The only difference between what we did and the real thing was that we used lead instead of plu-tonium."

"I'm almost afraid to ask if it worked," Deidre said with a shudder.

"We were assembled in eight teams," Lance told her without a trace of levity. "After we built the bombs, the military took them out to their testing ar-eas and substituted plutonium for the lead, and test-fired the bombs."

The relationship to the present was almost unbear-able. "Dammit, Lance, what happened?" Dirk snapped.

Lance shrugged at the inevitable. "Six of those bombs went off. Six out of eight. The best one turned in a yield twice as powerful as the bomb that tore apart Hiroshima."

A deathly silence followed. Dirk and Deidre looked ill. Lance climbed painfully to his feet. He'd been sit-ting in that chair too damned long, and his muscles were pulling. "Do you have a car I can borrow?" he asked. "I don't want to use the truck, and I imagine I'd have to wait until morning to get a rental."

Dirk nodded. "You don't need a rental. We've got four cars. A Cutlass station wagon all right?"

"Of course."

Deidre brought him the keys. "You know where to find"—she paused, smiling thinly—"whatever it is you're looking for, I suppose."

He kissed her cheek. "Love, it's the body that aches. Not the brain. Thank you both for every-thing—and don't wait up."

Chapter 26

He drove east from the Martins' house, following the thickly wooded streets until he reached the main north-south artery of Gainesville. Highway 441 was also Thirteenth Street, and he recalled that the intersection of Thirteenth Street and University Avenue, at what was the northeast corner of the campus, was the center of traffic and business activity in the town. He turned right to go south on Thirteenth, stopped at an all-night convenience store, and bought a detailed map of Gainesville. He turned on the dome light in the station wagon and studied the map, noting main arteries and the location of what could be important buildings and centers to his future actions. For someone who'd studied architectural plans and schematics all his adult life, a city street map was a document committed easily to memory. And he had found just what he wanted. A major motel on the edge of town, and it lay straight ahead on Thirteenth. The Hilton, along the shores of the lake noted on the map as Bivens Arm. He pulled into the entrance and went inside to the registry desk. He had begun his new "career."

"You're very fortunate, Mr. Parker," the registry clerk told him. Caution stiffened him until he realized the pretty girl was sincere.

"How come?" he asked.

"No football games right now. Otherwise, we could never guarantee the room for the two weeks." She smiled brightly. "When we have the games, this town goes wild. You can't get a room for fifty miles in any direction from here. If you don't mind a slightly additional charge, sir, you can have a room overlooking the lake. It's really pretty."

"Thanks. It's a good idea. It makes the room feel bigger." He paid cash for his first week, pocketed the receipt, and studied the motel. Hotel was more like it. It had a coffee bar, a nice lounge, and an excellent restaurant. At the same time the Hilton was spread out over so large an area he could disappear from view, enter and leave his room without going anywhere near the main entrance.

He lay comfortably on the bed, propped up on pillows, his cigar drifting smoke through the room. No relaxing; his mind worked furiously, trying to weave together the sudden turn in his life. Early in the morning he had that meeting with the university president. Fine. His credentials would be checked out thoroughly. They'd investigate him, and it would all come up roses because it was all true. The organization he'd dreamed up on the spot was another matter. He'd have to keep moving fast on that one. It just wouldn't do, he laughed to himself, for the top people in this business to learn he'd snatched the whole thing out of thin air.

But there is an organization . . .

The thought startled him. Of course! *He* was that organization! Lee's laboratory in California. Unimpeachable scientific, technical, engineering background through her laboratory. The lab, and the production center, the contracts and bank references, and all of it tying in so beautifully with his own background. He sat up straight on the bed, nearly chewing through the cigar, so intent was he on the possibilities. For the first time since he'd emerged from blackness after having been chewed to bits under that mountain, he knew he could keep the promise he'd made to the woman who had been responsible for his rebirth. He recalled his words to her: *I'll have to work it out. I've got to make it on my own. I've got to be responsible to my own existence. I swear that when it happens, you'll be the first to know ...*

He reached for the telephone and punched in the numbers. The seconds dragged longer and longer, and then the phone rang in California. Three rings, and he heard her voice. "Hello." One word, and it hit him like a lead pipe in the stomach.

"Lee . . ." He choked her name, swallowed, forced himself to speak. "Lee . . . it's Lance." He heard a gasp but no reply. Suddenly he was frantic. "*Lee?* You there? It's me, Lance. For God's sake, *say something*."

"It . . . it's like a dream. Oh, my God, I love you! Is it really you? How are you? *Where* are you? Of course . . . I spoke with Dirk and Deidre. Are you in Gainesville?"

"Yes, I'm here. I love you, Lee. I miss you more than I can ever say." The lump in his throat nearly strangled him; then he fought it down, and he could speak. "It's all right, Lee. Really. It's better than I could ever have believed."

"Lance, you sound incredible. I can hardly believe it."

"I found something I've been looking for. I think it's what we've both been looking for. Call it, well, myself, I guess."

She was laughing and crying at the same time. "And they say prayers don't work anymore. . . ."

"Lee, I need you. Here, right away. Remember all those words that drove us crazy? Purpose and meaning, reality, challenge, making our own way. Remember?"

"Yes," she said quietly, "I remember. Of course I do. How could I ever forget? Lance, for God's sake, don't stop now. Tell me about it."

"I'll fill it in later, Lee. Just take my word for it. There's no time now, but I'm right in the middle of something big. Bigger than I ever thought would happen. Can you make it? I mean, just drop everything?"

Her laughter was crystal. "The way you sound, darling, I can do anything."

"Get a pen and paper. You'll need to write things down."

"Go ahead, love. I'm ready."

He went through a list that lasted nearly ten minutes. "I don't care what it costs, Lee. Beg, borrow, or steal the money. We can make it up as soon as you get here. Bring it on the plane as baggage or freight on the same flight. You can get a plane direct to Orlando. Don't bother screwing around with changing planes in Atlanta or anything like that. I don't want to risk delays. I'll meet you in Orlando, and on the drive back here to Gainesville I'll fill in all the details. The timing is everything, hon."

"I won't bother with sleeping tonight, my sweet. That fast enough?"

"It is, it is. I love you, girl."

"My God, this is like a dream. Lance, you sound like—you sound like *before*. I love you. I'll call Deidre and let her know the flight numbers and—"

"No, call the Hilton in Gainesville. Don't ask questions now. Just call, and if I'm not in, leave the information. I love you. I can't wait to see you. Don't drag this out right now, Lee. Saying good-bye is tough enough."

"I love you," she said, and hung up.

He returned the phone to its cradle, immensely satisfied. *He was rolling now, by God.* The fierce exultation of controlling his life and the events about him filled him with wonder. Well, enough of rose-colored glasses. There were other things to do. He called a number in Orlando and woke up an old friend with whom he'd spent time in Silverton, Colorado, more than two miles above sea level, where Ted Votoe had built his cherished cabin retreat. Ted was also passenger traffic manager of Eastern Airlines at Orlando Jetport, and he could pay special attention to the arrival of Lee Grazzi and her vital baggage and freight. He hung up with Ted and called Dirk.

"I need a lawyer here in town," he told his friend. "Someone I can call in the middle of the night, who's sharp and fast and also knows how to get big things done while he stays low-key."

"That's all, huh?"

Lance grinned. "For the moment, Dirk. You got someone?"

"Yep. Harold Silver. He's a close friend. Hal's a retired army colonel, an engineer, a former test pilot, and now he's an attorney because he loves a good courtroom brawl. Here's his number."

Lance wrote it down, held down the phone, and dialed Hal Silver. A sleepy voice answered. "Silver, the name is Lance Parker. Dirk Martin said that his name would wake you up quickly."

"Do you know what the hell time it is? Of course. You sound old enough to know where the big hand and the little hand go. You're a friend of Dirk's?"

"Way back."

"You in trouble? Maybe a night in jail would teach you not to call people at this bloody hour."

"No trouble." Lance laughed. "I need a pro. Dirk says you're the best. He gave me your background."

Silver's voice was fully awake. "Okay, spill it."

"How long will it take you to get to room 129 at the Hilton?"

"Jesus Christ."

"Just you, Hal."

"You're too quick to be an asshole. Thirty minutes. I'll bring a Thermos of coffee."

"You do good work, Charlie Brown."

Thirty-one minutes later he let Harold Silver into the room—along with the Thermos and two heavy coffee mugs. "Survival rations," Silver grumbled as he poured.

Lance laid $3,000 in cash on the small table before them. "The money's clean, and everything I need and want is also clean. It's aboveboard, but I want to buy a lot of circumspection."

"Nobody talks a lot with his fly glued tight. Lay it on me. And don't worry about my not taking notes. That's not circumspect, for one. And for two, I don't need notes. I can play it all back to you as if it were on a tape recorder."

"I need a branch office of an investigative firm. Here in Gainesville."

"Name?"

Lance laughed. "I hadn't even thought of that. We'll call it The Fifth Law."

"What the hell are you, a guru?"

"Well, that rhymes with gumshoe, anyway. I do, *uh,* special work. There are the three basic laws of thermodynamics and the law of entropy, and those four lead to the fifth law, which is my bag. Consider me the disturbing factor in universal harmony."

Hal Silver grinned at him. "You're as crazy as a bedbug, but you got style, and that balances the boat. I like it. The Fifth Law it is. What address?"

Lance tapped the stack of $100 bills. "That's for openers. You let me know when you need more. You've got secretaries, and you know the town. You do it, and you bill me. Get me an isolated office in a new building. Take care of the legal amenities, telephone, answering service, full security; the works. I'll need a realtor—"

"Tiffins and Owens," Silver said crisply. "Bill and Karl. The best. Mind their own business, too. What do you want?"

"Rental. Big house. *Very* big. Good security, buried away from the world, in the northwest section of town. By the way, I'm a house guest of the Martins. They don't know about this room, and no one else is to know."

—"Good enough. Mine is to do and not to reason why. Now, question from lawyer to new client. I don't care what you said before. All this is clean?"

"Whiter than virgin snow. You have my word on that, and you can confirm what you need with Dirk. For the record, and you may find it strange that it's the truth, I'll be running an undercover investigation office. I'll also be working *with* the local authorities. You know the local sheriff?"

"Edward Duncan is top man. Tom Harper is his chief deputy. They're fast, smart, top cops, and they know the political scene inside out. Why?"

"I want you to tell them about me. You frame the word package. Also, if you have a chance, the chief of police."

"Stan Corey. If they made all cops in his mold, most of the criminal lawyers in the country would be out of business. Him, too, with the phone call?"

"I'd appreciate it."

Harold Silver went quiet. He took a long drink of coffee and lit up a cigarette, finally pointing it at Lance. "You know something? I got a nose that smells things. A hangover from G-Two. Army intelligence. You, sir, are starting to fit in with certain disquieting, and very disturbing, rumors. Strictly off the record, I'd like to—"

Lance held up a hand. "Do yourself and a lot of people a favor. Don't speculate and don't ask, and if you figure out things, for Christ's sake, keep it to yourself, or talk to me and nobody else. When the right time comes, I'll lay it on you. Until then take the word of your newest client that I know what I'm talking about."

Silver stubbed out his cigarette. "Okay, I'm out of coffee and cigarettes. You want a receipt for your three grand?"

"Nope."

"I hate people who make me stand on my good looks. Okay, it'll be done by early tomorrow afternoon." He shook hands. "You owe me a pot of coffee. Night." He was gone.

Lance left several minutes later. To his surprise he found Deidre still awake. "I started your presentation," she explained. "I'm too keyed up to sleep. Why don't you dictate into that recorder, and while you catch up on sleep, I'll finish it? You can go over it at breakfast before you and Dirk go off to meet with Crippens."

He kissed her on the cheek. "Got coffee?"

"Hot and ready. I'll bring it. Here's your recorder. Ignore me, talk your head off."

He recorded for just over an hour, then went to his room. His last thoughts before he fell into exhausted slumber were a sleeping tonic.

It's working.

Chapter 27

He was moving with the efficiency of a supercharged automaton. First the breakfast review with Dirk. He scanned the papers and handed them to his friend. "Your wife's a miracle worker. Everything is perfect. The credentials even impress me."

Dirk scanned the neatly typewritten sheets already bound in a leather folder. "It's what we need. You ready?"

"Let's go."

Dr. Charles Crippens was a tall and very large man who carried his bulk surprisingly well for his sixty-two years. Dirk had filled in Lance on the way to the university. "Crippens is brilliant. He's an Annapolis graduate, and he flew fighters in the Second World War and in Korea. Sixteen kills; three times an ace. He went on to become assistant chief of operations for the Navy, was administrator at the Naval Academy, and then came here. His military background wasn't a problem. He's a brilliant scientist in his own right. He worked on several navy satellite programs and—"

"If he was in the high echelon of the Pentagon,"

Lance broke in, "that means we don't have to educate him about the danger of the plutonium. He'll know."

"He knows," Dirk confirmed. "He was operations officer at one of the series of atomic and hydrogen bomb tests."

"Good enough."

It went fast, efficiently, and with the desired effect. Crippens stood six feet four inches tall and had a head of wavy silver hair. He was a man very much in charge of himself. He read the presentation and laid it carefully on his desk.

"I could call in military security for this job," he said to Lance. "Everything we need and no fifty thousand dollars in the blind. With," he added slowly, "another quarter of a million if you deliver."

"Then by all means get your blundering brahmas," Lance told him.

Crippens didn't bat an eye. "What happens if you *don't* deliver?"

"Then, sir, I buy the farm along with everybody else. Part of my agreement is that I stay *here*, in Gainesville."

"I'm glad to hear that," Crippens said dryly, "because so will I. When will you need your answer?"

"I have people on their way here already. With special equipment I need. I need your answer before I leave this office. There's no time to screw around, to put it as bluntly as I can. The time for a caucus is long behind us." He grimaced. "If it wasn't, we wouldn't be here talking about this thing."

Crippens sat for a minute without saying a word. When he did, he had no reservations to bother him. "You'll be issued payment for textbooks. We'll attend to the bill of ladings and the paper work. How do you want the fifty thousand?"

"Cash."

"You surprise me."

"Good. I'll be able to surprise other people then."

"It will require several hours."

"That's fine. Have it sent by hand delivery to my attorney here in town. Harold Silver. He'll sign a receipt in my name."

"Consider it done, Mr. Parker. When do you start?"

"Last night, sir." Lance glanced at his watch. "I'm running seven minutes late. Is there anything else?"

"I expect to be kept informed at all times."

"You will be." Lance stood, shifted the cane to his left hand, and extended his right to Crippens. "Good day, and wish me luck."

Crippens held his hand. "I'll do better than that, Mr. Parker. I'm risking my life on you."

"So you are," Lance said with a crooked grin. "Good day."

The whole world could have been invisible or nonexistent; it didn't matter and no one cared as Lee hurried from the jetliner at Orlando. She knew the long walk through endless corridors to reach the terminal, and her heart pounded like that of a teen-ager in first love, but a man in a red jacket and a wide smile met her as she left the airplane. "Miss Grazzi? Hi, I hope your flight went well. Would you come with me, please? I'm Ted Votoe with Eastern." Strange. They left the passenger corridor as Votoe unlocked a service door and took her down a service stairwell and then outside to the ramp where the airplane that had carried her from California loomed like a small mountain over them, and standing beneath the nose was Lance. Votoe had arranged their first moments free of the crowded terminal and the noisy kids shouting and running wild as they neared Disneyworld. They looked at each other and saw only the other, and Lee clung fiercely to Lance, tears streaming down her cheeks, and it was incredible and marvelous and beyond all believing, and she kissed him wildly, and she turned to the grinning man from the airlines and hugged him as well. "Thank you," she whispered in his ear. Lance introduced them. "Oh, you're the one!" she exclaimed. She laughed. "I remember now. You fly those ancient bombers, planes that are fifty years old, and that's fun?"

"It's better than throwing yourself out of an airplane like you two," said the man with a twinkle in his eye.

"I can't argue with that. Where do we go from—"

"All you do is concentrate on that man over there," Ted Votoe said with a nod at Lance. "Just follow me, please." They were in an Eastern Airlines car and driving through a forest of enormous wings and engines and thick struts with wheels, emerging finally in a landscaped area hidden from the terminal. Votoe stopped by a tan and black van. "That's it, Lance. The rental's in my name, and you can use it as long as you need or drop it off with National at the Gainesville airport. Miss Grazzi, your luggage and freight are all aboard that van. I checked it through myself." He held the door open for them. "Now why don't you two just get lost? Call me when you're free." Before they could say a word, he was gone. They embraced again, more quietly this time, and then they were on the highway, rolling north through beautiful hilly country of citrus groves and then thickening forests and horse country.

Lance brought Lee up-to-date on everything that had happened. His recounting of arrangements with the university brought a low whistle from her. "You always did like to shoot dice," she said quietly. "Just like that, and they're dealing?"

"It's not so much a matter of 'just like that,'" he said firmly. "First, consider our credentials, the lab, your own background, and then do the same for me. Now put yourself in Crippens's chair. He knows the military, the Pentagon, and the incredible confusion of government investigations. Don't you realize the people from the Atomic Energy Commission are also on the hot griddle? They're ultimately responsible for the disposition of that material. Then the military comes in for its own share of the blame because it knows the plutonium could be made into a bomb and it didn't guarantee proper precautions. What we have here, my love, is a university-based plutonium Watergate. And if that thing ever does get assembled and detonated . . ."

"I can guess the rest," she told him.

"No, you can't. That's the worst of it. Books and pictures don't even remotely touch the real thing. That must have been the final cruncher for Crippens. He was part of some bomb tests. That man *knows*. So the fifty thousand to him is spit compared to the alternatives."

"Have they paid yet?"

"Just before I left to pick you up, I called Hal Silver. He'd been informed the money was on the way, and he arranged to have it deposited in a small bank in Gainesville. High Springs. The account is in the name of The Fifth Law, and when we get a chance, we go to the bank. Checks can be drawn on either of our signatures."

She laughed at his attitude. "Is this the same man who was so worried about what to do with his life? You know, the one I last saw in California?"

He glanced at her. "No, Lee, it is *not* the same man."

She touched his arm immediately. "Lance, if I said that wrong, I apologize."

"No, *no*," he assured her. "You said it *right*. I'm not the same man. Whoever I am, I'm *me*. No ex-

319

planations. You'll have to come to your own conclusions."

She leaned back, smiling again, "I like what I see, and hear, and feel, and touch, and—"

"And the man is horny," he said.

"I should dearly hope so. His lady friend is in the same terrible condition. You, *ah,* have a cure in mind?"

"We'll be at the motel in five minutes."

They both had the cure. And Lee was right. The man was different. He'd learned the secret of how to remove from his neck that ponderous albatross of self-doubt. The secrets of life were wonderful once you understood them. It didn't take an athlete to make love; it took a man who loved and was willing to *be* loved, for the act of receiving was so often more difficult, more satisfying, than the giving.

They drove toward the house in northwest Gainesville. Lance had explained that the motel was their private retreat in town, a place to go where no one would know them. For the moment it was just as well that neither Dirk nor Deidre knew. All that would come later. He couldn't afford certain amenities at this moment. There was too much to do and too little time in which to do it.

"You have everything I asked you to bring?" he questioned Lee.

"Everything."

"Okay. We spend some time with Dirk and Deidre. But please try to keep it short. They know what's going on, and they'll understand. They've closed off the workshop, which leads directly to the garage, and until we bring them in, they'll respect our confidence."

She looked at him, astonished. "They don't *know* about ManFac?"

"Not yet."

"How on earth did you manage to—" The answers were obvious. "Lance, I don't care if I step on your toes. I'm very proud of you for that. All they know, then, is what they see. You."

He had a lopsided grin on his face. "That's right. I love it."

"Do we tell them?"

"At the right time. I don't want to compromise their position in any way. Because as soon as we get through this hysteria of you seeing those two again, I have got to get to work *immediately*. Everything you brought is, I assume, sealed? Good. Then you play hello again with Deidre, and I'll get Dirk to unload with me. And then we go to work."

"Yes, sir. Just one question, sir."

He raised an eyebrow, waiting.

"Separate bedrooms, sir?"

"I'll break your neck," he growled.

"Yes, *sir*."

Afsar Husain looked at the auditorium with mixed emotions of pleasure and dismay. It was jammed. Filled to every corner inside, and the lectures and open debate had drawn a great crowd of milling students to a covered plaza before the auditorium where they watched and listened on a closed-circuit television to the events within. Afsar Husain was a very large man who didn't bother himself with the amenities of social conduct, and he elbowed and pushed his way through the crowd. "Make way!" he shouted. "Make way for Husain, or I will break your feeble necks!" Protests died away with the sight of his massive body, the thick neck and squared head, the fierce mustache and black curly hair. Afsar bulled his way through, intimidated a young girl acting as an usher, walked midway down the central aisle, and rudely shoved a student aside to take his seat. The

321

started curse ended when a steel grip squeezed muscle.

Afsar smiled a wave of garlic and onions into the student's face. "Be quiet." His tone brooked no argument. "I am your friend." The confused student nodded slowly, but Afsar Husain had already turned to study the panel.

Ah, the man on the left was Professor Dirk Martin. The sign on the table by his microphone identified him as an engineer. There was also Dr. Stephen Alsford, an industrial energy scientist, and Dr. Forrest Reed, a specialist in nuclear power systems. They had completed their formal presentations to the student body on the critical need of the nation for electricity-producing nuclear reactors. The students, almost instinctively prone to grasp controversial matters to lend them public voice, now had their turn. Microphones brought to them by other students were their signal to direct questions to the three-man panel.

Afsar turned to study this crowd. Oh, this was good indeed! These people were not merely angry. They were belligerent and even dangerous. Yes, yes. This university had always been known for the vociferous stand of its students against many causes and projects, and near the top of their list was the nuclear reactor. They wasted little time in hurling biting and incisive questions at the three men fielding their barbed lances. Afsar noted the presence of university security guards in unusually large numbers, and his practiced eye detected the plainclothesmen scattered through the audience. None would carry guns, he knew. That was like bringing dynamite to a bonfire. There would be Mace and clubs and lead saps, but not guns. Better they should have their skulls cracked. Their heads healed.

Afsar listened to Professor Dirk Martin responding to a shouted question that was as much insult as query on why nuclear reactors should not be abolished.

"Nuclear reactors, or the alleged terrible danger from them, are not nearly as dangerous as agitators have made them out to be. In this country our civilian reactors have not caused the radiation death of a single person, but rock concerts have killed more than two hundred young people. Nuclear reactors didn't kill the fifty thousand people who died on the highways last year or maim two million others in accidents; they don't pollute the air like the coal-fired plants or condemn people to early deaths from asbestos and lead poisoning or cause acid rain from pollutants or rape the earth with chemicals! We need safeguards, to be sure, and we should incorporate them into every nuclear plant we build, and we should do everything to create thermonuclear systems for cheap and safe electricity. May I have the next question, please?"

Afsar Husain smiled as a student took up the rebuttal. "Sir, your argument is empirical and even facetious. Highway deaths or bathtubs or rock concerts in no way affect what happens with nuclear reactors. *That* is the issue here tonight, not your own selected comparators." The student openly sneered. "How convenient it is for you to disregard completely one of the greatest of all dangers of your precious reactors—that criminal or terrorist elements could steal the uranium to produce atomic bombs. And if they do that and explode them in a city, what happens to those statistics of yours? Professor Martin, you are a perfect example of the old saw that figures lie and liars figure."

It took several minutes to restore order, so wild was the reaction to the student's remarks. Cheers, whistles, shouts, applause, feet stomping—they went on unabated like crashing surf. They began to ebb slowly as hoots and cries of derision, daring Dirk Martin to respond, still carried the room.

Now. The time is now, Afsar Husain said to himself. He rose quickly to his feet as a young girl carrying a microphone passed nearby. He tore the microphone from the grasp of the startled girl. Even in this mob of people, Afsar's size was impressive, and when he raised a mighty arm and a clenched fist, and his deep bass voice boomed from the speakers on each side of the stage, a thick accent demanded even more attention.

"Professor Martin! You will talk with me!"

Every eye in the auditorium turned to him.

The moderator, seated by himself at a small table near the panel, broke in hastily. "Sir, this chair has not recognized you. You will have to wait until—"

"The devil with your stupid recognition!" Afsar shouted. "This is not little games we play. I will ask questions none of these foolish children dare to ask—and see whether the equally foolish gentlemen on the stage dare to answer!" Silence fell as he stepped into the aisle, planting his thick legs wide and firm, unfettered by chairs and bodies about him.

"We forget all this talk about reactors. We are not concerned with the silly radiation they release into the air or leak into the ground." His tone carried with it an unmistakable pregnant fury. "You tell us of the efforts to prevent the proliferation of nuclear weapons. You assure us again and again that your government does everything possible to keep small nations around the world from getting atomic bombs. Why do you do this, Professor Martin? *Why are you so set against other nations having the very same weapons that the United States and the Soviet Union have by the hundreds of thousands!*"

He held up both arms and turned slowly, brilliant white teeth a blazing beacon set within his dark skin.

He stopped when he again faced the stage, and at a gesture from him the roar in the room went silent as though he had pulled a switch. "What harm is there in a few measly bombs by small countries? Are you afraid here in America that we will attack you? Or that we will smash the Russians? We do not have giant navies and huge armies and great air forces! We are no threat to the world."

He stabbed a thick finger at the panel. "You reassure these sheep that small countries shall not get or make atomic bombs. Yet the United States makes tens of thousands of the most advanced nuclear weapons in the world *every year*! You fire hundreds of missiles in tests. You hold great war games. You practice, again and again, the destruction of millions of people—and you condemn the little nations that wish only to give themselves some measure of protection. You are vile hypocrites!"

He waited out the human thunder reacting to his words, his message, his delivery. Again he gestured for silence, and when he spoke, his words came out lower, deeper, like verbal battering rams. "By your own words you condemn yourself. By your own words you have told us over and over that you have the power to destroy this planet a hundred times. And yet you sit before us like some exalted Buddha, telling us how backward and unfit we are. But the Americans, in their infinite wisdom, so wonderfully demonstrated in Vietnam as but a single example, have some divine guidance that is denied to the rest of the world. You are the shining angels, and we are the unclean. But *you* have designed and created and built and used these bombs to sear the flesh and blind the children and destroy cities!"

Afsar Husain's condemnation was hellishly effective in this emotionally charged atmosphere. Professor Martin was visibly pale, and the others were shaken

325

by the fury of his words. A buzz grew in the auditorium, and Afsar timed his renewal perfectly.

"Silence!" he roared. Now he spoke as much to the crowd as to the shocked professors on the stage. "Listen, you witless infants! Listen to these men of learning, who would teach us life, and how they speak!" He had the crowd mesmerized, swaying, breathless. "Listen to them tell us of why we should be frightened of proliferation! But the bombs they have tested, yes, *tested* in the ground and in the atmosphere and under the ocean *have already hurled more radiation* into the air and soil of this planet than if a hundred thousand of their cursed nuclear reactors blew up!" He spun to face the stage, and again his finger stabbed forward.

"Tell us, Professor Martin! Tell us why you still build the great hydrogen bombs and the missiles and the submarines and the bombers and in the same breath you condemn the small nations that would have only the tiniest fraction of what you have! *Tell us, damn you!"*

The silence was incredible. Time froze in the auditorium. Into this huge drop of limbo rose Dr. Forrest Reed, slow and imposing. "I will answer you, sir," he said, his voice gravelly and authoritative, recognized by many of the student audience. "I will answer you by telling you that your questions are impertinent and they are out of order in this room."

"Out of order!" Afsar shouted. "Oho, so that is the reply to the question. Avoid it! Do not answer! Shift and evade, but do not answer." His finger stabbed like a sword swinging in aim through the auditorium. "Listen to me, you children! *I* am out of order, and *you* are out of order, *and we do not receive an answer* to the real question before us!" He raised both great arms to heaven, his face for a moment benign, then as swiftly again furious. "I am sworn to Islam to speak only English in this satanic land while I am here as a student!" he shouted. "But if only I could speak in my native tongue where I have the words—bah! This meeting tonight is a farce, a cruel joke, an insult to all learned and devout men the world over. You men on that stage do *not* answer questions. You are minions of propaganda, and there is only one way to respond to your vileness—to leave you talking among yourselves until the odor from your minds chokes and gags you."

He turned to the crowd. "All of you," he bellowed, "leave them before you are yourselves infested with their harlotry!"

There was no more talking. Two large men rushed down the aisle at him, two husky football players. Before anyone moved to stop them, a fist smashed into Husain's face. The microphone flew away wildly, and the second man crashed a fist into Husain's stomach. He doubled up and fell back, his face contorted, blood bright red along the side of his mouth. The crowd screamed. They fell silent as Afsar Husain slowly came erect. He held up a hand. "Be quiet, please. Allah is with me." He beckoned to the two burly students. "Come then, little ones, when your prey is ready for you."

They rushed him again, and Afsar sidestepped the first, tripping him and sending him flying. The second man felt a fist close about his ear and spin him around, and then a tremendous open-handed slap split open the side of his face. Afsar hurled him aside as if he were a rag doll. He laughed as the other man came at him from behind in a choking arm grip about Afsar's throat. It was a deadly hold, but a foolish move against someone who was obviously well versed in hand-to-hand struggles. Afsar slammed an elbow into the other man's rib cage. As he gasped and released his hold, Afsar spun about and brought his fist crashing into his attacker's forehead. He fell like a poled steer. Afsar Husain held up both hands, blew kisses to the wide-eyed students, and walked slowly along the aisle to the exit, looking neither left nor right.

Afsar Husain drove away from the auditorium parking lot, swung off University onto Thirteenth, and turned into the parking lot of Brewmasters, the steak-and-ale favorite of the student body and faculty in Gainesville. Inside, he nodded to the hostess. His physical bulk towered over her, and she was caught by surprise with a gentle voice. "I would appreciate a table in the back, please. A large one, away from the crowd if that is possible. I will be having company."

She led him to the elevated deck of the restaurant. He seated himself slowly, back to the wall, his great body spilling onto two chairs. He ordered a pitcher of beer and drank slowly, dallying with a plate of cold shrimp, wondering how long it would take.

Nine minutes later his gamble produced its results. He saw the group take a nearby table. There were too many furtive looks cast in his direction for their table selection to be coincidence. Shortly thereafter a girl approached. "May I sit with you, please?" He looked into the dark eyes and nodded slowly. He poured a glass for her, pushed it before her. She held the glass in both hands, watching him. He saw a face dark and beautiful with incredible lashes. More important was the intelligence in those eyes. Full lips and high cheekbones. A proud beauty of desert sands; no mistake there.

"I am Laila Habail. I know your name, Afsar Husain. My girl friend, at that table—"

He broke in, unsmiling. "Bring her and the boy,"

he said tersely. She seemed stung by his brusque interruption but turned and motioned her companions to
join them. "This is Gawhar Shad. She shares my
apartment." Husain nodded, sizing up the girl, dark
and wiry and a bit too brooding for his liking. "Yasar
al-Milah is our friend and classmate," Laila said to
conclude the introductions.

"Sit," Afsar directed, motioning to the waitress for
additional beer and glasses. When the waitress was
gone, Laila looked about her. The nearby tables were
empty. Finally, she spoke to Afsar.

"We saw you tonight. We were there in the auditorium. We saw you, and we heard you, and we
have talked long of the things you said." She seemed
impressed with her own words. *Too much so,* thought
Afsar.

"You tell me nothing I do not know," he said
scornfully, and his words stung Laila. "Did you come
here to me to prattle the obvious? To parade your
memory? Ah," he said, gesturing as if already weary
of their presence, "tell me then. What do you want?"

They looked from one to the other, nervous, un-
sure of themselves. The boy licked dry lips. *So,*
thought Afsar Husain, *the quiet one is here to study
me. And what he sees frightens him. He thinks too
much for someone who has gone to all this trouble to
sit here.*

Laila Habail sat erect, stunningly proud, elegant, a
princess among puppies. "We are students," she said,
her eyes bright.

"I did not imagine you were professors," he said
sarcastically.

He applauded, albeit to himself, her strength in
sliding past his remark. "Perhaps it is clear to you,
Afsar Husain," she went on, "but perhaps not.
Tonight you fired many hearts. Those people never
heard such words! I myself was astonished."

He smiled, but the smile bore little humor with its expression. "The words have long been here, desert child, and the facts have been with us longer still," he told them. "You are awakened, like a blind beggar given a gift of sight, and so he is awed by the golden sun those around him accept as commonly as breathing. They are uncaring; the gifted one is smitten. So I ask you what may not be so obvious as you proclaim by your presence. Why do you sit here with me? Why have you deliberately sought me out?" He leaned forward, so intense he became suddenly ominous. *"Why do you try to compromise me?"*

"That is not true!"

"What is not true?" Afsar hissed. "Did you not follow me? Did you not select that other table deliberately? Did you not come here unbidden? Listen to me, you little children. I am in this country under a Turkish passport, but the authorities know I spent two years in Iran, that I was in the Iranian Army special strike force. People from Iran are not popular here. I hold a dual citizenship. It is honest. It is, as the Americans say, aboveboard. Now you come here for a meeting, in full view of people *who will report a possible conspiracy*, and by so doing you compromise me. Perhaps the sand has trickled through your ears and noses into your brains. You think like camels."

Laila fought for her voice, tried to suppress the sudden anger that flushed her face. "We do nothing of the sort!" she said in a hoarse whisper.

Afsar laughed harshly and gripped her arm in a steel clasp. "Fools!" He leaned forward and jerked her roughly, closer to him, lowered his voice. "I know all about you and your childish organization. Do you think you fool people like me? *Listen* to me, you silly servants of your passion. I was an ordnance officer with the Turks. When I went to Iran, I worked with all sorts of weapons. Radar, missiles, electronics, nuclear devices—*all* of it. When that plutonium disappeared from the university, who do you think was the first person they questioned? Ah, you do not need to guess, I see. By the grace of Allah, I was not here, but in Washington, attending a seminar, and the suspicions were dismissed. I was, as they say here, clean. And I wish very much to stay that way, and I want, I order, you to stay away from me, or I will snap your necks like dry twigs."

He released his viselike grip from Laila's arm, shoved away the table with a short and angry gesture that tumbled glasses and spilled the pitchers, and stalked from the restaurant.

Chapter 28

Afsar Husain drove his van slowly along the winding
and heavily wooded road. He turned left at a street
marked DEAD END and flicked a lever concealed
beneath the dash before him. An amber light glowed.
He nodded with approval, eased the van forward, and
turned into a driveway. He stopped before a closed
garage door, waited patiently for the door to open,
and then drove into the garage. He shut off the engine as the doors closed to seal off the world behind
him. Lights filled the spacious garage. He went
through another door into a laboratory workshop
filled with electronic and mechanical equipment.

"Ah, it is Afsar Husain himself," Lee Grazzi said,
smiling. "Did it work?"

The man with thick black curls nodded. "Like a
charm. We've made the first direct contact. Faster
than I expected, and frankly that disturbs me. I—"

"Better let the explanations wait," Lee broke in.
"Dirk and the others, including some people from the
White House, are waiting to talk with us."

Afsar Husain grinned. "Not with me, I daresay."

She shared his amusement. "No, not with you. Do

you have it? I can start the processing while you get ready."

Afsar nodded. He removed his clothes and slid open a panel of his rib cage. Lee studied the open space, reached in, and withdrew a microcassette. She studied it carefully. "Almost fully run out. Did you get it all?"

"Yep. Every bit. Their voices, their names, an emotional gamut. Everything we need for a complete psychological profile."

"All right, Lance. I'll make the arrangements for the university computer first thing in the morning, but please, do hurry. Do you need any help?"

"Thanks, love. I can handle it. You go on and tell them I'll be right along." He watched her leave, waiting motionless until he heard the steel bolt close behind her. He walked up to the metal overhead trapeze they'd rigged in the workshop, hooked the holding clamps to the ManFac, went through the steps he'd learned quickly, and stepped backward slowly to emerge from the now-motionless ManFac of Afsar Husain. Lance washed up and slipped into casual sports clothes and walked slowly from the workshop into the living room, where Dirk Martin and the hastily assembled group waited for him.

He looked about the room, meeting the eyes and studied review of the twenty people who watched his approach. "Gentlemen, this is Mr. Parker," Dirk said. "I won't bother with introductions. Please identify yourself as you speak. It will be much easier that way."

Lance caught Deidre's eye. "Coffee?" she asked. He nodded and took a seat held for him with a table by his arm. He made certain to pick out from the group Arthur Patterson, sent by direct order of the President. Lance sipped coffee, making the wait uncomfortable. He took extra seconds to light a cigar and then directed his gaze about the room.

"Short and sweet," he said without preamble. "Let's not have any Cabinet meetings. Has anyone found anything?" He finished his coffee and leaned both hands on his cane held between his knees, the cigar smoke drifting slowly away from him. The men in the room exchanged glances with one another, but the only response was a low buzz of murmured conversation. Lance locked eyes with Jack Beal, security director for the university. "You, Jack. How about it?"

Beal didn't hide his own disappointment. "Empty hands, Mr. Parker. We've been following anybody and everybody who might fit into what we're looking for—"

"Jack, that's half the goddamned campus. How do you follow twenty thousand students?"

"The FBI's been working closely with us," Beal said, forcing some steel into his voice. "They have a list of names that seem the most likely to be troublemakers and—"

"The list is so much crap, Beal."

The FBI man didn't appreciate anything about Lance Parker. But, Bill Schaefer swallowed his pride and presented a fierce glare to Lance. "You're talking awfully strong for a man who has only questions, Parker," he snapped.

"That your best style?" Lance goaded him. "Or are you trying to resurrect the ghost of Hoover? The last time I heard he'd crumbled to dust. Not even enough left to turn over in his grave." Lance gestured impatiently at the FBI agent. "You *don't* have the right names, Schaefer. That's the long and short of it."

"Then why," Schaefer sneered, "don't you tell us who they are?"

"The list is being drawn up right now. It's not

complete, but we have most of the key names." Lance let it hang in the air. "We're preparing a cross-check of the names with organizations, biographical material, cross-references with associates—the usual statistical structuring."

"Then why the hell haven't we gotten that?" Schaefer shouted.

"Because you'd rush out and arrest them and screw up the whole works," Lance said, his words stinging Schaefer. "Hasn't it gotten through to you yet? It's not the people we want. *It's the plutonium.* Grabbing the people could lead unknown confederates to set off a bomb." Lance turned from the FBI man to the group at large. "Who's here from AEC? And, *uh,* DOD?"

Several people from the Atomic Energy Commission and two men from the Department of Defense raised their hands. "Short and sweet, just like I asked before, if you please, gentlemen," Lance requested. "Anything?"

Bob James from the AEC shook his head. "There isn't an inch of ground we haven't covered with every radiation detector known to man," he said. "I mean that quite specifically. We've had Geiger counters and ionization detectors and everything else in cars, on bicycles, on security vehicles, even in the hands and in the backpacks of two hundred people who've been over every foot of the campus. All we've got are a bunch of radioactive watches. And," he added, "two .357 magnums used by the local police force with radioactive night sights. We even picked up *that* kind of low-level radioactivity. But nothing with the signature we need."

"Defense?" Lance asked.

Gerald O'Connor looked glum. "We've been working with the other groups. We thought about using the ROTC locally but decided against it. We don't know if someone with them might be involved."

"Good move." Lance turned back to Jack Beal. "You've done the vehicle checks?"

Beal nodded, grateful for the chance to say something positive. "Mr. Parker, we've worked with local police, the sheriff's department, the highway patrol. We've even used public works trucks and street cleaners and everything else. We've catalogued every vehicle in this whole place big enough to handle the weight and bulk of the plutonium. We can't get a single lead."

"Well"—Lance sighed—"it would be harder to be more thorough than that. But then, Jack, I never expected you to find a thing."

Beal was openly surprised. "Why's that, sir?"

Everyone else hung on the response from Parker.

"Because everything points to the fact that the people who took the plutonium are well organized. They're also smart. They have discipline, and they can add two and two and come up with anticipating everything—precisely—that you've done. Why would they then leave themselves wide open to being exposed through your very predictable methods? You're all thinking on the wrong wavelength. You're looking for the criminal mind. You won't find it. Now," Lance said with emphasis, "who's here from the university's maintenance section?" A hand went up. "Your name, please?"

"Roger Coats."

"Good. I want a breakdown and a schematic of all heavy power line systems, especially 220 volts and up, everywhere on this campus."

Coats couldn't prevent the shrill laugh he offered in response. "You must be kidding me, mister. Or yourself. I don't know which. This university is filled with research centers and laboratories and workshops and medical centers and—" He stopped and studied Lance. "Parker, we've got heavy power loads criss-crossing this campus in every direction. You know what it takes to run those stadiums alone?"

"I don't know, and I don't care. I didn't ask for a sum of your burdens, Coats. I asked for schematics."

"You couldn't even *study* all those sheets in less than a month if you worked twenty-four hours a day!"

"For Christ's sake, Coats, shortcut the routine. Get all your heavy power line usage from your metering systems into computer charts and graphs. Use flow data, that sort of thing. You know how to do that, don't you?"

"Well, yes, but—"

"Then feed everything you get into a comparator open loop line on the computer. Compare the usage for the last few days with the pattern established for the past six months. You can eliminate the peak loads and drops as based on football games and other events with obvious high-power output. Somewhere in that mass of raw data, something is going to stick up its pointed little head and tell us where we have to-tally unexpected and unprecedented power demands. We can then begin to trace it down, determine if machinery is involved. However it happens, we'll get some leads. Hard leads. They'll be lighthouses in all this darkness. Don't just *sit* there, man! Get the lead out. Get started right away."

"Do you know what the hell time it is, Parker?"

"Yeah, I know. Sixty seconds to midnight, and when the bell tolls twelve, you're liable to find a mushroom growing under your feet. The kind that goes up to forty thousand feet. Jesus, get cracking."

Roger Coats and an assistant stalked out. *Good,* thought Lance. *He's pissed off, and he'll break his chops to prove me wrong.* The room settled down, and Dirk Martin stood up, pacing nervously. He stopped and looked directly at Lance.

"Did you hear what happened tonight at that seminar in the auditorium?"

"No. I wasn't there, Dirk. I got back here and came right in to join you. Something special?"

Dirk shook his head in memory of the events. "Special, all right. It was incredible, that's what it was." He grimaced. "Some giant, he's listed in the school records as a Turk *and* an Iranian—"

"You mean dual citizenship?" Lance broke in. He saw Dirk nodding, and Lance showed contempt. "And the FBI didn't know a thing about him?"

He glanced at Bill Schaefer. "Maybe I was wrong. Maybe Hoover *is* spinning in his grave. Dirk, forgive me. Please go on."

Dirk shrugged in frustration. "He has a mind like a razor. I guess seeing him standing there bigger than life fooled us. He was so fast he kept ahead of us and whipped the crowd along as he desired. Then some football players, the asses, lost their temper and jumped him. He broke them up like they were children! I've never seen such strength like that."

"Who is he?" Lance pressed.

"Oh, that's no secret. He told us. He announced it, for God's sake. Afsar Husain. I know one thing. We've got to learn a lot more about him."

Lance exchanged a casual glance with Lee Grazzi. Only they knew that Lee had paid $200 to two rough-and-tumble players of the Gator football team "to teach that damn Turk a lesson." But right now both men were in the hospital.

"Never mind him," Lance said to Dirk. "If he's that willing to be publicly recognized, then he's no problem for us because he's not involved in it." Lance turned to Arthur Patterson. "Mr. Patterson, you've been very quiet. What's the question you've been waiting to drop on us?"

Arthur Patterson smiled as he stubbed out a cigarette. He couldn't smoke in the White House—the President was a fanatic on fresh air—and he made up for his loss by chain-smoking every chance he had. He still had the smile as he looked up at Lance. "A question I haven't heard voiced by anyone, Mr. Parker. I assume the group you're trying to identify as to its lair is the same group you believe has the plutonium and that they are attempting to assemble a bomb from this material. Of course, of course. But why, I wonder, did they ever take the plutonium at all? What are they going to do with it? And if they do put together their apparatus and they do have a bomb—what are they after?"

The people assembled in the living room exchanged embarrassed glances. It was a question astonishingly simple, and they hadn't voiced it aloud. Now it hung in the air like heavy smoke that wouldn't dissipate.

"Very good, Mr. Patterson," Lance responded in the silence. "First answer—yes, I'm convinced the student group we're tracking down as an undercover organization is the same group that has the plutonium. Second answer—they'll attempt to assemble their bomb because they haven't got enough crunch with just the plutonium. Let me stay with the bomb for a moment. It'll be a crude affair. A very heavy, bulky device with a hell of a lot of battery power. That limits their means of transport."

Lance shifted in his chair. "Now let's extrapolate in reverse, all right? *Where is there a target within the restrictions of movement of this bomb?*" He looked about the room. "Anybody got any favorites? The space shuttle facilities at the Kennedy Space Center? That bomb inside the Vehicle Assembly

Building could put us back for years. But," he said, his smile showing his sudden position as devil's advocate, "they'd never get into the area if we increased security. So that's out."

Dirk motioned to Lance. "What about a nuclear reactor plant? Ever since Three Mile Island and that *China Syndrome* movie, that would certainly have its effect on the public."

Lance shook his head. "Nope. Again, too much security to get into anyplace like that once it's alerted, and two, the story wouldn't hold together once scientists got through identifying the debris. It would be obvious the plant was blown up instead of blowing up on its own." His gaze went around the room. "Jesus, can't anybody here see it? The FBI, the AEC—*anybody?*"

Schaefer's face was contorted. "You've been making your digs all night," he snarled. "All right, you smart son of a bitch, *you* tell *us*."

Dirk Martin swung to the FBI agent. "One more name-calling like that and I'll throw you out of here myself," he warned.

Lance laughed aloud. "Simmer down, Dirk. The man is frustrated. I'll tell you what they're after. What their target is and always has been." He paused, the smile thin and cold.

"It's right here. *It's the university itself.* The entire city of Gainesville, in fact. Can't you see it? This place has been a symbol for all universities because of its highly organized radical student groups—most of them very serious and dedicated to building a better world than destroying it. So they've made the university extremely visible. Ergo—the best of all targets, especially because the place is so damned vulnerable. Another reason is that by our staying right at home, all the effort we've expended in searching vehicles and monitoring roads and figuring out everything else has been worthless to us and a beautiful decoy for them. Now everybody hold it down. I know you've scoured this place with radiation monitors. But if the plutonium is sealed in lead and other materials, you can hold a Geiger counter right next to the bomb and get nothing of a signature. So don't blame yourself for failure in that department. I—"

Schaefer leaned forward. "When do you translate your supposition into hard fact? Are you ready to support the bureau in rounding up these dissidents? We could do it in a matter of hours."

"Schaefer, the truth is that it wouldn't do us a bit of good. In fact," Lance said, "it would only make everything worse."

"How the devil do you figure that?"

"Because of what a group of us did many years ago when we worked on the government's program to see just how well engineering students could do in building their own nuclear bombs from information available to any informed person." Lance let his gaze cover every person in the room. "I was one of those young engineers, and while we've been hashing all this over in this room, the truth dawned on me. I'd like to say I knew it all the time, but that isn't the way it happened. It began to become obvious as we were going through our little family spat here."

He leaned back in his chair. Damn, he hated staying in one position too long. He sighed and looked up again.

"*Dammit, they've already built the bomb!*" He let the sudden uproar run its course. It didn't last long. They were hanging on the edge to hear the rest of it. "Don't you see? They, the student group, have known for a long time this program of energy output using plutonium would be coming to the university. They're smart. Smarter than I gave them credit for. They did exactly what we did years ago. Since they knew the plutonium would be coming here, *they built the bomb months ago.* They used lead as a dummy bomb material, assembled the bomb, and kept it hidden until they could grab the plutonium. Then they cut the plutonium in a machine shop to the sizes they wanted—which was easy enough, since they could spread out the work in home shops and garages—and brought it back together for assembly into the final bomb. *Which they most likely have already put together.*"

It wasn't a hot potato in their laps—it was a great lump of coal blazing fiercely. There were the obvious questions: Where was the triple-damned bomb? Were the students really capable of detonating the weapon? How great would be the damage?

And it all led to the question: *What do they want?* They had to get into the minds and thoughts of the student group, and that was a rocky pathway.

They couldn't act the role of the bull in the china shop by making sweeping raids and arrests. There was no way to make a lightning strike through the campus and the school buildings because first, it would take too long; second, the bomb might not be on the school grounds; and third and most important of all, that could force or panic the students to set off the bomb.

Lee seemed to be reading his thoughts.

"Lance, if they fire that weapon . . ." She hesitated, dreading to voice it aloud. "I mean, what happens? How bad would it be?"

He turned to her. "At the very least it would be pure hell. We got about twenty thousand tons' explosive yield from the bomb we dropped over Hiroshima, and that was set off very high above the city for maximum blast effect. This weapon, well, it's impossible to figure. At its lowest level they would have to get at least two to four kilotons, and at the high end, which I doubt, maybe fourteen kilotons. My guess is a bomb equal to about eight thousand tons of explosive force." He addressed the group. "Do you know what that means? *All* of the university will be torn apart. You'll have a crater several hundred feet in diameter. A good part of the city will be shattered. Because it will be a ground burst, the fireball will be somewhat contained, but most of Gainesville will be set aflame. And after the heat pulse and the shock wave and the thousand-mile-an-hour winds we have a ground burst dissemination of intensely hot, really dirty radioactivity. That will carry slightly upwind, maybe a mile to the side of the winds, and will dump heavy radioactivity for five to thirty miles downwind and minor hell a hundred to four hundred miles beyond that." He took a deep breath. "There are, let's say, a hundred thousand people in this town, including the students. If more than thirty thousand survive—and most of those will be burned and poisoned by fallout—it would be a miracle. You could kiss off this university and the entire city. Period."

"Then, as far as I'm concerned, we should evacuate this city immediately," announced Dirk.

"You might make them nervous," Lance said. "They need the city as a hostage. If you so much as start a mass evacuation—boom."

"But then they'd be killed along with the rest of us," Deidre protested.

"First, they might be willing to pay the price. Second," Lance added, "they could set it off by remote control. A radio signal, a coded telephone call; anything. No, sorry. That reasoning won't sustain itself with the kind of dedication we're facing."

"We still don't know what they want," Schaefer said.

"I've got to agree with you," Lance said to the FBI man. "That keeps us in a bind. We've got to find out

344

their plans, and that, in turn, may tell us where the bomb is located, and that, in turn, tells us their plans. I know, it's a crazy sort of Catch-22, but we've *got* to find a way to break that circle." Again he let his eyes rove the room. "There's one thing they can't escape," he told the group. "Wherever they have that damned thing, it needs power. It needs a minimum of physical space because of power and shielding. It's *got* to be so goddamned obvious we can't see that one tree because of the whole bloody forest surrounding us. But I know how these youngsters think, so it *won't* be where we'd look for power, like a generating plant or a machine shop or something so obvious. They are damnably clever."

The security chief for the university shook his head. "Then you'd better tell us how we find out what they plan without tipping our hand."

"There's a way," Lance said with a cold smile. "When logic and rational thinking and orderly progress don't work, you turn to raw emotion. And that's what we're going to use."

"You sound like you want a riot," Dirk said with concern.

"Want? I'm going to orchestrate it," Lance promised him.

Chapter 29

"Deidre, can you get me a list, quickly, of all the student organizations with any clout to them? Overt and covert, just so long as they have enough people and muscle to get things done?" Lance cupped a mug of coffee in both hands. The only people still in the house were Lance and Lee and the Martins. They were wrapping up, planning.

Deidre rifled through a file. "I already have it. It seemed an obvious reference to keep on hand."

Lance nodded to Dirk. "She's still more efficient than the both of us put together," he said. "Come over here and let's look at these names."

He asked questions, got fast answers. "You know, I'm starting to see the pattern," Lance said at last. "It's no longer a case of an Arab group from any one country or even a group of countries. The Indo-Iranians and Arab-Iranians have melted into the overall picture as well. Ever since Iran tore itself apart, that part of the world has been involved not only in turmoil and turnovers but in a whole new *pattern* of changing power and influence. The Middle East we all knew is gone."

"You mean, like Egypt and Israel?" Deidre asked.

"I mean Egypt and Israel as a single entity," Lance confirmed. "Not just in the let's-quit-fighting-each-other, but in the fact they've pooled their military strength, and with a lot of American help, and they dominate all military strength throughout what we consider all of the Holy Land. And what did that produce? Arab countries that didn't know which way to turn. Islamic soul suffering in a helpless urge to return to the seventeenth century. History against modern times. Arab solidarity brought on by cash flow from oil to suppress historical bonds. I'm not quite prepared to turn this into an all-night current events seminar, but the upshot of it all is clear. These students, from what we can call the desert worlds, have formed their own loose but clearly identifiable coalition. The people we're trying to pinpoint have transformed rhetoric into action. And that kind of action meant planning ahead, building the bomb, and grabbing the plutonium when it arrived. They're brilliant, but they don't have experience, and that means they don't have the savvy of really dirty fighting." He glanced at the others. "Like the house we rented here in town," he added.

"I've been meaning to ask you about that," Dirk said. "A thousand a month, and you've got someone else living there. Why?"

"Because I want this group, which obviously has identified me through its own undercover organization within the campus life, to believe I'm in that house. Me and Lee. That way they don't look for us here. If ever they decide to do something against us at the house, they'll find some very tough and well-armed mercenaries we hired to take our place there."

Deidre nodded. "I'll buy that. More to the point, I'm sure those students believe you're in that house."

Lance shifted ground swiftly. "How familiar are you with Hillel?" He directed his question to Dirk.

"I know them well enough," Dirk said. "Everybody does, of course. They're a strong Jewish group, fiercely proud of their heritage, determined to keep Hebrew studies as much a part of the school program as black studies or even Arab studies."

"Are they well supported?"

"They're not very large in terms of numbers of students," Dirk replied, "but yes, they're well supported. The men and women who supply the money stay out of the action, so to speak. It's the youngsters, the firebrands, who really run the organization, and like any other organization, there's always a small ruling clique. *That* bunch has the *chutzpah.* They act like sabras—right out of a battle in the desert. They're very proud, and—"

"How much anti-Semitism here?"

Dirk glanced at Deidre before answering. Her nod confirmed they shared the same opinion. "Some. It crops up every now and then. Mostly it's low-key. Every now and then the haters get fired up, and it gets a bit nasty. But the university steps very heavily on hate programs involving *any* group. In fact, that's one way they keep Matthew Krieger in line."

"You'd better spell out some more on him," Lance said.

"He's a young man, brilliant, really, who's the organizational power behind the scenes of Hillel. He's also a part of the Blue Key organization here. They're involved with the upholding of what they consider to be minimum standards for this university. They include many alumni from well back in the history of the university, but the aspect to which I'm referring involves current student activity. Special events, homecomings, tradition, that sort of thing.

349

Krieger is one member of this group, and he works hard for it."

"What does he do with Hillel?"

"He's the firebrand. In fact," Dirk recalled, "he's a cousin of Joel Katz, the man in charge of nuclear weapons security for Israel. He's hardly a stranger to any of this."

"Deidre, can you set up a meeting with him for me? Tonight?" Lance asked.

"I'll call. Anyplace in particular?"

"Let him pick it."

They sat together along a wall of the Olde College Inn on University Avenue directly across from the campus. Heavy wood decor, beautiful stained glass. The food was excellent, the bar renowned—and the heated debates as much a part of the local scenery as the lights overhead. Debating went on mostly in a convivial manner, but at times it could be heated, and the manager always studied any unusually large group of students. If he so much as smelled trouble, he prepared for it. But it was rare, and this night he relaxed. He'd seen Matthew Krieger, and that could always charge the air. But tonight Krieger sat with an older stranger, and they were deep into their own thing.

Then it started coming unglued. Four students, their sweater colors marking them unmistakably as from Hillel, were swiftly heating up an exchange with nearly a dozen other students the manager recognized as from the Arab student bloc. He signaled to his bartenders to be ready. They didn't wait long. The exchange graduated into insults, and the insults into shouts and then curses and threats. Immediately the manager switched off the music loudspeakers. He knew that sometimes hearing his own voice bouncing off the walls can quiet a man.

It didn't work. A Jordanian student spit into the face of an intense youngster from Israel. The sabra smiled at the Jordanian, but the smile disguised the fist that crashed into the nose of the other student. Blood flew, there was a yelp of pain, and the Jordanian boy flew wildly through the air to crash into the midst of his own group. Nine against four; good odds for the husky youngsters from Hillel. Chairs crashed into the Arab group, and the manager saw knives flash. "Holy shit," he swore, and motioned for someone to call the police. He grabbed a fire extinguisher and ran to the group, spraying into faces and eyes. It had always been his most effective quencher for this sort of fire. Hissing, foaming, and supercold carbon dioxide did wonders. It would have done the same tonight except that a half dozen additional Arab youths burst through the entrance doors and ran gleefully into the melee. The manager spun about, caught the newcomers flush in the face with freezing foam. They stopped, skidded, tumbled, and were booted out the door. The police hit the inn from the front and back doors and found a lot of people bloodied, one Hillel youth with a deep stab wound to the ribs, and no one, on either side, who knew a thing.

Not until the place was quieted down and the mess cleaned up did it occur to the manager that the worst troublemaker of them all, Matthew Krieger, had never budged from his chair the whole time.

The news of the brief battle in the inn, and the ugly mood accompanying its telling, spread swiftly through the campus. Reports ghosted through the university that violent reprisals, on *both* sides, were inevitable.

Dirk Martin slowly replaced the telephone on its cradle in his living room. "That's the fourth call.

The dean and the president are asking every teacher in the school to stand by for duty at any time to help quell the disturbances. They seem almost sure to happen. Lance, what the hell are you so pleased about?"

Lance smiled at his agitated friend. "Because it's going exactly as I planned."

"But that's crazy!" Dirk shouted. "Don't you realize there are forty thousand students on that campus? They're hotheaded, and the radicals are dancing jigs about all the hell they can raise, and you sit there grinning like a Cheshire cat and tell me it's all wonderful!"

Lance nodded. "That's right. The key to all this is that we've got to make them believe things are going the way they want—that they are in control. Then they'll reveal themselves. It's vital we let this thing take its own course. It's the one hope we have to open doors while there's still time."

"People can be killed!"

"So what?"

Dirk stared at his friend. "I can't believe you said that." His face had pain on it.

"You haven't been close enough to death on a large scale," Lance said quietly. "You can't measure this problem by trying desperately to prevent one or a dozen people from getting killed if that's the only way to find that bomb. This goes beyond your cherished principles, Dirk. Far beyond them."

"You sure as hell don't sound like the Lance Parker I know," Dirk said angrily.

"I'm not," Lance replied smoothly. "Let me try it your way. We stop the violence that's building. We arrest the ringleaders, lock them up. We put the lid on everything. *And then that goddamned bomb explodes and kills fifty or sixty or maybe eighty thousand people.* The university is destroyed, and so is the city. And then what are you going to do? Assuming, of course, *you're* not just so much glowing radioactive ash yourself. Wring your hands and wail how sorry you are?" Lance climbed stiffly to his feet, resting with both hands on his cane. "This is the only way we have to go. To get to the truth of it, it's our *only* hope."

He started for the workshop, stopped to look back. "The next phase is under way. Will you be patient with me just a bit? I have a friend waiting for me in the workshop. I want you to meet him."

Dirk nodded, unhappy. "All right. I'll wait."

Dirk climbed slowly to his feet. He stared at the stranger with Lee, exchanged a puzzled look with Deidre, and then turned back to the young man who accompanied Lee Grazzi. He dwarfed her with his great shoulders and bulk. "Dirk, Deidre, this is Moshe Greenbaum." She gestured to her hosts. "Moshe, Dirk and Deidre Martin."

The young giant with the bull neck, a thick black beard, and curly hair nodded. He extended a hand that enveloped that of Dirk. "It is my pleasure," he said in a rumbling voice. "Professor Martin, of course. I saw what happened during the seminar. I wish I could apologize for that night, on behalf of the students."

"Thank you," Dirk murmured. He turned to Lee. "Where's Lance?"

Moshe Greenbaum answered. "He had to go to a meeting with Krieger. He drove me here, and they left together. Something came up that demanded his attention immediately. He asked me to apologize for the way he left so suddenly."

Greenbaum wore about his neck a thick gold chain, at the end of which hung a gold Star of David. Dirk gestured to it. "Forgive what may seem a prejudiced remark, but with the mood at the university, after that fracas at the College Inn, wearing that symbol could cause you a great deal of trouble."

Gleaming white teeth appeared in a broad smile, all the brighter against the dark beard. "I hope so, Professor. I dearly hope so."

Deidre showed her surprise. "I don't understand. You *want* trouble? I should think we've all had enough of that."

Moshe shook his head. "No. Not yet. If trouble does not come to me, then I must seek it out. Make it."

"That's ridiculous!" Dirk snapped.

"I apologize for disturbing you," he was told. "But you made a promise to Mr. Parker, did you not, Professor?"

"I don't understand. What promise?"

"That you would not interfere. You see, I follow Mr. Parker's instructions."

"You know what I promised Lance Parker?" Dirk turned with undisguised anger to Lee. "How the hell can he know that? I didn't think Lance would compromise what went on privately in this house."

Lee remained unruffled by the sudden heat from her friend. "He knows everything, Dirk."

"Oh, does he, now?" Dirk snapped. "Does he really? Does he know that the Student Pan-Arab League is holding a rally tonight? That there'll be a thousand fired-up students, maybe twice that many, demonstrating against nuclear energy plants? Against our own nuclear program here at the university? Does he know that after what happened today, if he walks among that crowd dressed like that, with that Star of David, that he could *cause* a riot?"

Again Greenbaum rocked him with that dazzling smile. "Sir, that is my dearest wish. You will excuse me, please? It has been a pleasure to meet with you."

He was gone. They heard the car leaving. Dirk

looked at Lee, his frustration boiling within him. "Lance has gone crazy. That is the goddamnedest thing I ever heard of! He's not only happy about the idea of a riot—he's actually going to *cause* one!"

Lee laughed. "You went to school with Lance. *You* did the world tour with him. You jumped out of airplanes and climbed mountains and—well, what's a little old riot or two?"

Dirk looked at his wife, then pointed to Lee. "She's as crazy as Lance."

Deidre shrugged. "I get the distinct feeling, my dear, that we are not really in on what's happening."

Moshe Greenbaum parked his car and set off at a brisk pace toward the open field. The glow from floodlights was a wide beacon directing his movement. Then he heard the sounds and cursed. He broke into a swift run. Even from this distance he could hear the uproar. Damn! He was late. The rally had already disintegrated into a furious melee. He ran into the outer edges of the milling crowd and in a glance took in the situation. Clear enough, all right. The students from Hillel had gathered all their strength, maneuvering carefully into a well-rehearsed flying wedge and, armed with everything from baseball bats to brass knuckles and Mace, had charged the crowd, moving with military precision toward the speaking platform. In the process they were smacking aside startled onlookers. Some people were hurt, many were terrified, and all were excited. Screams and shouts sounded over the general uproar, drowning the shouting, garbled voices from the platform.

Greenbaum ran faster, his great bulk carrying him relentlessly through the crowd, knocking aside anyone in his way as he hammered his own path to the raised platform. Everything depended upon his reaching the small group who had assembled and were running

Martin Caidin

this rally. He needed desperately to identify them at just the precise moment, with emotion screeching raw and naked from their midst. Finally, he was far enough into the milling throng to see a ring of students, clubs and bats and knives and chains in their hands, forming a cordon before several people huddled beyond their defensive wall of bodies.

That's them. That's them—get in there fast! Greenbaum swerved without stopping in his run, his great fists and arms thudding and slamming people aside. He stopped suddenly as a thought pierced his own emotions. This was the wrong way to handle this. It wouldn't do for him to carry this act solo. He shouted to a group of Hillel students. "This way! This way, damn you! They're over here. Come on!"

He took off at a dead run again, students swarming behind him. Closer to the defending cordon he saw just how right he was. Behind the shoulder-to-shoulder guards, her face frightened and yet still in control of herself, was the girl. Laila Habail. And by her side, confirming everything he already suspected, was none other than her brooding compatriot Yasar al-Milah, his face already bloodied, his eyes wild.

Greenbaum rushed the group. He was moving too fast to sidestep a man who jerked a gun from his belt, raised the weapon, and in that single smooth motion fired point-blank at the human rhino charging him. The shot boomed through the shouting and screaming; people turned to see who would fall. Greenbaum grunted with the impact of the heavy slug into his leg, but he kept running forward, shouting curses, his great fist smacking the gunman along the side of his head before he could fire again. The gun flew wildly in one direction, and the man tumbled crazily in the opposite direction, blood already staining the side of his face. Greenbaum bulled through the cordon of bodies, a wild-eyed demon throwing aside tables and

356

kicking chairs from his path. Then he was towering over Laila Habail. Screeching madly, Yasar al-Milah threw himself upon the big Hebrew, fingers clawing at his eyes. Greenbaum disposed of the maddened youngster with a single blow to his chest, and then his powerful hand closed over Laila's wrist.

He jerked her down brutally, dragged her to the back of the platform. He was unprepared for the fanaticism of al-Milah, who threw himself atop the big man's back, fingers clawing at his ears and eyes. Greenbaum had no time to waste. Still holding the girl, with his other arm he snapped al-Milah's arm like a stick. The boy screamed with the terrible pain and fell away. Greenbaum pulled Laila close to his face. She looked into the dark eyes, the fierce beard, into the face of certain death.

"The bomb," Greenbaum shouted over the din. "Tell me where it is, or I'll twist your arm out of its socket!" She pulled frantically, her eyes wide, terrified.

A club smashed against Greenbaum's head. He saw a great flash of red as he rolled aside instinctively, coming up with a spinning movement. Damn! He had no time— The club came down again, and he stepped inside the blow, his heavy shoe crashing into the groin of his attacker. There was a muffled gasp of pain. Greenbaum paid him no more attention and turned back to Laila just in time to see her pulling a revolver from her purse. She fired point-blank at the crazed giant before her.

The blow was like an anvil in his chest. Greenbaum staggered backward, fighting for air and cursing at the same time. Even through the woven metal and plastiskin of the ManFac that had been a terrifying impact. He roared with his rage and charged. Laila stared with disbelief, fired again. This time her aim was off as the shot thundered in Greenbaum's ears, but he felt the bullet plow into the same leg that had been struck before. The way the foot jerked, a sudden and violent spasm, he knew he'd taken damage to critical wiring. He smacked the gun from her hand, and without thinking, unable to stop the instinctive move, his other hand struck her harder than he intended along the side of her face. She whirled about like a rag doll and crumpled unconscious to the ground.

You fool! You—

Lance Parker's eyes in the face of Moshe Greenbaum froze on the purse of Laila Habail where its contents lay scattered by her unconscious form. A key with a tag lay in plain view. He sucked in his breath, an icy wind rushing through him. *My God, that's it . . . that's where they've got the bomb. Right under our noses . . .*

He turned and ran, feeling his left leg dragging, moving more slowly than the right so that his movement was a crazy scuttling motion. He heard sirens and police shouting for him to halt. He pulled his head down, forcing himself to run faster. Shots rang out, and he felt a mule kick him in his shoulder. Cursing, he rolled to the ground, beyond bushes, skidded down an incline, and then he was on his feet again and running in that crazy scuttle for the College of Journalism.

Chapter 30

He hit the main doors to the building at full speed, throwing his shoulder into the center. Glass shattered and metal screeched as the lock broke apart and he plunged into the lobby. He paused for a moment to find his bearings. All the time he'd been running for the college center he'd been thinking furiously. There would be one place and one place only in this building that had all the ingredients they needed to handle the bomb. Power, plenty of equipment to conceal the device, communications, and unnoticed and open access to and from the room where they kept the weapon. There was only one area that had 220-volt power cables in extensive use as well as workrooms and power systems and batteries—the television broadcasting studios of the College of Journalism. It fitted hand in glove. One large wheeled container marked "Video equipment" or "Film," kept locked, on wheels so it could be moved easily, wouldn't attract the first bit of attention, especially when you kept a group of your own people present at all times to keep an eye on things. He recalled something he'd heard in Dirk's house. The Arab students, especially

359

those working with Aramco, were producing Arabic-language television shows of *Sesame Street*, and that made the cover for the radical groups all the more secure.

Lance in the ManFac of Moshe Greenbaum pounded up three flights of stairs—and was appalled to find himself looking down a long corridor with television studios to each side. He went down the corridor like an engine of destruction, smashing open locked doors —he had no time for keys. It was in the sixth studio, pushed against a wall, and just as he'd expected— a heavy wheeled and locked case marked "Video equipment." What drew his eye was the combination lock; every other equipment case had a lock that opened with a key. It *had* to be what he sought. Why else lock the case with a combination lock inside a locked studio? He studied the case, forcing down his impatience. Thank God—there were no wires leading to the case and no antennas he could detect.

He heard feet pounding along the corridor, coming closer. Two students burst into the studio. "Hey! You're not allowed in here! Who are you?" The questions came in staccato fashion, and he felt relieved again. Their appearance meant no one else had been in here tonight to set up a booby trap detonator. Then he heard words that made him freeze.

"Dammit, Johnny, I'm calling the police."

Lance spun about. There wasn't time to explain. He hated what he had to do to innocent youngsters, but he stepped forward and dropped each youth with a ripping punch to the stomach. He dragged them out of sight behind a desk and turned back to the heavy case. Even the ManFac system couldn't break the lock, but these kids had made a common mistake. Their lock was many times stronger than the hasp riveted to the case. He grasped the lock and pulled, bracing himself for every ounce of strength those motors and cables in his arm and hand could supply. The metal bent, and then the rivets tore loose. He opened the case carefully and laid the cover all the way back against its hinges.

He couldn't believe the pounding of his heart. He tried to convince himself that if he made a single wrong move, he'd never know it, would be reduced to free atoms before the first trickle of thought could move through his brain. It didn't help. He looked down without moving, studying, trying to remember the bomb systems he'd worked on in the past. The equipment was just as he'd figured. The students had access to published material on the original bomb design used against Hiroshima. Simplicity itself.

Grooved chambers. The plutonium halves well separated and shielded from one another at opposite ends of the long shotgun type of barrel. On each end of the shotgun system, at the back of each half of plutonium of subcritical mass, there was a rocket-boost unit and—

"Good God," he murmured aloud. Those rockets . . . he knew them. RATO systems to assist aircraft in making short-field takeoffs. Common enough, and safe. *But these were old surplus units, and that meant they were unstable. The bloody fools!*

If the rockets fired properly, each ignited with the same electrical charge, they would ram the two halves of plutonium together and keep them together long enough to reach the K factor—when the plutonium achieved sufficient mass and size to release an uncontrolled fission reaction. The big bang itself. Sixty or seventy or a hundred million degrees in a self-contained eternity. The exact temperature determined the overpressure and the force of the killer shock wave booming outward. And the earthquake shock and all the other effects associated with the nuclear detonation.

361

He was mesmerized by the rocket boosters. They scared the absolute hell out of him. The longer they were kept beyond their "to be destroyed" date, the more brittle and unstable they became. If one of them were fired accidentally, and you could do that simply by jarring the goddamned thing, it would slam the two plutonium halves together and create, at the minimum, a fiercely radioactive soft explosion. A sort of "nuclear pop" that would still kick out an explosion greater than a thousand tons of nitro. A jarring impact, static electricity, even a microwave beam—almost anything would set off these suckers. He studied the mechanism with more deliberation, found the connecting wires. He had no tools, and there wasn't time to find any. The ManFac fingers would have to do.

He unscrewed the hold-down bolts to the wires and removed them with infinite care. His breath released in a gasp. There, he'd disconnected the batteries. That was one step on the way to immobilizing this hellish contraption. But it wasn't enough. He didn't even dare try to remove the rocket boosters. If he slipped . . . The only way to make this thing safe, without the right time and tools, was to get the whole works under water. Immerse it completely. Water soak would soon cut the whole assembly into a safe mess.

He strained against the casing. At least five hundred pounds. Normally the exoskeletal framework of the ManFac could handle the weight. But not now. Not with that left leg jerking in fitful spasms he couldn't predict. He had to reduce the weight. He removed the heavy batteries. Okay, now for the lead shielding. He hesitated. Plutonium was a metal. Its radioactivity wasn't dangerous in a pure form. You could hold a chunk of it in a leather or asbestos glove at arm's length and be safe. But this wasn't pure, and it lacked that comfortable safety margin. *Screw it—you've got to gamble. Besides, the ManFac provides some shielding.*

Lance rolled his eyes to whatever deity above was exercising its macabre sense of humor. He reached into the mechanism, freed the clamps for the lead shielding. A Geiger counter immediately sounded a rash of clicking sounds, a billion radioactive crickets that wouldn't go away. "Oh, Jesus," he moaned. He'd flashed back to that sphere beneath the mountain. *Got to stop that. Concentrate on now. Now. Now.*

The batteries were gone. The heavy lead shielding was gone. He could lift the bomb mechanism from the case. He reached down, balancing himself as best as he could on that damned twitching leg. He lifted slowly, figuring the weight at two hundred pounds. Normally he would have heaved that weight into his arms like lifting a small child. He still had the arm power, but unbalanced as he was, the weight made his leg as slippery as a greased pig beneath him. Still, time was running out, there were police on the way, those students might revive, and the longer he delayed, the worse that leg became.

He lifted the bomb so that it was cradled against his chest and resting on both arms. He tried to force himself not to think of that radiation streaming invisibly from what he carried like an infant before him.

Through the doorway, moving sideways, into the long corridor.

His left foot began to drag behind him. Balance was a nightmare.

He scuttled carefully along the corridor, close to the wall in the event his balance went. He could always try to cushion any impact from setting off those rocket boosters. *You won't feel a thing, sweetheart. Don't even give it a second thought.*

The stairway before him. He made the turn slowly.

He took the steps only one at a time, leaning his shoulder against the wall, descending in a strange shuffling, slow slide. It seemed an hour before he reached the second floor. Two more flights to go.

One more flight.

He slipped, jammed his weight against the wall. The leg wanted to jitterbug beneath him. He pressed hard, using the friction of weight and strength against the wall as he went down the last flight of stairs. Before him were fire exit doors. They could be opened only from the inside by the pressing of a door-wide lever. But they'd set off the night alarm.

No way out of that. He went through the door sideways, his hip shoving the lever forward and down. Alarm bells clamored about him. *Forget them. Keep going.* He perspired profusely within the ManFac, salt stinging his eyes. The ManFac was still functioning, but his own body was draining away its energy like water through a fire hose.

He was outside. Maybe two hundred yards to go to reach the shore of the campus lake. He speeded up. If he went partially sideways, he took some of the weight off the leg. His movement was a swaying, drunken, half-running gait. He saw flashlights coming around the corner of the building. He forced himself to keep his pace. Any faster and he might fall. *Goodbye, university. Good-bye, Gainesville. So long, Lee. It's been great. SHUT UP!*

Voices shouted at him. Feet pounded, running, after him. The lakeshore was closer. He saw streetlights reflecting from the water.

A warning shot cracked through the night air. Shouts, another shot. He kept going, desperate, crazy to reach the lake. He was close now, the water beckoning to him.

He blinked, cursing the sweat in his eyes. The ManFac life-support system was shorting out from the damage to the leg, and he was heating dangerously. But now he was at the edge of a grass slope leading directly to the water. He summoned all his strength and made a last desperate run, a maniacal motion just short of stumbling helplessly. A bullet crashed into his right shoulder. It deflected from the suit with a metallic scream, but it threw him off-balance, and he was falling. He threw himself *into* the fall, going with it, lunging for the water and at the same time twisting so that he would fall backward to protect the hellish mechanism in his arms. He braced for impact with the ground.

Water splashed heavily all about him. *We made it!* He went under the surface like a boulder, twisting again, easier this time. He felt soft surface beneath him. He knew he must keep moving to prevent sinking into the mud near the shoreline. He must get the bomb into the deepest water possible. It would need at least twenty minutes of soaking to dampen the rockets so they couldn't fire. If he remained by the shore, they might unwittingly retrieve the bomb before the rockets were disabled. He pushed ahead blindly, leaning like a deep-sea diver into his movement. He could barely guide himself by the lights wavering and dreamlike from the lamps along the campus walkways. Then he could carry the weight no more, not his own weight, another foot. He bent over to lower the bomb gently to the mud. Exhaustion scourged him. He felt the cold touch of water coming into the ManFac. He *must* keep moving. He flailed with his arms, kicking with one leg, the other sparking from the now-soaked short circuits.

Dizzy, exhausted, he heard a warning from his own mind that the ManFac had become a deathtrap. He must release himself. He took a final deep breath and pressed the switch for full manual override. If only the system still worked—

The backups came into play. The panels along the back of the ManFac slid aside, and he eased away from the now-inert form as it fell slowly into mud. He forced himself not to gasp for air as the water struck him like an icy whip. Then he was completely free, lungs bursting for air. He clawed at water to propel himself upward, shaking uncontrollably. He was shivering inside and out, and he knew his muscles were knotting and cramping. He had no more than a minute before he would double up into a pain-racked ball.

His head cleared water, and he gasped air like an animal, no thought behind his sucking, gulping motions. His head cleared, but the cold savaged him. He swam desperately for the nearest lights. Closer. He felt soft mud beneath one foot, and he grasped for a bush, dragging himself onto the shore like a dog with palsy. He heard sirens, men shouting. He retched violently as he made the campus walk, lying on his side. Everything blurred. The world was spinning, and a light exploded in his eyes.

"Over here! Someone get an ambulance!"

The flashlight was on him again, and he felt a policeman's jacket on his body. He looked up, teeth chattering, body shaking, his skin blue.

"Robbed . . ." he gasped out. "Two men . . . mugged me . . . stole clothes. Help, need help. Call . . . call Professor Martin. Hurry. Call—"

Blackness.

Chapter 31

The light coalesced from darkness, unfreezing from eternal darkness. Lance's eyes were locked open. He wanted desperately to close them, to block out the terrible glare, but he couldn't. He was being forced to watch the tiny mote blossoming outward, white beyond white, perfectly round, a sphere of pure energy. Then there appeared the first caress of pink along the edges of the expanding white, glowing within itself, and there was white, and then the pink and then orange and red and fiery glowing blood appeared, and he knew he was witness to the nucleus birth of the atomic fireball that spread faster and faster and became a great blossoming creature writhing within itself, a terrible rosebud unfurling with shocking speed, and he heard the thunder begin, the drumroll of the end and beginning of eternity, and the thunder broke apart into a dog screaming in pain, and there was a crazy strangling boom that came from within himself and—

"Easy. Take it easy. You're having a nightmare." Hands held him down, and he snapped his eyes open, looking into Lee's face. The strangling sounds had come from his own throat, and he tried to move, but her hands were strong, and her voice kept soothing him. Then he was back to reality, and he saw beyond Lee and focused on the pale green walls of the hospital room.

"My God," he gasped, "what a nightmare!" He shook his head slowly, still fighting off the horror. Lee held a glass and straw to his mouth, and he sipped water.

"Lean back," Lee told him, and he let himself collapse into the pillows. She dabbed at his face and neck with a towel. "You all right now?" she asked.

"Yeah. Sure, I'm out of it. Where the hell am I? It looks like a hospital and—"

"Alachua General. That was quite a night you had," she said with a smile.

"Are we alone?"

"Yes. Dirk and Deidre stayed with me, but I convinced them to go home when the doctors said you wouldn't be awake for several hours. A great many people are frantic to talk with you, but the police put a guard outside the door, and we won't be bothered."

"I need some damned coffee. And a cigar," he said.

Lee went to the door, spoke with the police officer. She returned with a mug of coffee. "I brought along your cigars. God knows you deserve one."

He sipped slowly, waited as she held his lighter for him. He took a long, deep, shuddering breath and let it out slowly. It was okay. It was good. *Relax. Relax, man.*

"The last I remember," he said slowly, "was lying on that sidewalk, freezing to death. And, and,"—he fought for memories—"yeah, I remember now. Police. I told them I was mugged. Did they buy it?"

"They did. They brought you here in an ambulance. They called Dirk, and we got here as fast as we could. By then you'd been given a shot, and they had you pretty well under control. Shock, exhaustion, cramps—what you would expect." She kissed him gently. "I am *so* pleased about you. Not what happened. About you, yourself. Your recovery is marvelous. And what you need now is a long hot bath. Maybe even another cigar when this one is done."

"I thought you hated these cigars."

"Of course I do. They smell like— Never mind. I love you. The cigars come with you."

"Damned right," he growled, but couldn't avoid the smile. "By the way, what time is it?"

"Four thirty."

"In the morning?"

"*Uh-huh.*"

"Can you fill me in? It's important. Let me finish this coffee while you speak."

She brought a chair to his bedside. "Everything ended perfectly, Lance. Placing the bomb in the water was sheer genius. You—"

"Not me," he interrupted. "Moshe Greenbaum. Does anybody know yet about me?"

Lee shook her head. "I was going to tell Dirk and Deidre about ManFac, but decided that was up to you."

"We'll see later. Go on, hon."

"They pulled the bomb from the water about two hours after they found you. I saw it, by the way. Not the bomb. One of those rockets. Soaked through. They couldn't have fired."

"Thank God," he murmured. "It was so damned close."

"Yes, it was," she agreed.

"What about the ManFac?"

"No one knows it's in the water. It's about fourteen feet down. We can arrange to have it removed one night."

"Are they still looking for Moshe Greenbaum?"

369

She laughed with delight. "Are they ever! The whole town is going crazy trying to find him. He's the new hero of Gainesville."

Lance smiled. "They've got a long look ahead of them."

"I've got better news. They've identified the students leading the group that stole the plutonium. You were right. That boy and those two girls were running the whole show. They're in custody—hospital custody, I should say. Greenbaum was pretty rough on them. You ready for more good news?"

He took a long, comfortable drag on the cigar. "Try me."

"Dirk called a while ago to say that the university has drawn a check for two hundred and fifty thousand dollars." She squeezed his hand gently. "Lance, we've done it. We've opened the door to our future. And in the process, I might add, you saved a university and a city and perhaps a hundred thousand people from a horrible death."

Lance looked about him. "I hate hospitals, Lee."

"I know that. And you want the hell out of here, and right *now*, right?"

"Right. Where the hell are my clothes?"

"In that closet."

"Please, lover. Help me get dressed. I don't think Dirk will mind if we show up at this hour."

"Mind? They're going crazy waiting to talk with you." She brought his clothes to him. "You start getting dressed. I'll call Deidre and tell her we'll be there soon. And don't worry about checking out of here. The police are handling everything."

He sat on the edge of the bed. Just those few hours of sleep had done him a world of good. He was beset with a flood of emotions that challenged rational thinking. Lee had said it simply but so very well. *I am so pleased about you. . . . About you, your-*

self. That meant more to her than everything he'd done in his astonishing performance to recover the bomb, find the subversive group, save the city and—God, he'd come full swing, all right. He dressed slowly as Lee spoke with Deidre, hung up, and returned to him.

"Need some help?" she asked.

He waved her off. "I'm still a bit rocky, but it feels so damn good to do this by myself. Except that I don't have that cane and—"

She held it up for him.

"Thanks." He slipped into loafers. "I know this sounds crazy, especially after everything we did with those ManFacs, but being *me* is pretty damned great."

She seemed to sober her mood. "Don't *ever* forget what I once told you. ManFac can't do a thing for you. It's the other way around."

"It sounds good. But without what you did—" He shook his head. "No one has tied us together? Really?"

"Really," she said, her own self-satisfaction radiating from her. "There'll never be any doubt anymore. You changed from one person to another right under their noses, and they have no idea, absolutely none, that you were—" She stopped short. "Something I read," she said, speaking slowly. "Some wild stories out of Atlanta. It's beginning to fit. Is that where you—"

He grinned impishly. "Sure was."

"How incredible. How *beautiful*. The strength of that system is so beyond anything I ever dreamed it could have."

"Well, we know one thing for sure. ManFac system or not, you can get hurt, even killed, in that thing." He rubbed several places on his body. "My chest feels like it was hit by a—"

"Bullet," she finished for him."And it *was*. Remember?"

"Do I ever. We ready to go?"

"In a moment. I want to ask you something. How in the world could you carry that bomb with one leg shot up the way it was? The story is everywhere that Greenbaum was shot several times, including several bullets in one leg."

He nodded. "The crazy thing about that is that it felt as if *I* were shot. I mean, that ManFac should have felt pain, and I *did* feel the pain. I—"

The telephone rang. Lee answered the call and Lance waited. "Of course, that will be all right. I think it's wonderful. . . . Yes, yes, we'll wait here in the room. Bye." She hung up and turned to Lance. "That was Deidre. She says they're going crazy waiting for us and they'd like to pick us up personally. I couldn't tell them no."

He waved aside any objections. "That'll be great. In the meantime, I could use another coffee."

"Coming right up, Mr. Sherlock Holmes, sir!"

He sat quietly on the bed, feeling his strength returning slowly but steadily. Every time he tried to think coherently he found his mental track besieged by feelings of accomplishment, wonder, even awe at what he had managed to bring off. He mused about their future. If they had been able to do so much on their first try, why, there was no limit to what they might accomplish in the future. They could set up a complete investigating team, bring in all the startling developments of Lee. He looked up as she returned with the coffee. "I think I'll share this one with you. I could use a pick-me-up."

They were content to sit for several minutes without speaking, enmeshed in their own thoughts. Then they heard the police officer. "Go right on in, Professor, Mrs. Martin. They're waiting for you."

A jubilant Dirk and Deidre rushed into the room, to throw their arms about Lance and smother him with a bear hug from Dirk and wild kisses from his wife. They laughed like children. It was several minutes before they managed to calm down enough to speak coherently with one another.

"Lance, I spoke to one of the policemen who saw Moshe Greenbaum carrying that bomb," Dirk said with excitement. "He also said it was the most incredible thing he'd ever seen. Greenbaum took several shots, and he somehow managed to keep right on going. And then he just *vanished* into thin air after getting the bomb into the lake!"

"He'll show up," Lance said quietly.

"You know where he went? They'd like to hang a hundred medals around his neck," Dirk said.

Lance shook his head. "I know that youngster. He's, well, 'very special' is a good phrase for it."

"Very special?" Dirk laughed. "He's astounding! To think of the punishment he went through, and yet he carried that bomb down three flights of stairs, and was shot again, and still managed to get a bomb weighing two hundred pounds down to the water and—"

Lance waved a weary arm. "Later, Dirk, okay? Let's just get home first."

Dirk nodded, apologetic. "Sometimes I forget what you just went through," he said quickly. "You're right. Home it is."

He hurt in every muscle as he walked the long corridor to the elevator, and he had to use his cane, but it was a sweet trip indeed.

Chapter 32

Lance sprawled on the couch, luxuriating in the plush softness about him. Dirk hung up the phone, looking slightly bewildered. "I just spoke to Edward Duncan, the sheriff. He's in his car, on his way here. And so is Stan—"

"The chief of police, right?"

Dirk nodded. *"Uh-huh.* I thought I'd get some statie, I mean, with its being almost dawn, but they couldn't wait to get here to find out *how* you and your team did what you did." He laughed, just a bit nervously. "For that matter, I'm on pins and needles myself."

Lance exchanged a glance with Lee. *They* were the entire team. If you didn't count the ManFacs.

Soon they were assembled together in the living room, coffee and some needed brandy shared by all. Stan Corey leaned forward in his seat. He was a powerful man, and muscles bulged beneath his uniform. "I don't mind saying, Mr. Parker, that I've been in this business a very long time, like Ed here, and neither one of us knows quite how the devil you managed what you did."

Duncan gestured to break in. "Where, Mr. Parker, is that fellow Greenbaum? A gnat couldn't hide from us in this city, and no one has the slightest idea where he is. Let me ask you directly. Is he still here in the city?"

Lance shifted position. "I don't want to seem evasive," he said slowly, "but I'm not going to answer that. It's, well, let's call it playing the matter close to the chest. Greenbaum is no longer a factor in this conversation. That's the way we work."

The police chief and the sheriff exchanged a glance, accepted the inevitable, and nodded. Corey set aside his coffee cup. "All right, sir. It's your ball game. Would you mind telling us how you knew where to find the bomb? Or how Greenbaum or your other people pulled it off?"

Lance looked about the room, absolutely silent, waiting for his words.

He smiled. "I had to go back to square one. The old saw of starting at the beginning. And the first thing I told myself was that you should never underestimate the opposition. But that works *both* ways. The opposition, in this case, had its own mental Achilles' heel. They looked on us strictly as police, the law, the higher authority, and they forgot that we would think just like they did. For some strange reason, the kids always forget that *we* went through the same drills they go through, and not all of us forget what we did. I put myself in their place, and then I added what they lacked."

"Experience, for one," Duncan tossed into the conversation. "And knowledge beyond their reach."

"Precisely," Lance confirmed. "Technical knowledge peculiar to this specific situation. The convolutions of nuclear danger are endless, and I'm a hell of a lot closer to its horrors than these kids. They've never seen a nuclear bomb explode. I have. They haven't been drowned in radiation. I was. There's also common sense, if you can detach yourself from

376

the immediacy of your problem. Now let's add that intrinsic working knowledge of how to think *like* a student. And never forget these were damned *smart* students. I had to get back to their level but be even smarter. For quite a while they were leading me down the primrose path."

"You've lost me," Deidre broke in. "You always seemed to be one jump ahead of them. That student organization, I mean."

Lance shook his head. "Not for a while, love. Because these kids figured out how I, we, would react to given situations. So I had to change the situation and force them to act emotionally."

"How did you manage that?" Dirk asked.

"You know how. I started a riot," Lance said casually.

"*You* started that riot?" Corey demanded. "But that was a Pan-Arab rally—"

Lance shook his head. "No, it wasn't. The kids thought it was because we, my group, orchestrated it that way. You were supposed to think the same thing."

"But *why?*" Deidre asked, almost visibly floundering to find sense in the machinations Lance was describing.

"We knew which ones we believed *must* have the plutonium, had the means and the reasons to build the bomb. But we still had no clue to where they had it or how they were going to use it. All I could gamble on was that in the excitement they'd give us that clue. They had to be carrying with them anything important to them." He took a deep breath and went on. "As it turned out, Moshe Greenbaum pulled it off. We used Afsar Husain to time the rally, to fire up the kids. Then Greenbaum made his move. He went through the crowd like a steamroller. When he found the girl, Laila Habail, by the speakers' platform, she was carrying a gun—and tried to kill him with it. He knocked her to the ground. Her books fell, and her purse burst open, its contents scattering. There it was right in front of Greenbaum—a key marked 'Property of the College of Journalism.' It didn't take much to add up the elements of electrical power, heavy equipment, lots of storage room—well, Greenbaum went right to the bomb. You know the rest."

"Jesus," Dirk said, shaking his head. "If that thing had ever gone off—" He let the unnecessary words hang unsaid among them.

Lance climbed slowly to his feet, accepting Lee's help. He couldn't sit in one position. He was still too fired up, too tense, to remain any longer in one position. He had his own private bomb to drop on them. He stopped in the room center, leaning with both hands on his cane. The expression on his face was so unusual it seemed to mesmerize them.

"There's the beginning of *another* atomic bomb here in Gainesville." As he expected, no one spoke for a moment, and the only audible expression was a gasp or two.

Finally, Stan Corey spoke. Briefly and to the point. "Where?"

"Most likely in a garage, a workshop, or something," Lance said.

"You seem awfully damned casual about it," Duncan remarked.

"Because everything points to the fact that they haven't assembled it yet. We'll find out where the plutonium is sometime today or tomorrow at the latest by putting full surveillance on the airport."

"How do you know about it?" Dirk asked.

"All of us missed the obvious," Lance said, obviously with some self-chagrin. "We have the bomb Moshe Greenbaum carried into the lake. It weighed two hundred pounds, we were missing two hundred pounds of plutonium, and it all evened out. But we forgot the weight of the bomb mechanism and the rockets." He let it hang in there until Stan Corey looked in self-amazement at Edward Duncan.

"How could we have been so blind?" he asked the other man.

"Don't blame yourselves," Lance broke in. "I asked myself the same question, and not until I realized that the total package Greenbaum carried weighed two hundred pounds did I see what should have been obvious. That we were still missing two hundred pounds. You see," he said dryly, "those kids were smarter than we thought. They played us for suckers and nearly got away with it. From the very beginning they planned to build *two* bombs. They planned way ahead. They figured we'd be supersmart, so they built the first bomb and expected us, sooner or later, to find it, and that would be the end of the story. For all I know, they were going to lead us to it. They certainly wanted us to believe they were going to use it here. All their demands were against the university. In the meantime, they'd shaped the rest of the plutonium for shipment to their real destination, probably as components of industrial machinery, and were preparing to ship it out. Assembling the bomb at this point would have been foolish since all they wanted abroad was the plutonium. The smart thing to do was to conceal the plutonium in lead. That way it could be broken down into packages, each easily handled by one man."

Edward Duncan gestured. "You figured out where they were shipping it? What they planned to do with it?"

"Generally, yes," Lance responded. "The key to that little puzzle lay in the nature of the student group."

Deidre broke in. "I think I see your point. The nature of the student group. They weren't from any one country."

"A cigar for the lady," Lance complimented her. "Radical students, right? What's been happening to that long-lived goal of the Arabs to wipe Israel off the face of the earth? Egypt and Israel with American support are allies. They pulled Jordan's teeth and have the Syrians almost catatonic. Saudi Arabia needs American assistance, so they've laid back. Libya's all hothead and backstabbing. To an Arab youngster who believes in the grand old traditions, the new leaders are toothless old hags. To these kids Islamic morality was being sold out for the big oil buck. Iran fell apart, the Russians are scaring the hell out of everybody, and the Arabs are sitting on fences."

Lee brought fresh coffee to Lance and took over. "These kids were going to break some fences," she added on. "They would pick up the cudgel by setting off an atomic bomb somewhere in an Israeli city. An enraged Israel would go all out, and you can bet a few Arab cities would have gone up in nuclear blasts. One more element began to fit. It takes money and organization to do all this. Do you recall Yasar al-Milah, one of those student leaders? His father is an OPEC billionaire. The kid has scads of money and the use of his father's jet to return home when he wants. So he arranged a holy visit—and the bomb would have gone with him. As a sheikh's son, all inspection requirements would be waived. He would go right through in his father's airplane. Instead, he's safe inside a hospital."

Lance shook his head slowly. "I have to give that kid credit. He wasn't much of a talker, but he was willing to die for his beliefs."

Stan Corey showed open disbelief. "*You* give him credit, Mr. Parker? Not me. Not Ed either. He could have wiped out all Gainesville, killed a few hundred thousand people back home, maybe started a war, and you give him *credit*?"

Lance smiled. "I didn't say I liked him," he retorted quietly. "I never thought Napoleon was personally appealing, either, but I gave *him* credit for shaking up the establishment." Lance returned slowly to his seat. "Chief, Sheriff, I'm wrung dry. Whatever you need to know, it comes later, okay?"

They shook hands. "You're one hell of a guy, Parker," Corey told him.

Duncan stood by. "Let me put it another way, Parker. Forget the big numbers. My family may be alive just because of what you did here. Thank you."

Lance and Lee told the Martins the next day. He dropped it on them with the subtlety of a left hook. Dinner was behind them, and they were enjoying brandy. "You two," Lance said carefully, "will be the only people besides Lee and myself who know the truth. We trust you." He paused. "Afsar Husain and Moshe Greenbaum are the same person."

Dirk and Deidre nearly dropped their drinks. They received only a smile from Lee. "It's his story," she said.

"The same person?" Dirk echoed. "That's impossible."

"Hang on for the next one." Lance chuckled. "Husain, Greenbaum, and Parker are *all* the same person."

Deidre looked at Lee. "He's flipped out."

Lee only shook her head.

"Lee made it all possible," Lance came in quickly for her. "You know the work she was doing with her Automated Human Systems. What you didn't know was that she made a quantum jump in her work. She integrated human-exoskeleton-android systems into one which we call ManFac. Short for Man Facsimile."

"It's more than that really," Lee offered. "Lance can be virtually anyone he selects to be."

Amazement crowded Dirk's voice. "But how could *you* be *them*? The differences in size, in voice, facial expressions—everything! It can't be possible!"

"It *is*. I was *in* those ManFacs. They're tailored, so to speak, to the *n*th degree of compatibility, or symbiosis, with Lance Parker," Lance said of himself. "That's why I asked you to give me your word never to go into your own workshop. The ManFacs are in there."

"My God," Deidre murmured. "You mean Husain, and Greenbaum, are right in that next room?"

"Afsar is. Moshe is still at the bottom of the lake, where I had to leave him. We'll have to work out a way to recover the system one night. There's no rush. We'll let things calm down first."

"I confess," Dirk said slowly, "that with everything I knew about you two, I am still flabbergasted."

They watched in silence as Lance demonstrated the ManFac in the person of Afsar Husain. When he finished, they returned to the living room, for a while strangely quiet, engrossed in their thoughts about the Man Facsimile system.

"I have some ideas," Dirk blurted out suddenly. "I'm sure that with some developments we've had on the back burner for a while I could increase the versatility of the system."

"I'll take them," Lance said quietly.

"What are your plans now?" Deidre asked. "You know you're welcome to stay here with us. You also have that big house you rented here and—"

Lance shook his head. "Short and sweet, Deidre, as soon as we find that plutonium, it's time to move on. We have plans."

"Tell us?"

Lance took Lee's hand in his own. "Some plastic surgery for one. We have the money to get into it, to start rebuilding this mangled carcass of mine. New bionics, prosthetics, you know. I want to walk without this damned cane."

"And I want a new lab," Lee said. "No matter what you've seen so far, ManFac right now is just a beginning. Lance has proved we have something absolutely unique in the way of special investigation and undercover operations. There are a great many people and corporations that'll pay handsome sums for services that *only* we can deliver." Her excitement showed through her faster speech and shining eyes. "What would you think of an electromagnetic field lifting system, for example?"

Dirk looked at his wife. "You realize what she's saying? In effect, that they can levitate the ManFac." He turned to Lee. "What about balance?"

She shrugged. "Details. Small hundred thousand RPM gyros. Autostabilizing systems we can improve from satellite balancing mechanisms. That's just for starters."

"Levitation," Deidre said in awe. "The dream come true."

"*Not* levitation," Lance said firmly. "Scientific—"

She waved off his correction. "To anyone who doesn't know, it is damned well levitation, and it could have tremendous psychological effect as well."

"Well, it's as practical as going to the moon," Lee chimed in, "and *that's* ancient history by now."

Lance drifted through his own thoughts as the others talked. The possibilities truly were incredible. He'd made that fifth law of his mean something. They could do a lot with that. And there should be a sixth law just around the corner, and there were always more corners to turn. Because the sixth law, if he had his thinking cap on straight, should be his own determination to live meaningfully. He *knew*. He'd been to the brink and beyond and he'd come back. Now, however, there was that long-awaited and deserved vacation and—

The phone rang. Dirk took the call, and they looked at him with questions in their expressions. It wasn't often you heard every other phrase out of Dirk Martin as "Yes, sir."

Dirk cupped the mouthpiece. "It's for you," he said after a pause. He had the strangest look on his face.

"Who is it?" Lance asked.

"The President."

"Oh. The university, of course."

"No. The President of the United States."

"You're kidding."

"No, I'm not."

"You've *got* to be kidding."

"Will you, for God's sake, talk to the man!"

Lance took the phone. "This is Lance Parker."

"Lance, this is the President. Can you hear me clearly?"

"Yes, sir."

Several minutes later he handed the telephone slowly to Lee, who grabbed it from his hand and replaced it on the table. He stared at the others. "*He* has a problem. He says he was kept fully informed of how we handled the bomb problem here in Gainesville, and he's intrigued by our special staff." Lance blinked. "But it's just Lee and me!"

Dirk shook his head, and he smiled. "No, you're wrong about that. Don't you understand? It's you and Lee and ManFac—as well as many of those alter egos of yours as you need. I'd say that was one hell of a special staff."

"Amen."